The Red Staircase

THE RED STAIRCASE

The Ascension of Peter the Great

A Novel

Kirk Anthony Vollack

Anthony Shelton Publications, LLP
ASP

2017 Anthony Shelton Publications, LLP

Published by Anthony Shelton Publications, LLP
P.O. Box 1347
Golden, Colorado 80402
www.anthonysheltonpublications.com

The Red Staircase: The Ascension of Peter the Great is a work of historical fiction. Except for the well-known actual people, events, and locales that figure in the narrative, all names, characters, places, and incidents are the products of the author's imagination or are used fictitiously. Any resemblance to current events or locales, or to living persons, is entirely coincidental.

ISBN-13: 9780999423202
ISBN-10: 0999423207
Library of Congress Control Number: 2017914589
Anthony Shelton Publications, Golden, CO

Printed in the United States of America

Dedicated with all my love to my father and mother,
Anthony and Imojean Vollack
--the greatest people I've ever known.

They were in possession of the most extensive dominions in the universe, and yet every thing was wanted amongst them. At length, Peter was born, and Russia became a civilized state.

Voltaire

Moscow, The Great Sovereign's Palace of the Kremlin

May 17, 1682

Artemon Matveev moved down the corridor with trembling determination, still unsure of whether each step brought him closer to his own demise or took him farther from it.

I will face her and then I will know, he told himself, listening as the frescoed Palace walls brought him grim news from Red Square below.

Exiled, Matveev had been allowed to return to Moscow only after Tsar Fedor's death, called back on the same day young Peter had been named Tsar of Russia. He returned to find the city in chaos, the opposition bearing axes and, however improbable it seemed, a woman standing poised to rule the Motherland.

She holds the favor of the mob, he thought, quickening his pace, trying to match his fear with anger. *Calling for the head of a man like me is expected...but Peter? He is chosen by the Holy Father, ordained by the Patriarch. Can she rely on her Strel'tsy to commit such a heinous act against the Church?*

The sooty air still reeked of conflict, a constant reminder of the preceding day's blood. The armed revolt had claimed several members of the Naryshkin family and many of their closest comrades, men who had committed no crime other than association with the Naryshkin government. Twenty or more had fallen, unpopular officials handed over like sacrifices, lives wasted in an effort to appease Moscow's armed Strel'tsy militia.

And sitting atop it all, blooming like a flower as she stirred the bloody soup with her own hand, the twenty-five-year-old sister of dead Tsar Fedor, Sophia Alexeevna Miloslavsky.

The thought of her made Matveev fearful. Sophia was a bull of a woman, healthy but hardly fair of face, her stern and cloudy countenance erasing any beauty that might otherwise have crept into her visage. She was a woman of purpose, a quick thinker, acutely aware of her prominent position in this struggle.

With the Strel'tsy leash in hand, she will get what she wants…her dim brother will sit drooling on the throne as Sophia claims Russia.

It seemed somehow appropriate that the influence should fall into Sophia's delicate lap. After all, the controversy had begun with two women--wives of the late Tsar Alexis, the mothers whose names divided the Palace and all within it. One, Maria Miloslavsky, the late mother of Sophia, Ivan, and the recently deceased Tsar Fedor. The other, Tsarista Natalya Naryshkin, the living matriarch of the Palace and mother to Peter, the ten-year-old heir to the throne of Russia.

It had been little more than a month since Tsar Fedor's death, a sad but not unexpected day that marked the rise of the Naryshkin clan. Tsar Alexis still had a living son by his first wife, but Ivan was known to lack even the meager intellect required to rule. By comparison, Natalya's son Peter was bright and healthy, already tall enough to command respect with his presence alone.

As the better of the two candidates, Peter had been named Tsar of Russia. It was a logical decision, but his appointment united the fading Miloslavsky clan and set the city afire. Artemon had been told of the riots with time enough to escape Moscow, but declined to leave, bound by both duty and devotion.

The mob answers to their new savior, he thought. *They thrive on this treachery! Those she cannot inspire, she buys with gold and promises.*

Forward still, his weary eyes finally spying Naryshkin. The large man waited for him in the corridor, his overgrown silhouette bearing the posture of defeat. The uncle of Tsar Peter, Ivan Naryshkin was a figure too important for the mob to ignore. As Artemon came closer, the dim light revealed the fear in Naryshkin's eyes, his thick eyebrows knit into worry.

"Artemon, my friend!" Naryshkin reached out to grab his shoulder. "I thought they'd found you."

"No, thankfully." Matveev returned his grip, finding none of the familiar constancy in the face of his friend. "And I am grateful to see you as well, but you must calm yourself--and lower your voice."

"Yes, of course." Naryshkin looked suspiciously down the corridor. "Have you heard the rumors?"

"Regrettably, yes."

"Artemon, they'll have our heads! Do you know what we've been accused of? The rumors alone will earn us a spot on Sophia's list."

"If there is a list, my friend, we are most certainly on it! Rumors also say that Ivan is murdered, yet the boy is alive and as healthy as can be expected. The sight of him may be just enough to temper the fury of the mob. We must sway Sophia."

"You risk too much on your silver tongue, Matveev."

"Risk? Our lives are forfeit. What more can we lose?" he replied, growing resolute. "Sophia holds the strings. I see little else for us to do but hide. Hold your tongue and we may just survive. But let us waste no more time. How many Strel'tsy stand at her door?"

"Only two, but others have been coming and going all night."

"Good. Wipe that cowardly frown from your face. Adopt a calm look, or better, a scowl. She can tell if you're afraid." Artemon lowered his voice. "She senses it--like a dog."

"It shouldn't matter what face I try, then."

Perhaps not…

Matveev's heart pounded in leaps within him, beating as though it were smart enough to seek escape from his chest and flee the tyranny of his irrational mind.

"They will kill Peter." Naryshkin continued, barely speaking the words.

Matveev forced a grin, shaking his head. "Your mind is clouded with fear. He is sanctified, named Tsar by the Patriarch himself--and even if he were not--Sophia needs Peter as badly as she needs Ivan. Together, they will get her what she wants. Peter will live…he must… even if we are to die for the purpose."

"But--"

"No more talk."

They walked together in silence the rest of the way, stopping only when Sophia's guards moved to block their path.

"We are here by request of the Princess," Matveev told the bearded Strel'tsy, ignoring the probing stare. "Step aside."

Looking him up and down, the red-coated guard sniffed and stepped back into place, allowing the two to pass.

Glancing at Naryshkin, Matveev stepped forward and offered a few solid but respectable knocks on the door, clearing his throat one final time.

Oh Holy Father, please guide my words.

The carved wooden door opened to reveal the rounded form of Prince Vasily Vasilyevich Golitsyn, leader in the Duma and Sophia's advisor in the wake of Tsar Fedor's death. Not far past his prime, Golitsyn had become a fixture in the Palace following Peter's ascension. He openly supported Sophia's agenda and was rumored to have engaged in more than simple politics with the Princess. Knowing Sophia, it was hard for Matveev to imagine.

"Gentlemen?"

"We require an audience with the Princess. Immediately."

"Oh?" Golitsyn raised an eyebrow and offered a slight shrug, stepping aside to allow them entry.

She has the boyars and the Strel'tsy, both, he thought, avoiding Golitsyn's gaze. *Sanctity or not--we should let her idiot brother be Tsar! He will not last long.*

Sophia stood from her chair to face them, her expression even but unwelcoming. She remained in grieving dress, dark hair pinned back from her wide face and falling in uncharacteristic tangles past her thick shoulders.

"Did Lady Natalya ask you to come?"

"No, Princess."

"Odd, then," Prince Golitsyn commented, "that you should arrive at such an inappropriate time."

"You have our apologies, Princess," Matveev answered, "but the crowd…the Strel'tsy are crying for Prince Ivan. They claim he's been strangled."

Sophia's face bore little surprise. "Oh?"

"Yes, Lady. We were hopeful that Prince Ivan…" he hesitated, fumbling for the words, "and perhaps Tsarevich Peter, could be shown to the crowd to affirm in their minds that they are both alive and well."

"Ah, now I see." She stepped toward him. "They're accusing you of this treachery. Am I right?"

"Yes. Well, they have named us both. Naryshkin has been accused of trying on the crown and--"

"Lady, they create their own conspiracies!" Naryshkin burst out. "No sooner do the words slip from their imaginations than they find bloody purpose in the blades of the mob! To accuse members of the royal family? What can be called treachery, if not this?"

Sophia's eyes narrowed a bit.

Temper your words, friend... Matveev tried to catch his eye, wondering if Naryshkin had said too much.

"Our needs are selfish," Matveev offered, placing a hand on Naryshkin's shoulder. "To this, Lady, we must confess. But, begging your indulgence, Princess, our very lives are at stake. In the ears of the mob, an accusation is the same as a sentence of death."

Sophia showed no reaction, her stony gaze now weighing heavily on Artemon.

"We appeal for ourselves, Princess," he resumed, measuring his words before speaking, "and appeal humbly on behalf of any other innocents in this matter. Many have fallen already, yet Prince Ivan lives. This trouble can be easily remedied."

Sophia stepped closer. "Your selfish motives need no explanation. But I ask you with consideration, sir--why come to me with your appeals?"

He began to speak, then faltered, realizing the trap in her words.

And what would she have me say? Because you command the mob, Princess? Because the murderers look to you as their savior? Because you hold the bloody list in your hand?

"You are Prince Ivan's sister and his caretaker, Princess--"

"Because the crowd screams out your name," Naryshkin added, loudly, his irritation now showing.

"You are a Miloslavsky," Artemon continued, "and given Prince Ivan's...condition, the most capable. They look to you as they would your mother, God rest her soul. They look to you for guidance, Princess--especially now."

Sophia glared. "The Strel'tsy seek to put Ivan on the throne, sir. The rumors and accusations are merely symptoms of their grievances. And, while the sight of Ivan may be enough to save your selfish necks, we are still far from your easy remedy."

"But Lady…"

"You are far too wise to actually believe that a woman could hold the reins of the Strel'tsy," she said, her face never changing. "If you are hoping I can save you, you are mistaken."

"You're a shameful woman!" Naryshkin cried out suddenly, his voice raised to a perilous level. "Look at you--flushed with the heat of influence! Ambition! And you may hide your motives behind the shields of the Strel'tsy, but your part in this slaughter has not gone unnoticed! The blood is on your hands now! Where is this list we've heard so much of? Or are all the murderous thoughts confined to your heart?"

Sophia's face changed now, feigning offence, her cold eyes gleaming with venom. "You wrong me, sir. You would accuse me of murder? I simply seek to equal the demands of the State. Ivan is Fedor's brother and next in line; he is rightly Tsar."

Naryshkin pointed angrily. "Trust this, Lady Sophia--your course is flawed. Peter has ascended with divine mandate and there is no reversal. And, with respect to the Strel'tsy, Ivan is a half-wit! I'm not afraid to say what we all know. Peter was named Tsar for this very reason!"

God in Heaven, he's just killed himself!

Matveev paled, stepping closer to his comrade. "Princess, you must forgive him! The thought of the axe is maddening! Friend, hold your temper!"

"For what purpose?" Naryshkin returned, his face red with the flush of free will. "Because I'm worried that our dear Sophia is going to order my head removed? Better to simply ask her and save ourselves the difficulty." He looked at Sophia, palms extended. "What will it be, Princess? Am I to live or die?"

The question lingered in the air like reeking pious incense, too strong to be ignored. Matveev grimaced, the blood draining from his already pale countenance.

Sophia offered no response, passing an offended glance to Prince Golitsyn before turning away.

The Prince advanced in her defense, shaking his head in disapproval. "You do her great injury, Naryshkin. You would protest your supposed persecution by casting about accusations of your own."

"I voice the truth that the rest are afraid to speak." Naryshkin stood erect, still enrapt in the exaltation of courage.

Sophia moved to the window, her back turned. Golitsyn glared but said nothing.

It was apparent that Ivan Naryshkin was a man in need of defense. Gathering courage, Matveev willed his legs to step forward, past Golitsyn, bowing like a timid pup as he approached the Princess.

"Lady, I--"

"I would appreciate your absence," she interrupted, her head never turning.

"As would I, Princess, but our purpose remains incomplete. We seek merely for Prince Ivan to make an appearance, nothing more, so the crowd may see."

"I have already made arrangements, Matveev. Your appeal is unnecessary. Both Peter and Ivan are being delivered here, and Lady Natalya will accompany us as well."

Thank the Holy Father! Artemon's spirits leapt. *Sophia summons Natalya and Peter--capitulation must already be planned.*

He bowed. "We are grateful, Princess."

"Then leave, gratefully."

Golitsyn gestured toward the door. "Dos vidanye, Matveev…"

Artemon's feet remained steady. "Lady, if I may entreat, I would consider it an enormous favor if I could be allowed to wait for Lady Natalya and stand behind the two of you--as a sign of my loyalty. A...reassurance."

She paused before answering, staring at him. "You may remain if you wish. Your companion must leave. I am blessed with the strength to bear his insults and his accusations, but there are not enough blessings in all of Russia to endure his presence."

Sophia was staring out the window as Naryshkin huffed and turned for the door, offering a forgiving nod to Matveev. Artemon made no gesture in reply, acutely aware of Golitsyn's watchful eyes.

Golitsyn shouldered past to console the Princess, the two of them carrying on as though Artemon were no longer present. Uninterested in creating any more ill will, Matveev gladly pulled away, securing a chair on the opposite side of the chamber.

Only minutes after Naryshkin's departure, Tsarista Natalya arrived, dressed respectfully in modest black silk attire, unattended and unadorned. Her dark eyes reflected no emotion. Matveev rose immediately to greet her, hesitating only after catching the scolding look on Prince Golitsyn's face. Sophia stepped forward, offering her greeting in a warm, courteous tone.

Beside Natalya, dressed in nearly identical fashion stood the two boys--Sophia's brother Ivan and Natalya's son, the Tsar of Russia, ten-year-old Peter. Both looked petrified, holding hands and struggling to understand why they'd been pulled from their beds and made to wear their heavy ceremonial kaftans.

Ivan was the elder of the two but slouched in his stance, making the taller and straight-shouldered Peter seem older. Peter was inquisitive and bright, vigorous and fit--everything that Ivan was not. Sophia's younger brother was considered a half-wit by most, barely capable but obedient enough to follow instruction, a quality not often attributed to young Peter. Were it not for his lack of patience with ceremony and religious rites, Peter would be the ideal candidate for Tsar. As the scene unfolded before Matveev, however, it appeared more and more as though Peter would become a pawn in Sophia's ambitious design.

Even if he survives this day, Peter will live only by Sophia's mercy…

A quiet execution could be passed off to the people as a riding accident, or untimely death the result of a fever or a piece of bad meat. His death would be questioned, but the Strel'tsy were more than capable of quieting any dissent. Barring a compromise, treachery seemed the only way that Sophia could insure Ivan's rule. Natalya had already realized this.

Matveev watched. The young Tsar was adding things up. Peter remained close to his mother, his wide eyes fearful but searching the chamber, scrutinizing Sophia and Golitsyn. He paid close attention to the words that passed between the Princess and his mother as though trying to find meaning in the cordial conversation.

All the bloody contention… Matveev's stomach clenched again. *Too much to place on the shoulders of a boy.*

The Princess excused herself to finish preparation, led by an attendant into the adjoining room. The Tsarista's face warmed as she turned to greet Matveev.

"My dear Artemon…"

"Tsarista Natalya." Matveev bowed respectfully, the sound of her voice enough to restore hope within him. "And Tsarevich Peter."

"Papa Matveev!" Peter wrapped his arms around Artemon's waist, embracing him tightly. The boy's eyes bore a serious, knowing look.

Matveev returned the boy's embrace and reached out to Natalya.

"You are unexpected," she said, taking the cold fingers of her guardian into her palms, "but a welcome surprise, certainly. How are you, my dear father?"

"Your arrival is a blessing, Lady. My spirit suffers horribly from worry, yet I am gratefully alive."

Matveev passed her a fearful look, wanting desperately to tell Natalya of her brother Ivan's outburst, believing her intervention might save him from the Strel'tsy blades. Had it not been for Golitsyn, Artemon would have spoken.

Prince Vasily, however, stood confidently beside the Tsarista, arms crossed, grinning with the arrogance of victory. His loyalty to Sophia and the Miloslavsky clan had never been more apparent.

"And how is the young Tsarevich?" Golitsyn asked Natalya, tilting his head as though interested.

"I'm standing right here," the child said, staring with contempt. "Do not speak as though I am not."

Prince Vasily nodded with a smirk, bowing in deference. "My lord, you have my most sincere apologies. I have been told it is hard on one's constitution to be awakened suddenly from sleep."

"That sounds foolish," Peter said to him plainly. "And I wasn't sleeping, so I wasn't awakened."

Bless that boy, Matveev thought, staring down with pride.

"He was sleepless and frightened," Lady Natalya added, "I don't see how anyone could rest on this evening."

"I was listening to the noise in the Square," Peter said angrily. "I kept praying that the heavens would send down a bolt of lightning to kill them all!"

Sophia returned to stand beside the Prince, her hair now covered respectfully, her traditional gold silk okhaben conspicuously understated, devoid of any excess ornamentation save for narrow gold and silver braid down the long front opening. After leaning in to whisper a few words in Golitsyn's ear, she turned back to the Tsarista. The Prince excused himself and stepped out into the corridor.

"Prince Vasily will return with our escorts," Sophia said to Natalya. "Lady, you have my appreciation. Regrettably, we have been delivered to this odd moment."

"We will be glad to see this tragedy brought to a peaceful end," the Tsarista replied, her eyes never wavering from the persistent stare.

With no regard for Matveev's presence, the two women began to speak cautiously and politely, keeping mainly to the topic of the children's welfare. Artemon watched quietly, knowing that the subject of their discussion was unimportant when compared to the tone of their words, the extent of their kindness, the understanding that this was the first conversation of a new relationship. Their posture, their expressions, their responses--everything had changed.

Natalya and Sophia were equals now. Like generals from opposing armies, they conversed with dignity and mutual respect, face-to-face, their comments born in strength and bathed in diplomacy.

Finally, a bit of civility in the midst of all this barbarism! With her destination in sight, Sophia is willing to end the bloodshed.

The thick-shouldered Princess leaned down to wipe the corners of Ivan's mouth, explaining to him that he should remain quiet and stand where he was told. Peter listened, moving closer to his mother and taking her hand.

Matveev tugged at his beard and drew a deep breath. He looked to the Princess. Sophia was comfortable now, as comfortable in her burdensome frame as she'd ever been, her eyes brimming with hopeful aggression as she straightened young Ivan's robe. Educated alongside her brother Tsar Fedor, the politically shrewd woman understood the workings of the Kremlin and knew what she wanted.

She had calculated the risks, made her play, and was now savoring her moment of importance, openly allowing the Tsarista to recognize her satisfaction. The role suited her well.

Despite his curiosity, Matveev was careful not to stare too long or meet the Princess' gaze. With good fortune, her attention would not return to him. For the moment, he was happy just to remain in the chamber.

Safer in here than out there, he thought, wondering again where Naryshkin had gone. The sounds of dissent rose again seeping through the windows, an audible reminder of Sophia's influence. Artemon stepped closer to Lady Natalya.

Sophia needs nothing more. She'll be satisfied with a Regency and no one else will have to die. For now.

Heavy footsteps sounded from the corridor.

The doors behind Matveev burst open without warning. Prince Golitsyn re-entered in uncharacteristically frantic condition, his confident look absent. Behind him stood two loyal Strel'tsy captains.

"The mob has breached the gates, Princess."

Artemon's heart dropped, his mind flooding with new, perilous possibilities.

Sophia received the news as though she'd expected it, her sullen face barely wavering in reaction. Her squared jaw remained firm, her eyes neither widening in surprise nor dropping in mournful acknowledgement. Sophia required only a moment to assimilate the news before calling for action.

"We will take the boys to the Red Staircase," she commanded. "Lady Natalya, perhaps you would be safer elsewhere. I would offer you an escort back to your chambers."

"I will go where my son goes," the Tsarista replied promptly, looking at Peter. His face now absent of wit or charm, the boy squeezed her hand and stepped closer.

"Are you certain, Lady? We cannot risk to have you injured."

"If Peter can be risked," Natalya responded, "then certainly--so may I. Respectfully, Sophia, I will remain with my son."

"Ah, fine then. Vasily, how many are in the Kremlin?"

The Prince shrugged. "By this time? Nearly all of them, I expect."

Sophia shook her head sadly. "We must remedy this trouble before it overcomes us all. We leave then."

With this, Sophia took Ivan's arm and marched out into the corridor, leading the boy toward the Holy Antechamber and the Red Staircase. Prince Golitsyn followed her, gazing around before motioning for Natalya and Peter to move. Lest he be forgotten, Matveev followed the Tsarista closely.

Outside the chamber, the echoing shouts were frighteningly real, now accompanied by the smell of smoke and the constant clatter of blades and axes.

He stumbled along behind Lady Natalya and Peter, craning his neck to search the corridor for surprises. Every instinct cried out for flight, his rational thoughts countered with the notion that his fate had already been decided.

Are they calling for my head? And where is Ivan Naryshkin in the midst of all this? Dead already? Merciful God, we're walking right into them!

Sophia turned back, still holding Ivan by the sleeve, motioning for Golitsyn to hasten the Tsarista's advance. For a moment, her gaze reached past the narrow shoulders of Lady Natalya and landed on Matveev.

Keep your place, he warned himself, moving behind Peter and placing his hand on the young boy's shoulder.

If Peter can survive this day, he may still be Tsar…

They were close now, hateful cries echoing around them. He looked to their escorts, wondering what instruction they'd been given, guessing at what lay behind the calm looks on their faces.

As they reached the top of the Red Staircase, Matveev heard the cries and recognized the voice.

Ivan Naryshkin stood backed into the corner of the courtyard below them, surrounded by Strel'tsy aggressors. Blood flowed from his head, his face a shining mask of crimson as he held out his hands in unarmed defense.

"Ivan!" Matveev pointed frantically. "Lady Natalya!"

The Tsarista was already watching, tears welling in her eyes. She attempted to pull Peter closer, but the young Tsarevich was held in place, his eyes wide as he watched.

"Uncle! Someone help him!"

Naryshkin heard the familiar voice, looking up through the mask of blood to see the group at the top of the stairs. The Strel'tsy were looking up as well, turning at the sight of Sophia to voice their support.

"Do something!" Matveev shouted to Sophia, his own voice failing in the tumult. "For God's sake, Princess, call them off!"

Sophia turned to look at him, her gaze tempered with inappropriate calm. "There is nothing I can do. I am a woman, Matveev. Do you think I command the will of men?"

Despair flooded through him. *If Naryshkin is to die, then so am≈I…*

As the royal party watched, the mob collapsed on Ivan Naryshkin.

He fell beneath the rain of fists and feet, clinging to the bloody brink of consciousness before being raised from the floor, held up by his arms at the mercy of eager pikes and axes. The loyal Strel'tsy Captain ran the first of them clean through Naryshkin's stomach, the blade dumping blood and entrails as it exited his back.

Another assailant stepped from the rear to run a knife across the side of Naryshkin's throat, loosing a spray of scarlet on the ravenous mob. They roared with delight, raising their fists in exaltation.

The young Tsarevich screamed, his hands balled into white-knuckled fists, his eyes flooded with tears. Natalya held him back, pulling him into the folds of her dress. She kissed his forehead and whispered calm reassurance, promising that soon it would all be over.

Sophia turned, her hand still gripping young Ivan's arm, reaching for Peter. He glared with accusatory fire, slipping from her grasp and clinging to his mother.

"Peter, come!" the Princess commanded. "Come with me! Natalya, you will be escorted to your chambers. Peter will be delivered when this is complete."

The Tsarista's arms remained tightly wrapped around her son. "I refuse to leave him."

"There is no more time for this idiocy." Sophia scowled, firmly taking Peter's arm. "You have no option to refuse, Lady. I cannot risk your welfare."

She nodded to the escorts, who moved behind the Tsarista.

"Peter, come with me."

"No!" the child shouted back at her, pulling away from her grasp. "I want to stay with Mother!"

Sophia reached out again, this time gripping his arm with the strength of her weight, jerking him away. Reluctantly, Natalya released him, her own arms held back by the Strel'tsy escorts.

Matveev was dizzy, his legs trembling so terribly that he could barely stand. His heart, however, was still strong enough to shout.

"You traitorous sow!" he screamed, provoked by terror. "You'd call for all our heads and then claim victory! You're a murderer, Princess! The blood of the Naryshkins will forever stain your hands!"

His words seemed to disappear into the din of shouts, their potency dulled by the smell of ash and fresh blood. Sophia stared at him for a moment, this time with a look of wonder and surprise, as though amazed by his sudden lack of timidity.

And then, Artemon saw it.

The slightest of glances, a subtle look passing from Sophia to Prince Golitsyn. The Prince looked to the escorts and offered a nod so slight as to be almost imperceptible.

A simple nod, and Matveev's fate was sealed.

They meant to kill me all along...

He began to back away but was claimed from behind by the Strel'tsy escorts, large hands grabbing his arms and tearing him away from the Tsarista's side. Sophia watched for a moment, one boy in each hand, her face bearing the look of satisfaction he'd expected. Peter was no longer struggling in her grasp, his gaze fixed on Matveev.

He looked back at Peter, connecting with the young boy's teary eyes. Restrained, wrapped in despair, Matveev realized that he had no profound final words, no single bit of wisdom to impart.

Born into this brutish world...how can he hope to survive? God save the Naryshkins and poor Tsar Peter...

Sophia was finished with discussion. With her two charges firmly in hand, she turned to stand at the top of the Red Staircase, displaying the boys for the mob. Victorious shouts and accolades filled the air, greeting her with the reception she desired.

Pulled away from Natalya, Artemon's legs finally gave out, leaving him limp in the arms of his captors. They said nothing as they threw him over the parapet and into the mob below. Mercifully, as though graced by God for his loyalty, Artemon was unconscious as the first of the axes chopped into his noble flesh.

Moscow, The Palace of Tsarista Natalya in the Kremlin

May 25, 1682

Tsarista Natalya gazed out the window as she waited for her visitor, her weary eyes scanning the courtyard and wondering at the swift change of season. Trees that had been bare only days earlier were now colored with leaves. Beneath, newborn flowers sat wide-eyed and staring at the sun, enjoying their fleeting moment of glory. The world had changed in what seemed a single night, transforming from drab brown to vibrant green, exploding with color and life. This tragically short spring would soon give way to the long days of summer and ultimately fade again in deference to another dark winter.

This kind of change was expected. The seasons would turn and this turn could be counted on, relied upon, prepared for. Welcome or unwelcome, the seasons were consistent and certain, incorporated into traditions and counted as landmarks of the days and years.

The change of seasons, she could tolerate. Considering herself to be typically Russian, Natalya Naryshkin generally disliked anything less predictable.

She had been trained to be a lady, a finished work of art, believing for most of her life that her position would be one of changeless consistency. She'd imagined tireless, steadfast duty beside a man of noble birth, a pious, respectable, and generally uneventful life within the walls of a mansion somewhere in Russia. Destiny had other plans for her.

Natalya was married to Tsar Alexis in 1671, less than two years after the death of his first wife, Maria Miloslavsky. A beloved figure in Moscow, Maria bore the Tsar thirteen children, leaving behind two sons and six daughters. Following such an esteemed lady was worrisome at first, but Natalya soon learned to disregard the cool affect of the Miloslavskys and quietly bear the insults. She was safe in her marriage and the birth of her first son meant respectability for her entire family.

A healthy heir. A healthy Naryshkin heir.

Tsar Alexis was pleased. Natalya's side of the family prospered. Men like Ivan Naryshkin and Artemon Matveev made their names in the Court. She was a respected lady and would be so for the rest of her life. All this, because of Peter. The days seemed to stretch out endlessly before her, as predictable as the turn of spring to summer.

Tsar Alexis' death in 1676 was tragic and sudden. He'd been claimed by a deadly mix of ailments only five years into their marriage, leaving Fedor, his eldest living son by Maria, as successor. Since that day, nothing had been predictable.

"Counselor Golitsyn has arrived, Lady."

"Yes, yes. See him in."

Boris Golitsyn stepped through the door, his face reflecting the serious tone of the day. The cousin of Prince V.V. Golitsyn, Boris was a skilled diplomat and loyal supporter, now Natalya's closest confidante within the Kremlin. A prudent soul, he bore little of his famous cousin's flamboyance and was scarcely as popular. Still, Natalya trusted him more than any other man in Moscow.

Boris waited for the attendants to leave before greeting her. His grin was typically forced.

"Tsarista, if only you had seen! A spectacle, it was! Unabashed theatrics, posed and painted to resemble history."

"This is nothing surprising," she reassured him, warming his cold thin hands with her own. "Calm yourself and tell me what happened."

"The Strel'tsy delivered a petition--borne on the blade of a pike, I expect--a petition asking that the government be administered by the Sovereign Lady. No, no, I misspeak--it was the pious and wise Sovereign Lady, the great Princess Sophia Alexeevna! After all the killing, after all the grave-digging and tears, the Strel'tsy bastards marched up the bloodstained steps and presented the petition to Patriarch Joachim as though they were foreign ambassadors!"

"And Sophia?"

"Enjoying it immensely, of course, though she couldn't show it. She played her part very well. Solemn. Honored. She looked over the crowd, took a breath into her warrior's breast, nodded as though she were mourning the fact and said--and I remember the words perfectly-- 'I agree to take upon myself this great labor'. Take upon herself, indeed! Need I say more, Lady? I think our dear Sophia has labored hard enough already."

Natalya drew a deep breath. "The circumstance is unimportant," she said finally. "Did Sophia speak of the resolution?"

"Yes, just as before. Ivan will sit as senior Tsar, and Peter as junior. The wise and pious Sophia Alexeevna will oversee as Regent. Senior and junior…mere words, but the Strel'tsy colonels seemed to enjoy the distinction between the two. Anything that can be called a victory, I suppose."

We must pray that Sophia holds to her promises, Natalya thought. *Whatever the distinction, Peter will be Tsarevich and the rest of my family will be graciously spared.*

"We should thank the Almighty for bringing this terror to an end. Trading influence, I expect, will be the least burdensome of their demands. For Peter's benefit, I would have gladly conceded more."

Boris frowned angrily. "The Strel'tsy may keep Sophia's hands clean, but everyone knows of this treachery. Surely, someone will think of revenge."

Natalya glared at him. "Please, don't even suggest such a thing. We have suffered more than our share of loss, and conflict can only serve to hurt Peter. As weak as we are now--are you capable with a pike, Boris?"

"Yes, you're right," he replied, raising his palms in surrender, "The thought is horrifying."

"Well, you have little to worry about," she told him. "The matter is settled. The people are not so fond of conflict that they would support another change. Ivan is fifteen and will be of age soon. Sophia needs Peter's youth, lest her Regency be unacceptably short."

He nodded his understanding. "The ghosts of our comrades are not enough to stir the blood of revenge--even the spirits of Artemon Matveev and our dear Ivan. Perhaps they will move Peter's hand when he is older..."

Golitsyn drifted a bit, lapsing into thoughts, his features bending with melancholy. "You know, when they told me that Ivan and Artemon had been murdered...the very instant I heard the words I felt my own life to be forfeit. I was certain, Lady, that my door was about to swing open--that the Strel'tsy would march in, behead me in a single stroke and move on to the next chamber! I dwelled on this thought so completely that even when you told me--even now, when I know a resolution has been reached, there is part of me that still carries this lingering sense of dread."

"Poor souls," she said mournfully, pressed to the verge of tears at the sound of her brother's name.

"They were torn from us out of spite."

"Not spite," she replied, raising a finger. "Shrewd sensibility. Ivan was our family's heart, and Matveev its head."

"Artemon should never have returned from exile," Boris responded, now pacing, his feet set in motion by the passion of his spirit. "He should have remained in Pustozerk where Fedor sent him--at least for a few more months. They may call it an uprising, but the blow was directed at the Naryshkin clan and no one else! All our progress, flooded away in a crimson stream, and all for a half-wit who probably won't live to see his twentieth!"

Natalya stared coolly. She grew weary of the dissension and struggle, the continually voiced complaints and promises of revenge. At this moment, she wanted nothing more than to mourn in peace and pray for the safety of her children.

She looked at her devoted advisor, wondering how quickly he would collapse if the tide of rumors turned against him. Matveev had been implicated for possessing an astrological chart, and Naryshkin for standing alone in the presence of the crown. And despite his grumbling about his cousin V.V.'s alliance with Sophia, Boris would admit that the Golitsyn family name and Prince V.V.'s influence had likely spared his life.

"We are finished," she announced, drawing a quizzical look. "I do not wish to speak further of this incident. Of my courtiers, Boris, you are the shrewd one--practical enough to realize that whatever the injustices of the past, our priorities now lie with Peter."

"Agreed."

"He is beautiful," she continued proudly, "bright like his uncles, a healthy boy who will rise to his position despite Sophia and Ivan. Of this, I am certain. If they wish us to address him as junior Tsar, then we will do so. He is still a child and can avoid the further stain of this trouble. The rest of us will hold our tongues and, for now, allow Sophia to make her own decisions. We will attend to Peter and insure his security above all else. He is our heart and, God willing, our strength for the future. If not for yourself, you will hold your tongue for Peter. Am I understood?"

Boris looked down at his feet. "I would think of nothing else. Peter is our devotion, our very purpose. He has been through too much already."

"Good, then." She smiled warmly, again taking his hand. "You're far too valuable to allow your passions to consume you now, Boris. We need you. Russia needs you."

Golitsyn shrugged modestly. "I strive only to serve Russia and the Naryshkin household. I am eternally yours, Tsarista."

"You are a blessing, Boris. Will you accompany me to the teremok to see the Tsarevich?"

Calmed by her words, he nodded, shaking away the look of embarrassment. They walked arm in arm, exchanging fond memories and speaking of the future. Sophia's name entered the conversation only once and was quickly dropped.

They found Peter alone, dancing around with a mason's spade, brandishing it like a sword as he vanquished invisible enemies. He'd been fond of the implements since the day he'd first seen them and had his selection of wooden swords and carpentry tools laid out respectfully on a fur-lined cloak beside him. Aware that he was being watched, Peter stabbed at the air a few more times and looked up at his mother.

"I'm killing Strel'tsy," he said plainly. "Strel'tsy and Turks."

"You shouldn't say such things, Peter."

"Yes. Keep to the Turks," Golitsyn added. "There lies the true threat."

The young Tsarevich frowned. "But the Strel'tsy are closer."

"Peter, the Strel'tsy are not your enemies. You are the Tsar and they serve you."

"If they serve me, then I wish them to disband," he replied. "They killed Uncle Ivan and Papa Matveev. I saw them."

Golitsyn nodded to him. "It would be nice if things were so simple, eh? We are all mourning the loss, but you must be careful what you say, my lord. You've seen how angry the city is. Keep your deepest thoughts to yourself and you'll be far better off."

"What do you mean?"

"You're scaring him," Natalya said, stepping between them. "No one is going to harm you, Peter. You are Tsar by God's will. No one can change this."

"If I am Tsar, then I wish to rid Russia of the Strel'tsy. And I wish for Sophia to be exiled, far away."

"Someday, perhaps," Boris replied, arms crossed as he evaluated the child. "But you must never say such things. Be respectful to the Regent, even when she becomes intolerable. You know this, don't you?"

"Of course," Peter said, resuming his swordplay. "I've been told a thousand times how to act."

He grinned. "You're not frightened by Sophia, are you?"

"Boris!"

"Lady, if you please, let the boy answer the question."

"I'm not afraid," Peter answered vehemently. His eyes betrayed the truth.

"Good boy, Peter. Never admit you're afraid, even when you know in your heart that you are. The Tsar shows strength, not weakness, because he knows that his example inspires others."

Peter nodded dutifully. "I know."

Boris passed a look to Natalya. "Perhaps it's time for him to start playing with real swords instead of wooden ones."

Peter halted mid-strike, turning wide-eyed to Natalya. "Oh Mother, please! I'm big enough to handle a sword! And I've been practicing!"

She looked down at her fair-faced son, wondering how long it would be before he was fighting his own battles. Given the renewed authority of the Miloslavskys, it seemed only prudent that he learn to wield a sword. She realized the day Tsar Fedor died that, no matter how hard she tried, she would never be able to keep him from the brutality of his homeland.

Peter has inherited a world filled with turmoil; he must be prepared to rule it.

"We shall see. I will speak with Captain Zubarov."

"Oh, yes, Mother!" Peter cheered at the thought, leaping excitedly to the center of the chamber and stabbing again at the foes surrounding him. The boy possessed boundless energy and the resourcefulness to occupy himself at all times. It felt good to see him happy again, even if just for a moment.

"He's been studying with Nikolai Zotov," she told Boris. "He uses prayer books and the Psalter as texts, though Peter seems to have little use for words or poetry. Still, he reads well enough, I think."

"With respect, Lady, it may be time to enrich his education a bit. Perhaps we could call in an additional tutor--and if I may, I would recommend that he be trained in the martial code, and perhaps some artillery."

"I hate to think of him that way," she said, watching as Peter sharpened his imaginary sword. "Soon enough, I know, it will be my reality."

"He will make us all proud, no doubt."

She looked to him. "If you don't mind, Boris, I wish to speak with Peter alone."

"Certainly. We will speak again soon, Lady. Summon me if you require anything." Golitsyn bowed, offering a smile to the young Tsarevich before excusing himself. As the door closed behind him, Peter turned solemnly to his mother and looked up at her.

"Mother?"

"Yes, Peter?"

"I want to ask you a question," he said, "but I don't want you to be angry with me for asking."

"I won't be. I promise."

"And I don't want you to think I'm angry, either…"

"Peter, what is it?"

He paused, tilting his head reluctantly. "I just keep thinking about Uncle Ivan and Papa Matveev. They were killed because of me, weren't they?"

"Certainly not," she replied confidently. "They were killed because the Strel'tsy believed they were traitors. They thought that Matveev and the others were trying to steal the throne. Matveev was even accused of strangling you, and of all things, necromancy."

"But none of it was true. None of it. Those things were lies, weren't they?"

"Of course," she replied. "The two were very loyal to the family and to your father. They wanted nothing more than to see you as Tsar."

"But they were killed…because of rumors?"

"The Holy Father has a place for them, Peter. The Strel'tsy were wild that day, like wolves in a pack. They acted without proof, as a mob is wont to do. But the trouble has passed now. You and Ivan will sit as co-Tsars. And have no worry, Sophia will not be Regent forever."

He looked up at her with the serious, angry look she'd seen so often in the face of her husband. Peter's young mind was hard at work assimilating the bloody events of the past week, trying somehow to reconcile his destiny with the outcome. It would be impossible to make him understand completely; she hoped only to ease his spirit and prepare him for the future.

"Why didn't someone do something, Mother?"

"What?"

"Why didn't you do something?" Peter asked her, angrily raising his voice. "Why didn't you tell them Uncle Ivan was innocent? You're the Tsarista! Why didn't you stop them?"

"Lower your voice, Peter." She moved to sit down on the bed, motioning for him to sit beside her. "Come here and listen carefully. I will explain to you because you of all people must understand."

He obeyed her, looking sadly curious. The Tsarista took his hand in hers and looked on him with warmth, offering a smile as reassurance before she began.

"When you were born the whole of Russia rejoiced. I know I've told you many times, but oh, Peter--if you could have seen the parade, the feasts, toast after toast, all in your honor! They predicted that you would be great. Court Poet Polotsky made all the proper astrological calculations, and he proclaimed that you would be the New Constantine, a great man who was destined to conquer Constantinople. But we didn't need the stars to know that you would be special. You brought new hope to everyone in Moscow. Your father was very proud of you, and it is my firm belief that he intended you and you alone to succeed him as Tsar. Had you been older, you surely would have."

"I told you!" he burst out. "Uncle Ivan was killed because he wished me to be Tsar. Matveev, and all the others, too!"

"Shhh," she rubbed the smooth skin of his hands, relaxing him as she'd done when he was just a baby. "Put the worries out of your mind. You are my smart boy, and I know you have seen enough to understand the trouble...but you are Tsar and you always will be. There will always be someone who opposes the Tsar, and you cannot carry the blame for those who choose to defend you. Think of this. Your father sent armies into battle, conflicts that claimed the lives of many loyal men. Do you think he should have carried the burden of their deaths?"

Peter shook his head. "No. They were serving the Motherland, and not just a Tsar. They're all heroes now."

"You see? Although we pray for it to be otherwise, there will be many who give their lives for Russia in your defense--and many more, regrettably, who die at the hands of your order."

He frowned. "I understand, Mother. But we saw it happen. If Father had seen the soldiers and could have done something, surely he would have. Wouldn't he?"

"I refuse to hear any more of it, Peter. As a person, as a woman, as a child of God, I wanted to cry out and tell them to release your uncle. You can look at me and know that this is true, Peter. But I am also the matron of our family, Tsarista and the mother of the Tsar. The welfare of the Motherland--your welfare--must always be my highest priority. Had I cried out, they might have implicated me as well, and possibly your Uncle Lev and others.

"When you sit in a position of influence," she continued, "you must learn to view the world in the terms of your position. As mother of the Tsar, I care for the Motherland by caring for you. Our whole family, Uncle Ivan included, owes its duty to Russia. As Tsar, you have the interests of the entire country to consider. You are the caretaker, and so your decisions must be shaped by what is best for Russia, and not merely what you see before you. You must understand the depth of the river and not just the speed of the current."

He nodded in reply, listening carefully, for a moment free from his questioning nature. She conveyed seriousness in her tone and he understood, waiting silently for her to speak again.

"You mustn't question Sophia about what happened. Do you understand? The conflict was resolved. Your uncle and the rest are blessed souls, Peter, but they are regrettably gone. If you wish to honor their memory, then do so by keeping with your lessons and becoming the Tsar they wanted you to be. Hold your tongue and mind your temper. Someday you'll have Sophia and these memories far behind you."

"Yes, Mother."

"You will be Tsar for your entire life, Peter. For now, it is simple enough to walk beside Ivan and allow Sophia her Regency. Do you understand?"

"Yes, Mother. I promise not to argue."

"Good, then." Natalya smiled warmly. "You are the Tsar, Peter, the Servant of God and the Savior of Russia. Never forget how much your family and your people love you."

"I know…I'm sorry about Uncle Ivan and Papa Matveev…"

"So am I, son."

"Mother?"

"Yes, Peter?"

"If Ivan is the co-Tsar, is he also the Savior of Russia?"

She grinned a bit, shaking her head regretfully. "No, the stars predicted nothing so grand for Ivan. He is just the senior Tsar and your step-brother."

Peter shrugged. "It's too bad. I like Ivan."

"But he's not like you," she said.

"No, I guess not. Mother?"

"Yes?"

"Will you talk to the Captain about the sword?"

She tilted her head. "Hmmm...I suppose. But first you must give me a hug and a kiss."

"Oh, thank you, Mother!" Peter's face lit back up, his smile contagious.

She pulled him close and hugged him tightly, feeling in his shoulders how quickly he was growing. Already tall for his age, Peter would likely grow to eclipse his father in stature.

Better that he grow to be an imposing figure, she thought, kissing him on the forehead before turning him loose again to play. *Ivan will always be stunted and is far too dim--he will pale in Peter's shadow. The years will pass quickly and the men in the Duma will grow tired of working with Sophia.*

Peter is courageous and holds a pious spirit. He will be strong, tireless and full of pride. In time, Russia herself will call for him to claim his rightful place!

Moscow, The Sloboda

Seven Years Later, June 1689

Theodor Sommer quickened his pace as he moved through the cobbled streets of Moscow, traversing the rows of wooden houses with little regard for what was occurring within their simple walls.

The city's indistinct dwellings were tacked together and patched with scraps of wood, topped with snow-ready peaked roofs that rose sharply like divine spires into the air. Their crude chimneys trickled thin streams of sooty smoke into overcast skies, piles of chopped and stacked wood waiting outside for the inevitable turn of season.

Initially, Theodor was indifferent; he neither liked nor disliked Moscow, though he would admit that his time there had given him an understanding that tempered his view. The city was founded on a common brew of politics and religion, its citizens composed primarily of civil servants, clergy, and their servants. Such a singular hub, the capital, that it often seemed more like a carriage house than a city--comings and goings, with no one truly in residence. Moscow may have been the point upon which all else turned, but the heart of Russia lay elsewhere. This much was obvious to a foreigner.

As for Sommer, he had grown accustomed to living in the East despite the cold weather and brutish politics. As odd as it may once have seemed, he could command a brand of respect here that he would never have been able to forge at home. For the moment, at least, Sommer was prospering--tutoring the future Tsar of Russia was a notable accomplishment and had proven far more fulfilling than he'd first expected.

The mere idea of it--to have the willing, curious mind of this young ruler in his care and custody--was itself so alluring as to spark his immediate interest and keep him in Moscow despite the inconvenience. Sommer found the young Tsarevich to be surprisingly bright and eager to learn; unlike the vast majority of his aristocratic brethren, Peter was devoted to his own betterment. With the exception of his impatience, the young Tsarevich was an ideal student.

The rest was of no consequence to Sommer. The tales of Peter's carousing and his penchant for cruel practical jokes never really turned the mentor's ear; none of those in the foreign quarter had ever fallen victim to the boy's temper, and nearly everyone recognized their own Franz Lefort as the most notable tutor of the baser pursuits. If there were anyone to blame for Peter's behavior, Lefort would certainly have been the first suspect. There was no question, however, in Sommer's mind or anyone else's, about the boy's enormous sense of self-determination. With very few exceptions, no one influenced Peter more than Peter.

If Peter drank, it was because he wished to do so. If Peter taunted, it was because he wished to do so. If he ate a meal, rode a horse or carved wood with the carpenters, it was by his will and his will alone. He did what he wished and would often go to great lengths to see his desires become reality. Even in studies, the mentors only taught subjects Peter desired to learn.

The work was challenging as Peter proved to be a ravenous student. Thankfully, the young Tsarevich was rational and shrewd. Even in his disobedience, there seemed a pure motive in his mind and a heart that beat double-time with conviction. There was an intensity within Peter that kept him devoted to whatever task he chose to undertake, and the same perseverance was present in both his work and his play.

As a military man, Sommer understood this kind of passion. There was more to victory than maps and maneuvers.

If only his people shared his spirit, Theodor thought, his gaze straying to meet the sour expressions of the Muscovite locals. *How soon before this mire of tradition reins him in? How can Peter resist it when following his true will would mean disenchanting his country?*

But there was no reason to question Peter's assertiveness. By the age of sixteen, the boy had already recruited a small army of 'toy' regiments that numbered in the thousands. He'd staged parades and maneuvers, enacted mock battles, and had even requisitioned cannons from the Moscow armory with the grudging approval of Regent Sophia.

Cautiously aware of his surroundings, Sommer struggled to keep his inquisitive eyes on the ground until he was well within the suburb that made up the foreign quarter.

The Nemetskaya Sloboda. In Sommer's eyes, the pearl in the oyster--an oasis of European culture and style in the midst of Russia. Created by Tsar Alexis in an effort to segregate the non-orthodox, the German quarter had flourished, growing brick by brick from the memories and longings of its inhabitants. Englishmen, Danes, and Scots came to settle in Moscow as well, many of them royalists or Catholics seeking a fresh start.

They created a second home, a world which, in both appearance and spirit, resembled their native Europe. Broad, tree-lined avenues stretched in every direction, supporting rows of two and three-story brick houses with wide European style windows. The mansions were decorated with columns and cornices, hiding secret gardens with pavilions and reflecting pools. Even the carriages that traversed the streets were crafted in London or Paris, carrying their owners through the decorated squares and past ornate fountains. A small world, recreated so thoroughly that once inside, one could easily forget about the oddity and isolation of Moscow. A slice of Europe. Here, the only reminders of Russia were the golden onion domes that rose in the distance.

But the beauty of the Sloboda went far beyond its stately accommodations, particularly for a man like Sommer. His joy came from the companionship, the spirit of Europe that lingered behind these painted doors. The company was the best in all of Russia--by the Tsarevich's own admission. The greatest minds in Moscow lived and thrived here, worshipped and raised families away from the persecution of the continent. And though these minds well understood Alexis' original intent, they never failed to raise a glass to the late Tsar in thanks.

Rejuvenated by the sight of home, he hurried to the meeting place, driven by thirst and the dust that rose with the wind.

The Dutchman Karsten Brand was the first to stand, his face flushed with inebriation.

"Ah, Sommer!"

"Hello, my friend."

"You have arrived just in time." Brand took Theodor's arm, gripping his shoulder in friendly gesture. "Surely, you are the ideal arbiter to settle this dispute. Lefort and I were discussing the condition of Moscow."

At the opposite end of the table sat the indomitably cavalier Franz Lefort, an impressive figure in any setting, known to all as the favorite of the young Tsarevich. Worth every inch of his girth, Lefort was a great man among the well-traveled bunch in the foreign quarter.

Sommer shrugged a bit, acknowledging Lefort. "I should be able to assist you, then--there is little of consequence to consider."

"Hah!" Brand pointed gleefully. "You see, Franz? Sommer would agree with me. Moscow is backward, to a pitiable degree. A capital city, a ruling city, admittedly--and no one can deny the Kremlin its dominance over the landscape."

"You are stepping backward, sir."

"But if he is to look closely," Brand pressed, "a man who has traveled will see that there is little to distinguish the minds of these city-dwellers from those working in the fields. Backward, I say."

"You would deny Moscow its prominence?"

"No, sir. Not entirely. A center, Moscow is--in history and size only. But as for culture? Well, culture certainly fears this place. No theatres, no guilds, no suitable courts...and no schools beyond the oaken trunks of the clergy. This you cannot deny. Moscow, with respect to our benefactor and the roof settled over our heads, is a city without significance."

Theodor was inclined to agree. The Dutchman's enthusiasm, however, seemed overly rude.

"Considering that the finest minds in Moscow already sit at this table," Sommer replied, "my opinion is very humbly delivered. I do think, perhaps, you accuse the Muscovites of too many things. 'Backward' is a mere matter of perspective."

"Hah!"

"Truly, sir. Bring me a native of Paris or Vienna--they would undoubtedly agree with your opinion. There's no argument in the fact that Europeans would be uncomfortable here, and perhaps a bit uninterested. A European gentleman would think these people far too devout, and the cities too small. I do not question this. But...to another man, in another place? To the countless villages of the Baltic, however, I am certain that Moscow appears as big as a mountain."

Brand shrugged a bit, nodding in concession. Lefort grinned from the end of the table.

"If you wish to speak of culture," he continued, inspired by the topic, "I will gratefully concede that these Russians have yet to find the taste for such things as theatres…but we're dueling with words, Karsten. You've traveled enough to know that in the heart of every backward village rests a church, a shining beacon of God, a pillar on which every village is centered. The Russian people are fond of shouldering themselves with lists of rituals and pilgrimages, ceremonies and the like. Rituals are their bread and prayers their broth. The hearty soul of a Russian needs little else."

Brand rolled his eyes. "Not that I lack admiration for the persistent piety of the Russians--but Theodor, do you know what they call a city that has a church but no theatre? I'll tell you, my friend. They call it a village. There! Moscow is a swollen village. That is my current estimation. To any cultured man, it can never be anything more."

"Where is my drink?" Theodor looked around the table, pointing to the pitcher at the opposite end. "My thirst must be satisfied before I explain the wonder of Moscow to our comrade Karsten…"

"Here, my friend." Lefort stood and poured, handing over a cup. "We eagerly await your words."

Sommer nodded to him. "You've been here as long as any of us Franz. What keeps you in Moscow?"

Lefort grinned. "I would have to blame the lively company… and of course, the accommodations."

The group responded with a burst of knowing laughter. As the favorite of the young Tsarevich, Lefort had been gifted with a palace-sized mansion in the foreign quarter, a place where, to the consternation of the ruling family, Peter was known to spend considerable time.

Theodor chuckled before downing his drink. The kvass was not of good quality, but he was accustomed to the taste.

"Do you remember, Karsten," he asked, taking a new tack, "the best Russian vodka you've ever had? Is it possible to do such a thing? To remember the finest glass of wine that ever graced your lips or recall the sting of the finest--"

"I do remember," Brand interrupted, his eyes glazed with memory. "Exquisite. Shared with the Tsarevich only last year at the onset of the Azov campaign. He was greatly pleased with the work at Preobrazhenskoe and shared his best vodka with the lot of us. If I recall, we toasted Golitsyn!"

"The vodka. It was good, then?"

"Oh, yes. Very."

"And would you be able to find such a taste in Paris?"

"Well, no. But who needs vodka in Paris? The wines, friend, the wines!"

"Yes, yes, the wines," Theodor pressed, "but vodka belongs here. Vodka is native to the East."

Brand made a face. "Either I've had too much to drink or you're drowning the conversation, Theodor. And considering that the first rarely happens..."

"I'm saying that if you seek culture, Karsten, then you only need to open your eyes. We're encircled by it, surrounded--the vodka you drink, the bread that fills your formidable stomach, the samovar, the center hearth, the men with their proud beards and the women with their covered hair...everything around you, friend, it all belongs here. Culture in every corner, every breath of air. The Russians are steeped in it, full to the top with it, so much so that there is very little room for anything new. A Westerner considers culture to be comprised of new things--of new statues and new buildings, new styles and methods. Innovation, you see? The Easterners, however, the old, the staid, the traditional. Well, they define themselves by different means."

"Here, here." Lefort nodded his consent. "Well stated, Theodor. The statuary and architecture are little more than landmarks when matched against the mighty will of a people! Perhaps that explains why I'm so fond of the Russians. They're solid, solid as the ground they stand on. They strike an odd balance between willful and stubborn, and hold fast to their traditions. They're seasoned, reared with an immovable regard for custom--"

"Preserving the strength of what makes them Russian!" Theodor interjected eagerly. "I am pleased to see that you agree with me, Franz."

"Not entirely, I'm afraid." Lefort stepped back to his chair and sat down with a grunt. "Russia lives on its customs. You've made this argument quite well, I think. I would, however, propose that Russia's sturdy customs are also its weakness."

"Weakness?"

"Certainly." Lefort scratched at his jaw. "You know better than I--the Russians' frosty diplomatic reputation on the continent--and we've all seen how the Catholics are treated. But I see much more that would offend the West. The long beards, the icons, the solemn, robed figures--they appear more like Mongols than Lutherans, friend. Few foreigners love Russia the way we do, Herr Sommer. Not that I'm discounting you, but the very customs you praise are the irritation of sods like Karsten here, and ever will be. Weeds in the garden. And thorny weeds--however strong their stalks--must eventually be pulled."

The table remained quiet for a few moments, Lefort's words ringing clearly enough to stifle the usually ample chorus of rebuttal. Sommer thought immediately of Peter.

"It doesn't surprise me that the Tsarevich enjoys your company," he said, feeling a bit thorny himself. "You foster his restless spirit."

"No, you have it wrong, sir." Lefort flashed his contagious smile. "It is most certainly the Tsarevich who fosters me. That boy is willful enough to drive the chariot of the sun, complete the Herculean tasks and have more than enough left over to spell Atlas in his duties! Willful like his brethren, yet his spirit is not chained and grounded. His headstrong ways may be just enough to keep him afloat."

"Or sink him," Theodor countered, finding it irresistible. "Another double-edged difficulty, Franz."

"Ah, we dance in circles!" He threw up his hands in futility. "And we worry too much about tomorrow. Better that we live today. If we want the Tsarevich to accomplish all the great feats you imagine, then we must first be mindful of his present situation."

Brand's expression drooped. "What? You've heard something?"

"Oh, nothing more than we already know. But I would lay a wager that our current situation does not last the year. Peter grows strong while his opposition weakens and becomes more desperate. The stronger our Peter gets, the less sturdy the branch on which Sophia balances. If Peter is restless, it is rightfully so."

Sommer nodded his agreement, suddenly wanting another cup. "The boyars grow weary of Sophia's womanly presence."

Franz shrugged. "It was the defeat in Azov that changed things. Had Prince Vasily returned on a white horse with a victory to his credit, I'm certain the boyars could have swallowed their offence. Sophia chose to tie herself to that buckled rat and now she reaps her reward. No surprise, really. Prince Vasily is not a proper general; no surprise that the Turks were too much for him--"

"The Turks had little to do with our defeat. If we cannot reach our enemies, we can never hope to defeat them."

The unfamiliar voice sounded behind Lefort, stopping him mid-sentence and drawing the attention of the group.

Sommer looked over Franz' thick-shouldered jacket to see a dark-haired man in plain dress, his accent betraying his European heritage.

"I apologize for the intrusion," the stranger said amiably, "but I could not help but reply. It was dysentery and short supply lines that did us in. Given the poor planning of Prince Golitsyn, I don't believe Caesar himself could have pulled us through."

Lefort stood, looking over the man before offering a slight bow. "Ah…General Gordon! Someone who truly knows! You must forgive us, sir--we are drunken men who enjoy conjecture. Our opinions may be strong, but they are certainly no more valuable than the inferior ale we drink. Please, join us. Gentlemen, a man of renown…"

The General nodded, bearing a knowing look. "You are far too modest, sir. As well-known a man as Captain Franz Lefort, your own reputation extends far beyond the borders of Moscow."

Lefort smiled widely, pausing to enjoy the thought. "Hah! They talk more of my mansion than anything else, eh?" He reached out an arm to wrap around the General's shoulder. "I like this fellow. Let us get him a cup!"

"Your hospitality is appreciated. I regret to say that I cannot join you, however." The General's cloak remained buttoned.

"Don't be foolish." Lefort waved him off. "Karsten, pour this good veteran a cup."

Brand complied, passing a glance to Sommer before reaching for the pitcher. "You must excuse Lefort," he said pointedly. "He is terrible with introductions."

"My name is Patrick Gordon, sir."

"General Gordon," Lefort added. "He has just returned from the Crimea."

Brand nodded. "Ah, yes! A name I recognize. You're a Scot?"

"Aye, sir," Gordon answered. "Though I often find myself forgetting the fact."

"Understood. This country has a way of turning us all into Russians, eh? And in this spirit, we cannot let you depart without sharing a toast. In the name of our dear Tsarevich Peter. Or should we drink to Ivan? Perhaps we should each simply pick one of the two and keep him in mind as we drink?"

More chuckling from Brand as he poured a cup for the General.

The officer smiled politely. "I would truly rather not."

"A pity." Lefort shook his head sadly. "But I'm afraid, sir, I must insist."

General Gordon nodded his consent. "I will comply, then, out of respect for your generosity."

As they offered a toast to continued fair weather, Sommer tried to remember all he'd heard about the foreign-born Strel'tsy officer.

Sophia may fill his pockets, but no one speaks ill of him.

Given the shrinking support for Sophia's Regency, the strained relationship between the Naryshkins and the Strel'tsy Guard was quickly repairing itself. Prince Vasily's military failures stirred the fears of the people and rankled the hearts of the soldiers, turning many away. And now, Patriarch Joachim's support for Natalya and the Naryshkin cause was proving too much for the Miloslavsky government to resist. God himself, it seemed, was again choosing Peter over Ivan.

He was married, a man now, and with a child on the way would likely beat Ivan to fatherhood. Peter was strong and able, and commanded his own personal army. It had been a good run for Sophia and the flagging Miloslavsky house, but suddenly their support was falling out from beneath them. Sommer reminded himself that, at its very core, the Strel'tsy Guard was a militia. In the end, they would lean toward strength.

"You see, my friend?" Lefort slapped Gordon on the shoulder when the round and the introductions were complete. "A little sip can make us brothers!"

"If only it were so," Gordon replied. "Admittedly, I come to your table with more than the simple motive of sharing your company."

"You've come looking for me, then?" Lefort pulled away, delivering a comedic glare. "Confound it! I'll have to move away! Trust me--when the Strel'tsy come calling, I know enough to run!"

Brand laughed out loud, enjoying the comment immensely. His laughter seemed a bit of a challenge to the Scot, but Gordon smiled and nodded as though he understood.

"Nothing so threatening, I can say, but I do come with a matter of a very serious nature. I ask only that you hear my request."

"Ah…" Lefort paced back to his seat, extending a hand toward the chair closest to him. "Perhaps our toast should have waited, eh? Have a seat, friend."

General Gordon sat in the chair beside Lefort. Theodor and Karsten followed, taking the seats beside and across from the Scot, their loudly spoken toasts suddenly quieted to a conspirator's hush.

"I will make this as tidy as possible," Gordon began quietly, "for I fear my presence alone may be enough to cause difficulty for you. Still, I was obliged to seek you out on behalf of my men, and perhaps more important, for myself."

"Speak freely, friend. No explanations are necessary."

"I am sure it comes as no surprise," the officer continued, "but confidence in the Regency is lower than ever. Word travels that Regent Sophia has lost support in the Duma. The Strel'tsy Guard grows restless and the army fears another ill-fated campaign in the south.

"But more than this, sir, regardless of this, Tsarevich Peter is a man now and his endeavors in Preobrazhenskoe have not gone unnoticed. He is clearly capable and, at seventeen, well old enough to rule. In the minds of common types like myself, it is time for the Tsarevich to take his rightful place. Perhaps what I'm trying to say is that there are many among the Strel'tsy who look to the future and find their favor resting with the young Tsarevich. The foreign commanders, certainly, but I also believe that many among the ranks would support Peter given the circumstance."

Sommer sat expressionless but not entirely surprised, watching the officer's face for a disingenuous tick or downward glance, finding nothing physical that would lead him to believe that the Strel'tsy officer was being deceptive. Even the stubbornly loyal Strel'tsy could smell it in the air--this was a year for change.

Lefort paused, his brow leaping up and down. "I see, then, why we're speaking in whispers. But General Gordon--may I speak frankly?"

"Yes, sir."

"General, I appreciate your visit and I understand why you would seek me out, but I'm afraid that my influence in matters concerning the Tsarevich is a subject well overdone. Well overdone, truly. And while it may be true that I would run to the ends of the earth at his request, I cannot claim responsibility for any of his actions, particularly in something as vital as the militia."

Lefort was being overly modest…and safe.

The officer shook his head. "I fear I may have misrepresented myself. My offer…my words were only my explanation and not my request. What I ask of you is far simpler and, I hope, less burdensome. I merely seek an audience with the Tsarevich, a discreet audience in which I may be able to voice my support."

Lefort looked over at Theodor, their stares connecting as the Scot finished speaking. Sommer shrugged a bit in reply, his own mind still undecided. It seemed wiser to remain out of this, yet the officer seemed quite honest and by all means generally likeable. If what he claimed were true, there would be precious little support for Sophia when the turn came.

When the Tsarevich had moved out of the Kremlin, miles away from Moscow, Theodor understood, believing it an eccentric but symbolic act. When Peter demanded the construction of a fortress and began recruiting young men of all stations, he wondered at the Tsarevich's grasp of the situation, amused at the thought of a make-shift militia defeating the mighty Strel'tsy Guard. But here, right before Sommer's eyes, was proof of Peter's long-reaching vision.

Lefort waved for another round, staring at the Scot. "I appreciate your ingenuity, sir. And judging by the weight of your avowal, I think the Tsarevich would be more than interested in speaking with you. I shall oblige your request, but you must travel to Preobrazhenskoe with me--I'm certain he won't meet with you in Moscow."

"Certainly. I understand."

"You see, the Tsarevich only travels here for meetings of the Duma, and even then we rarely get the pleasure of his company. Despite the prevailing thought, I do not entertain the Tsarevich to supper on a nightly basis. Besides, he is in much better spirits when he's not in Moscow. So I'll take you to him, but I will offer a single piece of advice that you should take to heart, sir."

"I would be grateful to hear it."

"If the Tsarevich offers you a drink," Lefort said, "I suggest that you accept it."

Moscow, The Great Sovereign's Palace of the Kremlin

June 1689

Evdokia Fedorovna Lopukhin sat quietly as the Kremlin stirred about her, a solitary and beautifully adorned figure placed amidst the finery of her chamber. She moved very little save for her pearl white hands, well-kept fingers working tirelessly embroidering intricate floral motifs on a shirinka handkerchief. Comfortably secluded within the damask-covered walls of her chamber, she counted down the minutes with every stitch and pull.

Soon, she reminded herself. *Surely I will see him soon.*

She received many compliments on her work but couldn't bring herself to believe them, knowing that many would applaud the wife of the Tsarevich simply to gain favor. In her current condition, her ladies were expected to say such things.

She paused, sitting back to examine her work, not liking what she saw. Every stitch and color seemed in place, just as it should be, done competently and with care...yet the pattern seemed lifeless and amateurish compared with others she'd seen. Enough that all the stitching and pulling allowed her to escape from the bustle and noise of the Kremlin and pass the long stretches of solitude and loneliness.

Thinking again of Peter, Evdokia scolded herself for being too needful and prayed for forgiveness.

She couldn't ask for more. Evdokia knew as much and truly appreciated the beauty and comfort that surrounded her. She'd been chosen by the Tsarista and was well versed in the importance of her position and the responsibility to her small but suddenly relevant Lopukhin family name. She knew her role and expected to play it perfectly.

After all, she was the wife of Tsarevich Peter, soon to be the Tsar of all Russia. The thought alone was enough to encourage patience.

Rising from her seat, she set down the embroidery and walked slowly to the large gilt-framed mirror, her round figure hidden far beneath the layers of fine fabric. Her red silk okhaben was trimmed with jewel-encrusted embroidery and worn over a brocade kaftan. Her costume was cumbersome but beautiful, and she often dressed in her finest robes even when alone, walking the parquet floors of her chamber and imagining herself at Peter's side, attending religious ceremonies and presiding over name day celebrations. There would be many such occasions and it seemed only fitting that she practice being Tsarina.

It made her feel closer to him, even now.

The Palace itself was still alien and uncomfortable without Peter, but she didn't mind the seclusion, especially here. At least in the Kremlin, she felt safe.

Her twenty years seemed hardly enough to prepare her for the challenges of this mighty house. The daughter of a state servitor, her family home had been quieter and far less contentious, leaving her ill prepared to deal with the ongoing rivalry between the two clans. It did not, however, take long in Moscow for Evdokia to realize the extent of the trouble in the Kremlin.

The men may have cried out for Miloslavsky or Naryshkin, but the true trouble seemed to lie between the two women who personified this clash: Regent Sophia and Tsarista Natalya.

With Peter, however, there was never any worry. She'd been delivered into his unexpecting arms and felt comfortable immediately. He was a giant of a man and the peculiar look of his eyes often gave the impression that he was angry. One smile, however, would dispel such thoughts and bring her immediately to his side. And though it did feel a bit odd looking so far up at him, Evdokia had to consider herself fortunate.

After all, she had seen Tsarevich Ivan's true condition. She'd seen the slump of his back as he stepped in turtle crawl and heard the slurred speech he used even in the most formal of circumstances. Ivan was married now, as well. Evdokia pitied the elder Tsarevich's poor wife, Praskovia, and used the thought to boost her own spirits in the darkest of the lonely hours.

Thus, she supposed, were the fortunes of a royal bride. She had arrived as a mere accessory to Peter, a means by which to secure his lineage. The wedding, though pleasant, had seemed a matter of course, and Peter's absences became routine less than three months later. While welcomed and respected, Evdokia had never felt truly appreciated until the announcement of her impending motherhood.

Within a matter of days, she had become the talk of the country, and few neglected the opportunity to pay their gracious respects. Natalya's stern countenance had changed a bit, taking on additional politeness and an almost motherly air, her temper now wholly restrained. The prospect of an heir was exciting to most, but none seemed to cherish the thought more than Mother Natalya.

Evdokia was glad to be in the Tsarista's favor. She'd witnessed the shouting matches between Natalya and Sophia, and had no intention of trying to cross the wishes of the iron-eyed matriarch. For Evdokia, it was frightful enough to know that she was tied to Peter's side, inextricably placed in the midst of the Naryshkin clan. Her mother had commented that Evdokia lived in the den of a bear, and Evdokia spent days afterwards wondering whether the comment was in reference to Peter, Sophia, or the Tsarista.

She experienced nightmares in her first weeks in Moscow, horrid dreams in which the Strel'tsy would storm the Kremlin, seeking to slaughter the Naryshkins. Evdokia would see herself running, searching for someone to save her, finding one empty chamber after another, helpless against those who pursued her, incapable of defending herself against certain death. She would awaken to the distant bustle of the Kremlin, knowing that her nightmare could one day become reality.

The bad dreams were a distant memory now. Her blessing had changed everything and would eventually lure Peter back to her side.

Why worry about such things? It is not my place.

There was much about politics that Evdokia didn't know, and even more that she simply ignored. For her there seemed only one relevant fact: within her innocent body she carried the future of the Romanov line and the heir to Peter's throne.

She heard the door open and turned to see Anna slip inside, their eyes immediately connecting. The chambermaid rushed to her side bearing an impatient look.

"Lady, I beg your forgiveness…"

"What is it, Anna?"

"I rushed ahead to tell you. Lady Natalya approaches with the intention of speaking to you. She was not far behind, Lady."

"Lady Natalya?" Evdokia asked.

"The younger Natalya…the Princess."

Little Natalya, Evdokia thought, her pleasant mood fading. *What could she want with me?*

"What is it, Anna? You look odd."

"Forgive me, Lady--"

"Anna…"

"It is nothing, my lady."

"You're frightening me, Anna. Tell me!"

The girl looked toward the door before lowering her eyes. "I am told that the Tsarista intends to move the entire household to Preobrazhenskoe--every last one of us! Forgive me, my lady."

Anna looked down, her eyes fixed on the floor.

Evdokia had no more than a moment to think before the door opened to reveal Peter's sister, Natalya.

The Tsarevich's favorite, little Natalya resembled her mother to a great degree, appearing as a slimmer, youthful version of the Tsarista in her drab black Polish clothes. She'd been lucky to avoid her brother's prodigious height and was, in Evdokia's estimation, fair of face, or at least fair enough not to be considered ugly. Natalya's faults lay elsewhere.

Natalya strode through the doorway as though the chamber were her own, her narrow eyes fixed directly on Anna.

"I believe I just saw you, Anna," she stated pointedly. "Are you considering changing professions? Enlisting as a spy, perhaps?"

Anna hesitated, frozen in place. "No, Princess. I wished only to prepare the Lady for your arrival."

Natalya stared for a moment, her very presence making Evdokia feel weak and small.

"Hmm, yes. Your lips move faster than your feet. Don't they, Anna?"

"Yes, Lady. My apologies, Lady." Anna backed away to the edge of the chamber, not daring to match Natalya's stare. Evdokia remained frozen as well, her anxiety rising to claim any words.

"Yes…" Little Natalya surveyed the room, her eyes finally resting on Evdokia. She paused, looking a bit confused. "My dear, what is that you're wearing?"

Evdokia stared down at the delicate fabric of her beautiful okhaben, never having considered that there might be something wrong with it.

"I--"

"You look ready to march into the Assumption Cathedral! Really, Dunka--there are no ceremonies today."

How could she say such a thing?

"I thought it was pretty," she stammered finally, the words spilling in a rush from her lips. She motioned for Anna and turned for the dressing room. "I shall change immediately."

"No, no," little Natalya protested, stepping forward to block her path. "We have no time for that. My mother wants to see you."

The Tsarista.

Anna tells the truth. When the Tsarista sends for me, she always speaks seriously.

"Allow me to change my attire. It will only take a moment--"

"I told you--we have no time," Natalya returned, taking her arm. "Besides, I suspect Mother will appreciate your choice."

"Truly?"

"Come then," Natalya pressed, tugging on her arm. "I am certain she will like it. As you are, you can do no wrong in Mother's eyes."

Evdokia relented, following her out the door and into the corridor.

"I meant no offense," she said, hurrying her pace to walk beside little Natalya, "but there are few who share your fashionable tastes."

Should I have changed?

Natalya grinned but kept moving. "Should I be offended? Are you making attempt at an insult, Dunka?"

"What? No, Sister. Where your family is concerned, I am incapable of such an offence."

Natalya wrapped an arm around her shoulders, leaning close. "My family is yours, Sister. Lopukhin, yes. Your family name is more important than ever before. But you are the wife of Peter, and soon with the blessing of the Holy Father, you will have his child. This makes you Naryshkin, my dear. Naryshkin, as well. You bear everything that comes with the name."

Evdokia nodded, not knowing what to say.

"You must think of us as one family, dear Sister. Our lot is cast together. If tonight the Strel'tsy come charging through slaughtering Naryshkins, do you think they will leave you out?"

Of course not…

"You are frightening me, Natalya. Please stop."

"I will," she answered, seeming pleased, "but you must think of these things. You are a Naryshkin, and that means supporting those who support you, even if it means wearing something fashionable."

"Yes, Sister."

I should have changed, she thought, her hands feeling the smooth silk of her robe, knowing she wouldn't be wearing it again soon.

Preobrazhenskoe? Is it possible?

Evdokia moved quickly to keep pace with Natalya, Anna's words still sounding in her ears.

"Are we in danger?" she asked, her voice just loud enough to be heard.

Natalya frowned and looked over at her. "No more than ever, Sister. Why would you say such a thing? Has Anna been filling your ears with some lowly gossip?"

Evdokia nodded slightly. "She never stops talking. I really have no means of avoiding it."

"Come, now. I imagine her dialogues are solicited more often than not. Still, you shouldn't be troubled so."

Summoning her strength, Evdokia swallowed and turned her head to look at her sister-in-law.

Out with it! She scolded herself. *There is no offense in asking. If I am wrong, she will simply laugh at me.*

"Anna said that the household is moving to the country, to Preobrazhenskoe."

Natalya showed little reaction, answer enough.

"Mother will tell you the rest," she said simply, "but suffice it to say that Anna speaks the truth."

Evdokia's heart sank.

"But when? And how long are we to remain?"

"Immediately," Natalya replied quickly. "We will depart as soon as things are arranged. You needn't worry--I'm certain you will be treated like a goddess."

"We will stay at the summer palace, then?"

"No," Natalya said, smirking. "I think we will be staying at the Fort."

"The Fort?" Evdokia asked, her worry growing with each moment. "Truly?"

"Ask Mother if you don't believe me. Really, Dunka--I expected you to be overjoyed at the thought of seeing Peter again, whatever the accommodation."

Peter! What was I thinking?

With the advent of a single notion, Evdokia's world brightened.

"Yes, yes," she answered eagerly. "Of course. Will we be...close to Peter?"

Natalya nodded. "I expect so. If he chooses."

Reunited, at last! Will he think me beautiful? He must!

I must prepare. I must be perfect. I will ask the Tsarista for her help.

She felt dizzy and unprepared, joyful but intimidated by the thought of following the Tsarista into the country. The fear remained, at least now tempered by the glossy sheen of hope. She would endure and await Peter's even hand.

As they neared Mother Natalya's Palace, Evdokia saw a gathering in the courtyard outside the entrance, three men whose laughs and conversation echoed throughout Cathedral Square. She recognized two elder boyars in the group, their ample forms flanked around the striking figure of Lev Naryshkin.

"Quite stunning, isn't he?" Natalya asked, lowering her voice.

Evdokia agreed but held her reply, knowing it wouldn't be appropriate.

Handsome, but nowhere near the man that Peter is. Naryshkin is little more than an attendant to Peter...

"Uncle Lev!"

Natalya rushed forward, locking her arms around him in childlike embrace. Naryshkin returned her gesture, laughing out loud.

"I am assailed!" he teased, picking her up and placing her back on her feet before kissing her on the cheek and smiling around to the group. "She looks more like her mother every day, yes?"

The boyars smiled and agreed, nodding their heads in greeting. Evdokia could feel the weight of their glances as they looked past Natalya to the spot where she stood.

"You seem in high spirits, Natalya. You are prepared for this transfer, then?"

"I have been to Preobrazhenskoe many times," she replied, wearing a brave face. "I could practically lead the train myself!"

"And dear Lady Evdokia…" Naryshkin turned his attention. "Our beloved mother-to-be. How lovely you look."

Evdokia curtseyed quietly, suddenly quite happy that she'd chosen to wear her fine clothes. Men of distinction appreciated such things.

"I pray you are in good health."

She nodded coyly. "Yes, sir. You are kind to ask."

He flashed an attractive grin, meeting her eyes, the kind of look that he saved for his favorites. "You are an inspiration to us all, Lady. Truly. I was commenting to Lubov just the other day how our fortunes turned on the day you arrived. The Holy Father blesses us with your presence."

She nodded meekly and looked down to hide her blushing face. "I am flattered, sir."

Following Naryshkin's lead, the other boyars proceeded to deliver their own sincere but less artful compliments, bowing before her like servants. Evdokia kept her humble pose and delivered them sheepish smiles in payment for their deference.

Is this how the Tsarista lives? Will I command such respect when I no longer carry this child?

Evdokia glanced over to see Natalya staring back at her, the look on her face showing little of her uncle's ardor. She glared sternly, tilting her head toward the entrance.

"Ah, ladies, please forgive my rudeness," Lev said, noticing as well. "I have kept you from the Tsarista."

Natalya smiled. "You have never been rude, Uncle. On some things we may always depend."

"Indeed, I do my best," he returned, reaching out a hand to touch her cheek. "I am blessed that my faults are not as evident as most. Dos vidanye, ladies. I expect I shall soon be seeing you in the country."

With that, Lev Kyrilovich Naryshkin bowed and made his exit, boyars in tow. Natalya waited until they were out of sight before turning to Evdokia, her look severe.

"You should strive to be more humble, Sister," she said, reaching out to straighten the shoulders of Evdokia's robe. "Especially when in the presence of someone as important as Uncle Lev."

"Was I not humble?"

Without answering, Natalya moved toward the entrance.

The Tsarista's servant Leszka greeted them, her pale face brightening at the sight of Natalya. She ushered them into the large chamber where the Tsarista stood waiting.

Mother Natalya was by no means a statuesque woman, though she possessed an invaluable quality that made her seem larger than she actually was. The Tsarista was eternally in motion, her primal vigor spurred by movement and conversation, her world kept in motion by her own two feet. Evdokia had rarely seen her sitting. She spoke firmly and persistently, and possessed an opinion for every topic.

"Must you keep me waiting?" the Tsarista asked, stepping forward. She wore a drab black dress that matched that of her daughter.

Evdokia felt immediately overdressed, her stomach cramping at the sight of Tsarista Natalya. The chamber felt odd, larger and more spacious than usual. At a glance it was obvious that some of the furnishings were absent.

"I'm sorry, Mother," Little Natalya answered, moving to her side. "Uncle Lev caught us in the courtyard and he simply wouldn't stop pouring compliments on Dunka, telling her how she is sent straight from heaven!"

"I would expect nothing less," the Tsarista answered, her eyes looking past Natalya. "This is her time for such praise. Evdokia, come in, my dear."

"Yes, Tsarista." Evdokia kept her quivering chin up as she approached Mother Natalya, clenching her jaw to hold it steady. After only six months, she was still far from comfortable in the presence of greatness.

"You are feeling well, I trust?" The Tsarista looked her over, squinting a bit.

"Yes, thank you. I am grateful for your concern."

"You needn't thank me, dear. Your welfare is the first of my prayers in the morning and the last of my thoughts before I lay my head to rest at night. You know this, of course."

"Yes, Tsarista."

"Very good." Mother Natalya offered a pressed grin. "Your costume is inappropriate, dear."

Evdokia looked down at herself, feeling ugly, defeat flooding through her. She fought to keep from crying.

"I'm sorry…I thought it was pretty…"

Natalya smirked. "I told her! I told her she looked li--"

"Natalya, be quiet." The Tsarista hushed her with a raised finger. "Now Evdokia, there is certainly no call for tears."

She was unable to comply; the mention of tears was enough to bring forth the real thing.

"Oh, my dear girl!" Mother Natalya reached out to put a hand on her shoulder. "I know how you endeavor to please us. You are a dutiful soul, but you simply must understand that, in times like these, appearances are so very important. We strive to support Peter through our unity, both inward and out. Do you see?"

"Yes, Tsarista."

"You are, my dear, the sun in the Naryshkin sky. Your child will be the most blessed and loved in all of Russia! Think of it! You carry the future of this land, and the hopes and dreams of our ancestors! Still, such responsibility requires prudence and judgment. The boyars, the nobles, the people--all of them look to see you, Evdokia. Just as it did at your wedding, your appearance sets a standard, a level of respect which spreads to everyone within our family. This will grow tenfold when you become Tsarina. Conversely, if the people think you vain or too extravagant...well, you certainly do not wish to feel their wrath."

Evdokia sniffed and swallowed, her tears all but evaporated by the Tsarista's lecture. She nodded obediently, looking up to meet Mother Natalya's eyes.

"Much better. If we wish to cry, there is certainly enough time away from the eyes of others, yes?"

"Yes, Tsarista."

"Very good," she returned, pacing. "I suppose I should be willing to take the blame for your lack of proper dress; I promise to be more diligent in the future. I will have some clothes sent for you immediately."

Polish clothes. I'll look like an old woman in those hideous things!

"Thank you, Tsarista. I am undeserving."

"Nonsense," Natalya snapped in reply, touching a finger to her face. "No more weeping, dear. It makes others worry. Chin up and smile. With the blessings of the Holy Father, you will soon be standing before your husband again."

"It's...true, then? We're leaving the Kremlin?"

The Tsarista nodded, glancing over at little Natalya. "I meant to tell you myself, but I see our resident nightingale has done the work for me. Yes, dear, it is true. We will remove ourselves to

Preobrazhenskoe to accompany and support our beloved Peter. We shall leave as soon as the arrangements are complete."

Evdokia struggled against her fear, thinking of Peter.

"But Preobrazhenskoe…it is a small summer palace, is it not? Is there enough room for all of us?"

"Quite," the Tsarista replied. "And we will not be going to the summer palace this time. Peter has built us a house at Fort Presburg, something safe for now. We shall, of course, have to sacrifice certain luxuries, but I can think of nothing as uncomfortable as remaining here with the Regent. You will soon be as comfortable there as you have been here. But for now, I need you present and looking appropriate, Evdokia, and no tears. Crying is a public weakness we certainly cannot afford. You are a pillar now, my dear, and you will act accordingly. Soon, our Peter will be Tsar."

Evdokia listened, now beyond her tears, balancing the wondrous thought of seeing Peter with the stifling fear of leaving the protective walls of the Kremlin. His image dominated her thoughts, his encouragements continuing to ring in her ears. Whatever the difficulty, Peter would be waiting with his even smile and steady hand, waiting only to sweep away her worry and keep her forever.

Outside Moscow, Fort Presburg at Preobrazhenskoe

June 1689

The Preobrazhensky Regiment flooded down the hill like marbles poured from a bag, each matching green-coated figure followed in smooth succession by the next, bobbing over rocks and craters as they rolled toward their imaginary enemy. They strode proud and eager, brimming with angry confidence, their eyes fired hot with the will of their leader. To an outsider, these soldiers would have seemed no different than a genuine army, a true regiment training for a real war.

For now, the battles were staged. Performances, like the numerous parades and drills, were becoming more and more authentic with each rehearsal. Even Boris Golitsyn's skeptical mind realized that soon the charge would be more real than imaginary. He'd known Peter long enough to know that even the boy's wildest whims were usually created with a practical purpose. The question seemed evident enough and the answer quite obvious: why raise an army without planning to use it?

The offset cracks of cannon fire sounded in the humid air, smoking projectiles forcing their course above the men and landing with concussive claps on the hill opposite, many finding their mark among the wooden target structures.

Sommer would be proud, he thought, sniffing at the sooty air. *They're getting much better.*

The aim of the Preobrazhensky artillery was steadily improving and with it the level of anxiety in the Kremlin, a worry that had grown from curious conversation to envelop the Regency in fear and suspicion. For now, the simple truth was more than enough to startle Sophia and her flagging group of supporters. Peter's 'play' army was growing into a legitimate threat.

Golitsyn spotted the young Tsarevich riding at the head of the flanking cavalry, dressed in an identical green uniform yet standing out by size alone. Peter's excessive height demanded a large mount, and on his golden Akhal-Teke stallion he seemed to ride three heads taller than the rest of the battlefield. His legs were unusually long, spindly long, stretching down into stirrups that often seemed to reach the ground. Peter shouted orders, his distinct voice the only allowed among the flutters of hooves and tack.

Boris Golitsyn stood patiently as an observer, robed and sweating in the warm sunlight, keeping his distance but impressed nonetheless with the potent leadership qualities exhibited by the Tsarevich. The men scrambled harder when in sight of Peter and constantly looked to his upright figure for direction.

He inspires respect, be it adoration or merely ambition--we must remember to put him atop a horse whenever possible.

The regiments had been gathered through the diligent recruiting efforts of the Tsarevich himself, a varied group of green soldiers composed of everyone from chamberlains to serfs, men of both foreign and native background. In their midst Boris even recognized a few of the lesser nobility, former Miloslavsky loyalists who now believed Peter was about to ascend to his rightful place.

Golitsyn didn't begrudge shifting loyalties. He considered himself a rational man and figured that many others must be equally so. Even the Regency's most solid supporters could read the writing on the wall and were hedging in flocks toward the Naryshkins. Rational men who formerly stood against Peter were realizing that aligning with the future Tsar was the only politically shrewd move. Knowing how badly the Naryshkins needed rational men, Golitsyn was willing to forgive.

Peter's glance leapt up toward Golitsyn before returning to duty. The Tsarevich raised his sword arm, waving the charge forward.

The non-wooden members of the opposing 'army' braced for impact, their unfortunate ranks composed of a similar number of 'enemy' Preobrazhensky, unlucky soldiers who were routinely required to play the part of the besieged in Peter's training exercises. With the exception of several errant artillery deaths, the fatalities were few.

Golitsyn watched as Peter's charge came down like an unkempt avalanche, rumbling over and past the opposition, the enemy dropping in submissive pose when confronted by the overwhelming numbers.

The greencoats pressed, stomping back up the enemy hill in broken formation to seize the artillery positions, whooping with delight as more of their enemy folded.

All in all, the mock attack was undisciplined, yet the worth of the exercise was not difficult to measure. Rough in form, yes, but to Golitsyn it seemed an impressive display nonetheless. The lot of them appeared to be angry, enthusiastic and devoutly loyal. Like real soldiers, however, these men were thirsting for a real fight.

Peter, apparently, was thirsting as well. His expression showed that he was hardly pleased with the day's performance. He nodded stern acknowledgement to Golitsyn before spurring his horse and charging toward the enemy artillery positions.

Golitsyn could hear Peter shouting support to his victorious invaders as he passed through their midst, their line respectfully straightening at the sight of him. Every head turned to watch as he charged up the enemy hill on a mission of his own, the pace of his ascent indication enough that someone was about to feel the lash of his tongue.

Like the rest of the men, the Counselor found himself wanting to follow the Tsarevich so as to hear what was about to be said. He kept his place, however, tugging at his sweat-soaked collar and hoping for a swift resolution to the dilemma.

Peter leapt from his horse as soon as he topped the hill, his arm reaching out to point down at the 'dead' enemies. They rose and stood before him, eyes guiltily averted.

Even from a distance, it quickly became apparent to Golitsyn that Peter was dissatisfied with the effort of the enemy opposition. His comments were straightening the backs and bending the necks of the guilty parties into remorseful drooping heads. Golitsyn strained, but couldn't make out the words.

With an authentic sigh, he found a tree to lean against, regretting his decision to arrive so early in the afternoon. Peter was far more amenable when the sunlight was fading, but the endeavor often involved drinking and he wished to spare himself the arduous merriment on this day. As it was, he'd been standing patiently for the better part of the afternoon, watching as Peter completed his exercise from beginning to end, taking no shortcuts on Golitsyn's behalf.

The Counselor leaned back, closing his eyes to escape the sunlight.

Immediately his mind filled with visions of the Kremlin--soft beds and well-prepared meals, comfortable chairs and the ceaseless feeling of importance.

When Peter moved from the Palace to his Fort at Preobrazhenskoe, it seemed a shrewd political statement and a symbolic expression of the young Tsarevich's independence. Now Lady Natalya had followed her son out into the wilderness, despite Boris' stern recommendation. Golitsyn deferred to her, however reluctantly, and kept his comments to a tolerable minimum.

"Counselor, I see you're enjoying this fine day!"

Golitsyn opened his eyes, immediately recognizing the hearty voice as that of Franz Lefort.

"I confess I'm much the same--it only takes a warm afternoon and a slight breeze to send me off into the deepest of slumber. I don't know where I developed my love for sleeping under the sky."

Lefort approached in his customary brocade and lofty wig, accompanied by a plain-coated man with dark hair and a clean-shaven jaw. Somehow familiar, the man was obviously another foreigner though at first glance he seemed too proper to be one of Lefort's cronies. The Counselor strained for a moment to place the stranger's face, soon realizing that the common dress had fooled him.

General Gordon. Alexis' mercenary from the British Isles and the head of the foreign command. Friend to cousin Vasily…

"Captain Lefort," Golitsyn nodded his greeting, "if I may make a confession of my own, I don't enjoy this sunlight a bit. I'm far better off in winter, both in body and spirit."

"You say that now, sir, but I will remind myself to ask the same question of you in another few months. I suspect you'll be as sour over the cold as you are over the heat."

Golitsyn smiled uncomfortably. "My profession requires me to find complaint and voice it whenever I see fit. I suppose my vocation cannot help but spill over into my character."

Lefort grinned back at him. "That, or the opposite--your character is spilling into your vocation. Counselor, you are perfectly suited to the task as stated. I, for one, would hate to contend with your complaints on a regular schedule._Peter is still in the field, then?"

Golitsyn nodded, gesturing toward the hill. "Yes. There. Do you see him?"

"Ah, yes." Lefort nodded, smiling a bit. "Of course. He doesn't look pleased. Are things going poorly?"

"Not in my eyes," Boris replied quickly, looking past Franz to the General. "I almost failed to recognize you without your uniform, General Gordon."

Lefort bowed his head in apology. "Yes, yes. I was coming to the introduction, truly--although I thought that the two of you might already be acquainted."

"Not formally," he answered, grinning politely. "But all in Moscow are aware of the General's good work."

"And likewise the name of Golitsyn," the man said, extending an arm. "I am, of course, well-acquainted with your cousin Prince Vasily."

Yes…but is he Vasily's man?

"Side by side in the Crimea, eh?"

Gordon nodded solemnly. "Regrettably, yes. We have certainly seen better days. I suppose I must accept a measure of fault for our failure, though I have rarely seen a more poorly managed campaign."

"I am certain you performed admirably, General."

Franz patted his shoulder. "Not your first time against the Turks, if am correct…"

Gordon nodded in agreement. "We attempted to take Azov when I was first commissioned to serve the late Tsar Alexis, many years ago. I'm afraid the outcome was no more successful then than it has been of late."

Golitsyn's memory stirred at the mention of Tsar Alexis. Peter's father had been a progressive as well, often promoting talented foreign men to lead the vastly inexperienced Russian forces.

"You're a Scot. Am I correct?"

Gordon nodded. "Aye, sir. Much seems to be made of the fact. I suppose I'm such a novelty as to be interesting without having done a thing."

He raised an eyebrow. "And still a Strel'tsy General…"

"Yes, sir." The soldier looked down at his plain coat, rubbing his chest as though wishing to feel the buttons of his uniform. "I admit, I spent hours debating the wisdom of wearing my proper dress this afternoon. I realize I'm improperly clothed for such a meeting."

"Think nothing of it," Golitsyn said, waving it off. "No one could blame you for leaving your uniform where it belongs. It certainly would not be the first occurrence. And I believe your arrival may be fortuitous, General Gordon. I'm curious to see what you think of our own green-coated Preobrazhensky."

Gordon looked out to the field, his eyes never straying far from the silhouette of the Tsarevich.

"Admittedly, I've heard far more than I've seen," he replied politely. "But I think I would be confident in claiming that your artillery men are well trained."

"Ah, I see you're now consorting with Herr Sommer."

"Aye, sir." Gordon's face broke into a slight grin. He seemed a measured sort, amiable enough for an officer. Judging by first impressions, Golitsyn liked the Scot.

"Yes, Boris," Lefort patted the taller man on the shoulder. "He's already been indoctrinated into the decadent ways of the Sloboda. I saw to it!"

"Oh?" Golitsyn shook his head sadly. "A pity."

"Indeed, sir!" Lefort returned, chuckling. "Like Virgil into Hades, I was poor General Gordon's guide through the fiftieth ring--a place where foreigners are forced to suffer Russian hospitality and drink inferior kvass with Danish scholars!"

Golitsyn smirked through a whiff of the Captain's breath, looking back with practiced politeness. Despite his variety of faults, Franz Lefort was a tolerable man. His drinking and lewd behavior were hardly enough to offend a man of Golitsyn's experience.

To Boris, it seemed almost natural that Peter would admire a man like Lefort. It was easy to see what the Tsarevich found so attractive in the Swiss adventurer. The Captain was an extrovert of the highest degree, a figure who glowed with charisma even when stinking and dirty. He was a stranger's best friend and could strike up a cordial conversation with anyone. Perhaps more important, Lefort seemed to be everything Russia was not--Westernized, European in thought and dress, adventurous and bold.

And whether the thought was agreeable to him or not, Golitsyn was forced to recognize that this Swiss drunkard was theoretically one of the most powerful men in all of Russia. Boris could only dream of having such sway over the Tsarevich.

Golitsyn shook his head, looking to Gordon. "I would be cautious in my association with Captain Lefort. He's been known to keep a perilous pace and his poor Russian dialect is horribly infectious."

"What?" Lefort showed his palms in mock defense. "I'm just a simple man at heart! And I'll have you know I speak many languages far worse than Russian! If only you could hear my Dutch!"

"For my part, I would hardly be able to discern your skill in that regard," Gordon added, "My command of language is poor."

"I suffer from the same affliction," Golitsyn said.

Lefort reached out to pat Golitsyn on the shoulder. "Do not allow Counselor Golitsyn's humble nature to deceive you, General Gordon. He is quite an important man. Soon, I suspect, even more so. If he gives warning about me or anyone else, then I suspect you should listen!"

The Scot nodded and chuckled only slightly, looking a bit uncomfortable.

Boris watched closely, sizing up the General. His demeanor seemed appropriate given the circumstance, his manner genuine enough. Shrewd, prudent and obviously educated--few of the foreigners Golitsyn had known were so well spoken.

Has he been searched for weapons? Boris wondered, the suspicion lingering despite his appraisal. *Is it ridiculous to think that Lefort would have done so?*

"It may be nothing to a military man," Golitsyn began, "but it seems quite a long ride from Moscow. I know for a fact that you're not fond of the ride, Franz."

Lefort tilted his head a bit. "Aye, customarily not. Odd, then, that I enjoyed the ride so much today. I suppose it all depends on the company one keeps."

Golitsyn brightened falsely, sneering at Lefort. "Your wit is surpassed only by your desire to use it, Herr Lefort."

At this, Franz burst out laughing, pointing a finger. "Hah! You're a wonder, Golitsyn! It's no mistake that you're a great man, and I refuse to torment you ever again!"

Boris kept the grin. "You have my thanks. If I may continue, I realize--"

"You know it is far too long a ride for mere pleasantries," Lefort interrupted genially, "and you want to politely ask why in hell I would deliver a Strel'tsy General into the heart of Preobrazhenskoe. Is that it, Boris?"

"You are embarrassing your guest, Captain."

General Gordon looked at the ground. "I certainly meant no intrusion," he replied quickly, "and I fully understand the…discomfort with my presence here. I confess I'm unable to speak with the ease and expertise of a diplomat, but nonetheless I arrive on a mission of political significance. Trust that I bear the Tsarevich no ill will. Certainly, quite the opposite."

At this, Boris' mind set to work, his authoritative half-grin changing little as he considered the possibilities.

Is Sophia finally losing the Strel'tsy? Are we prepared?

Another clapping round of cannon fire sounded from the hills, preempting Golitsyn's reply. The three watched as the shots landed in erratic pattern around the wooden targets.

"Pitifully astray, most of them," Lefort commented, chuckling. "Perhaps I shouldn't be so quick to shower compliments on Sommer. Apparently, he has much work to do!"

"Customarily, they perform much better," Boris said, glancing at the Scot. "These regiments are composed of young men of varied stations, all of them chosen by the Tsarevich himself. Quite young, most of them--many who would not be otherwise fit for this duty. If nothing else, they possess the passion of their leader."

"Understandable," Gordon returned, "I have many young men in my command."

"Their number would certainly benefit from the presence of a veteran with your experience, General."

"You are most polite. My aim, of course, is to speak with the Tsarevich."

Boris stared for a moment into the field, still undecided. He spotted the dark green jacket of Peter's uniform, the clean white shirt beneath glaring like a light among the soiled dress of the others. Peter would undoubtedly wish to hear the Scot's proposal, but it seemed best not to appear too eager.

"Admittedly, it can be hard to pry him from atop his horse…"

The General looked suddenly guilty, as though he'd offended his hosts.

"Of course," he said quickly, "I would be more than willing to discuss the matter of my business with you--prior to speaking with the Tsarevich. You would know better than I whether it deserves his attention."

"He is a young man," the Counselor answered, "but shrewd, nonetheless. If it concerns the Strel'tsy, then I'm certain Peter would find interest."

"I'm pleased to hear this."

Golitsyn's attitude softened a bit. "My approval is certainly no requirement, but I would be more than happy to hear your news. Perhaps I can help you phrase things in a way that the Tsarevich will find more…palatable."

The Scot nodded back at Golitsyn, then cast a glance toward the Captain. Lefort turned the corner of his mouth and winked reassuringly.

"You needn't worry about Franz," Boris said. "If there is one part of the Captain's character that is beyond reproach--and there may be only one left--it is his sense of loyalty. Your words are safer here than anywhere in Moscow."

"I meant no disrespect to the Captain," the General replied immediately. "He, perhaps better than anyone, knows of my purpose here. In truth, I would like him to stay."

"No worries, General," Franz replied, bowing slightly, "At your request, I will gladly remain."

"Given the nature of my visit," the Scot began, turning back to Golitsyn, "I would imagine that you've already guessed my mission. I suppose I should begin by saying that I do not speak for the whole of the Strel'tsy, but only for my regiment."

A whole regiment. He doesn't know how few we are…

"The Strel'tsy are restless," the Scotsman said with a reluctant tone, lowering his voice, "and a majority of the boyars grow weary of the Regency. Many feel Sophia has overstepped her bounds--"

"He speaks the truth," Lefort burst out. "I overheard that she has taken to calling herself the Tsarina!"

"That bit of information is terribly stale," Boris snapped. "Would you kindly allow him to speak?"

Lefort raised a palm. "My apologies. Please continue, General."

Gordon cleared his throat. "Admittedly, I am likely best served by limiting my discourse to a few words, as I tend to stray from my purpose if I explain too much. Spoken quite plainly, sir, I wish to convey my…confidence in Tsarevich Peter. Despite the general opinion of the Strel'tsy, my men are an honorable lot and quite proud of what they feel they've earned. With respect, Counselor, I survived both of your cousin Prince Golitsyn's failed attempts against the Turks--as did many of my men. I assure you, these defeats are not forgotten easily. After wearing home the blood of their dead comrades, my men were subjected, twice over now, to the disgrace and injury to reputation caused by such losses."

Gordon paused a moment, appearing a bit embarrassed. Sensing that his appeal remained unfinished, the two remained silent and attentive.

"I often feel as though my speech sounds far too selfish, although, I assure you, I speak on behalf of many a man. And though I may never be considered a Russian patriot, I would certainly figure that my own fears for the safety of this land are echoed loudly by its countrymen.

"Tsarevich Peter possesses the spirit of Moscow," Gordon continued without pause, "even in his absence. Peter's name resides on the lips of every breathing soul, from the well-fed boyars to the starving administrative clerks. Certainly, the Regent and Tsarevich

Ivan continue to fulfill their duties in Kremlin ceremonies, yet there is an odd feeling that accompanies them--a feeling that we are all merely waiting, that the Regency is nearing its end. The people know that Tsarevich Peter has come of age, and the rumors of what occurs here at Preobrazhenskoe are numerous and varied. In short, the Tsarevich is a great unknown and, therefore, most compelling."

Counselor Golitsyn nodded diplomatically, holding back the fountain of enthusiasm that accompanied visions of the Strel'tsy riding at Peter's back. With Sophia's formerly loyal Guard behind him, the Tsarevich would scarcely need his rogue army at all. Golitsyn thought of Lady Natalya and delighted in the prospect of delivering her the news.

"You have my thanks, General. I am very pleased with your appraisal of the situation in Moscow." Golitsyn tempered his tone, not wanting to sound too eager. "Given your credentials--and your task, of course--I can hardly deny you audience with the Tsarevich. Ultimately, of course, it will be Peter's choice, but I expect he will be eager to meet with you."

"You have my thanks, sir."

"Admittedly," Golitsyn added, raising a finger, "this is a most surprising development...one which could greatly swing things in favor of the Tsarevich and, humbly, the whole of the Naryshkin clan. Your mere presence here would cause a panic in some circles. At the risk of sounding too threatening, General Gordon, I wish to impress upon you that should you make a promise, the Tsarevich will be most determined that you keep it."

Again the notion struck Golitsyn, the worrisome voice crying out within his conscience, questioning whether any Strel'tsy officer, foreign-born or otherwise, could possibly wish to align himself with Peter and the Naryshkins.

Has Sophia's control deteriorated so thoroughly?

"I want to assure you," the Scot replied, his face never changing, "I would never have embarked on this endeavor had I not been certain. Respectfully, I would remind you that my military career sits in a tenuous position. Personally, sir, I risk all by being here."

The Captain nodded, squinting his eyes and allowing Gordon's words to linger in the air. Both men looked to Golitsyn.

"I appreciate your candor," he said, nodding as well. "We must all be vigilant concerning our place in this world, particularly in such unpredictable times. Russians are not unaccustomed to such worries. Indeed, our country itself seems to linger in melancholy and restlessness. If it eases your mind at all, General, I would suggest that every soul in Preobrazhenskoe feels the same. From the lowest up, we all risk our futures here. Regrettable, certainly. Such fear can be stifling, I think. This is our condition, however. Until Peter sits in his legitimate place, we must all consider ourselves at risk."

Outside Moscow, Peter's Cabin at Preobrazhenskoe

June 1689

"Are you certain? I'll pour you one if you wish."

"No, no thank you, Captain." Patrick dipped his head and raised a hand in appreciation. "From what you say, I can expect to be drinking my share when the Tsarevich arrives. I should wait for his arrival."

Franz shrugged. "As you will…though I fear that we have all pressed the issue of vodka too far. You needn't worry so much, friend. Peter is quite good-natured with men of your make. For your service if nothing else, I would guess that he would be fond of you."

"Your confidence is appreciated, sir."

Gordon enjoyed Lefort's company. It was difficult not to like the man; Lefort was perpetually bright and possessed a happy, restless spirit that could not be repressed. He drank, danced, laughed, and argued with precisely the same vigor, his face bearing a familiar quality that made you feel as though you'd known him for years. Never disinterested nor overly offended, Franz could hold a spirited conversation and often turn a witty, albeit crude, phrase.

At their first meeting, the General enjoyed his discussions with the Captain but estimated that Lefort's nature would be too much to tolerate at length, that his vigor would soon become tedious and his wit tiresome. The opposite proved to be true. Lefort was animated and verbose, but possessed a keen awareness of his own personality. His comments were often sharp but never injurious, and when exposed over a long period of time, Lefort showed a willingness to amend his extroversion and make himself a joy rather than a nuisance.

Their time had passed pleasantly enough, tempered only by the knowledge that the meeting with the Tsarevich was imminent. Now, with his introduction only moments away, Patrick felt quite unlike himself. The changeless, calm exterior that served him on the battlefield was conspicuously absent in this diplomatic circumstance. Despite the kind reassurances of Lefort, he was filled with trepidation as he sat waiting on the stiff-cushioned chair.

"Odd, that I find myself in this position," he said, thinking aloud, regretting the comment as soon as he'd uttered it.

"Eh?" Lefort sniffed, rubbing at his nose. "How so?"

"My apologies, Captain. I speak out of nervous anticipation."

"What? No apologies--go on, friend. You make me curious."

He shrugged. "Had I your wit, I could surely explain myself better, but suffice it to say that the irony is not lost on me."

"Irony?" Lefort frowned quizzically.

"That of a Scottish soldier who finds himself in some authority regarding the politics of the Russian Tsarevich…and in what seems a vital role as well."

Franz began with a single huff which rumbled back inside him and emerged as a short burst of chuckling. His eyes narrowed happily as the chuckles multiplied, growing quickly into a shower of laughter.

"My apologies, General. I have no intention of belittling your cause. I laugh because you give me perspective on my own position. Given your words, my entire life could be considered an ironic occurrence!"

"I meant no offence--"

"Oh, of course not! None taken, my friend. Trust me, you have my sincere sympathies. Who could understand your dilemma better than I?"

"No one, certainly."

"Indeed." Lefort chuckled again. "I've often felt like a fish out of water in this bundled-up country. And being the man that you are, I suspect that you know a bit about me already. Considering the fact that you sought me out in a tavern, I feel it safe to assume that you are aware of my reputation. General, I have been told that I am the most favored foreigner in the dubious history of this land… something for which I am greatly criticized."

"I heard no criticism, Captain."

"Eh?" Franz grinned in reply. "Well, you must have failed to solicit anyone of worth! But trust me when I tell you that you and I are not the first. This country has a history of employing foreign souls like ourselves to do the work of the State. You know this, of course--you have been here longer than I. The Sloboda exists only because there are enough of us to warrant it.

"The people of this land are forged in stone," he continued, "changeless in both thought and action. Hardy, yes. Capable, certainly! The perfect slab of stone, perhaps, if only they were more malleable…but desperately in need of sculpting, nonetheless. If a Tsar is observant enough--if a ruler possesses enough vision--he can see his country for what it is and truly know that he commands not a gem, but a slab.

"Knowing he needs tools to sculpt such impermeable rock, he calls upon the West. Expertise, culture, finesse--the qualities poor Muscovy lacks. European men, then. A veritable drawer of knives, eh? Sharp tools, capable of understanding what a country must look like. Men like you and me."

"Sculpting tools," Gordon replied, lamenting his inability to trade elaborate metaphors with the Captain. "Yes, I suppose. I have heard armies spoken of as swords."

"And so the same here, but with individual men," Lefort said, nodding. "Left alone, Russia does not move. And it must be moved! It must be prodded, pushed and pulled--by the bit, like a well-fed mule! We are the ones to accomplish this. And thankfully, Tsar Alexis was shrewd enough to realize it. Peter, as well. And I tell you, the boy is not without compassion. He treats foreigners kindly, in general--the lot of us."

"Considering his past with the Strel'tsy, I would think the Tsarevich…" Gordon hesitated, measuring his words. "What I mean to say is--"

"That Peter won't like you?" Lefort responded, chuckling with his mouth full. "It is a distinct possibility, of course, but not for the obvious reasons. After all, you served under Tsar Alexis. Tsar Fedor as well. You're a military man and foreign-born."

"Aye."

"Harbor no worries, General. Be respectful, but don't kneel or grovel. When he questions you, speak your mind. When he presses, politely back down. Not that you'll have any trouble, eh?"

"Your counsel is appreciated, Captain."

Lefort grinned. "Yes, I know. Think nothing of it--my charity is nothing more than penance. And you seem like a straight enough fellow, Strel'tsy or not! Tsar Alexis was said to like you, and that speaks plenty loud enough for a man of my dubious station. I shall do what I can to facilitate your success." Franz reached for his cup, downing what remained.

Gordon nodded his acknowledgement. Despite the sincere reassurance from the Captain, Patrick felt restless, unable to master his thriving trepidation. There was hope in the Captain's words, but Lefort was very fond of the Tsarevich, perhaps too fond to be taken seriously when considering Peter's temperament.

Lefort's insights were always delivered with a willing air, and alone they often seemed unimportant. When taken collectively with those of others, however, they presented the General with a very indistinct portrait of the young Tsar. The descriptions of Peter ranged from sublime to abominable, with seemingly everyone bearing a unique and distinct opinion.

Some considered him the perfect candidate for the throne--restless, yes, but capable, sharp like his father. Others interpreted his indomitable spirit as frivolous and lazy, denouncing Peter for his absences at church and his continued fraternization with foreigners. Of late, the rumors spoke of a German mistress in the Sloboda and questioned where Peter was resting his head at night.

In general, the negative comments were uttered by supporters of Sophia and the Miloslavskys, delivered with the same passion that stirred the accolades from supporters of Lady Natalya and the Naryshkin clan. Loyalties were deep and cleanly divided in Moscow, making the truth an interpretive judgment. Yet, despite the fact that factionalism ruled opinion in Moscow, Patrick had listened carefully to everything he heard about the Tsarevich, knowing that this decision would be the most important of his time in Russia.

Still the mercenary foreign general, Gordon was now moving from relative obscurity to the forefront of this decisive conflict, casting his lot as the crucial moment arrived. Patrick was happy to see the Tsarevich was preparing his 'play' army; the boy was shrewd and, like Gordon, recognized that the time for change was approaching.

A gamble, yes, he thought, trying not to stare at the Captain as he ate. *But the better side of the wager. Is it truly wise to oppose this young lion?*

There was no need to argue, even with himself. The die had been cast; his mere presence here was proof of his new loyalty.

The door opened suddenly, startling Patrick out of thought.

He squinted into the late burst of sunlight that shone through the door, staring up at the tall silhouette that stepped through the opening. The figure filled the doorway, hands on hips, forcing the sunlight to find its way around him into the room.

"My friends…"

"Peter!"

Lefort stood from his chair with a grunt. Patrick did the same, waiting as the Captain rushed over to greet the Tsarevich.

Stepping out of the shadow Peter seemed a colorful giant, almost too big for the room itself. His long dark hair curled wildly, hanging loosely about the shoulders of a green Preobrazhensky coat that bore no medals or sign of rank. His uniform was stained with mud, his smiling face smudged and dirty.

Despite it all, Peter seemed every bit the Tsar. His charismatic air was undeniable, his youthful spirit infectious at once. This much was apparently not just rumor.

"Franz! I meant to come sooner. I hope you've been treated well."

"Yes, Peter. As always, my friend. You may regret treating me so well--today I come bearing a dangerous gift!"

Peter grinned, his wide eyes turning to meet Gordon. "Welcome to Preobrazhenskoe, General Gordon."

Remembering Lefort's instructions, Gordon did not kneel. He offered a short and respectful bow. "You have my thanks, Tsarevich. It is an honor to be received."

Peter returned the gesture. "Your politeness is appreciated, but I believe that the honor is mine. After all, you bear decoration and battle the Turks. My battle is still confined to conquering wood and bags of dirt."

Lefort laughed, patting the Tsarevich on the back. "Your imaginary prisoner count was formidable, sire."

"Where imaginary foes are concerned, we take no prisoners, Franz. Now let the General speak."

Boris Golitsyn entered behind the Tsarevich, closing the door behind him. His eyes met Gordon's, and the Counselor offered a nod of greeting.

"I am flattered, sire," Gordon replied, "though I must protest that my decoration was in large part due to the generosity of your father."

"A soldier, nonetheless," Peter returned glaring. "And an honorable one, from all I hear of you, General. I am told that my father was very fond of his foreign officers, but spoiled none. Your accolades are well earned, I'm certain."

"I fear our last effort against the Turks was a failure. For that, Tsarevich, I must rightly take my share of blame."

Peter nodded. "An honorable thought, General, but you were hardly culpable. From all accounts, the skirmishes were well executed. Watering the troops proved your end! Prince Vasily was the commander and organizer, and from what I hear, he is already bearing the brunt of the blame."

"You have my gratitude, sire."

Peter stared back. "You and I will certainly talk of the Turks. I have much to learn from you, I think."

"Yes, Tsarevich."

Taller than most, General Gordon was unaccustomed to looking other men directly in the eye. He had always enjoyed his height advantage and could honestly say that he had found a significant benefit to being taller, in both his public and private relations. Never before had Gordon felt physically outranked by another man.

It was these thoughts that passed through the General's mind as he looked up to match Peter's stare, feeling suddenly very small and unimportant. He'd seen the Tsarevich from a distance many times before, but the young man's true size was much more impressive up close.

Already almost seven feet tall, Peter stood on spindle thin calves, his stockinged legs seeming to take up most of his height. His torso was thin but carried the sinew of youthful muscle, strength brimming beneath the pale flesh. His visage was uncommonly intense for an aristocrat but reflected no anger or opposition. He brushed a wavy brown lock from his eyes and surveyed the General with a satisfied look.

A shiver--of all things--traced down the General's veteran spine.

Odd, unfamiliar, the rush of intimidation was palpable, and intriguing.

"Please, General," the Tsarevich said, leaning toward him, "if you would give me your honest opinion of what you saw on the field today--your professional opinion, of course--I know I'm certainly no commander and that, compared to a legitimate army, we still lack considerable ground, but a few simple directions might be enough--anything, really, that would--"

"Peter, Peter," Lefort interjected happily, "perhaps we should allow our guest to regain his seat. I believe he was waiting for your arrival to taste the food!"

The Tsarevich nodded, shrugging a bit. "Yes, yes, of course. Sit, please! Of course. You haven't eaten, General?"

"No, sire," Gordon replied, taking his chair. "But not for want of encouragement. The Captain has taken very good care of me."

"We shall drink, then."

"Certainly, sire."

Lefort chuckled, reaching for the vodka pitcher. "Notably, I have also taken care of myself. Pleasure before work, eh? This is the sensible course. How is a man supposed to devote a true and honorable effort to work when the passions of his body and spirit are screaming like sirens?"

"Franz is right!" Peter exclaimed, taking the chair beside Gordon, pulling it out from the table to accommodate his long legs. "We cannot rightly speak of serious subjects with our stomachs groaning. You'll see, General. I've sent for something--I think you will be surprised at how much better everything tastes when you're away from Moscow!"

The Captain nodded his agreement, passing a drink to each of them. This time, Gordon readily accepted, as did Golitsyn.

"To our esteemed guest," Lefort said, raising his cup, "and to the continued welfare of the Strel'tsy, wherever their loyalties may lie."

Gordon drank without making comment, unsure of how to interpret the toast. Lefort passed him an amiable glance, offering a slight wink.

The vodka was cold and fine, the beautiful taste that Gordon had learned to appreciate since coming to Russia. He drank little else now and was relieved rather than concerned when he learned of the Tsarevich's propensity for the same.

Peter set down his cup, motioning for Lefort to refill it. Gordon followed, wanting to taste more.

"Franz, Franz," Peter scolded, shaking his head. "Regrettably I must tell you that you managed to combine two toasts into one. General Gordon and the Strel'tsy. We must drink again!"

"I cannot argue, nor do I wish to."

Lefort poured a second round for everyone but Golitsyn, who turned down the offer with a stern glance. The Captain shrugged and offered his now familiar chuckle, taking pleasure in his task.

Peter raised his glass again. "Hush, now, my friends. Drink."

Before he'd even finished the second cup, Patrick was feeling the effects of the drink, his tired joints loosening a bit with the warmth.

I should have eaten, he lamented, watching as the Tsarevich finished with a shake of the head.

"Much better!"

"Indeed."

The Tsarevich lifted his chair and moved it closer to Gordon, leaning forward, his face bearing a radiant eagerness. Patrick held the younger man's stare comfortably, his own age seeming more evident in the face of such vitality.

"Admittedly, our performance in the field is far from what it should be, particularly in the eyes of a true soldier like you. Embarrassing, truly. Many of the boys are quite green, but I refuse to blame them for my own shame--our deficiency can be singly attributed to a lack of quality command."

"You seemed to do your part well, sire."

"Oh, no, General." Peter shook his head a bit. "I must ask for your apology--you've mistaken my passion in the field for rank."

"Peter is but a private," Lefort interjected. "His shouting was spurred by frustration."

"I've earned no command yet, and I should rightly keep my mouth closed in exercise."

A private? The General paused, not knowing how to react.

"Well, you certainly earn respect with your presence in the field, sire, regardless of rank."

"Do you mean my shouting?" Peter replied, his focus still on the Scotsman. "Bah! You're being complimentary. I will likely be confined to artillery for now. This must seem ridiculous to you, General. Here you are, an accomplished officer, fresh in the afterglow of my wretched exercise, listening to us babble."

"Oh, not at all ridiculous--"

"I would benefit from even the slightest measure of your expertise."

"I would certainly offer what I could, sire."

Peter stood suddenly, as though unable to wait any longer. "Have you had your fill, General?"

Gordon nodded. "Yes, sire."

"Let us walk, then."

"Well, yes. Certainly, sire."

Gordon moved to stand from his chair, accompanied by the others.

"I know you've traveled today, General. I've been inconsiderate not to let you address your business." Peter leaned down a bit, tilting his head in Golitsyn's direction. "But I think we would speak more comfortably alone."

The General turned in time to see Golitsyn's eyes roll a bit. The Counselor offered no verbal protest, stating only that he had important matters awaiting him. Lefort followed in kind, proclaiming that he was still a bit hungry and would rather wait for the honey cakes he'd been promised. The two stood politely as General Gordon and the Tsarevich stepped out into the fading afternoon light.

"I prefer the air out here," Peter said to him, leading the way. "Moscow is filled with soot. After spending time here, it is difficult to breathe the aged wind that never leaves the Kremlin. Dead air, it is. Stifling. Not like this."

Gordon nodded, moving to keep pace as they stepped down the path toward the tiny fortress Peter had named Presburg. For all its inexperience, the camp at Preobrazhenskoe was orderly and well-maintained, comfortably holding Peter's 'play' army. The small village had grown much in the last few years and was, at the moment, host to the majority of the Naryshkin clan and their many attendants and staff.

The General looked over to the line of wooden houses that comprised Preobrazhenskoe, marveling at the Tsarevich's effect on the area. The sound of new construction ground and popped in the distance, hammers and saws still working in the early evening to keep up with the population boom. The Tsarista's household alone was enough to double the small population of the village.

Natalya Naryshkin is here somewhere, he thought wondering at the sudden importance of this little village. *Golitsyn, and all the others. They've moved their entire world out to this village. Surely the Tsarista sees an end to all of this.*

"I am quite aware of the Strel'tsy's feelings for my side of the family," Peter began quite candidly, speaking without restraint. "I was born into the Naryshkins, placing me at the opposite end of the Strel'tsy's desires. I realized at an early age that, although I am neither the cause nor the reason for this anger, I am most certainly its target."

"My lord, I fear that you misinterpret my motive."

"Certainly not, General," Peter replied immediately, raising a finger. "But please, before we go any further, I must ask you not to use formalities when addressing me. I don't like them. Titles have their purpose in the proper setting, but we don't need them here. Call me Peter, or Tsarevich, if you wish."

"You have my gratitude, Tsarevich. And, of course, you may call me Patrick, though I'm more often called by my last name."

"There is so much I wish to ask you, General--and I wouldn't want to disrespect your rank. You've seen the poor condition of my regiments and our startling lack of skill. I know that they call this my 'play' army--as though I were setting up wooden soldiers for amusement. And though I cannot deny my pleasure, General, I wonder what you think of Presburg and the Preobrazhensky and Semyonvsky Regiments. I wonder what purpose, if any, you think I give to this endeavor?"

"To defy the Strel'tsy," Patrick answered honestly, "Or to defend yourself from them."

Peter nodded, smiling. "Good. I'm so glad that you understand. You won't blame me, then, for being suspicious where the Strel'tsy are concerned. They have never been my allies nor do I ever expect them to be. When I was a child, General, I lived in constant fear that they were conspiring to kill me. Now, less so--the fear, not the suspicion. It is only through a man like you would I ever have believed such a proposition as Boris has relayed to me."

The General cleared his throat, prepared to make his appeal.

"Tsarevich, you know perhaps better than most that the Strel'tsy Guard has many faces, and that to test the temperament of any one man is not to know the whole. Some are, regrettably, still the monsters which you built all this to oppose. I speak, of course, of the Russian colonels and their loyal Muscovite brigades. Tradition runs deep in their ranks, fathers and grandfathers, generations that keep them in place. Their hierarchy has forgotten their purpose and long ago abandoned their common pursuits, becoming little more than professional bullies.

"But the Strel'tsy as a whole? We must remember--the Strel'tsy Guard is comprised of individual soldiers but acts as a mob. The

Russian colonels still wield great influence, but at the end of the day, it is the temper of the whole that rules their actions. Gratefully, I believe the majority now lean in your favor."

"Truly?"

Gordon paused, considering his words, trying to remember what he'd practiced. "The musketeers have been furious with Prince Vasily since our embarrassment in the steppes. Their confidence in the Regency has disappeared, Tsarevich, and you stand ready, of age, bearing the poise of your father. You are prepared to lead, by all measures. The blessed addition to your family could be seen as nothing less than divine validation.

"There is change in the air, Tsarevich. Even an old dog like myself can smell it. I was rightly contracted to serve the throne and I believe that you and Tsarevich Ivan will soon sit as co-tsars, without Sophia. As the Regency falters, I find myself disappointed in the current command and looking to the future. Your future, sire."

Peter offered a serious look but said nothing, allowing the General to finish.

"I am but one commander of many," Gordon continued, "but I believe my regiment to be unified. With their leave, I have come today to humbly express our confidence in you, Tsarevich. You were ordained as Tsar long before Sophia took her place--and seem quite ready now to rule. Should you seek the throne, Tsarevich, I feel comfortable in saying that my regiment would attend to your orders."

Having said it, Gordon paused, watching the Tsarevich to gauge his reaction. Peter's serious look deepened, his jaw clenching as he nodded in respect.

"You have my gratitude," Peter responded, his eyes never breaking stare. "I am honored to have your confidence, General Gordon. I cannot say what is to come, though I suspect I shall have to take you on your offer."

"Although I speak only for my regiment, I believe many of the foreign colonels to be of like mind. I will aid in this endeavor, certainly, but you would not be wrong to count them among your supporters."

The Tsarevich paused, his face growing serious. "Thank you, General. I will treasure your offer."

I must not spur him to fight, Gordon thought, receiving the Tsarevich's embrace.

"If I may ask one question, sire?"

"Certainly, General! You may ask a thousand!"

"I do not wish to offend, but I wish to know whether you intend…whether it has ever been your intent to attack the Regent with your regiments and take the throne by force."

"You wish to dissuade me from such thoughts," Peter replied, speaking frankly.

"I meant only--"

"Fear not, General," Peter said, grinning a bit. "I am a rational man--green, but wise enough to see that my army is no match for the Moscow Strel'tsy. The Preobrazhensky? Call it an army of defense, or as some believe, an army for novelty. Or perhaps more accurately--an irritation, a fly in Sophia's wine. I cannot speak to my intent, but I am well aware that attacking Moscow would prove futile."

The General lowered his eyes. "I meant no offence, Tsarevich."

"None taken, General!" Peter placed a hand on his shoulder. "None at all! We must speak of these things openly. Trust that I will ask you often for your opinion."

"And I will gladly offer it," the General responded, renewed by the Tsarevich's words.

"Excellent." Peter nodded. "Tell me, did you attend the victory parade?"

"Yes. I regret to say that I was compelled to take part. Your absence was noted, Tsarevich."

"Ah--that's what I was getting to!" Peter smiled again.

"I dare say that your absence at the parade was the stone that tipped the wagon."

"Ah!"

"Miloslavsky and Naryshkin. Regent Sophia and Tsarevich Peter. Whether truth or not, the two of you have taken opposite sides in the minds of your people. And respectfully, sire, no sane man would choose a childless Ivan over a vibrant Peter. For the time being, Tsarevich, the Strel'tsy are wavering."

Peter nodded slowly. "Your candor is appreciated, General. I suppose I knew this would come."

They walked for a while without speaking, taking survey of the Tsarevich's proud little fortress, led only by the occasional gesture from the young man as he pointed out the finer points of Fort Presburg.

The General soon felt comfortable with Peter. The Tsarevich was larger than Patrick, but did not seem to use his size to intimidate. To the contrary, there was a distinctly humble and personal air to this would-be tsar, a provincial coat that covered him from the dirt on his face to the buckles of his German boots. He smiled when he was amused and frowned when in disagreement. Peter moved and expressed, thought and acted, served his emotions instead of disguising them.

Whatever the outcome, General Gordon had decided that he liked Peter.

If the boy can survive, he may just turn into something exceptional…

Gordon had never presumed to know the hearts of men or believed that he could sway anyone's opinion but his own. Yet, standing in the presence of this brimming young heart, feeling the effect of the spirit he'd been told so much about, Patrick knew that it would be his job to keep the foreign Strel'tsy colonels in line.

To convince them that it will be worth it to risk their lives for Peter.

He heard a bell in the distance and thought of the Patriarch.

With the Holy Father's blessing, he will be Tsar.

As they reached the boundaries of the encampment and turned back toward the Fort, Peter broke the silence with a question, and followed it with another.

Curious, the young Tsarevich continued, discovering every detail of the failed campaign, asking for Gordon's opinion alongside the facts. The boy devoured the information and only became quiet when the subject turned personal.

General Gordon had expected to leave the next morning but spent two additional days at Preobrazhenskoe, leaving himself entirely at Peter's disposal, answering questions and soaking in the youthful light of Russia's future Tsar.

Moscow, The Great Sovereign's Palace of the Kremlin

Early July 1689

Sophia rolled in the bedclothes, resting her head in the soft pillows, allowing herself to linger in the sleepy state for a moment longer. She felt tired and, for the first time since taking the reins of the Regency, was actually considering how it might all come to an end.

She closed her eyes, trying to clear her mind, feeling only the soft linen beneath her cheek, drifting on the edge of sleep. She dozed a moment longer, her thoughts flying far above her troubles, escaping for one weightless instant before falling back down to the cold earth.

A clatter from across the chamber opened her eyes.

Sophia sat up, exhaling her frustration.

"Must you make so much noise, Vasily?"

Prince V.V. Golitsyn stood tugging on his stockings, hopping recklessly on one leg. He sneered and sighed before falling back onto the velvet-cushioned seat, unfinished.

"I detest dressing myself," he said, not bothering to look at her.

"Odd," she quipped, "considering how fond you are of undressing…"

She threw back the bedclothes and set her feet down on the small silk Persian rug, watching for his reaction. Knowing he was under observation, Golitsyn frowned appropriately and continued struggling.

"Vasily?"

He didn't respond, mortally focused on straightening his seams. The sight of him brought a smile to Sophia's face, the sour mood quickly fading away.

"You're a competent man," she teased. "Surely you can negotiate an agreement with your own hosiery."

"Your faith inspires me, Lady."

She gathered her robe and stepped past him to the wash basin, the polished parquet floors cold on her bare feet. Even in the summer, the floors of the Kremlin seemed to hold their chill, making it impossible to ever feel entirely comfortable.

As a child, she'd been told that the palaces of the Kremlin were kept cool by hundreds of spirits, ghosts of the past who inhabited their walls. At the time, she believed the stories and wondered if one day she, too, would haunt the chilly corridors. Now, years later, she was sure of it. For Sophia, it had always been home, her cage and her castle, the pleasant memories living comfortably alongside the horrid ones. After all she'd seen and done, there would certainly be a spot waiting for her amongst her ancestors.

The corridors had been uncommonly quiet of late, a calm condition which Sophia would normally have welcomed. The solitude, however, did little to ease her worry. The showy departure of Lady Natalya and her household seemed at first to be a gift of divine providence, yet Sophia soon realized that she was merely trading one problem for another. Natalya's absence would mean less drama in Moscow, but the boyars and the Strel'tsy were wavering in the face of such clan division. Sides were being taken. Peter and Ivan were being openly compared.

Sophia was no fool. In fact, she considered herself the most practical and rational of her family, a pillar of strength who understood the role she'd been born into and gladly accepted her burden. She was more than shrewd enough to realize the widening gap between Ivan and his famous brother, the fact that despite Ivan's consistency, despite his reverence and dutiful presence, he was dim and inferior in the eyes of the Russian people. Brother Peter had strength and wit, influence and the will to oppose.

And an heir on the way, she thought, lifting her heavy fur-lined robe onto her wide shoulders, hating the sight she saw in the mirror.

"I will wear my hair down again," she announced, expecting a reply. "After all, I'm still unmarried."

"But you are Regent." Prince Vasily glanced up at her. "You know I support you, but perhaps this would be the time to…lean toward the appropriate?"

She turned, staring. "What?"

"I mean, simply, that in light of the Duma's criticism, perhaps you shouldn't be overstepping your bounds again so soon."

"Do you honestly believe that they would continue to press this piteous complaining? Why should I consider their opinions at all? They allow me to bear the burden, to act as Tsarina, to legislate and negotiate as Tsarina, to carry the weight of decision--yet let me sign as Tsarina and I am condemned!"

"Please don't yell, my sweet--"

"A bit of ink, yes, but much more, Vasily." She uncovered her hair and let it fall, shaking her head a bit. "In action, I am Tsarina. Yes?"

"Certainly."

"In name, I can be nothing more than a woman."

He shrugged again. "Perhaps, but what can you do?"

"I will wear it down," she repeated. "I am as pious as any."

Vasily rolled his eyes and turned away, leaving his wig on the bench. "You cannot hope to keep the boyars with such audacity. You did sign, and you did call yourself an autocrat. You tempt difficulty, my love."

She stared at herself, still displeased with what she saw.

"I refuse to be scolded by you, Vasily." She stepped toward him, her frustration awakening into anger. "The boyars are far less troublesome than your failures. A victory parade? I should never have listened."

"The festivities were well received, I thought."

She shook her head. "Well received?"

"Well enough," he amended, turning away as though knowing he couldn't contend with her.

The victory parade in Red Square had not been able to erase the stigma of the second failed campaign against the Turks. To the contrary, the display had proven insulting to the Strel'tsy, magnifying the army's lack of adequate command. Peter's notable absence only made things worse.

Was I so foolish to put Vasily in command? she asked herself, looking him over and wondering what she'd ever seen in V.V. Golitsyn to make her think he would be a competent military leader. *Might it have been different without him?*

A knock on the door sent Vasily scrambling for his wig.

"Who's there?"

"It is Fedor," came the muffled but unmistakable reply.

Vasily rolled his eyes again. "It is Fedor…with all his grace."

She raised a finger to hush Vasily.

"Come, Fedor."

The door opened to reveal the sloping girth of Fedor Shaklovity, a man who, despite his tendency to slouch, was tall and thick enough to be described as statuesque. Imposing in size and consistently sour in demeanor, Fedor always left an impression on those he touched. His loyalty was unwavering and, therefore, good as gold. There was no question, however--beneath the calm exterior lurked a mean spirit and a violent bent. If Vasily was Sophia's face, then Fedor was no doubt her fist.

"I had no intention of intruding," he said with a bow, acknowledging her. "Still, we must have our priorities, yes?"

Salty as ever, she thought, returning the gesture. *He cannot help himself.*

"You are looking well today, Fedor," the Prince said, crossing his arms. "Have you been resting?"

"Certainly not," Shaklovity growled in reply. "And no festivals have been thrown in my honor."

Vasily smirked. "Did you not enjoy the parade?"

"I did not," he said, looking to Sophia. "May I speak frankly?"

"Please do."

"Yes, yes!" Vasily added. "Please favor us--"

"Vasily!"

Shaklovity's pock-marked face reflected no reaction to the Prince's taunting; a general disregard for Golitsyn had rendered him immune long ago. In Shaklovity's estimation, the trouble began where it always began--squarely in the lap of Prince V.V. Golitsyn.

The Prince's 'triumphant' return from the southern campaign was being ridiculed in the Duma, and the Strel'tsy ranks writhed with embarrassment at the thought of their failure being paraded as a victory.

Shaklovity, of course, had not been present, but foot soldier and officer alike testified that the Prince's second campaign consisted of a few minor skirmishes and a major shortage of supply. Water was scarce and the swamps of the south took their toll on the health of an unprepared army. Disease and dysentery claimed far too many lives to continue, and the entire effort was scrubbed long before the cannons ever reached their destination.

Despite Shaklovity's best efforts, the truth spread quickly throughout the city, so thoroughly saturating the public knowledge that, by the date of Golitsyn's victory parade, even the lowest serfs and laborers knew of the charade. The day went poorly. Many Strel'tsy stayed away from the ceremony, and when the crowd looked to the podium, they saw Ivan and Sophia…but no Peter.

His absence sent a wave rippling through the crowd, validating the soldiers' stories of a failed campaign and sending fear into the hearts of Sophia's supporters. As though in a dream, the unthinkable was happening: Sophia was actually losing the Strel'tsy Guard.

"Granted, the parade was poorly planned," Fedor began morosely, "considering that the campaign…need I say…but it was Peter who delivered the blow, Lady. I needn't tell you--his absence was the insult that rang throughout the ranks."

"I was not expecting him to attend," Sophia commented.

"Then, respectfully, you should not have held the parade."

The Prince looked amused. "You worry far too much, Fedor. You see traitors behind every bush!"

"Laugh if you wish," Fedor replied, "but consider that Peter sits waiting with his army, his wife with child and his clan firmly behind him, waiting for his chance! And now we find ourselves weakened by rumor and insult--"

"The Strel'tsy will not desert me," Sophia interrupted in loud voice, shaking her head. "And my spies report that Peter's army is made up of fishermen and boys, cannons they cannot use and muskets they cannot aim."

"If you trust your informants."

"I do," she answered.

"Certainly." Fedor nodded, his stare unnerving. "I wouldn't question their honesty, Lady. But how can they know enough to make such a judgment?"

"I am satisfied they are correct."

"Perhaps…but what of your own musketeers? And the nobles?" Fedor's face changed a bit, darkening. "The campaigns have destroyed their faith. Tsarevich Peter will find sympathy among them, Strel'tsy or not. Would that the Holy Father strike them dead for choosing to follow that impious boy!"

Sophia raised a hand. "Fedor, please. You go too far in condemning the Tsarevich. He is certainly less dangerous than the Tsarista."

As the words left her lips, Sophia realized she was lying.

"The Regency has made you dull," Fedor said flatly, glaring at her.

His comment was pointed enough to draw a gasp from Vasily, but Sophia never broke his stare, attempting to show no sign of offence.

"Vasily, I wish to speak with Fedor alone. Leave us."

Knowing when not to argue, Prince Golitsyn bowed and quickly made his exit. As soon as the door closed, Shaklovity let out a deep exhale, as though he'd been holding his breath waiting to have Sophia to himself.

Fedor's eyes were as serious as ever, his expression one of contemplative sorrow. "The fool has jeopardized the loyalty of the Strel'tsy," he stated, stepping closer. "You know this, yes?"

"You truly doubt the Strel'tsy?" she returned, allowing her own irritation to show.

"Without them, the Regency is lost," Shaklovity said, pacing past her into the chamber. "My fear, Sophia, is not simply for you, or for Tsarevich Ivan, but for the future of Russia itself."

Fedor is vengeful, but his fears must be genuine, she thought, watching as his face changed again.

"Tsarevich Peter is rarely present for Kremlin ceremonies anymore," he continued, "and his attendance at worship...well, you know how rarely he stands before the Patriarch! He marches around in German dress and allows himself to be seen in all states--dirty-faced most of the time and stinking with mud! He makes a mockery of every tradition and retreats to his 'play' fortress, luring everyone he can to follow. You've lost members of your own household! Are you aware of this, Sophia?"

"You needn't attack me, Fedor."

"Nay, not an attack, Lady. I offer only an appeal. Russia has a great difficulty and we are about to lose our advantage in finding a remedy. Peter is impious, disrespectful, willfully disobedient! When he does come to Moscow, he spends time in the foreign quarter cavorting with his European friends." Fedor produced a handkerchief, wiping his forehead. "Forgive my anger, Regent, but to think of our Mother Russia given over to someone as dangerous as Peter..."

"There is still Ivan."

"Yet to produce an heir," Shaklovity countered. "And there is great question in my mind as to whether he is capable--"

"We must have an heir," she snapped, raising a palm to silence him.

"But, even so, what are the chances that Ivan outlives Peter? Eventually, Peter will rule."

What is he trying to say? Sophia's mind began to turn, swirling around a notion she had abandoned long ago. *Could it actually be done? Is it too late to rid ourselves of Peter?*

"We share the same fears," she said finally, carefully considering his reaction. "And you know the nature of the Naryshkins. I am loath to think what they will do to the pitiful few of us who remain. The Tsarista has plans for those who stand in her way."

Shaklovity paced, popping his knuckles one at a time. Sophia could almost see him thinking, worrying, growing more resolute with each step.

"I have done my best, Lady." Fedor began, his tone growing louder from a growl. "I have spread the word wherever I could and stood beside you to preserve the integrity of Ivan's throne and your Regency. Would that I could save Russia from the fate I so dearly dread. Short of calling a bolt of lightning from the sky to strike Peter dead, I can do no more.

"This is my appeal," he continued, opening his palms to her and bowing. "My talents are yours to command."

She stared for a moment, the silence awaiting her reply.

He opens the door and waits for my order. After all this time, could it possibly be so simple?

"I wish only what is best," she said, pacing her words, "for the Regency, for Ivan…for Russia. We must be vigilant and strive to do everything in our power to ensure her safety. Do you agree?"

"Yes, Lady," he answered, the words escaping as he exhaled.

Outside Moscow, Fort Presburg at Preobrazhenskoe

July 1689

The cannon fire clapped like strikes of lightning, the waves of sound arriving in a succession of blows that shook their bones and passed through the bits of cloth stuffed in their ears. Many crouched or held their hands up to their heads in defense against the thunder claps while others stood tall and tried to remain composed as though they didn't mind. A third smaller group was oddly inclined to enjoy their work, welcoming the sound of the cannons and the ringing in their ears.

Of the three groups, Alexander Danilovich Menshikov was decidedly a member of the latter. He treasured his green Preobrazhensky colors and welcomed any task, however small, in the service of Tsarevich Peter. Tall and sharp-featured, Alexander bore thin lips and a high forehead capable of a scowl that could humble the best.

"That was pitiful," he told the others, pointing. "You girls will get shot in the ass cowering like that! Shall we try again, Captain Bruce? Sir?"

The Captain stepped forward, chuckling a bit, bearing the invigorated air that all Scotsmen seemed to possess. To Menshikov, Jack Bruce looked typical of his kind, red-haired and a bit round-faced, shorter than Alexander but much larger in stature due to his reputed friendship with the Tsarevich. The son of a refugee from Protestant England, Bruce had been with the Tsarevich when Menshikov first encountered Peter.

"I think not," he replied with a half-grin. "The rest have quit, and I believe the hillside has taken enough damage for one afternoon."

"Of that there is no question," Alexander replied, covering his disappointment with a grin. "At least we saved ourselves the trouble of re-setting the targets."

The Captain laughed. "Aye, that you have. You two--go fish the shot out of the hillside. Fourteen. Get them all."

The recruits nodded and set out into the imaginary battlefield, taking a small handcart to accommodate the cannonballs. Menshikov calmed the urge to offer his service, knowing that the Captain had purposely excluded him.

A bit of respect, certainly, he thought. *I should take it where it comes.*

"I don't know which you like more, Menshikov, hitting the targets or calling your comrades down when they miss."

"The bastards deserve it," Menshikov stated with a chuckle. "They need to grow some balls. Their cowardice will kill somebody."

"A common man like you?" Bruce smiled. "Friend, you simply like giving those fancy boys a twist. I don't blame you a bit."

Menshikov grinned back, shrugging. "At Preobrazhenskoe, rank is all that matters," he answered. "As long as I keep within my rank, I can say what I will. You will kindly notice I never insult you, Captain Bruce."

"Aye, it is true. Don't mistake me, Alexander, I think you're quite a miracle, actually. You have a way about you that I admire--an air that speaks experience, even in a place where you have none. You are as green as either of those two, and yet, from the first moment here, they both would have sworn you to be a veteran. A wonderful trait, no doubt!"

"I am accustomed to fighting for what I need," Menshikov answered, not knowing whether to be offended or proud. Bruce had an odd way of delivering his lines that made it seem as though he were perpetually amused. An astronomer by study, Bruce was also fond of tricks and sleight of hand, qualities which had undoubtedly endeared him to the Tsarevich.

As for Menshikov, he considered himself to be in possession of no special tricks or talents, nothing which might otherwise distinguish him from any of the others. He had always compensated with undying effort, thinking that hard work was his best path to success. For the most part, his work had proven to be profitable. He'd risen from selling pies in the street to manning the cannons for the Tsarevich's treasured Preobrazhensky Guard. He'd been granted the title of Private Bombardier and was nurturing relationships with anyone reputed to be close to Peter.

But as he stood watching the two dig the shot from the hill and load the cart, Menshikov dwelled on Bruce's words, adding up the events of his recent past and realizing that the Captain was correct.

"I don't begrudge you," the Scot continued, patting him on the shoulder. "In fact, I thoroughly enjoy your company. You are, however, a wolf within a horse. You know this, eh?"

Menshikov paused. "If you say so, Captain, then I must agree. As I am obligated to obey, I will happily be a wolf and willingly be a horse."

"Hah!" Bruce laughed again, shaking his head. "You are indeed a singular sort! Your wit is so sharp that I find myself looking for the motive. With all the time we have spent together, still I suspect that you may secretly detest me."

He's smarter than he looks, Menshikov thought.

"I have been told that my face is unkind," he responded with a half grin. "But you may trust that I hold nothing but respect for you, Captain. And as for my wit? I admit…it causes me trouble more often than not. I do, however, graciously accept the compliment despite your butchery of the Russian language."

Another laugh. "Ah! You see? You're a sharp one. The Tsarevich has the same kind of humor. You know, I suspect he would be quite fond of you."

"Oh? Truly?" The comment sounded like a divine song in Alexander's ears.

Bruce smiled back at him. "Aye, you're the kind of young man who gets on well with the Tsarevich. He keeps many such friends--Herr Lefort chiefly among them. You've heard of the All-Drunken Assembly, haven't you?"

"No, sir."

He shrugged. "Well, I suspect you will. No matter. You would get on well with the bunch, I'd say."

"What is it, then? The All-Drunken Assembly?"

Captain Bruce raised his hands. "Oh, no. I shouldn't be the one to tell. Trust me, friend, I have every confidence you'll get there on your own."

"Your discretion is appreciated, but surely it would do no harm to tell me."

Bruce shook his head, squinting beneath the point of his cap. "You will know soon enough."

Menshikov looked down at the stack of cannon shot, wanting to pick one up and toss it at Bruce.

How dare he keep it from me! he thought, wondering if he should press the issue. Bruce had been kind enough and his recommendation would no doubt work wonders with the Tsarevich. Menshikov, however, longed to know everything about the mysterious workings of Peter's inner circle. Gaining such favor would be a blessing indeed; there was no higher achievement in his mind.

As for the All-Drunken Assembly, Menshikov had certainly heard the whispering. Peter's reputation extended far beyond the ceremonies and the throne room, the gossip including rumors of parties and debauched costumed celebrations that mocked everyone in authority, including the Tsarevich himself. Peter was said to be the instigator of such charades and his friends were always present.

"Do you know Captain Lefort?" Alexander asked.

"Of course," Bruce answered, nodding. "The Sloboda is not big enough for someone like Lefort to hide. A right pleasing fellow, the Captain. Have you met him?"

Menshikov nodded his head, looking down. "They say he turns the Tsarevich's ear."

"And not for the worse, I assure you," Bruce told him, cooling a bit. "Tsarevich Peter has his own mind."

"Certainly. I meant no insult to the Tsarevich."

"You are very curious about him."

Menshikov shrugged. "Yes, I suppose. Who isn't?"

Bruce grinned. "An excellent point, Private. You are not alone in your curiosity, certainly. On the other hand, I would guess that you are the only soul in all of Russia who can claim to have assaulted the Tsarevich and lived to tell of it!"

Alexander clenched his jaw, biting back a rude reply. "With all respect, Captain, I would prefer that we not speak of my troubles."

"Troubles?" Bruce chuckled. "Nay. Rather you should call it a stroke of luck, or a miracle, or whatever you will. But if my eyes don't deceive me, I see you standing here before me." He reached out to pat Menshikov lightly on the chest. "Yes, there you are! Private Menshikov, standing right here in the flesh."

Alexander glared. "Your meaning, Captain?"

"Don't you follow?" Bruce asked, tilting his head. "Had you offended Peter, friend, you would certainly not be available. Jailed, at the least. Your very presence tells me that the Tsarevich has forgiven the incident."

Menshikov's spirits lifted, pulled skyward with the Captain's assessment.

Each time I begin to hate him, he tells me something I want to hear…

"It relieves me to hear you say so, Captain. And if the Tsarevich changes his mind and chooses to punish me, I am nonetheless grateful for your part."

"You have no worry," Bruce told him. "The Tsarevich never changes his mind."

"I hope as much."

"You may count on it, Private. You needn't worry--your skin is safe."

He thinks me a coward.

"I am not afraid to accept punishment," Menshikov told him, straightening. "I will willingly take what I have earned."

"Of that I have no question," the Captain replied, his tone still bearing amusement. He turned to place a hand on the cannon, staring out at the target range. "Tsarevich Peter wouldn't trust these beauties to just anyone."

Following Bruce's lead, Menshikov turned his attention back to the hill where the two recruits labored. They seemed to be working far too slowly but he held his comment, knowing that the Captain already considered him to be something of an ass.

The cool breeze signaled the onset of evening, the last of the sun's light chased from the field by shadows. Like farmers in the field, they crept steadily onward, claiming the last remnants of daylight in long strips of darkness. Alexander watched without seeing the sunset, his mind too preoccupied to appreciate the palette of red and orange that colored the sky before him.

If I can be forgiven, truly...then the Scot is correct! I sit in better position. In Peter's clear view, no longer just a face in a uniform. With the grace of the Holy Father, my mistake becomes a blessing!

"I hear no cannons!"

A voice sounded behind them, the tone unmistakably that of the Tsarevich. Menshikov turned stiffly and stood at attention, his heart pounding at furious pace.

Before him stood Peter, dressed in a green Preobrazhensky coat, a clean white shirt shining bright beneath it. A giant of a man, always larger than Alexander recalled, Peter's impeccable posture only served to make him seem taller. Such height was enviable, as was the penetrating stare that topped his vertical frame, a gaze that seemed to command all that it fell upon.

"Have you vanquished all our enemies so quickly or did you simply surrender to the targets?"

"Neither, my lord." Bruce answered. "Regrettably."

Behind Peter stood an oddly matched pair of figures. On his left, the familiar yet still unpleasant face of Prince Fedor Romodanovsky, a son of one of Moscow's elite families and a friend of the Tsarevich. When Menshikov joined the Preobrazhensky, he had been overjoyed to discover that a Romodanovsky would share his rank. Fedor was known to be ill-tempered, but in his short time in the regiment, Alexander had seen nothing out of the ordinary.

On Peter's right, a stately figure Alexander did not recognize, a well-dressed man who, though somewhat plain in his features, reeked of experience. The foreigner lacked a beard, his pale skin making him appear almost ghostly beside the vibrant flush of Peter's features.

One of Peter's tutors, surely, Menshikov thought, straightening. *I must strive to impress.*

The Captain bowed. "The battle remains at a standstill, my lord."

"Excellent!" Peter said, stepping forward. "Then there are still shots to be fired. I am confident that we can still pull this one out! How many men left on our side?"

Bruce grinned, playing along. "Four, Tsarevich."

Peter knit his brow in comic fashion, pausing. "Down a few, certainly. No matter--our enemy seems to be holding their position. Am I right, Alexander?"

Menshikov looked up to see Peter staring at him.

"My lord, our enemy may seem a bit wooden," he told the Tsarevich, "but I assure you, they are tricky. No sooner do we fire a shot than they move!"

Romodanovsky chuckled.

"Hah! I see…" Peter rubbed his stubbled chin. "Confounded things! Have no fear, gentlemen--I have delivered aid in the form of an expert. We shall have to consult Herr Sommer on how to hit a moving target."

With this, Peter delivered a deep bow, extending a hand toward the foreigner.

Sommer removed his tricorn hat and offered a forced grin. "I fear your enemy may have outwitted this group," he said, "but I can assure you that the only way to hit a moving target is with the aid of providence."

"Herr Sommer." Captain Bruce removed his own hat and bowed. "A pleasure to see you out here in the countryside."

"The Tsarevich was growing weary of conjecture," Sommer replied.

"Why sit indoors talking when we have cannons ready?" Peter asked, walking to where Menshikov stood. He examined the artillery pieces, patting the barrels as though they were his pets. "You said there were four. Where are your other two?"

"In the field, my lord," Bruce replied. "Fetching cannon-shot from the dirt."

Peter stared out into the fading light, pointing as he spotted the pair. "Ah, yes."

Do I dare mention the past? Menshikov thought. There seemed nothing to indicate that the Tsarevich held any resentment, but he had been warned against Peter's quickly turning temper.

Better that it remains unspoken. Perhaps it shall simply pass of its own accord.

Peter turned suddenly, as though reading his thoughts.

"Cannons are beautiful things. Do you agree, Alexander?"

"I do," Menshikov replied, trying to keep his voice from trembling. "Particularly beautiful when they behave properly. No wonder they give them women's names."

Peter stared happily. Bright-eyed and smiling, he wrapped an arm around Alexander's shoulder and turned him to face the foreigner and Romodanovsky.

"Theodor, I want you to meet the man who nearly broke my back!"

"Ah," Sommer's face finally broke from its droll expression, stopping at a wry grin. "The pie-boy, you mean? How very interesting."

Romodanovsky chuckled, staring.

Peter squeezed his shoulder. "Alexander Danilovich, this is the great Theodor Sommer--without question the finest of my tutors. He has come to correct us."

Sommer nodded politely. "A pleasure."

"And you know good old Romodanovsky, eh?"

Fedor tipped an imaginary cap, a glint of contempt lingering in his gaze.

Privileged little louse!

"Yes, my lord," Alexander replied dutifully. "Private Romodanovsky has trained by my side."

"Captain Bruce tells me that you're fond of shouting at the others."

Alexander tensed, not knowing how to respond. "I only shout when necessary, my lord."

"It is no shame," Peter said, releasing his grip. "From the number of standing targets, I suspect you should have bellowed even louder. A pitiful result, truly."

"Yes, my lord. We strive to improve."

Romodanovsky stepped forward bearing a mocking grin. "My lord, perhaps it would be best if you stood away from Private Menshikov, lest you become the victim of his exuberance once again."

"Worse that I become sick at the sight of your face, Fedor!" Peter clapped Menshikov on the back. "I should not have to worry about Alexander again, I think. His assault was an act of devotion and duty. And Fedor, you would be blessed to possess Alexander's bravery."

"Considering his past, I cannot question that."

"Shall I tell you, then?" Peter asked, directing his stare to look at each of them. "Shall I tell you of the assault? I think our Private Menshikov deserves that the story be told properly."

Romodanovsky looked bored with the thought but didn't respond. Bruce held his tongue and said nothing, quiet in the presence of the Tsarevich.

As for Menshikov, he was loath to relive the tale of his embarrassment but was enrapt in the presence of the Tsarevich and the undo attention being granted him. If Peter wished to recount the incident, then he was certainly welcome to do so.

"Captain Bruce could no doubt depict the events with more style," Peter began, extending a hand, "but I will endeavor to tell the tale as best I can. The Captain and I were out walking the boundaries--quite absently, to be truthful--eh, Jack?"

The Captain nodded. "We were talking more than soldiering. Yes, my lord."

"Precisely. Talking and admiring our work, strolling in the fading light, much as it looks right now. Stricken by Mother Nature herself, the Captain was taken with an urge to piss and wandered off to manage his comfort. Being quite dry myself, I waited for his return, strolling and thinking, not aware that I was walking into the domain of sentry Alexander Menshikov."

"A near fatal error, my lord," Romodanovsky quipped.

"It was nothing so severe," Peter replied immediately, waving away the comment. "But I had most certainly wandered from the path and remained just within the sight of our friend here. I was staring at the moon, I remember, when I was struck."

Menshikov cringed inwardly at the words, wondering if the Tsarevich could be playing him into another humiliation. It seemed odd that Peter should depict the incident with such pleasant regard, but he sensed no animosity from the giant.

"Right here," Peter continued, reaching up an arm to pat his own back. "A blow so solid and determined that it sent me to the ground. I fell to my stomach and rolled to my back just as he descended upon me. Quickly, I tell you! Without giving me so much as a chance to defend myself!"

Sommer looked on dispassionately. Bruce and Romodanovsky were not as composed, their own amusement written in volumes in their eyes and smiles.

Alexander dropped his head, staring shamefully at the ground, wondering if he should offer another apology.

What can I say? Am I to laugh or be ashamed?

"Admittedly," Peter continued, "I did strike him once before poor Alexander recognized who I was. Truly, Herr Sommer, you should have seen his eyes widen when he found me staring back at him!"

"I can imagine," Sommer responded.

Romodanovsky shook his head. "The poor fellow must have thought he was done for! Eh, Private?"

Alexander nodded regretfully, his heart pounding as never before. "I thought so, yes."

"What then, my lord?" Romodanovsky urged, now enrapt. "Did you stand and beat him with your fists? I have seen no marks upon his face, so I may only assume that you punched him in the ribs."

Peter shook his head "I tossed him away but pressed no further. The predatory look was still in his eyes and I dared not test him in such condition. Is that not true, Alexander?"

Menshikov paled. "My lord, I know not what look I was wearing, but I can assure you that I meant no offense."

"Certainly not. You were doing your duty and with passion. Better to face the task bravely and fail than to sit back and hope for success, Alexander."

Romodanovsky offered a confused look, shaking his head again. "My lord, without being too contradictory, may I ask--do you truly considerate it bravery to strike the Tsarevich from behind? I would think there might be a better word for Menshikov."

"Ah!" Peter held up a finger, waving it at him. "But it was not the act itself that I consider brave! It was after the fact that Alexander showed me his courage. If you will allow me to finish, I will explain all."

Romodanovsky bowed. "Certainly, my lord. My apologies."

"Just shut your mouth, Fedor."

"Yes, my lord."

Peter paused, glaring at Romodanovsky for a long moment before resuming. Even through the flood of anxious thoughts, Menshikov found himself suddenly hating the young aristocrat.

"You know me," Peter told them, resuming his tale. "The three of you are certainly accustomed enough to my company to know that my immediate reactions are often my most severe, and this instance was no different. I admit I haven't been given such a shock since I fell from that hateful little horse last summer. I was stirred, certainly, and angry enough to fight! I leapt up to my feet and scowled back at my unknown assailant, realizing, of course, that he was one of ours.

"My temper, however, was still too hot, and I began shouting him down and threatening his arrest. The scene was drawing others to our side and, by this time, poor Alexander realized that his own comrades would be only too happy to take him into custody.

"I was vicious, in truth," Peter continued, nodding his confession. "I was stirred, mind you, and I quite expected Private Menshikov to buckle and submit to my torrent of insults. In this, I was sorely mistaken. Here, I say, is where Alexander's courage came charging to the front! He stepped forward, puffed his chest out as though he'd been slapped in the face and delivered an impassioned defense that would have won the day in the English Parliament! He told me in no uncertain terms that he had done nothing but his duty and scolded that I should have announced my presence to avoid such trouble!"

Peter paused, the group silent around him. "There was an apology, certainly, but Menshikov never kneeled or cried--never threw himself at my feet. I was slow to accept his defense and I shouted back. I was angry, I tell you--more from the comment than the injury--but he held against me like a soldier, accepting his punishment but steadfast in the belief that he was right.

"I was correct about the other sentries," he said, nodding to Menshikov. "Seeing my anger, they immediately pounced on him and took him away. For the rest, I suppose we would have to ask Alexander himself, for my part was almost done. It didn't take me long to reconsider his arrest, and I sent word that he was to be released and promoted to Private Bombardier. I have only seen him once since that day, and then only briefly. Isn't that right, Alexander?"

He despises weakness, Menshikov thought, lifting his chin.

"Yes, my lord," he replied. "I am grateful for the opportunity to redeem myself."

"I should think so!" Romodanovsky spouted bitterly, rubbing his hands together. "You could certainly have been executed for such a turn!"

"He has proven an excellent soldier," Captain Bruce interjected. "In my estimation, the choice was a wise one."

"Certainly," Fedor snapped back, his voice thick. "The ranks of the Preobrazhensky would be far too thin without dedicated members of the peasantry to fill it. When someone of his birth shows as much promise as Menshikov, it is only wise to use him--"

"Don't be an idiot, Fedor."

"Yes, my lord. I shall try."

"Fedor's ramblings aside," Peter said, turning to the others. "I will embarrass Alexander no further. I do warn you, however, to watch for him. Look upon him and make note--Alexander is a true

Russian. This is what one looks like. Men of his kind have risen to great heights in this country."

"Why, certainly, my lord!"

"With your recommendation, Tsarevich, he cannot help but go far."

Menshikov glanced over, sensing defeat in Romodanovsky's forced grin. Fighting his instinct to gloat, the Private calmed himself and reveled in the simplicity of the moment, taking his role as humble servant.

"I am flattered and grateful, my lord." He addressed Peter with a look of humility. "I have no words to express this feeling."

"Well, I suspect a few cups of vodka will loosen your tongue. We'll sup and drink a few together. You will like Fedor much better when he is drunk."

Romodanovsky nodded his agreement. "My natural condition, it is true."

The sound of the recruits' return quieted the conversation. Laboriously dragging the cart of spent shot, they stiffened quickly from their hunched posture at the sight of the Tsarevich.

"You two--what are your names?"

"Private Bombardier Ilkovansky, my lord."

"Private Bombardier Zotov, my lord."

"Did you get them all?" Peter moved to inspect the load.

"Yes, my lord," Zotov answered. "Every one, sir."

"Good. I shall soon be loading beside you. When we stand together here, I am Private Bombardier Peter. Is that understood?"

"Yes, my lord." Zotov looked around uncomfortably.

As though knowing what was about to happen, Captain Bruce stepped forward and looked out into the darkness.

"Right, then," Peter exclaimed clapping his hands together. "Now that we're all present, let us fire off a few! We'll need torches or lamps for the hill. Do you agree, Captain?"

Bruce grinned politely. "Without question, Private. I cannot see a thing out there."

Romodanovsky stepped to the Tsarevich's side. "Surely it grows too dark for maneuvers, my lord. Let us retire for supper and return in the morning, invigorated and full of blood--"

"Ridiculous! There is plenty of light left," Peter contradicted him immediately. "Herr Sommer did not make the long journey here to partake in a quiet meal! No, we will certainly fire a few off before anyone sees anything to eat. Take heart, Fedor, the darkness will serve to ease your disappointment when we miss!"

As they moved to load the first shot, Peter clapped Alexander one final time on the back, looking down at him with reassuring expression. "We'll vanquish these bastard targets and then have our long-awaited talk!"

"Yes, my lord." Menshikov nodded his assent, his heart now pounding in anticipation, for the moment all worries chased away by the presence of the Tsarevich and the warm glow of his favor.

Out in the field, the pale wood of the remaining targets faded into the grey of the hillside, the cover of night no worry for the young Tsarevich. With Sommer's instruction they loaded and fired, again and again, the men losing track of time as they reveled in the elation of their companions.

Peter shouted his joy each time as the cannons exploded and launched their shot into the black, his enthusiasm infectious to all. Beside him, filled with a pride and contentment he'd never known before, Menshikov stared out into the darkness, searching for targets but seeing only his own bright future.

Moscow, The Assumption Cathedral in the Kremlin

July 18, 1689

The crowd of parishioners at the revered Assumption Cathedral continued to stand as the mass entered its third hour, the lengthy ceremony accompanied by the choir's anthems, their ceaseless song interrupted only occasionally as Patriarch Joachim chanted prayers before the altar. Held captive before the myriad of candles on the massive, glimmering iconostasis, the worshippers endured, their weary legs eased somewhat by the warmth of the late summer, a condition that made the service far more tolerable than usual.

Regent Sophia stood dutifully in place, a spectacle of piety in her crimson gown, her mind focused on more important thoughts than her aching feet. She listened and watched with unchanging, pleasant expression, enduring the tedious parade in the name of the Holy Father.

And though she could be called a pious woman, Sophia nonetheless found herself wishing the service would end quickly.

So patient and perfect today, she thought, glancing at Tsarevich Peter. *He hasn't moved a bit...not a single shuffle. He behaves like a hero to keep me the villain!*

She fought the urge to scowl, seeing the obvious difference between Peter and his slumping, bearded half-brother. Peter stood with his shoulders straight and his eyes awake, the determination in his gaze serving to enhance his intimidating height.

He plays with me now, like a true rival. Where is the little boy I so stupidly spared?

She glanced out to the congregation, her eyes finding Lady Natalya and the Naryshkin entourage. The Tsarista was conservatively dressed, standing amidst a group that included her daughter Natalya, Peter's wife Evdokia, and Boris Golitsyn.

Natalya flaunts her advantage. She wields a plump little mother-to-be and a vibrant young heir. She strikes with a golden rapier…

A loud hiccup rang in the air, followed by a second.

Tsarevich Ivan nodded in apology to the Patriarch. Sophia glared, unable to catch his glossy stare.

…and I defend with a wooden spoon.

She looked away, breathing the scented air and trying to calm herself, not wishing to earn a scornful glance from Patriarch Joachim. The curiosity of the congregation had once been so welcome--now it seemed a weighty burden upon her. Shaklovity often spoke of rumors and criticism, but never had Sophia so acutely felt Moscow's disapproval.

Natalya and her people glare--as though they could wound me with their eyes. The rest gaze in adoration at Peter!

The festival celebrating the miraculous appearance of Our Lady of Kazan was an annual event, a summer occasion which Sophia eagerly anticipated, an opportunity to see and be seen by the people of Moscow. Routinely kept hidden by command of her sex, she welcomed any opportunity to present herself to the public. Of late, it was Peter who won the attention of the crowds but Sophia persisted, wanting desperately for the boyars and Strel'tsy to remember who held the reins of Russia. Save for religious events and festivals, Moscow may have forgotten that she existed.

For Sophia, above all else, was a woman. She had negotiated a treaty with China, placed diplomats in Europe and had been the architect of the 'Eternal Peace' with Poland, yet remained bound by the restrictions of her sex. Allowed few leniencies beyond those of her less noble sisters, Sophia neither lived nor dined in the same place as the men. Even in official capacities, the Regent was forbidden from appearing in public, forcing her reliance on male courtiers and family supporters.

Early in her Regency, she had commissioned the creation of a special double-seated throne for Ivan and Peter, a broad-backed creation with a hidden seat to facilitate her presence in official capacities. On Peter's side, she had installed a small sliding door disguised with a velvet covering through which she could offer counsel and direct the Tsarevich. In the first years, Peter had been far more amenable to such things. Now the throne was little used but for Ivan, and the boyars knew better than to approach the senior Tsarevich with issues of a serious nature.

Ultimately, Sophia had been forced to rely, both politically and personally, on Vasily Golitsyn. In turn, the Prince had become the most notable man in Moscow and Commander of the country's armies, wealthier and more popular than ever before. As much as Sophia, Prince Vasily had become the face of the Regency.

And so it was that her public appearances became extremely important to the young Regent. Denied the respect of standing before her peers in truth, Sophia found it enough to suffer standing before them at celebrations and religious rites. Here, at least, they could see their Regent, tall and unyielding in her rightful place.

Peter stands so proudly today, she mused, her thoughts never straying far from the Tsarevich. *He bears that serene look as though he were born with it! Mother has prepared him well.*

Patriarch Joachim continued the service, the lull of the prayer echoing tirelessly, carried up on streams of scented smoke into the peak of the cupola. Driven by the bloody events that brought Sophia to the throne, the Patriarch had reluctantly supported her in the early years of the Regency. Now, after suffering through years of her tolerance of outside religions and expansive foreign policy, he found Sophia far too progressive.

She spied Vasily in the crowd, his dress far less ostentatious than usual, his manner subdued of late by negative public opinion. The bitterness surrounding the Turkish campaign still lingered in potent quantities, providing a common point of dissent for those who opposed the Regency's actions. The Prince had been the obvious target for the complaints, but Sophia knew that she would ultimately be the one to shoulder the blame.

He looked up from his place, his eyes meeting Sophia's for just a moment before looking away. She saw a glimmer of recognition, perhaps, but the Prince's face changed little and he did not return her glance again.

He acts strangely…even Vasily cannot remain himself.

They had exchanged glances in this manner hundreds of times before, and Sophia had always relied on the depth of his stare, the reassuring wordless replies he was always able to provide. More than anyone, Prince V.V. had been her support, her benefactor, her male political face in a man's world. And despite his eccentricities and faults, Prince Vasily had always been consistent in his devotion. Until today.

She subdued her rising emotion, trying again to connect with him. Vasily's eyes remained averted, his lips moving slowly as though in prayer.

She waited, her eyes lingering longer than appropriate, her vision blinded from all but the face of the Prince. She could feel the scorn of the Naryshkin congregation but ignored it, needing only a single look from her beloved to set things back in balance.

How can he deny me this! I ask so little. I need so little and he denies me!

Vasily maintained his posture, his eyes fixed on the floor. Given nothing to feed on, Sophia's hope for solace faded, her mood turning quickly to anger.

Sophia tore her gaze away from him, catching the unwelcome glare of the Patriarch. Averting her eyes, she pretended to mouth a prayer.

How dare he show such fear when I bear the same burden! Does he seek to deny me now? What good will it do?

She could feel the flush in her cheeks, her bilious nature rising from within to replace her rejection with resentment. Fuming through her pious posture, Sophia kept her eyes focused on the ground.

Let him try to find me now. Let him look up to see me angry.

She fought the urge to glance back at the Prince, taking a silent, deep breath.

I must persevere, she told herself. *I cannot fail in my duty, especially not now.*

Weakening, she looked over to find Vasily's eyes still downcast.

Bastard! Let him put on a remorseful act for the congregation. If he dares try to leave me, I'll saddle his cowardly back with all the blame!

Sophia battled back her furious tears, closing her eyes as though lost in prayer.

Everyone will see my weakness. I cannot allow this now.

She thought of her mother and the day she'd been granted the Regency. She thought of her counselors and supporters, men like Shaklovity who had risked their lives and reputations for her cause.

I am bigger than Vasily. Sophia opened her tearless eyes and looked out at the congregation.

And for now, whether the Naryshkins approve or not, I am bigger than Peter and Ivan. Let them feel safe. They gamble on their absent heir and his child-to-be. Were she to lose that child, we would be restored in an instant!

She glanced up at Peter. He remained devoutly straight and attentive, perfect in every way. Even before his arrival in Moscow this morning, news of Peter's appearance buzzed on the lips of boyars and merchants alike. In the wake of his absence at the victory parade, Peter's popularity was climbing and the Naryshkin clan was certainly shrewd enough to capitalize on the temper of the city. They posed him as a hero now, a strong young leader who would ultimately fulfill the prophecies of his greatness.

Peter, apparently, was agreeable enough to play his part. Whether for purpose or merely for spite, he was performing expertly. He had been gracious and personable at every turn and was now fulfilling the role of devout and humble servant of God. The majority of concern surrounding Peter-the-boy had been in regard to his attitude. Now, suddenly, Peter-the-man seemed cured of his restless spirit and ready to lead.

Look at him! I contend with every complaint and tend to every difficulty while Peter plays with soldiers and cannons in the country--and they look to him for inspiration! He knows nothing of what I endure! The people forget about their work horse Sophia! So easy to fall in love with the pretty young Isarevich and forget that he is still a selfish boy…

The service was nearing its end, the faces of the congregation growing more devout with the knowledge that the waiting was over and that the celebration would soon begin. Only the recessional remained.

Sophia kept her eyes from searching for Vasily, her patience waning amidst the rain of bitter thoughts and worries. She watched along with the congregation as the Patriarch moved to say a prayer over Peter and Ivan, clearing their way.

He skips on his duty whenever he wishes...yet when he finally makes an appearance, they all applaud! I toil and worry every moment of every day, but let Father Medvedev compare me to Queen Elizabeth and they claim I'm mad with power!

Peter knows me far too well, she mused, the corners of her mouth turning slightly downward in sneer, her polished veneer growing dull in the heat of resentment.

Peter had barely acknowledged her all morning and, despite her attempts, had refused to match her stare before or during the ceremony. Had he remained aloof, the rest of the day may have proceeded as planned. As it was, Peter chose to look back at her, for just an instant.

Later, Sophia would replay the incident again and again in her mind, searching for the answer, trying to discern what precisely had provoked her. In the end she would reconcile that it was Peter's look that set her off--that he was ultimately to blame for her subsequent disgrace and embarrassment.

At the time, she saw only a glance from the young Tsarevich, a look that might have passed between the two on any other occasion. It was little more than a slight expression, a glance that, given all they had been through, might not have struck her so soundly in different circumstance.

But it was a piteous look. Peter stared with a sad expression that reeked of sympathy and condescension.

Sophia's spirit stood up on its hind legs and roared in defiance. She stood speechless as he looked away, fury flowing hot in her veins.

Pity? How dare he pity me!

She had borne the worst of his childish insults and scornful glances--shouldered the brunt of the Tsarevich's considerable anger on many occasions. Sophia knew the intricacies of Peter's temperament and would never have believed that he could affect her so. Yet where she expected venom, Sophia found only pity. This, she could not bear.

He has planned everything, including the look on his face! He devalues me beneath his own contempt!

Peter gave Ivan his arm for support as the two slowly stepped forward, the congregation turning to watch the procession move down the aisle.

And though she certainly knew better, Sophia chose not to wait her turn.

She felt herself moving forward, her body taking the initiative despite her indecisive mind, the crimson-gowned figure of the Regent moving to walk beside, not behind, Peter and Ivan.

Even as she acted, Sophia was aware of what she'd done. The moments seemed to slow around her as she cast aside all thoughts of repercussion and submitted to her vengeful grace.

She fell in step with the two, her eyes forward, focused on the sunlight that poured through the arched portals at the end of the aisle. The gasp that rose from the otherwise silent congregation was quieter than she expected.

Sophia persisted, rage and liberation coursing through her. *There! Let us see if his look changes now! Let them all see!*

Beside her, Peter halted his slow march. She could feel the weight of his stare as he turned to look at her.

Sophia stopped alongside the two, but kept her eyes forward.

If he thinks his glare will change things, he is mistaken.

"Regent."

Sophia held her pose.

"Regent," he repeated, his tone quiet and calm, bearing no anger.

"Yes, Tsarevich?"

He leaned down to put his head close to her ear, placing a hand on her shoulder.

"You've overstepped your place," Peter whispered, the words like poison in her ear. "I wish you to stand back. You may exit with the rest."

And though she would deny it later, Sophia's jaw dropped wide at the sound of his request.

She turned to look at him, her stomach churning, the tears she'd battled earlier now finding their opportunity to well in her eyes. The weight seemed unbearable now.

"I will not," she replied, her feet moving again out of spite, not waiting for his reply.

Back she marched, plodding under the watchful eyes of the stunned congregation, avoiding the scornful glare of the Patriarch as she neared the iconstasis.

Let them see me now! Let them see the devotion of their ruler!

She grabbed an icon from the hands of Patriarch himself, clutching it proudly to her chest before turning to face the congregation.

Sophia paused there for a moment, surveying the scene before her, the Russian saint pressed devoutly against her bosom. Calmly, her heart pounding in her chest, she took a deep breath of the scandalous air and began her own procession.

She stepped quickly down the aisle, keeping her eyes focused on the glow of sunlight, unwilling to grant Peter the satisfaction of another look.

She moved--past the congregation, past the mystified Peter and Ivan, the icon firmly wrapped in her arms as though it could protect her from shame.

Finally she reached the portals, her head held high as she crossed the threshold.

Let them talk, she thought, grateful as the welcome warmth touched her face. *Let them say that the Tsarevich tried to command his superior and that she refused! I am Regent of Russia and God's servant!*

Let them talk. Tonight, let them all talk of Regent Sophia!

Outside Moscow, Tsarista Natalya's House at Preobrazhenskoe

July 1689

"And you should see the list of recruits, Mother. You would surely be surprised at some of the names. Golovin, Prozorovsky--of course I haven't seen them on the field, but the numbers are reassuring. Can you imagine the sight of Shein charging in the van alongside the carriage boys?"

Tsarista Natalya Naryshkin listened as her son paced and talked, thinking how healthy and able he looked at the age of seventeen. She had once worried that his prodigious height would make him look freakish or ridiculous, but she could see that Peter was growing into his size, training himself in the art of using it to his advantage. Natalya approved; to ignore such a conspicuous trait would be ridiculous.

"They enlist as a show of support," she reminded him. "Even in the most dire of circumstances, I would not expect to see Shein or Prozorovsky standing beside you in the field. They join you in spirit…and as support in the Duma, of course."

"I understand, Mother," he answered immediately. "I was speaking in jest."

"Ah."

"They sign the roster as an insult to Sophia, clearly. I admit, I do like the sight of their names, whatever their intent. If they wish to play politics to our advantage, then let them. If nothing else, this posturing must worry Sophia."

"It does."

"All for the better, then." Peter paused, shaking his head a bit. "I do, however, admit to my suspicions of Shein. The man is far too shrewd to be so gracious."

"Nevertheless, you would do well to acknowledge their loyalty. Tell me, when does the Duma meet next?"

"Have no fear, Mother--I shall attend on schedule. They have come to expect me."

"Good. The boyars are important allies to the Naryshkins. Do not forget this, Peter."

"Allies?" Peter scowled. "They are self-serving, most of them. Their support comes with a motive…and they change with the seasons."

"This is the nature of alliances," she answered plainly. "Do not place too much value in the loyalties of men like Shein. Let it be enough that his motive benefits you and that your cause is in season."

"Yes, Mother," he nodded dutifully. "I shall endeavor to match Shein's vigor when I greet him."

"In light of what occurred at the Cathedral, I am certain their opinion of you has changed." Natalya thought back to the sight of Sophia's face as she floundered before the congregation. "Peter, we have not yet spoken of that day…"

His reaction was odd, his brow folding guiltily like a child being scolded. He moved to her side as though ready to take his punishment.

"I should have mentioned it sooner," he said, lowering his eyes. "I apologize for any embarrassment you suffered, Mother, but I have no regrets. She did it purposely and deserved the repercussions. Even Shein would think so!"

"Peter."

"For our entire lives, year after year, ceremony after ceremony, we walk the same paths--always with Sophia behind us! Behind! So how, Mother, how can I see it as anything but an insult when I turn to see the 'autocrat' marching along beside us? I refused to attend her charade of a victory parade and I refuse to sit by as she makes herself Tsarina in our place! I had no intention of spoiling the ceremony. I wasn't thinking about the ceremony at all--"

"Peter!" she snapped, quieting him. "There is nothing to be angry about. The embarrassment, as I see it, was certainly Sophia's. Ours was the victory."

He paused, his anger quickly subdued. "I thought you would be annoyed."

"You should know better," Natalya told her son, reaching out a hand, "Seeing Sophia trotting up that aisle was the most joy I've had in years."

He smiled brightly, taking her hand. "I know the boyars are pleased, but I was unsure of your opinion. I couldn't have planned such a thing."

"I am proud of you and Sophia is certainly deserving. I believe it to be a coincidence of fate, a moment of divine favor in which you stepped in and proved your worth. But be cautious. I ask only that you remember that all eyes are on you--it will always be so. Your actions speak volumes, Peter. Always consider the circumstance before choosing to act. Once you act, do so without regret."

"Yes, Mother." He waited for her step as he walked her to the window, staring around the room as though seeing it for the first time. "Your accommodations? I hope they are not too terribly crude."

"Meager, when compared to what we are accustomed to in Moscow," she replied honestly, "but certainly tolerable. My health has no doubt improved without Sophia to aggravate me."

His eyes widened. "You don't like the house? I'll have another one built immediately--"

"No, Peter, there is no sense in it. The accommodations are fine. They are not, however, truly fitting for a person of your rank. You will soon be Tsar. Your place is in Moscow, in the Kremlin."

"If I am Tsar, Mother, then I am Tsar everywhere, including Preobrazhenskoe."

"True, but the Tsar must be seen, Peter."

"They have Ivan to look at. Let Ivan be seen in his golden robes. I have many more important things to do."

She looked up at him, wondering at his restless spirit. The boy made a good impression on others, but was rarely around long enough to nurture the truly important relationships.

"Mother, I wish to travel to Archangel," he said before she could reply, his eyes brightening with the words. "Perhaps I'll arrange it for the spring."

"Archangel? For what purpose?"

"To see the ocean," he replied, pointing toward the window, his tone suddenly full of fire. "To set foot on the shore and see the open water! To finally set foot on the deck of a ship and feel the motion beneath my feet! Surely I've spoken of it."

"I was unaware," she said, unwilling to respond in kind. "Regardless, you will not be traveling to Archangel, Peter. It would take months and there are far too many concerns in Moscow for you to leave."

"Nonsense. Ivan does a perfectly good job."

"Come now, Peter."

"You wouldn't forbid me from traveling, would you?"

"You know I don't make such demands of you," she told him, her tone still bearing weight, "but I simply won't hear of your sailing--that much I cannot bear. Do you hear me, Peter? You are in no position to travel."

"Not now, then," he answered, acknowledging her with a half-grin. "I will plan it when I find myself in a better position."

Does he understand how close we are? Does he understand that he won't simply wake up one day and be Tsar?

Natalya was at a loss. She'd played out this conversation hundreds of times in her head, thinking of how to impress upon him the urgency of their situation, realizing that however persuasive her argument, she could ultimately offer no solution to their dilemma. Peter remained distracted by his 'play' army and cannons--too comfortable, in the Tsarista's estimation, for his own good.

She could think of little else to say. Peter cared for family politics and was shrewd enough to understand policy and etiquette. He had already spoken against Prince Vasily and opposed Sophia in both word and deed. Even the presence of his 'play' regiments seemed to suggest that he intended, at least in theory, to act. Still, he spent the lion's share of his time focused on cannons, military maneuvers and, since discovering the remnants of an old English boat with his tutor Franz Timmerman, shipbuilding. Like a child caught in the joy of a new novelty, Peter was content now and, with his life entirely before him, could see no reason to rush things. His mind was right, but his spirit was yet to be moved.

With an heir on the way, there is little time left, she thought, looking up at his face, noticing how much older Peter now looked. In just over a year, he'd grown out of his boyish size; the playful, wide-eyed cherub had turned into a man--leaner, sharper, carrying the weight of knowledge and a look of maturity. The glint in Peter's eye was ever-present, now hiding a world of thoughts instead of innocence, a deep pool of emotion and the knowledge that he would one day rule all he surveyed.

So much for a willful boy to conform to, she thought, wondering if she should approach the subject of his 'play' army but reconsidering in favor of a different topic.

"Have you been to visit your wife?" Natalya asked, speaking as only a mother can.

"No," he answered simply. "I have not."

"She will be disheartened to hear that you stopped without visiting her. She does so depend on you for her happiness."

"I know, Mother. She makes it quite clear to me how terribly sad she is the moment I walk away. In fact, we seem to spend most of our time speaking of that very subject."

"You must visit her, Peter. She is fragile in her condition and must be kept happy. Do you want your child to be born frightened and sickly?"

"She is fragile enough without the benefit of the child."

"Peter!"

"I treat her wonderfully, Mother. You know that I do."

"When you are by her side, you are kind, I know. But you neglect her, still. You must take more time to visit her, Peter--at least until we see this through. You do understand how important your heir is, do you not?"

"Of course," he answered, showing a bit of frustration.

Natalya caught his eye. "Sophia would execute a hundred of her most loyal if it meant gaining an heir for Ivan. Do not underestimate the power of such a thing."

"Odd, that I have yet to take the throne and we are already so concerned with who will replace me!"

"It is the way of things," she told him. "This, you know."

"I will make every attempt to see her. I promise."

"Promise to see her today. Promise me this."

He rolled his eyes but raised his palms in capitulation. "Yes, Mother. Today."

"What is it that you so dislike about Evdokia? Tell me!"

Peter shrugged a bit, clearing his throat. "I cannot say, specifically. Certainly, there is nothing despicable or loathsome about her, and she treats me as though I am the sun itself. But Mother, I find myself continually restless in her presence, eager at every moment to be away from her. She speaks of little but her own condition and complains if I don't compliment her at every turn. You know her better than I, Mother."

"I do, Peter, but these things make her no less your wife."

"Worry not, Mother. I will smile at her and make everything better. When she stops talking, she can really be quite pleasant to be around..."

The girl is too slow for him, Natalya thought, reminding herself of the Lopukhin family's service, knowing in her practical mind that some situations were simply made to be tolerated. *We may only hope that the child takes after his father.*

Footsteps sounded outside the door, followed by the unmistakably regimented knock of Boris Golitsyn.

"Boris, come in."

Golitsyn stepped through the entry, offering a slight bow. Well-groomed, Boris wore a new gray silk justaucorps and matching waistcoat, his stockinged legs stretching down into a fine pair of square-toed buckle shoes. Even Natalya had to admit that the rivalry with Lev had been a good thing for Golitsyn's wardrobe, and though he would never possess Naryshkin's flair, Boris nonetheless matched the younger politician in taste.

"Tsarevich, Tsarista," he greeted them simply, bowing again.

Peter grinned at him, opening his arms wide. "I must say, Boris, you look very well put together this afternoon."

"My thanks, Tsarevich." Golitsyn shifted uncomfortably. "It is of little consequence. I do not wish to interrupt."

"Nonsense," Natalya said, waving him in, "I sent for you not an hour ago. I appreciate your dedicated response, Boris."

"Always at your service, Lady. The distances to travel are so much shorter here than in the Kremlin. I rarely have far to go."

"You look a bit flushed, Boris." Peter grinned at him, eyes shining. "Boris misses the comfort of the Kremlin. He has grown so accustomed to the chill that he finds the rest of the world to be unbearably warm."

Golitsyn offered an uncomfortable grin. "Ah, yes. Quite true. I have been told that I possess thick blood."

"Words you will never hear from the lips of a Georgian!" Peter laughed. "A valued Russian trait, no doubt. You see, Boris, you were destined for such a life!"

Natalya drew Peter close, kissing him on the cheek.

"Leave us. I shall see you in the morning, I expect. God watch over you."

Peter returned the kiss. "Farewell, Mother. You do look beautiful today--did I tell you?"

"Go, flatterer," she ordered with a smile, waving him away.

Peter nodded to the Counselor. "Boris."

Golitsyn bowed. "My respects, Tsarevich. My regards to Lady Evdokia, as well. I imagine you will be seeing her."

Peter glared at his mother, serious at first, then fading into a slight chuckle. "Yes, I will. Though I believe this to be nothing short of a conspiracy!"

"Dos vidanye, Peter."

Collecting his plumed hat, the Tsarevich bowed before exiting, closing the door behind him. Natalya could see Boris relax in Peter's absence.

"You seem so uncomfortable in his presence," she said immediately, speaking her mind. "You know Peter likes to spar with you--really, Boris, you used to be so good at it."

"It is his youth, and little more," Golitsyn answered. "Seventeen is a defiant age. For a boy as restless as the Tsarevich, I think it especially so."

Restless, she thought. *Again, that word.*

The Tsarista turned. "I am restless as well, Boris."

"Oh?"

"Yes," she nodded, now commanding his full attention. "I worry that all our efforts may soon be wasted."

"Lady?"

"We cannot sustain another winter of Sophia," she answered, her temper rising as the name crossed her lips. "By then, the failure at Azov will be all but a memory. She will have the city infested with the Pope's bloody Latins. And do you plan on braving the cold in this place?"

Golitsyn shook his head. "Certainly not."

"No, I thought not." Natalya moved to her chair. "Peter is passionate and of the right mind. I truly believe this, Boris. He may not be quite ready to rule, but his ability is hardly the issue. Sophia's ill fortune cannot last forever. I have no doubt Ivan will eventually sire a boy and things will be equal. Without Peter to push her out, Sophia will be entrenched."

Golitsyn continued to nod, listening to her words with a dispassionate look, pausing as though considering her trouble as an expert. "Admittedly, I was hoping to speak with you about this very subject. I have never seen Sophia so weak, Lady."

"The incident at the Cathedral?" she asked feeling a bit better.

"In part, but I believe that her greatest problem lies with the Strel'tsy. They waver, Lady--they fear more unsteady campaigns at the hands of my cousin Vasily. Already we have the loyalty of the Sukharev Regiment and I believe Peter has ingratiated General Gordon, though I would offer no promises on that front. Gordon is a mercenary, strictly."

"There is no better time," the Tsarista announced, only half of her listening to him. "Ready or not, there is no better time for Peter. He is of age and quite capable. He possesses the support of the Duma, the aristocracy, and thanks to Sophia, the sympathies of many Strel'tsy. He is God's chosen, with a wife and a child on the way. Given all this, Sophia cannot continue to stand in our way."

She could see that he agreed with her, his thoughtful look taking on an air of vision and foresight. If anyone could unravel this dilemma, it was Golitsyn.

"You speak my thoughts, Lady, almost to the word. And you are correct--we cannot hope to revisit such fertile ground."

"Peter's little army is hardly enough to take the Kremlin by force."

"Whatever their disposition, the Strel'tsy will defend Sophia against attack. You may depend on this. Our solution must be more…imaginative."

"We do think alike," the Tsarista told him, her spirits lifted by his words. "What is your suggestion?"

He stepped back for a moment, looking at the ceiling and crossing his arms. "I confess, Lady, this is not the first time I have considered the subject and I'm afraid that I have been unable to come up with a foolproof notion. I do, however, have a few valuable ideas, I think."

The Tsarista smiled. "Ah, Boris. Tell me."

He cleared his throat. "Well…in my humble opinion, we must take advantage of Sophia's greatest weakness. She has grown unpopular, even among the rats that follow her. She is seen as ambitious and covetous of the Regency. All of this against her…yet, if we attack her, we make her a martyr. The Strel'tsy will come to her defense and we will lose our advantage. But if we turn the situation on its head and make Peter the victim? What support, then, will there be for the Regent?"

"We will never provoke her into attacking," Natalya answered. "She is far too shrewd to make that mistake."

"Respectfully, Lady Natalya, I do not speak of armies. I describe a far more subtle action. Simple, but possessing all the impact of a battle. More, perhaps."

"Do not be cryptic, Boris," she scolded. "Tell me what you would do!"

Boris cleared his throat again, brushing a speck from his sleeve. "I have no desire to anger you, Tsarista, and I think that my idea may seem cruel or unwarranted. I do not wish to insult you or cause Peter any undo dis--"

"Boris! Why are you stuttering? Will Peter be harmed in this plan of yours?"

"Certainly not."

"Then tell me," she ordered, her patience waning.

"Well, quite simply, if Peter, for example, received word that Sophia intended to harm him, would this not move his spirit? Shaklovity enacts similar treachery quite often. It would have to be something dramatic, of course, something more urgent…perhaps assassins on their way to cut his throat. We would all need to be prepared to react appropriately, of course. The better we react, the more true it becomes. Sophia would rightly deny the charges, but I see few who would believe her now."

He paused as though finished, dabbing at his brow with a handkerchief and offering a half shrug in expectation of her response.

Natalya restrained the currents of hope that flowed beneath her powdered skin, allowing the repercussions to play out in her mind, enjoying the possibilities that rose to greet her.

"Yes, I see! Her denials will be irrelevant. Boris, your plot has promise! It could actually work."

"Well, Tsarista," he replied, sounding a bit prideful, "There are certain conditions that need to be fostered. The Strel'tsy must be ripe for rumors."

"With the majority of the work done, surely you will sort out the details. Do you think it possible?"

"Certainly," he said finally, his tone hardening, "We shall find a way."

Moscow, Cathedral Square in the Kremlin

August 1689

Boris Golitsyn spied his target long before the carriage circled the final turn, a sight that failed to placate his troubled mind. He cleared his throat and prepared for the encounter, reminding himself of the greater purpose.

Lev Kyrilovich Naryshkin was never early. It was hard to believe that the news would be favorable.

The little drunkard commands a harem of followers...

As was his custom, Naryshkin had arrived in the company of several courtiers and their attendants, the collective entourage creating what resembled a small but refined crowd. The lot of them waited for Golitsyn there at the foot of the Red Staircase.

How important he must feel--leading about such a group! He talks of politics and speaks the words as though he were the first ever to mouth them.

The carriage hopped on the gaps in the cobbled Square before rolling to a stop. Leaning back out of sight, Golitsyn took a deep breath and gathered himself.

At least they will know that Naryshkin waits for Golitsyn!

Boris waited patiently for the driver to open the door, lingering for an additional moment before stepping down from the carriage.

Prince Boris Alekseevich Golitsyn, Commander of the Kazan Palace, Counselor to the Tsarista herself. I need no entourage.

The face he wore today was not his customary guise of impatience but rather a stoic attempt at noble grace, a condition he thought far more fitting. With cousin Vasily bearing the brunt of the Duma's complaints, it was becoming evident to Boris that deeds alone were not enough to separate his good name from that of beleaguered Prince Vasily. Even now, he would have to set himself apart.

Lev Naryshkin offered an unfriendly smile from beneath his plumed brim. Seeing that Golitsyn was not moving to greet him in the middle, the younger man stepped slowly to match the distance.

Look at him! Golitsyn thought, fuming inside. *The new champion of tradition!*

Despite their anti-reform tendencies, the Naryshkin clan was avidly fond of European dress, routinely importing clothes from Poland and Germany. Lev Kyrilovich was no exception, and only Prince V.V. himself could have been called more extravagant in his love of Western fashion. Only seven years older than his nephew Tsarevich Peter, Lev's political reputation already far outweighed his competence. Given his name and prominence, however, Naryshkin was the most obvious choice to lead the Duma against the offences of the Regency.

Young, brash, green--everything they require in such a position!

"Greetings, poor Boris!" Lev spoke as though it were an announcement, his voice loud enough to be heard by all. "Always traveling, always alone. Is there no one who will ride with you?"

"Often, yes. When I find someone deserving," Golitsyn replied without a flinch, his expression unwavering. "My responsibilities are too numerous to allow time for socializing--a problem you apparently do not have."

"My agenda is quite full, I assure you," Lev answered, now staring unabashedly. "Still, you know I always find time for a friend of the family and loyal supporter like you, Boris."

"As gracious as ever, my boy. I'm honored that you could spare a moment."

"Think nothing of it, Counselor."

Boris bristled. Lev's entourage eyed him curiously, as though waiting for him to explode with rage.

"Do away with the dancing troupe," Boris whispered as soon as Naryshkin was close enough. "We must speak alone. Perhaps the carriage would be best."

He didn't wait for Lev to respond but turned instead for the welcome discretion of his carriage, wanting only to be away from Naryshkin's cackling chorus. There was, no doubt, a deep appreciation within Golitsyn for the part that Lev played; in his estimation, Lev Kyrilovich would have a considerable role in the future health of the clan and, with the exception of Peter himself, was easily the most likeable of the family. Lev's popularity was understandable. Predictable. Good for the family and Mother Russia.

Boris Golitsyn was, if nothing else, a practical man, and well understood the benefits of having a character like Lev in confidence. He recognized Lev's popularity and agreed with his rational side that the younger, better looking, quick-tongued advocate was precisely what the Naryshkin cause needed in the Duma. By all accounts, Boris realized that he should have been reconciled with Lev Naryshkin's swift rise in politics. Yet somehow, he was not.

Boris hated the whelp--despised every clever turn of speech and fashionable ensemble. He cringed when Lev boasted and refused to address him by his full name. He watched with a hawkish, suspicious eye when the young boyar was in the room, knowing that beneath all of the politeness and etiquette, Lev equaled him in hate.

A rivalry born of jealousy, perhaps. Golitsyn was big enough to admit it, yet from the view of the elder statesman the offence was simply one of service and dedication. In his estimation, politics always seemed to favor the least qualified while leaving the most experienced used and forgotten. He was determined, however, that his would be a notable life, despite the long line of Lev Kyriloviches dancing in his path.

Golitsyn clenched his jaw. Perhaps for the first time in his long life, the administrator was surveying his own emotions, understanding the swells that shaped his temperament. Within him there were deeper levels of satisfaction, laboriously earned, needs that could not possibly be satiated with the notion of collective success. Boris wanted, quite simply, all that he had earned.

As Lev backtracked to deliver apologies to the crowd, Boris reentered his carriage, eager for the privacy of the coach. Kyrilovich was more docile without an audience, and Boris knew he would surely have the advantage in a private setting.

The door opened and Lev stepped into the coach, taking the seat opposite Golitsyn in a fragrant rush of wind. He lifted his chin and stared, a grin spreading slowly across his bristled face.

"You stink of wine," Golitsyn said in welcome. "It shall accompany me home, I expect. What could possibly make you smile so?"

"I confess to the wine, sir, and I apologize for the offence. You would certainly know the scent."

"You are drunk."

"No, no-no--merely drinking. I celebrate a victory for our cause, brother! I drink to our shared prosperity! For this, you cannot condemn me."

"Your plea to the Colonel was a success, then? Colonel?"

Lev smiled again. "Success? Success is far too mild a word, sir. And you refer to Lieutenant Colonel Larion Elizarov. He is a patriotic, if not brilliant, man!"

He's done it, Boris thought, wondering how the drunken politician was capable of achieving such personal feats. *Even the Strel'tsy are charmed by him!*

"Naryshkin! Wake up and give me the details. Tell me what was said."

Lev tilted his head in offence, his eyes glaring back but revealing little. "I am not as drunk as you would think, Boris. To state it simply, he will be our eyes within the ranks of the musketeers. If they plan to march, we will know."

"And their temperament?"

Lev paused. "Oh, to find the ideal word…should I say cautious…or frightened?"

"Did you express our deep concern for Peter's life?"

"Yes, of course. Lady Natalya's exodus to Preobrazhenskoe only furthers their suspicion. I told him that we fear treachery from the Regency, that Sophia grows desperate."

"This Elizarov is solid, then?"

"Quite. I assure you, I explained everything."

"Good. The time, as they say, is ripe. Commander Shaklovity has been stirring the pot more than is his custom, and the embarrassment at the Cathedral has flowered into a vine of rumors."

"Sophia oversteps her rank. There is no longer any question."

"And what of the Boyar Council?"

"Ahh!" Lev smiled again, confidently. "They remain as irritable as ever…you've seen the portrait of Sophia, I assume."

"Indeed."

"If the crown of the Monomakh sitting on her head were not enough, that idiot Medvedev added a verse to the bottom, comparing the 'Grand Autocrat' with Queen Elizabeth, no less!"

"Yes, yes." Boris suppressed his irritation. "But what of the Duma? Can we count on their support?"

Lev nodded convincingly. "Once the scandal begins? Surely! Even her closest comrades will desert her. If you need proof, then you only need look at the roster of new enlistments out at Preobrazhenskoe. Peter's 'play' army grows and grows. Many names, some of them boyars and sons of elite families."

"All for the best. The Duma will serve us later. For now, however, they are unimportant compared to our Strel'tsy allies. Without the riders, our plan has no legitimacy."

"I told you, we have Elizarov now and the riders have been selected. Dependable men."

"I must rely on your word…"

Naryshkin stared, looking a bit offended. "You needn't worry--I have done my part! And what of you, Boris? Were you successful as well? We must have a villain! Tell me of your plan to implicate Commander Shaklovity."

Boris cleared his throat, feeling a bit proud.

"We must lure the Strel'tsy from Sophia's side," he began thoughtfully, "and leave Shaklovity stranded in the middle. The musketeers are loyal to the Regent and the Miloslavskys. To break this bond, we must press them to test a higher loyalty…that of their duty to God."

Naryshkin started to speak, silenced by Golitsyn's pointed finger.

"We know that the Strel'tsy would defend Sophia, but they would never attack Peter."

"Certainly not. Peter's rule has been ordained--"

"Precisely," Boris snapped, interrupting. "If pushed to the edge, if pressed to the point where they truly believed that Sophia was about to engage Peter? They would never support Sophia to oppose God's will."

"This is not an answer," Naryshkin protested. "How do you intend to press them?"

Golitsyn leaned back in his seat. "With a simple letter, my boy. With a letter, sent at just the right moment. We will stir their hearts and make that scourge Shaklovity our scapegoat in one clean stroke of the quill. The good Commander is already known for spreading rumors. Our conspirators will do the rest."

"Explain," Naryshkin responded, tilting his head. "What do you mean, a letter?"

"Lev, you must assure Lieutenant Elizarov and the others that Peter has no intention of attacking Moscow. Can you do this?"

Lev shrugged, nodding. "Yes, of course. But Boris, what do you mean, a letter?"

"I will explain everything. I have already spoken with the Tsarista. You will see how beautifully everything fits..."

Moscow, The Great Sovereign's Palace of the Kremlin

August 1689

Fedor hesitated for a moment, staring out at the formidable size of the Palace, deciding to blame the carriage driver for his tardiness. He slapped away the driver's hand and hopped down from the carriage.

"Be waiting," he ordered simply, raising his chin and stepping confidently toward the entrance.

He nodded his way past the guards and headed straight for the Regent's chambers, noting the odd silence that permeated the once murmuring corridors.

A man of two minds, Shaklovity strode with determination toward his target, half of him conscious of his duty and half anticipating a warm reception from the Regent. He'd been certain to insure that his visit to Sophia coincided with the Prince's weekly absence and had taken extra time with his grooming. With two shots of vodka warming his stomach, Fedor was feeling more like himself, half angry and half amorous, ready to face her.

Poor girl--forced to shoulder all this burden.

Many considered Sophia ugly and thought her features to be masculine, but Fedor had always considered her beautiful in her own way. She was still young, smarter than most men and could keep her stride with all of Russia in the palm of her hand. More than just a woman, Sophia was an office, a clan, an icon. What could be more inviting?

With Golitsyn away, she'll be alone.

Dismissing her attendants with a wave, he took the liberty of entering without knocking, creeping through the door and closing it behind him. The chamber was dark, lit by a single candle and a few thin strips of light intruding through the window coverings.

"You're late, Fedor."

He heard her voice, squinting as his eyes adjusted. "Yes, my dear, you have my most sincere apologies."

She's in the bed! That lovely girl!

His spirits taking flight, Shaklovity moved quickly to Sophia's side, opening his arms to hold her.

"I wish to know why," she snapped, evading his embrace and offering only her cheek.

He kissed her cheek but stopped short of touching her. Waving him back, she stood from the bed.

Beautiful and furious, the sight of her stirred him. Sophia's hair fell to her shoulders, the most complicated of her stockings and under-garments already removed, white snowy flesh visible beneath what remained. Her eyes were wild, bearing a fiery depth, like a lover jilted at the height of passion.

"Why, Lady? I am here now."

"You took too long, Fedor! I wish to know what bit of business is more important than I!"

"Why, none! Of course, Sophia."

"I promise, if you tell me I will most certainly find a remedy and rid you of that business! You are to come when called, Fedor!"

"I am ever loyal!"

"You are ever tardy! And ever salty!" Sophia paused, looking him up and down.

She sees I've dressed for her.

Fedor stepped closer, risking to reach out and touch her bare arm. To his surprise, Sophia allowed it.

"Sophia, you must forgive me--this was hardly my fault! My driver is the one to blame! He had me waiting to depart, waiting and waiting. Really, dear, you don't understand how difficult it can be for a man like me."

"Difficult?"

"I try always to make myself available to you," he told her, "particularly in times when Prince Golitsyn is visiting his wife."

Sophia's eyes narrowed.

Even as he uttered the comment, Shaklovity commended himself for being so clever. Mentioning the Prince's wife was always the quickest path to Sophia's bed; she was still young enough to hate the things she could not control. He wanted to remind her that, ultimately, Prince V.V. would never be hers.

"You speak of her too often," Sophia said to him, too quick to allow his game. "In truth, I need you no more when he is gone than I do when he is present. You are cruel to remind me of her. Still, I wish you to be available."

"Yes, Sophia..." He pressed closer to her, placing his hands on her thick bare shoulders and caressing the pale flesh. "There are so many unnecessary burdens placed on these beautiful shoulders. You must relax."

"There is no time," she replied sleepily, her eyes closing.

She enjoys my touch.

"Of course there is," he whispered. "There is always time for the Regent, Come, Sophia, lay with me for a while."

She moved with his hand for a moment, a beautiful instant that changed suddenly.

"I was waiting for you," she said to him, moving away. "And now I don't see how I can find the inspiration. As you just said--I am Regent. There is much to do."

"Sophia, please." he advanced but stopped quickly, held in place by a single raised finger.

"Blame your driver if you wish, Fedor, but I am no longer of a mind to enjoy myself. My blood cooled, I suppose, the very moment you were late."

The measure of her glare warned him to stall his advances. Undaunted, Shaklovity conceded the battle but remained hopeful for the outcome of the war.

She stands from the bed but does not dress.

"Is there no way I can persuade you, Lady?"

She frowned. "Perhaps with some good news. What have you from the ranks? What is their temperament?"

I must be honest with her, lest she be too passive.

"Regrettably, their temperament is cool. Their allegiance is still as strong as ever, I believe, but their temperament is decidedly cool. Fragile is the word to describe an army that fears it cannot even muster an attack against its greatest enemy. I know you are loath to hear these words from my mouth, but the blame belongs to the Prince. His farce of a campaign has wounded you with your people, Lady."

"You are too fond of blaming Vasily," she replied, ever defensive of her favorite. "His endeavors, however ineffective, are well intended. I was the one who allowed the celebration. Peter, however, was the one who caused this mess."

"I worry too much," he said in his defense, shrugging sympathetically, "and trust that I blame Peter as well."

They're both at fault, he thought. *We should have killed the boy long ago.*

"Peter is too much a man to ignore. And now, apparently, he is willing to speak." Shaklovity stared, measuring his words. "Given your performance at the Cathedral, I should think it obvious to everyone."

Sophia turned on him, her eyes blazing. "I refuse to speak of that day. You are cruel to mention it."

The events at the Cathedral lay heavily on his mind. It was not Sophia's embarrassment that disturbed him, but rather Peter's sudden assertiveness. Certainly, the Tsarevich had disagreed with Sophia before, but never anything so public, never anything more than childish complaints. This insult was the act of a man, not a boy. This was a young Tsar asserting himself, posturing shrewdly as his father had.

"It was not my intention to scold you," Shaklovity replied, backing down. "I merely meant to suggest that Peter's aggressive tongue makes me wonder what he has planned for his army."

"Peter's army is little more than a rabble. He would not and cannot hope to take us by force."

Fedor shrugged. "He may not have need of force, my dear. He is winning in tiny increments, hundreds of them, weakening you at every turn."

She lifted her chin. "We have borne his insults and borne them well, I think."

"Perhaps, but given Peter's character, who knows what to expect? Respectfully, Regent, he has become a threat to your stability. There is little time left to kill him…"

She moved suddenly as though leaping toward him, her brow bent in anger. "Fedor! You are to cease any thoughts of assassination!"

He shrugged, unaffected. "Well, of course, an outright assassination would be far too incriminating and difficult to manage. I was thinking of an accident, perhaps, something involving those bloody exercises at Fort Presburg. With a single stray cannon shot, Peter could be--"

"Enough! I forbid you!"

He frowned back at her. "What? You don't like the idea? I have many more."

"And you will keep them to yourself from this moment on," she ordered, clenching her jaw. "You are to drop all thoughts of treachery and put aside any plans you have already made."

"What?"

"I have changed my mind," she stated. "I know what we spoke of, Fedor, but now is not the time. Our opportunity passed us years ago."

"But Lady, we could still be successful!"

"We could not," she countered firmly. "Are you a fool? Were one hair on his head to be harmed, you would be the first culprit and I the second! My reputation is soiled at the hands of the Tsarista--the wretch made a fool out of me by taking her household to Preobrazhenskoe. And, given what occurred at the Cathedral, I'm certain the Patriarch and the boyars are all foaming at the mouth!

"We cannot risk such scandal now," she continued. "I must attempt to repair my relations with the Patriarch and win back the trust of the Duma."

"And the Strel'tsy as well," he added.

"I see that you understand."

"Respectfully, my lady, I do not."

She stared back without responding, delivering only a molten glare.

"Sophia, it could be done! Cleanly, without incident--an accident! I can see you now, speaking warmly about him at his funeral--"

"No more plots!" she hissed, her whisper bearing weight. "I cannot trust you to succeed. All talk of murder ends here. And keep your lips shut tight. I don't want to hear of your speaking in public against the Naryshkins."

"They will think me sick if I don't."

"Nonetheless," Sophia returned, her look serious, "You will cease any and all public speaking. And that goes for Father Medvedev as well. Be sure he knows. Remember this, my love. With all you've said against him, Peter would afford you little leniency!"

Shaklovity bristled at the visions emerging from her words. He'd spoken against the Tsarevich in public, accusing Peter of everything from laziness to heresy. He'd crafted the anonymous letters that threatened Sophia, rallying the undisciplined Strel'tsy Guard to her side. When Sophia's popularity waned, she could always count on Shaklovity to invigorate and excite the Strel'tsy mob, the source of her bloody control. Shaklovity was the problem solver, the originator of fear.

The most likely conspirator…

Shaklovity exhaled, feeling the hope leaving along with his sour breath. The path ahead was darkening, his visions of the future suffocated beneath Peter's engulfing shadow. And now, though he could hardly believe it, Fedor found himself in far too deep, stuck in the position of sacrificing everything in the name of the Miloslavskys and Sophia.

As hard as he was, Shaklovity was not immune.

I have failed.

Peter and Natalya should be dead, by my order. Now it is too late.

"I am driven by thoughts of our fate!" he rattled back, his temper spurred. "I am infected with them, consumed! You are cruel to restrain me, Sophia. Given all I have done, I find it unthinkable that we could simply abandon our last hope."

"Respectfully," she shouted, screaming the words at the top of her lungs before quieting. "You will do your duty and respect my orders. And I won't hear any more about Prince Vasily's failed command. I have enough aggravation without dealing with the two of you growling at each other."

"I suppose I shouldn't blame the Prince when Peter has an heir waiting to be born."

Sophia's look changed. "On this, we are of like mind. When compared to the threat of Peter with a male heir in his arms, a victory on the field means nothing to us."

"Regrettable timing," he replied, thinking aloud. "Better that the Lopukhin bride be further along. We might be fortunate enough to lose both mother and child at birth."

Sophia frowned. "God does not provide such blessings. And there is no doubt in my mind--by the time Evdokia gives birth to this child, we will be in the midst of an entirely different dilemma."

"Lady?"

"Ivan must have a male heir. For now we require only the blessing, and not the end result. Praskovia must be as blessed as Evdokia. She will equal Peter's wife, then, and Ivan will equal Peter."

He thought of Tsarevich Ivan, imagining the dim bearded fool writhing naked atop his wife. *He must make a mess of things...poor little dog.*

"Ivan has tried his best, no doubt," Shaklovity conceded, "and I would commend his wife for being such a dutiful soldier in the cause of Russia. Respectfully, any woman who could tolerate Ivan is surely a patriot soul!"

"Ivan has a benevolence about him," she said, her tone bearing offence, "a kindness that you are simply unable to appreciate."

"Ah, I see." Fedor scratched his beard. "I am too coarse for such things. I see. But Sophia, I am merely speaking in truths. If your plan relies on Ivan to carry through with his wife, then I would certainly reconsider. You would do better to find some strapping young peasant to plant a seed in Ivan's place!"

The Regent fell quiet, offering no immediate reply.

At first he thought Sophia's silence a sign of offence, but quickly realized that she was considering his words.

"I aim to amuse," he told her, "though I think you take me quite seriously."

She looked back at him. "The idea is not without merit."

He shrugged, considering it himself. "I suppose so, yes."

Sophia stepped closer, her look serious. "This, at least, is an option…"

She's growing desperate, he thought as he watched her speak. *We cannot rest our strategy upon ridiculous hope.*

Ridiculous or not, Shaklovity knew he could not question her. There was only one path for him, that which he had already been walking for years. He would do his best to carry out her wishes, knowing in his heart that every man eventually has to choose a side.

My lot was cast long ago…

"Very well. I will endeavor to find a worthy candidate, Regent."

"Be discreet." Sophia turned her back, returning to the bed. She sat down on the edge, patting the corner with her hand.

Shaklovity stepped forward reluctantly, his amorous intentions now caged and sleeping.

"Of course," he answered with a servant's smile, bowing. "I strive only to serve your cause. Regarding Peter, however, if you would reconsider…"

She stood immediately, her scowl returning. "Certainly not! I won't tell you again, Fedor. Truly, you are persistent like a child!"

She moved away from him, her gaze regally absent. "I am tired and need to rest. I trust you will not forget to make arrangements for my pilgrimage."

"Forgive me, Regent, but in light of what happened at the Cathedral…I assumed it would be--"

"Certainly not!" she returned angrily, raising her chin. "I will attend as planned. All the better for the Regency."

"Yes, Regent."

"We must rebuild our reputation and show strength, this I know. Our isolation accomplishes nothing. I will be part of the pilgrimage and the Patriarch will know it. Do what you must to prepare. You are dismissed, Commander."

Shaklovity said no more, bowing respectfully and carrying his rage with him, his tortured thoughts building as he stepped out into the corridor.

I search for bastard fathers when I should be plotting to cut Naryshkin throats!

Sophia casts away our opportunity. Her fear shackles her!

Fedor paused, resting against the wall. His thoughts clouded with dread, his spirits sagging beneath the weight of practicality.

The Cathedral has made her timid. She seeks to play the middle when she's always prospered on the edge.

The Regency weakens with each day, and we counter with nothing, no measure of control, no affirmation of our strength.

The warrior within him twitched, now bound at the wrists, neutered and caged by policy and perception. On fire with futility, Shaklovity straightened his posture and counted his assets.

I am yet Commander of the Strel'tsy.

Thousands upon thousands serve at my call, while that arrogant boy commands nothing more than a rabble.

Peter's light blinds all of Moscow. The city must be reminded where the power truly lies.

Moscow, The Naryshkin Estate

Late Afternoon August 17, 1689

Lev Naryshkin was dozing drunkenly in his favorite chair when the doors burst open and Boris Golitsyn came striding in, his heels popping like musket fire on the parquet floor. He looked oddly unsettled, his face flushed and bearing an uncharacteristic eagerness that Lev didn't recognize in the statesman. Golitsyn's coat remained half-buttoned and his wig crooked, thrown atop his head as though it were a cap.

From the look of his guest, Naryshkin could see that the news was profound, be it terrible or glorious.

"Boris?" Lev rose on shaky legs, using the back of the chair to steady himself.

"We must speak," Golitsyn announced. "Time works against us."

"Doesn't it always?" Lev replied, smirking. "Boris, catch your breath before you speak. You look as if you pulled the carriage yourself! And what of my staff? Did you not receive a greeting?"

"I did," Golitsyn replied quickly. "They were far too slow to wake you. But Lev, listen to me. Are you listening?"

"Yes, yes. Of course."

Golitsyn stared. "An opportunity awaits us--the kind we have been longing for."

His head spun a bit, his stomach growling for nourishment.

"What? Boris, take a seat so we may speak. I do not wish to stand at the moment."

"Our dear Regent has planned a pilgrimage for tomorrow," Golitsyn pressed, "and Shaklovity called up not one, but two battalions to escort her. There haven't been this many troops in Moscow since Sophia ascended! Apparently, Shaklovity claims that he is guarding against a murder that occurred on the road to the Donskoy Monastery. But to bring in additional arms as well? I would say he intends a show of power in the wake of Sophia's grand performance."

"Is that all?" Lev chuckled, shaking his head and moving toward the vodka. "Boris, I was here in Moscow all day and I promise you I wasn't drunk until evening. I know about the military parade--they caused quite a clamor."

"They did," Golitsyn quipped, looking pleased. "Though apparently you fail to share my enthusiasm. Perhaps you are still too inebriated, Lev. You did not walk the streets as I did! Lips are buzzing with worry. And best of all, the Strel'tsy themselves seem to be wondering what is happening. The sight was inspiring!"

Lev poured himself a small taste and downed it quickly, shaking off the effects of sleep. Like flame to powder, the strong vodka awakened his mind to Golitsyn's implication.

Lev stepped closer, lowering his voice. "You mean to say…you think the Strel'tsy ripe tonight?"

"Yes. I do. I told you--there have not been this many soldiers in Moscow in seven years, comrade. The city is perfectly uptight, the soil plowed and ready to be planted!"

"I have never seen you so lively, Boris."

Golitsyn scowled. "Can you possibly endeavor to keep your thoughts focused on our task, Lev?"

"Certainly, Boris."

"You may mock me at some other moment if you wish."

"You don't have to go on so, Boris." Naryshkin flashed his diplomatic smile, raising his hands in surrender. "You have my apologies. I am beside you in this."

"I expect you to be, comrade." Golitsyn moved to the table. "We have little time to act."

Lev straightened, the vodka taking effect. "Then we shall do so quickly. What do you have in mind, Boris?"

Golitsyn sighed, reaching for the feathered quill and lifting it for Naryshkin to see. "There are moments, Lev, occasions when you and I are speaking when I must stop and ask myself if you are listening at all. Your talent for persuasion, however, will not be lost in this endeavor."

"Ah, yes…you intend to pen the letter now."

The Counselor nodded, his eyes still bright with anticipation. "We will plant our seed in the hearts of the Strel'tsy."

"Indeed."

"You'll have to work as well, Lev. We will need several copies of the same note. The city must be equally convinced."

"Yes, yes!" Lev grinned now, seeing the possibilities in Boris' plan. There was an element of gamble, certainly, but his partner's enthusiasm was rubbing off on Naryshkin. The outcome would take one of many paths, all of which seemed to lead in their favor. "There is a good chance, undoubtedly."

"The rest will be in the hands of the Holy Father and our dear Lieutenant Colonel Elizarov, but we must prepare for success. Now, think--help me pen the lines. We have little time."

Naryshkin reached for the vodka but hesitated, caught in the sudden realization that the end of the Regency was near.

Moscow, The Kremlin

The Night of August 17, 1689

"I told you all I know! Please, sir, have mercy!"

The prisoner sat strapped to a chair, his eyes and mouth horribly swollen, his nose dripping a thick trail of blood that streaked down to his chin. His head lolled in response to Shaklovity's voice, rising with the effort of a man who knew his life was in the balance.

"You seem to have a bit of breath left," Shaklovity snapped in response, his patience all but gone. "Answer my questions truthfully and we can be finished."

"I spoke the truth, sir. I know nothing more!"

"I would know the status of the Preobrazhensky Guard and their readiness at the moment you left for Moscow."

The prisoner hung his head for a moment before looking back up, wincing as though expecting another blow. "I know nothing of the Guard, sir."

"Again," Fedor pressed. "You will tell me--do the Preobrazhensky plan to march on Moscow?"

"I am only a chamberlain, sir. I came with a routine dispatch. You've seen the message, sir!"

"Answer the question!"

"I don't know, Commander! Please, I told you! They pulled me from my horse and began beating me! I know no more!"

"Silence!"

Shaklovity raised his hand and turned his back on the messenger, his line of questioning proving wholly unfruitful, serving only to muddy the already clouded waters. He considered pressing further; by most standards this interrogation had been mild and there were certainly more tortuous means of persuasion at his disposal. Still, he could not deny his instinct. The young man seemed truthful and, despite his fear, had remained consistent in both tale and tone.

Only an hour before, the chamberlain had been rudely dismounted by a group of overly eager Strel'tsy Guards who, driven by the events of the evening, mistakenly thought him a Preobrazhensky scout. The courier suffered a cruel beating before being dragged to the Kremlin and held for questioning.

Pleased with the actions of the vigilant Guard, Shaklovity had immediately ordered an interrogation, thinking he'd found the key to unlocking the mystery of the letter now circulating throughout Moscow. Suddenly, Shaklovity felt defeated and foolish. The courier was telling the truth.

And what if this is just a distraction? he thought, his worry springing to the fore. *I've wasted time with this nobody while the real plot progresses without me! I must speak with Sophia before anything else happens!*

Captain Fedorov stepped to his side. "Sir, if you give us a few moments..."

"No more for now," Shaklovity replied, not bothering to look back at the man. "Put him back in the cell. I will return later."

"Yes, sir."

"You two--come with me."

Fedor stepped to the side of the hall, tapping his chest as though he were short of breath. Still shaken by the events of the night, the accompanying Strel'tsy allowed him a moment to gather his thoughts. The guards he'd chosen were capable and had performed well at the interrogation, though little had been revealed about Peter's intentions.

A trick, surely, he thought, still seeing the messenger, knowing that despite his lack of confession, something odd was indeed occurring.

Not an attack. That headstrong boy is incapable of such a military action. It must be something else...a diversion, perhaps. Do I deny the truth? Does Peter try to defeat us with guile?

Fedor sniffed and cleared his throat, wondering how to advise the Regent. His suspicions ruled him now, and despite the most rational of his thoughts, he found himself being more and more certain that a real threat existed.

He thought back, searching for the cause.

The events of the day had begun simply enough, in the same manner as many days before. Regent Sophia's excursion to the Donskoy Monastery was planned for the following morning, and as was his custom, Shaklovity was to commission a battalion of Strel'tsy to accompany her. Instead, he'd used a murder on the road to Donskoy as his rationale and summoned an entire regiment.

His true motives seemed important at the time, a display of authority in the wake of Sophia's embarrassment at the Cathedral, a simple reminder to all of Moscow that the Strel'tsy were still in control. Now, however, the Commander could see his decision for what it was--a foolish bit of arrogance, a trap of his own making into which he'd fallen.

The soldiers had most certainly been noticed, clamoring through the streets on their way to prepare for the morning journey. The city had come to their windows and doors to watch as the red-coated Strel'tsy marched by in number, the overwhelming military presence stirring the populace into a round of murmuring doubt and question.

Fedor sighed. On any other occasion, their alarm would be inconsequential. On this night, however, the rumors seemed aligned against him.

My enemies seized the opportunity I gave them.

A letter, he thought, shaking his head. *Of all things!*

Not long after reaching their barracks, the soldiers had received a letter, a treacherous note claiming that Peter's army was preparing to attack the city. From what Fedor could ascertain, additional copies had been circulated throughout Moscow.

Like a wind-swept fire the rumors spread, soon filling every head in Moscow with fearful, perilous thoughts. From house to house the rumor claimed devout believers, especially among those who had seen the parade of military might earlier that afternoon.

It was not the first time. Similar letters had appeared before, notes much like this one, the majority claiming that Peter sought to have the Regent murdered. Shaklovity knew well of the prior letters, for he had been the author and arranged for their surreptitious release, knowing that rumors written in ink spread much faster than those which came from his lips. The pen had been his favorite method of stirring a bit of sympathy for Sophia when she most needed it.

Tonight, however, the letter was unknown to him, written in a hand he did not recognize. Given its crafting, there was no doubt in his mind that the letter was malicious.

They dare steal my methods! They rest their success on the foundation I have laid!

But does it tell the truth?

Do I dismiss the second battalion? he wondered. *Or is their presence fortuitous? If the letter tells the truth, we will certainly need them.*

Which preceded which--the battalion or the letter?

Suddenly, it struck him. If the letter had been delivered as an act of opportunity, it could not have come from Peter; the ride from Preobrazhenskoe would have taken too long.

He nodded to himself. *The traitors are in Moscow, then. Surely, the letter is a lie. Peter has no plans for attack.*

"Sir?"

"Yes? What?"

"Are you ailing, sir?"

"More than I wish to discuss," Fedor replied, his tone bearing no levity. "I will persevere, as is my custom. And the Strel'tsy will not be outdone! We must keep moving."

"Yes, sir."

As they continued on, Shaklovity spoke little, immersed in his thoughts, his mind playing out possibilities and finding little comfort in any scenario. As he neared the Regent's chambers, his thoughts shifted to Sophia and how he would explain all the confusion.

She will blame me, but her pilgrimage must be canceled. If we are granted a peaceful night, she will deliver a speech in the morning...with an explanation.

He expected the Regent to be angry. He expected Sophia to be her usual perturbed self, brimming with pride and vitriol.

The woman he found awaiting him, however, was not the Sophia he had come to know. She sat slumped at the small desk, her hair down and uncombed, her large hands holding a crumpled piece of parchment. As she looked up at him, Fedor could see that she had been crying.

He ordered the guards to wait at the door, insuring privacy before approaching her. Never had he seen the bullish Regent in such condition, the effect on him so profound that for a moment Shaklovity hesitated, not wanting to speak to her for fear of how she might reply.

"Where have you been?" she snapped, her eyes incriminating him. "You are horrible to leave me sitting here alone--without knowing anything!"

"Lady, I was with the courier."

"Yes, but you were away for nearly an hour! What if something had happened in your absence?"

"I have returned now, Sophia. The courier claimed to be one of Peter's chamberlains--said he was bringing a routine dispatch."

"And his message? What did it say?"

Fedor shook his head slightly. "Routine, my lady. Just as he claimed."

"Are you certain?" she asked standing from her seat, the confusion creeping into her tone. "There was no other message?"

"No, my lady."

"But…how can it be? What was his purpose?"

"I was not able to extract his purpose," Shaklovity answered curtly, "But you must cancel your pilgrimage."

She paused. "I expected as much. But what of the interrogation? Did he speak the truth?"

Fedor scratched at his beard, wondering how to answer. He couldn't honestly incriminate the chamberlain, but the thought of making such a careless mistake plagued him with worry and doubt.

Do I tell her he was just a courier? It makes things no less dangerous…yet, the letter remains.

"He was convincing," Shaklovity answered her, hesitating, "though I think this man may very well have been sent as a distraction or perhaps as a way to allay our fears in light of the letter."

"Ah, yes!" she snapped, her gaze seeking him. "How can I forget the letter...the one you knew nothing of!"

Fedor's jaw dropped, his offence blooming to life. "What? Sophia, do you not believe me?"

"I fear that you planted the letter and now fear to admit to it."

"I had no part of that letter!" He turned a shoulder to her, stomping a boot on the floor. "How could you accuse me?"

"You are fond of your letters, Fedor. And I promise not to be angry or to punish you, but knowing that the letter came from your hand would serve to ease my worried mind."

"Your worried mind?" he shouted back, allowing his anger. "My every thought is for your preservation! I have been wringing my bloodied hands for years in your service, Sophia, and tonight is certainly no exception. If I say that I composed no letter, then you may count it as truth!"

"I believe you, Fedor," Sophia said, lowering her tone, the frightened girl absent now in favor of the seasoned monarch. The color rose in her face, and he could see that his angry rant had awakened the Regent. "But your innocence in the matter of the letter only complicates. If not you, Fedor, then who?"

"Someone in Moscow, my lady. A Naryshkin clan member or one of your opponents in the Duma. That is my belief."

She paced now, brushing the hair from her eyes. "They mean to weaken us?"

"Yes, my lady. I believe so."

Sophia stopped, bearing an odd look. "But...could not the letter have strengthened us as well? I see no sense in it. How do they benefit militarily by warning us of attack?"

Has she come so far as not to see? he thought, staring at her. *Do I really have to explain?*

"I believe they mean to shake the faith of all Moscow, Lady, but most certainly your Strel'tsy. Put plainly, the Guard do not wish to face Peter. Thoughts of doing so are quite upsetting to them. You must remember, Sophia, the Strel'tsy are sworn to defend the crown, and does that not mean Tsarevich Peter as well as Ivan?"

"You needn't remind me."

"Still, Lady, the Guard is of two minds. They must defend the Regency, but are unwilling to stage an attack on the chosen. Should they believe that you intend to attack Preobrazhenskoe, well, the results would be...unpredictable."

"I have no such intention," she responded, speaking the obvious as though it needed to be voiced. "To think I would do such a thing would be foolish! Fedor, the Strel'tsy are loyal, are they not?"

He nodded. "As loyal as ever, I suppose," he answered, unable to confess the truth this time. "But they are like no other army, Sophia. They have their own mind and they are easily swayed, particularly by the sight of a willful young Tsarevich."

"Your recommendation, then?"

"It is odd to me that you ask for my recommendation now, Sophia. Certainly, I understand that Prince V.V. is absent tonight, but given that so many of my prior recommendations have gone unheeded--"

"Fedor, do not play with me tonight."

"Oh, I play at nothing, Lady. I merely seek to remind you that I recommended the cure to this problem years ago, and I've done so many times since! I told you that we would be better without the Tsarista, without Peter--"

"I won't hear this!" Sophia screamed at him, the animal now unleashed. "Watch your tongue, you lice-ridden bastard, because I refuse to be scolded by you tonight! Had you not ordered an army into the Kremlin, we would not be in this position! And understand that I am not so stupid that I fail to see the connection between your passion for rumors and our opponents' choice of weapon this evening! The letter, Fedor, is your fault and your responsibility! They are your Strel'tsy, and you must be the one to pull on the reins! Now, what is your recommendation?"

My responsibility, he thought. *Where is the autocrat now? She places it all on Fedor Shaklovity!*

"The letter is malicious," he said, his tone now absent of anger. "But we can neither dismiss it as a ruse nor confirm it as a genuine warning. In either case, shaking the faith of the Strel'tsy serves Peter. We must take a defensive posture and make no effort to mobilize further. I will pull on the reins what I can, but I suggest that you deliver a speech in the morning to calm the hearts of the people."

"Oh? Will you compose my speech?"

"No, Lady," he answered without affect. "Perhaps Prince Golitsyn can aid you with that."

"And if Peter's threat is real? I am more concerned with cannons than I am with speeches."

He paused. "Odd, how quickly things can change."

"We must close the Kremlin gates," Sophia announced. "Without question."

Shaklovity hesitated for a moment, thinking it through before deciding to err on the side of caution.

"Better to be safe," he said, voicing his thoughts. "I will order the gates closed and go immediately to speak with the Guard."

If we make it to morning without incident, they will be easily tamed. Until then, we pray that Peter is as smart as his reputation would have us believe.

Moscow, The Kremlin Barracks

The Night of August 17, 1689

Lieutenant Colonel Larion Elizarov brushed the ashes from his lap and set to reloading his pipe, keeping his hands busy in an attempt to quiet his worried mind. He pulled a pinch of tobacco from the pouch and packed it into the bowl, his eyes searching the crowded barracks for anything unusual. He felt like pacing, but remained seated to give the impression of calm.

Tonight, the wooden walls of the barracks creaked with doubt and apprehension. The normally stoic men were buzzing like gossiping babushkas, their murmurs combining to create an emotional, fearful hum. The soldiers took turns deciphering the meaning of the night's events, seeking desperately to tell their own futures.

The commonly vicious musketeers were known for their willingness. Their strength in Moscow was complete and unchallenged, their impudence already part of history. Yet on this night, the Strel'tsy were enwrapped in an unfamiliar spell of fear, an odd feeling that left some angry and others despondent. Had it been any other opponent, the Strel'tsy would have been willing. Were it the Turks or the Cossacks, or even Odin himself, these soldiers would have been eager to engage.

But to fight Peter? To challenge the will of the Holy Father himself? Here was an opponent they dare not challenge.

The long Strel'tsy barracks reeked with apprehension, filled with ranks of chipped and rugged men who suspected that they were being deceived. And though he had done his best to allay their fears, Elizarov couldn't blame them. Like caged dogs, the Strel'tsy Guard sat captive, confined to the barracks, none of them knowing what the morning would bring. To the Lieutenant Colonel, it seemed natural that they should bark.

In his heart, Larion truly wanted to join the chorus. For the moment, however, he was still in the service of the Regent and under orders to remain ready.

And so he sat, puffing his pipe and tapping the toe of his boot on the planks of the wooden floor, the persistent sound lost amidst the yapping kennel of soldiers. Officially, they were to stand down until morning when they would escort the Regent to the Donskoy Monastery. Given the circumstance, however, there was little chance; many still wore their overcoats, and none had gone so far as to remove his boots or recline on a bunk. They gathered instead in small groups, talking and thinking, trying to piece together the truth.

He thought of Boris Golitsyn and Lev Naryshkin, wondering if they were in Moscow. *Do they know anything of this letter? Am I alone in defending Peter? Holy Father, bless me!*

They are proven right, Elizarov thought, fearful but proud. *Horribly right. Everything we feared blooms now before my eyes!*

He thought of his trusted fellows, knowing that they looked to him for guidance. Seven of them in all, bound by their devotion to the greater cause and to Russia herself, sworn to maintain their silence until the moment arrived. There were many more, surely, who felt this allegiance to Peter, but Larion had only been brave enough to approach his most trusted comrades. His confidantes were few, but it seemed fitting that someone in the Strel'tsy should be looking out for the interests of Tsarevich Peter.

I will commend them for their courage.

Tonight, the Lieutenant Colonel was of two minds--one that clung to the duty of his rank and another that called from his conscience, reminding him of his promise to the Naryshkins.

He had seen the letter and had confirmed its existence with the rank and file. Yet even with his word, the soldiers had demanded to see it for themselves, passing it around before consenting to believe. Now they waited, unable to move or act, without a voice to respond, their opinions of the Regency growing more sour every ignorant minute.

Already, the talk of desertion was beginning. He could hear the doubt in their voices. Were Sophia to call for an attack, how many would remain to fight?

They told me Peter would not attack. The letter is meant to provoke us.

He sat up, setting down the pipe and pushing it away, thinking of his promise.

Peter's life may rest in the balance. All in the hands of Larion Elizarov.

If tonight is the night, so be it. Alena and the children will be proud of me--they all will.

Naryshkin had been quite specific. If the Lieutenant Colonel suspected that Sophia intended to act against Peter, couriers were to be sent to Preobrazhenskoe to warn him.

If Peter is in danger, he must be warned.

At the time, the order seemed quite clear. Now, however, Larion was realizing its true difficulty, the confounding subtlety of the command that left such an important judgment in his control. Who was to know how much danger existed, and more important, when to act?

If I wait too long, it will be too late, he thought, scratching at the surface of the table. *If I act too early, I may cry attack where there is none and be seen as a traitor!*

Where could Dmitri be?

He scanned the room, finding no one he wanted, wondering where his comrades had gone in his time of need. The Strel'tsy who filled the room were friends and allies in most situations, but there was no predicting how some would react if they knew he was consorting with the Naryshkins. For a group that had been the Miloslavsky clan's greatest supporters, the Strel'tsy Guard was still grudgingly accepting the notion that Peter would be a good Tsar. The hatred born in 1682 had faded considerably, yet a long-standing loyalty still swayed most. Taking orders from a Naryshkin family member would be seen as a traitorous act, particularly by Commander Shaklovity.

I could be executed or worse, tortured.

It was not the first time that such thoughts had entered his mind. Larion knew of the risks, but, like the others, recognized that in a short time the tables would be turned. Those who opposed Peter would soon have to answer to him. Larion was not a politically astute man, but had already resolved in his heart and mind that Peter would and should rule. Above all else, the Church commanded it.

And so it was that, when he first received the news of the courier's arrest, Elizarov's initial and most persuasive instinct told him to act. Whether defending herself or preparing for war, Sophia was surely planning something. Lacking any sign of the Turks, there could be only one enemy.

Dmitri appeared from the door at the back of the barracks, moving quickly through the groups of men, not stopping to respond to questions or return the greetings offered him. His face looked serious but bore no fear, his eyes never leaving those of the Lieutenant Colonel as he strode through the long room.

"Dmitri, sit at the table." Elizarov pushed out a chair, realizing that the room had quieted considerably, eyes turning to watch his reaction.

He glared at the Captain. *Be smart, Dmitri. Don't spark their fire!*

"Colonel," Dmitri said, trying to catch his breath. "The interrogation--"

"Sit down, Captain." Larion glared again, his words measured and calm.

Dmitri understood this time, sitting and clearing his throat. The Colonel nodded approvingly and offered a grin, sliding the bottle to the other side of the table. He paused a few moments, waiting for the curiosity of the room to fade before beginning.

"Now, Captain, if you would discreetly tell me your news."

Dmitri swallowed. "The whole place will know soon. The interrogation offered nothing, but Shaklovity kept the poor bastard alive. They'll torture him, surely."

"Nothing? What do you mean?"

"The man claimed to be a chamberlain. He told them he knew nothing of a plot."

"Of course not," Larion replied, whispering. "The plot belongs to Shaklovity."

"What?"

"Dmitri, I was assured that Peter has no intention of attacking Moscow. The letter, then, is a ruse. Sophia makes her bed for her own offensive; she feigns a threat so she may attack. Or perhaps the letter is an attempt to make us fearful and angry--ready to defend the throne. Whatever the reason, it appears we are being duped by the Regent."

"And you are certain of this?"

"No," Larion answered calmly. "I am certain of nothing, but our orders are quite clear. In my mind, little has changed."

The Captain paused, his face etched in worry.

"It has all played out as Naryshkin feared it would," he continued. "He warned that Sophia would roust us with talk of war before sending out her assassins. She feigns a threat to justify defending herself--"

"Then why do we wait?" Dmitri snapped in reply, interrupting him.

"Calmly, Captain."

"With respect, sir, our duty is to Tsarevich Peter. Should we not do our duty?"

"I waver, Captain," he admitted. "We have no proof of the letter's author."

"But sir, the Regent could call for an attack at any time! All the Commander has to do is whisper in Sophia's ear. Shaklovity has been waiting for a chance like this."

"Lower your voice," Larion ordered, glancing around the room. "You'll stir them to anger. We have an anonymous letter, a lone courier and nothing more. The Regent has called up troops before."

"But sir, two battalions in Moscow? It has been seven years since this many Strel'tsy walked the streets together! It may already be too late!"

"You have my agreement, Captain. But until I see some action from the Regent herself, I can assume nothing."

Elizarov leaned back, taking a deep breath.

Would that we had some sign...Lord, can you not show me the way?

Dmitri leaned forward. “What of the Naryshkins, sir?”

“I told you--nothing has changed, Dmitri.”

“You’ll go through with it, then?”

“I will do my duty, yes.”

Larion thought of his obligation. His stomach bent and clenched within him, his body fatigued from the beating of his own heart. He felt claustrophobic within these walls, ignorant of the facts and oblivious to the conversations within the Kremlin that served to shape his fate. Tonight, the Lieutenant Colonel’s warrior instincts had been subtly subverted by his sense of devotion and love for Mother Russia, combined with the burdensome knowledge that his actions carried repercussions for the throne itself.

The Naryshkins would never forgive me if I failed, he thought, trying to calm his beating heart. *They would take my head for revenge...if Shaklovity didn’t weed me out first.*

A commotion sounded from the opposite end of the barracks, the doors opening and closing several times. The shouts of men rang indistinctly above the din, raising the sound to an intolerable cacophony of dissent. Small scuffles began to break out as the hot-tempered soldiers came too close, their angst evaporating into physical rage.

“What is happening? Dmitri!”

Dmitri leapt from his chair and entered the crowd, emerging several moments later with a frantic, odd look on his face. He stopped before the Colonel, his eyes brimming with trepidation.

“What is it?”

“The Regent has ordered the Kremlin gates closed, sir.”

Elizarov’s stomach dropped within him, his heart leaping at double speed.

Need I any more sign than this?

Finally, the slightest feeling of control within the chaos of the evening. He swallowed and cleared his throat, knowing what he had to do.

They will not have Larion Elizarov to blame!

"Dmitri, come closer…"

"Yes, sir." Dmitri's eyes widened as he stepped forward.

"It is time," Larion continued, his voice barely breaching a whisper. "Do as we have discussed. Send Ilion and Vlas to Preobrazhenskoe. Tell them to warn the Tsarevich that his life is in danger!"

Outside Moscow, Fort Presburg at Preobrazhenskoe

Just After Midnight, August 18, 1689

Peter awakened from dreamless sleep to the clicking sound of the latch on his door. Instinct brought him up with a start.

He threw back the covers and stepped down to the cold floor, squinting in the darkness.

The door opened a crack and a column of yellow lamplight cut through the black, widening to reveal three shadows.

He stumbled barefoot to the end of the bed.

"Who's there?" he questioned into the darkness, recognizing Viktor's shadowed form in the wavering light.

"Sire?"

"Viktor, is that you? What is this?"

He glared as the three entered the room. Viktor first, followed by the two figures. They bowed meekly, palms open in apology. The strangers were young and wore Strel'tsy uniforms.

"We beg your forgiveness, Tsarevich, but these musketeers came from Moscow. I thought you would--"

"Explain! What is this?" Peter tensed, his mind still waking.

Viktor hesitated, as though unsure how to begin.

Have I no Guard?

"Please, sire!" The first of the musketeers pushed past Viktor and fell to his knees, his hands clasped in pleading posture. "We bring you news, Tsarevich, dire news that must be delivered! We fear you will grow angry or disbelieve, sire, but I swear in the Holy Father's name that our words are true!"

Peter's stomach tightened, suspicions creeping within. "Who are you?" he asked.

"Private Ilion Hohlakov, sire," the man responded immediately.

"Private, stand up. Tell me what brought you here."

"Yes, sire, we--"

"Tell me!" Peter ordered. "Quickly, and be clear!"

"Yes, sire." The man nodded and took a deep breath, his hands trembling. "We bring a warning from Moscow, Tsarevich. A threat from the Kremlin. Your life is in danger, sire. "

Peter stumbled backward, lacking the voice to respond, his knees buckling as though they'd gone back to sleep. His breath escaped in a suffocating rush, leaving him gasping and suddenly weak.

He dropped to his knees, his hands quickly following to meet the cold wooden floor. The room spun beneath him.

Viktor was by his side, a hand placed on his back. "Tsarevich… can you stand, sire? I beg your forgiveness--"

"Shut up, Viktor!" Peter barked between gasps, fighting the unfamiliar feeling. "Give me a moment!"

"Yes, of course."

Viktor stood and backed away a couple of steps, his presence no comfort.

As the dizzy feeling faded, Peter's thoughts began to race, a swarming sickness of fear that bounded from notion to notion, infecting all that it touched. His mind rushed back to the brutal despair of 1682, and the cold years that followed within the Kremlin walls. He had been plagued with nightmares in the wake of her rise to power; no childhood fairy tale could provide a villain as horrible as Sophia and her brigades of bloodthirsty drunkards. The better part of Peter's youth was spent in fearful doubt, never knowing when the Regent might call for his demise. Even in the best of moments, Peter had always believed Sophia capable of such treachery. The Strel'tsy had already proven themselves.

"Where is Golitsyn?" he asked, attempting to stand. Viktor and the soldiers moved forward to aid him.

His suspicions leapt again, and Peter pointed toward the Strel'tsy, staggering back beyond their reach.

"Do not touch me! Either of you!" he shouted, the force of his command sending both to their knees, eyes averted.

"We mean no harm, sire!"

"We mean to save your life, Tsarevich!"

"Hold your place!" he yelled down at them, anger now joining his mix of emotions. "Both of you! No matter your purpose, your presence binds me to act. Whether you lie or not, you leave me no choice! Viktor, answer me! Where is Boris Golitsyn?"

"In Moscow, Tsarevich."

"And Lev Naryshkin?"

Viktor shook his head. "Most certainly in Moscow, Tsarevich. Do you wish to travel there?"

Peter looked toward the door, the walls now closing in around him. Every instinct told him to run.

If these men ride from Moscow with news of my murder, then the assassins could surely be here as well!

He turned to the strangers, pointing. "You two--stay planted on your knees! Make no attempt to follow me or I will take your actions for treason!"

"Yes, Tsarevich."

Viktor stepped forward, confused. "Tsarevich?"

Peter stood, staring and unresponsive, trying to catch his breath. Viktor looked on, not willing to interrupt his silence.

Again, Matveev flashed in Peter's memory, his corpse dissected in a pool of fresh blood. Peter thought of the final glance that passed between them and the look of pure terror that appeared on the guardian's face as he realized he would not escape. Peter could still see the bloodlust in the eyes of the Strel'tsy as they carved into innocent flesh, the mob more powerful than the crown itself. In number, they acted without fear and without reason.

There is no choice. No decision to make. I cannot simply wait here to die.

Peter pushed past Viktor without another word, his mind in a fearful daze, his feet striding forward as though they knew their purpose.

"Tsarevich?"

Peter ignored him and kept moving, suddenly desperate to be away from the Fort. He pressed forward, his fear easing a bit with every step, opening doors and passing through them without looking back.

"Tsarevich…your clothes! You are still in your bedclothes, sire…"

Peter let the voices fade behind him, hearing but not caring, unwilling to be slaughtered while pulling on his stockings.

He wiped the tears from his eyes and continued, breaking into a run as soon as he felt the chilled night air on his face.

Leg after leg he raced, his bloody feet beating the ground beneath him, his eyes too terrified to look beside or behind for pursuers. Driven, Peter prayed for his salvation and kept pace, not stopping until he reached the darkness and cover of the woods.

Outside Moscow, The Monastery of Troitskaya-Sergeeva

The Morning of August 18, 1689

Boris Golitsyn straightened in his seat as the carriage neared the Troitskaya-Sergeeva Monastery, attempting to wake himself from the lull of the rocky cradle. After a sleepless night in Moscow, Boris now found himself weary but ready to play his part, surrendering to the elation of knowing that somehow, someway, their gamble had paid off.

In his mind, the result was nothing less than a miracle.

He'd been awake and waiting when the news arrived; Elizarov had acted, just as they had hoped. The messengers had been persuasive enough to send Peter fleeing for his life into the nearby woods.

The news had come like the voices of angels to his worried ears--word that Tsarevich Peter had fled his Fort and traveled to the Troitsky Monastery seeking sanctuary. Prepared for his own journey, Golitsyn moved quickly to insure Elizarov's confidence before heading out to Troitsky to console and support Peter.

All in all, Boris was quite satisfied. He was lucky, perhaps, but wise enough to know that a Russian seizes good fortune wherever he can find it. This time, he would choose to call it providence and attribute the night's events to divine intervention. How else could it all have happened so perfectly?

He peered out the carriage window as they passed the gates of the Monastery, his eyes searching for any sign of visitors.

I must be the first. Lev must not arrive before me. For once, Peter will be fearful, malleable, ready to talk of succession.

Troitsky had been standing tall for centuries, transformed from a monastery to a fortress by Ivan the Terrible, an effort that took decades to complete. Having served their purpose in defense of Moscow, the high white walls of brick and stone continued to mark the perimeter and dominate the landscape, their fourteen towers still manned and well armed.

Inside, the grounds were impressively large, hosting a variety of churches and holy buildings, the Troitsky population numbering more than many Russian towns. A bastion of economic wealth and power, the Monastery held a significant portion of Russia's gold and controlled much of the land surrounding it.

In Boris' mind, the location was ideally suited to their purposes. The Monastery was more than the simple structures of holiness that dotted the landscape and shared the holy name. Troitsky was the mother of all the rest, the greatest and most renowned, the center of the Russian Orthodox faith.

He steadied himself as the carriage pulled to a stop, encouraged by the thought that he would be the first to see the Tsarevich.

Natalya is depending on me, he thought, blinking to shake away the weariness in his eyes. *Peter, as well.*

The Tsarevich awaited him inside, fresh from the second worst night of his life, already welcomed into the protective arms of the Church. Knowing Peter, he would be bursting with the desire to tell his tale--fearful, anxious, vengeful perhaps--but certainly desirous of an audience. Golitsyn was happy to provide.

I must secure our relationship, he thought, stepping out into the afternoon sun. *He will need strength in the days to come. Sophia will not easily surrender the throne, and Peter will not obey if he suspects he's being manipulated.*

All this, left in my hands. If only the Patriarch were here!

The slumped figure waiting to greet him was instantly recognizable.

"Herr Golitsyn! We are overjoyed to see your arrival."

"Thank you, Viktor. Though I would think there to be little joy on this day."

Viktor shrank. "My apologies, truly. We are fearful, all of us. I meant only that we seek a sign of hope and the sight of you brings encouragement. Sir, if I may, I would like to ask a question."

"Quickly, Viktor! I have questions for you, as well."

"Of course, sir, of course. I wish only to ask--do the Strel'tsy mean to attack Preobrazhenskoe? Do they, sir? Can we never go back?"

Golitsyn paused, frowning a bit. "Nothing is certain, Viktor. You've done well getting him here. I'm quite pleased that you remembered what we discussed."

Viktor nodded his head dutifully. "Thank you, sir. The moment I realized what was happening, I thought of what you told me.

"I have feared the worst all summer, Viktor. Did you suggest the Troitsky Monastery?"

"Yes, sir. I remembered you saying it was the safest place in all Russia for the Tsarevich. Peter was more than willing to make the journey once we got him dressed and mounted."

"In what condition will I find his spirit?"

Viktor looked down. "Poor condition, admittedly. He is quite difficult to speak to, and given our familiarity, I fear I am unable to provide any consolation. You will certainly fare better, sir."

"I was told that the Tsarevich ran from the Fort wearing only his nightshirt."

"It is the truth, sir. We collected his clothes and delivered them along with his horse and weapons. A small group of us rode here."

"And the messengers?" Golitsyn asked, growing more and more concerned with loose ends.

"Gone back to Moscow, I would expect. Peter would have nothing to do with them--he mistrusted them."

"Would you remember them if you saw them?"

"Yes, sir. I believe so. They were Strel'tsy, sir."

"Then you will forget their faces, Viktor. We would not want these good men to suffer for their patriotism."

"Yes, sir. I remember only that they warned Peter."

Boris took a deep breath. "Good, then. Send for the rest of the dentchiks and secure whatever he may require for comfort. We will undoubtedly be spending more than a few days."

"Yes, sir." Viktor turned, pulled back by the Counselor's hand on his shoulder

"Listen to me, Viktor," he said, staring with grim certitude. "You may trust that we are in the midst of a crisis. From what we know, the Tsarevich remains in grave danger, even here at Troitsky. There may be traitors in our midst, Viktor--we must keep our circle close. Trust no one, even the priests. Keep your lips tight and your eyes wide open. Your task is to make Peter comfortable here, and nothing more. The Tsarista is relying on you."

"Yes, sir," Viktor answered again, now a bit pale. "I always do my best, sir."

"Yes." Golitsyn continued to glare. "Be certain to give your best this time, for it will surely mean your life if you fail. I do not wish to risk catastrophe. Access to the Tsarevich will be limited to those whom I approve."

"Yes, sir."

"The Preobrazhensky are on the way and soon you will be assisted by a Guard complement to keep things secure. Fear not, Viktor. With the eyes of the Holy Father upon us, we cannot fail. Now, take me to the Tsarevich."

Viktor bowed. "Yes, Herr Golitsyn. This way, please."

Boris followed, anxious to see the Tsarevich, his weariness all but gone in the excitement of the moment. There were risks, certainly, but for better or worse, it felt good to be moving again.

Natalya will be overjoyed, he thought, imagining the moment of their reunion. *She must be as anxious as I...*

In a small room within the thick walls of the Monastery, Peter waited, his face flushed with anger. The young man looked older than his seventeen years, the deep circles beneath his eyes serving as evidence of his plight. He seemed smaller than normal, his height somehow diminished by the circumstance.

"Tsarevich..."

Peter moved forward to embrace him. "Thank the Holy Father! It seemed an eternity waiting for someone to arrive."

"I left as soon as the news reached my ears," Golitsyn responded, feeling the weakness in Peter's grasp. "My driver was capable--I'm not surprised that I'm the first. Tell me how you fare, Tsarevich."

"I am unharmed," he replied, the gratitude leaving suddenly, replaced by a morose stare. "Though I wait for the assassins."

Boris nodded, matching the look. "It is through divine grace that you stand here today, Peter."

"Had I not been warned..."

"We should have suspected," Boris replied with a tone of regret. "We should have been more vigilant at Preobrazhenskoe. Your mother has warned me often of Sophia's temper, though I never expected such rash action. Even before the incident at the Assumption

Cathedral…well, I mean to say that I knew she was desperate, but I never could have predicted this."

"What of Mother and little Natalya? And Evdokia?"

"They are all safe. They will be carefully guarded and will soon join you. Fear not."

Peter exhaled in relief. "Thank the Holy Father. I was halfway to Troitsky before I even thought of them. I'm ashamed to say it."

"You were wise to leave, sire."

The young man shook his head, tears welling in his tired eyes. "But why--why now, Boris? Does she think she can turn the world upside down?"

"We cannot know, sire. But we do know, you as well as I, that Regent Sophia has been through the worst summer of her life, beginning with Prince Vasily's return from battle. In truth he was a good influence on her--we all recognize this--and certainly his was the better part of her decision-making as Regent. Sophia, of course, feels no shame in saddling him with all the blame. I hear rumors that a distance has grown between the two of them, and I fear that Shaklovity has strengthened his control over her."

"An outspoken devil…"

"Precisely. Shaklovity has often spoken against you."

"He called me a heretic," Peter said pointedly. "I do not forget."

"Indeed." Golitsyn bore a mournful look. "To have such an opponent in charge of the Strel'tsy…well, who could trust Sophia with Shaklovity at her right hand? Whatever the circumstance, sire, we must consider Shaklovity to be involved. After all, the messengers who brought word of your peril are both members of the Strel'tsy Guard. It would seem to follow that the assassins would be Strel'tsy as well."

"Your point is well taken, Boris."

"Loyal to you, of course," Golitsyn replied, nodding. "But Strel'tsy, nonetheless."

Peter moved from Boris' side, kneeling in prayer before rising again to his feet.

"I could easily be dead," he said, walking slowly back, his stare distant and fearful. "They could have cut my throat instead of waking me! The thought pulls me ever downward. All that work, everything we've built, the entire sum of my life!"

Golitsyn waited, allowing the Tsarevich his speech.

"When I was younger I would dream about this," Peter continued, staring away. "Horrid, fearful dreams about Sophia sending the Strel'tsy to kill us all. I believed it then, Boris, I walked those cold corridors with the fear of death and the love of the Lord in my heart. But the odd thing about my nightmares was that I never actually saw the assassins coming for me. It was always Sophia and the sight of her smiling as someone whispered a grim warning in my ear! I remember waking up in a puddle.

"I thought it was over," he pressed, shaking his head. "When we came to Preobrazhenskoe, I was to be free of the Kremlin and the fear as well. I suppose I deceived myself into thinking that her murderous ambitions were behind her--that a few cannons made me strong, or that a few miles put me beyond her reach. All this time, Boris, I've lived without realizing: my very life rested in Sophia's palm! From the beginning, my life was apparently a gift from the Regent, left to be taken at her whim! The Strel'tsy were just waiting…smiling and waiting to cut me up!"

He paused, the rage passing as quickly as it had arrived. "I was so close. Another year and I would have been able to face them."

Golitsyn placed a hand on his shoulder. "You are alive, Tsarevich, and you will certainly be Tsar. Providence has granted us an opportunity. Sophia has made an irreparable mistake and she will have to answer for it."

"We cannot stand against the Strel'tsy. Even with General Gordon."

"If we manage properly, we will not have to fight, Tsarevich."

"What?"

"The Strel'tsy serve the throne, and not just Sophia. Trust in this, Peter--she cannot hope to stand against the will of the Holy Father. The Patriarch will not fail us. He will support you."

"You were in Moscow," Peter said, his mind now working. "I must know what happened. I've been waiting here in the dark, without the slightest notion of what was occurring outside. What of Moscow?"

"We couldn't believe our eyes, Tsarevich. At least two battalions of well-armed Strel'tsy marching in line into the Kremlin barracks, paraded through the streets as though they were headed to battle. They caused quite a commotion."

"Why? Was she planning to march on Preobrazhenskoe?"

Golitsyn shrugged. "We cannot know. The whole city was talking. There haven't been that many Strel'tsy Guard in Moscow since Sophia ascended."

Peter paled a bit, swallowing. "I have thought of Uncle Ivan and Papa Matveev many times."

"As have I, Peter. Their murders are fresh in my mind as well."

"Who else would she oppose with her Strel'tsy?" Peter returned, his temper creeping out again. "Not the Turks, surely! She lost that battle already!"

"There is other news from Moscow, sire--"

"Who else but a pitiful army of stable-boys could she hope to oppose?" Peter interrupted. "We could have shown her a battle, too! Had we another full year, we would be strong enough to take Moscow and send her cloven feet to running!"

"Your chamberlain, Andrei Golovin, I believe..."

"Golovin?" Peter hesitated. "What of him?"

"He was pulled from his horse as he approached Moscow--beaten rather badly and taken to Shaklovity for interrogation."

Peter's eyes opened wide. "Interrogation? But he was sent with a routine dispatch! What happened?"

Golitsyn shrugged sadly. "That, I am unable to tell you, sire. I would, however, suspect that Shaklovity may have been interested in insuring your location before sending his assassins. And, of course, other pertinent information they were interested to know... the state of our fortifications, for example."

"But Golovin knew little of that!"

"Thankfully, there is little he can tell yet he remains in their custody. We must be grateful that the circumstances were not different."

Peter turned, staring down at him. "Tell me--do you believe they plan to move against the Fort?"

"You are safe, sire."

"Call for a horse," Peter announced, walking to the window. "I must return to the Fort immediately."

"Impossible! We're not about to put you at risk."

"But you said that the Strel'tsy were unwilling to face me! Without me, the Preobrazhensky will be an easy target!"

"Without you, sire, the Preobrazhensky are, with all respect, not worth the time of the Strel'tsy. You, unfortunately, are the target."

Peter nodded gratefully. "You are likely correct, Boris. Yet, I cannot remain here just doing nothing."

"You must remain here," Golitsyn stated firmly, matching the younger man's stare. "On this, we must agree. You can do nothing from the Fort that you cannot do here, and Troitsky serves as a powerful symbol. We must bring the Patriarch to our side and force Sophia to respond to you."

Peter's expression fell again. "You speak the truth, Boris. A military venture would be suicide."

"I mean no insult to you or your troops, sire. In my estimation, you have performed most admirably. Truly, you've raised an army from the soil itself! And, I know we have grown fond of calling the Preobrazhensky your 'play' army and treating the whole affair as though you were simply looking for diversion, but I've seen a greater purpose all the while. You have as well, I think."

"As an army, we are weak," Peter said, nodding. "Yet our roster holds the names of some very important men."

"Ah, you understand my meaning!"

"I do."

"Good, good…" Golitsyn paused, looking at him. "Peter, I wish to impress upon you the fact that I have served your clan with loyal devotion and that your mother trusts my judgment routinely--"

"You don't need to list your credentials," Peter interrupted, snapping. "I have said nothing to make you believe that I think otherwise!"

"I will deliver my advice, then, and you can do with it what you wish. Our days at Preobrazhenskoe are at an end. You may certainly return there, but we are now in a position from which we cannot retreat. "

The Tsarevich nodded, standing and pacing away. "I will not simply wait."

"Certainly not. There is work to be done. We will do far more than just wait…beginning with a letter to the Regent. Something very cordial, inquiring into the reason for her military parade last night."

"I understand," Peter said, his mind now working as Golitsyn talked. Finally, it seemed, he was on the right path.

"You must make her respond to you, sire. Sophia is the one who must answer." The Counselor was calm and resolute. "You have the hearts of the people and the approval of the Duma--you need only the Patriarch and the Strel'tsy to complete the rest. Rejoice, Peter! You are Tsarevich. It is time we showed Shaklovity and the rest that you understand what that means."

Moscow, The Great Sovereign's Palace of The Kremlin

August 18, 1689

Sophia stood in silence, pulling an ivory comb repetitively through her hair, staring at herself in the small mirror that rested atop her dressing table. Frustration was the mood of the day, and she tugged and pulled mercilessly at the tangled ends, tearing out what she could not tame. The solitude of her chambers had been unbearable of late, and for want of more significant cause, she found herself dwelling on petty, annoying subjects such as beauty and grace.

She looked carefully at herself, mourning the tiny lines at the corners of her eyes, knowing that in her sadness there was something missing, a weakness of spirit that reflected in her face. Older, certainly, than she'd looked when she took her place as Regent, but still young enough to see the premature signs of age in her dour expression.

The Regency makes me old, she thought. *I criticize the artists, but their work is just.*

She'd been listening to the whispers since she was a child and had always known her reputation, that of a homely sour-faced girl. She also recognized quite early, however, that she was considered shrewd and smart, a force unto herself, the most capable of Maria Miloslavsky's children. Sophia listened as they called her 'fiery' and 'bossy', realizing that her role was not to be one of decoration.

Her mind skipped back to her prior affairs noting the prominence of her amorous conquests. *I have done well for myself. Ugly or not, I've had some of the greatest men in all Russia! Let them sneeze at the affections of Prince Vasily Golitsyn…or even Shaklovity, for that matter! What other woman can command the services of two such men?*

But for how long? Everything fades…

She pushed the mirror away and turned, marching to the open window and taking a deep breath. Closing her eyes, Sophia searched for a sense of relief, reminding herself that the night had passed without incident.

Shaklovity's letter was nothing but a ruse. I must see him.

She was yet to leave her bedchamber on this day. Knowing Vasily owed her a visit and was expected, there seemed no need in parading through the Palace. Had she a throne to sit on, Sophia would most certainly have waited there. As it was, she waited alone in her small world, having dismissed all her attendants.

The short rap on her door was followed by the turning of the latch, the sound serving as the only announcement of Prince V.V. Golitsyn.

He turned without acknowledging her and closed the door behind him.

"No one to see you in?"

"None of them willing," he answered, brushing at his sleeve. "Apparently you've frightened them all away."

"They were tedious and stupid."

"I thought perhaps I should leave and return later, but I decided that my presence might save them some misery."

Prince V.V. was dressed with his customary flair, his pale blue waistcoat and knee breeches matching identically, his plumed blue hat in hand. His expression lacked warmth.

"Always the charitable soul," she answered, approaching with her arms wide. "You should endeavor to be as charitable with me."

She leaned in to embrace him, offering a small kiss. His response was stiff and inadequate.

Sophia glared. "My love?"

"We must speak. Peter has fled to Troitsky."

The chamber darkened before her eyes, the sun passing back into the overcast skies. Sophia swallowed, trying to assimilate the news.

"Troitsky? What?"

"I must know all that happened last night," he said, pacing away, his voice bearing concern. "Tell me, so that I may unravel this--"

"Troitsky?" She descended upon him. "Vasily, what do you mean?"

"We are informed that couriers rode out to Preobrazhenskoe last night and delivered a message to Peter that he was to be murdered…by your command. He fled to Troitsky seeking sanctuary."

Sophia stepped back, lacking a response, feeling as though she'd just been hollowed out. Her composure wilted beneath the blazing sun of circumstance.

"Impossible!" She moved to grasp his sleeve, wanting to see his face. "What has happened? Why wasn't I told?"

"Sophia, you must be completely truthful with me. You know that they will seek my head before yours. It is only fair that I know what our dear Shaklovity has done! Did you call for this?"

Sophia dropped her jaw in offense. "Certainly not! No!"

"You must be honest with me--"

"I did no such thing!" she protested again, her bedchamber shrinking around her. "Sanctuary? From what? We were the ones standing at defense!"

"And Shaklovity?" Golitsyn glared with a knowing look, his tone serving to voice his suspicion.

Oh, please, no! Could he do such a thing without telling me?

"Impossible," she repeated, shaking her head. "Fedor has suggested it dozens of times, but he would never act without my consent."

"But he did take a prisoner, yes?"

Sophia paled. "It was a mistake and nothing more. The guards were provoked by the letter!"

"The man was interrogated, Sophia." The Prince exhaled, shaking his head. "Shaklovity told me nothing of the interrogation."

"You've spoken with him? Today?"

"Yes," Vasily answered. "He was too cowardly to bear the news to you himself. He thought it best that I be the one to advise you. There's a bit of bravery for you!"

"That dog!" Her temper flared, anger displacing the worry. "Did you ask him of his part in this?"

"He denied it all, though I remain unconvinced. He has been waiting to give such an order. There is no other possibility. Tell me--did you, you personally--did you summon the additional battalion?"

"No. It was Fedor--and he claims to have acted with good reason."

"Apparently."

"Troitsky?" her mind was racing, unable to contend with the torrent of negative thoughts. "Vasily, this is Peter's doing. It must be!"

"What?" Vasily frowned. "You think he would feign his own murder? What's more--to take this lie to Troitsky? No, I think not. It seems too cowardly for Peter."

"Perhaps," she replied, "But nothing is below the Tsarista's attention. Natalya would think nothing of such treachery!"

The Prince paused, taking a few steps before turning and offering a slight shrug. "You may be right, my dear, but I fear we have come too far already to begin placing blame. Remember, we are the accused, Sophia."

"Then we must respond!" she shouted, growing angrier by the moment. "We must offer a denial! The Kremlin acted in self-defense, and that is all!"

"And what do you wish to deny? There have been no formal allegations."

She nodded, pacing, a hand at her forehead to ease the aching.

There will be no one to support me but the Strel'tsy, she thought, looking at Vasily. His posture seemed weak today, his customary confidence deflated by the challenge.

"You realize," Vasily continued, turning back, "that this incident puts both our positions at risk. If you've forgotten, neither of us is winning support at the moment. I am still ridiculed for the victory parade and you for your episode at the Cathedral."

"I have not forgotten," she answered sternly. "Your point is understood. Still, we must claim our innocence before it is stolen from us."

He shook his head. "We cannot, Sophia. To deny something we have not been accused of--"

"Then let us apologize for detaining the courier!"

"Not a bad notion," he replied, "and were Peter back in his place at Preobrazhenskoe, we could perhaps pursue such a course…"

Again, the huge white walls of Troitsky came to mind.

"The Patriarch," she said, thinking aloud. "Where is Joachim?"

"In Moscow, thankfully," Vasily answered, nodding. "Now you're in the right mind."

"Yes! I will summon the Patriarch and explain our position! He will understand the circumstance, surely. We will say what we must, and then send him to Troitsky to reason with Peter. Who could deny Joachim?"

"There is, of course, a risk that the Patriarch may not favor your opinion."

"What?" Sophia huffed, waving a hand. "How could he not?"

"Come now, Sophia--the man despises you."

"He dislikes all progressives, but he is reasonable and believes in the order of things. I can talk to him reasonably when I must."

"We have little choice, it seems."

She scowled at him, perturbed with his weakness. "The Regency will not bear these false allegations, Vasily! Someone will hear my defense!"

"He will, Sophia. I merely think we appear better if we make his journey an order and not a request." Vasily bit his lip, now ignoring her anger. "Joachim should go to Troitsky on your command, on your behalf and not of his own accord. This will require swift action."

He makes sense. He wouldn't think to abandon me.

"Yes, of course," Sophia replied, calming herself. "I cannot allow these rumors to linger."

"The longer Peter sits at Troitsky, the worse the situation will become," he told her, offering a kiss on the cheek. "We will summon the Patriarch and you will speak. For my part, I will assess the damage among the boyars."

She embraced him, allowing her head to linger on his shoulder, knowing how few supporters remained. Above all else, Vasily had been true in his heart.

He will bear this as I do…

"We will overcome this," she told him. "You won't regret your faith in me, Vasily."

"I shall endeavor to keep your detractors at bay," he answered, his face bearing little affection.

She stepped back, pointing toward the door. "Go, then. I think better without you in my presence. And send me that bastard Fedor. He has much to answer for."

The Prince nodded and bowed politely. "Yes, Regent. Oh, and just one more subject, if I may. I think it wise to contain Medvedev as well."

"Medvedev?"

"Your illustrious poet-monk is at the center of every heretical notion in this city and is tied to Fedor, as well. His name has been mentioned and swirls in rumor with your own. Time to tighten the reins, I think. I should send for both--the monk and Shaklovity."

"Excellent," she answered, fighting back the urge to scream. "I have enough rage for both of them. Call Medvedev as well, but be quick. I must have time to compose myself before I meet with the Patriarch."

Moscow, The Great Sovereign's Palace of the Kremlin

August 18, 1689

"Hurry and finish, Sylvester! The longer she waits, the angrier she will be."

Strel'tsy Commander Fedor Shaklovity watched as Medvedev readied himself for an audience with the Regent, drinking his fill in an effort to sooth his fearful but still pious soul with the Kremlin's fine vodka. Summoned by Sophia, the two had been asked to arrive together.

"Don't rush me," the monk answered loudly, his voice echoing in the vaulted ceiling. He choked back his cup of vodka and grimaced, quickly pouring another. "I always steady myself before visiting Sophia, even in the best of her moods. Today is worse, of course, now that you've thrown me to the wolves!"

"What?" Shaklovity frowned back at him. "You cannot blame me for spreading your name to every set of lips in Moscow. Of all the clergy in this town--and how many would that be? Hundreds, perhaps? You, above all, are known as the enemy of the Naryshkins. The Patriarch himself despises you! That is certainly a life's work."

"You exaggerate."

"There is no blame here but our own, brother. I suppose I should have known that something like this could occur. We are the only culprits, friend."

Medvedev huffed through a mouthful of bread, drowning it with another drink of vodka. He was a man who looked older than his years, deep circled eyes set so low as to appear to be resting atop his formidable beard. And whether it was the robe or the drink, Father Sylvester was sweating miserably on this day, his bald head flushed pink.

The fool would turn on me in an instant, Fedor thought, shaking his head as Medvedev gestured toward an empty cup. *But the word of a renegade monk against that of a Strel'tsy Commander? There, he would have difficulty.*

"These rumors are the lesser matter," Shaklovity continued. "Sophia sent no assassins--nor did I. And though the boyars may think you capable of such action, I know that you were not responsible."

"An idiotic notion," Medvedev agreed, nodding.

"There is but one answer, then--and a quite troubling answer as well."

The monk shrugged. "The Naryshkins feign this treachery and make themselves the victims. Yes, yes, it's all very obvious."

"For military advantage," Shaklovity added with emphasis. "This is their purpose, no doubt. Peter may be resting at Troitsky, but I suspect that his army prepares for battle."

Medvedev frowned in disbelief. "He has no military advantage, surely."

"He has tainted the hearts of the Strel'tsy! Those fools would have willingly cut his throat but just a few years ago! Now, they wring their hands like babushkas! The Naryshkin influence prevails--spies among us, no doubt, even within the ranks. Trust this: if they know of our actions, then they know the hearts of the Guard. No, there is not a doubt in my mind, Sylvester! We must ready ourselves for blood."

"You are transparent. You seek to replace Sophia's anger with fear."

"In part, perhaps, but I speak my mind. I am convinced that this is much more than a simple plot to defame the two of us."

The monk offered a short belch and patted his stomach. "Yes, well, I am ready," he announced. "…for Sophia, that is. You may have all the blood."

He takes it lightly. He thinks I will willingly take all the blame!

Shaklovity stepped closer, popping his knuckles and focusing his gaze on the monk's weak eyes. "There is one more subject we must address, comrade. I find your manner quite troubling."

"Oh?"

"You seem to find amusement in this whole affair, Sylvester."

The monk rolled his eyes. "Fedor…"

"I will remind you again, dear friend, that we stand side by side in this, as we have done many times before. Even the washerwomen know that Shaklovity and Medvedev are in league, and there is no one in Moscow who has not listened to one of your belligerent sermons about the Tsarevich! I am loath to carry you through this affair, but judging by the rumors, it seems I have no choice!"

"Hah! Nor do I!"

"Good, then!" Fedor grabbed his shoulder, squeezing with intent. "I am pleased that you understand, Sylvester. For you may count this as the truth: I have no intention of bearing the full burden of blame. If Fedor Shaklovity goes down, friend, you may trust that Medvedev will be walking to the block by his side!"

The monk's eyes narrowed for a moment, then widened again in accompaniment to a forced grin.

"I would expect no less from you, Fedor," he replied without venom. "Though I think you worry far too much. You are the one who must remember--we have been accused before. Think, friend! The Regent cannot give us up; she would incriminate herself by doing so."

For a moment, Fedor experienced a rush of relief, a welcome breeze of comfort in Medvedev's words.

Sophia will do what she must, he thought, opening the door and waiting for the monk to exit. *Less would mean the end of the Regency; she will certainly preserve us.*

They spoke little as they made their way to the Regent's chambers, too suspicious of the attending staff to let their feelings be publicly heard. When they turned the final corner, Shaklovity could see the Regent's chambermaid Inna waiting to meet them. Her sullen face bore no ill will, yet her posture indicated a reluctance, a grim regard that Fedor noticed immediately.

Without a second glance, Inna bowed respectfully and turned to lead them in.

"Too warm for you, dear?" Medvedev asked, trying his familiar tone. "The heat has been unbearable."

"No, Father."

"Good, good. We shall require a flagon of wine before long. See if you can't stir us up something special."

Inna nodded, her regard unchanging. "Yes, Father."

A chill from Sophia's staff? Fedor wondered, realizing that his worry was growing with each moment, changing his perspective. *I see too many ghosts. Sylvester is right. Sophia's fears must be nurtured.*

Inna opened the door, stepping aside to let them pass.

The Regent was pacing as they entered, her thunderous strides betraying her mood. Her hair was pinned back and covered, her face flushed as though she'd been shouting at the top of her lungs. In her hand she held a piece of parchment, the edge crumpling under her grip.

"Ah! At last, the Commander makes his appearance!"

"I have been most busy, Regent."

Sophia glared. "You are a competent liar, but I have known you too long. You have been avoiding me, Fedor. You sent the Prince to deliver the bad news in your place."

"It seemed fitting," he responded simply, standing firm. "After all, you are closer to the Prince--"

"Be quiet," she snapped, silencing him. She held up the parchment. "Do you know of this, as well?"

"Lady?"

"A correspondence from Troitsky--from our dear Peter. He politely wishes to know why so many Strel'tsy were gathered in the Kremlin."

"You see! He plots to trap you with your own words! You must answer with caution, Lady."

Sophia looked over, acknowledging the monk. "Father Sylvester..."

"Our dear autocrat! I pale in your grace! This horrid accusation has burdened you unduly. May I help ease your troubles, Lady?"

Sophia smiled facetiously. "At the moment, dear Sylvester, the two of you are my greatest trouble. We are left to defend ourselves against rumors and your names are mentioned in every accusation. You will assure me, right now, that you wrote no letters and called for no assassinations!"

Medvedev raised his palms in defense. "In the name of the Holy Father, I swear that I did not!"

She stared for a moment, frozen as though trying to judge him with a look.

"We must think of tomorrow, Sophia…or better, of today," Shaklovity interjected, his tone pleading. "Medvedev and I are innocents, as are you. I fear this has all been a diversion--to weaken the Guard, to deceive us in preparation for an attack."

"Except my precautions, they would have murdered us all! Let him run. Let him run! He has plainly gone mad."

"Would that it were so simple," Shaklovity followed. "There is treachery afoot, Lady, and this has the marks of the Tsarista."

Sophia's look darkened, her hands clenching into fists. "Yes, of course. Natalya gives orders from her house in the country. The bitch would bring down the Regency from within. Yes, Fedor, you speak the truth. I can see her now, smiling somewhere, knowing the torture I endure!"

She is in perfect condition, he thought, dropping his eyes as though wounded at the thought of Sophia's strife.

"I wait here, endeavoring only to endure each hour, accused but unable to defend myself while the Tsarevich sits at Troitsky like a little wounded lamb!"

"He is contemptible, indeed," Medvedev added. "But he is far from a madman, Lady. I would be much relieved at the thought of it, actually."

Sophia paused. "A conspiracy, then."

"I fear you are correct, Lady."

He watched as the Regent lifted her chin, taking a deep breath. She looked strong, still defiant.

"We will answer their message with equal politeness," she said finally, setting down the parchment and bringing her hands together at her chin in a moment of silent prayer.

"Very wise, Lady."

"The pilgrimage was no secret; I will tell them the truth. The Strel'tsy were called to accompany me. If they wish us to answer accusations, they must first accuse us!"

"Precisely. An excellent course of action." Shaklovity tugged thoughtfully on his beard and nodded his approval. "I would ask that we also keep the Strel'tsy on double duty--to prevent against any attack."

She frowned back at him. "Are you still worried about the Preobrazhensky? Always the soldier. Eh, Fedor? No, Natalya cares nothing for the army. She would rather disgrace me with words than defeat me in battle. If you have prepared the Strel'tsy properly, our regular complement should suffice in defense of Moscow. I am far more concerned with treachery."

"Certainly. But I--"

"I want sentries posted to keep the assassins out," she ordered, pacing again, hearing only herself. "Someone you trust, Fedor. If they attempt to retaliate, we must be ready."

"And the Patriarch?"

"I will receive him this evening. As loathsome as it may be, I must impress the Patriarch. I will send him to collect the little lamb and put him back where he belongs. Now, the reason I called for the two of you--Sylvester, are you listening?"

Medvedev straightened. "Yes, Lady. Of course."

"Good, because I must have your compliance. Our relationship has been one of providence, and I would begin by telling you that I appreciate all you've done in the name of the Regency. But I would now ask--no, I demand that you both keep your silence. We cannot bear another incident, particularly with all the treacherous accusations. Offer no denials or accusations; speak nothing of our condition or our innocence."

Shaklovity frowned quizzically. *Does she think us idiots? Surely, she speaks more to Medvedev than to me!*

"You may rely on my discretion," Sylvester told her, kissing the hand held out to him.

"And mine, as well," Shaklovity added, his bitterness creeping into his tone. "As ever."

"Very good. I wish you both out of the Palace by the time the Patriarch arrives."

"And the Strel'tsy?" he asked, suddenly eager to leave.

"The Strel'tsy are my strength, are they not?"

"Yes, Lady."

"Have you not advised as such on many an occasion, Fedor?"

"Yes, Lady."

"Good! Then see to it that they remain so!"

"Understood, Regent." He nodded his consent, unable to voice the rest of his concerns, knowing she was hardly in the mood to receive them.

She refuses to acknowledge their indecision. To Sophia, the Guard will always be that raging mob at her back.

"You will leave me now," she said suddenly, waving them away. "I must meditate on my meeting with Joachim. Father, I would be appreciative if you could say a prayer for me."

"Certainly, Regent--and more!"

The door opened, and Inna entered with a tray containing a flagon of wine and three goblets. She paused, looking first to Sophia.

"Inna, who called for this?"

"I did," the monk interjected before Inna could respond. "Admittedly, I guessed that you would be troubled…"

"Very kind of you, Father." Sophia looked down at the tray. "I do not, however, wish to partake with either of you. Leave me."

A bit offended, Fedor attempted to catch her gaze before leaving the chamber, managing to claim only a short, severe glance as he turned into the corridor.

The Patriarch will be insulting, without fail. She will seek consolation and I'll be back.

"A shame," Medvedev commented once the door was closed behind them, "the wine here is quite exquisite. But then, you know that, of course."

"Just remember our discussion, brother." Shaklovity offered his own severe glance before marching ahead, leaving the toddling monk in his wake.

His head rang with doubts and regrets, his body aching from too much worry and too little sleep. Still, one thought prevailed:

If Peter triumphs, I am finished.

His hatred for Peter was greater than ever, a contentious pull that left him weak with unspent rage. Ever strong, his passion had once been a matter of political leaning and duty. Now, suddenly and with dire consequence, the matter had become intensely personal.

Outside Moscow, The Monastery of Troitskaya-Sergeeva

August 21, 1689

The Monastery of Troitskaya-Sergeeva buzzed with activity, its floors rumbling with the footsteps of monks and abbots collectively bracing themselves against the weight of Naryshkin hospitality and preparing for the arrival of Patriarch Joachim.

"You are to be commended, Boris."

From her high window the Tsarista looked out, her eyes following the dark, formless shapes as they moved against the towering white outer walls. Troitsky surrounded her, from the beauty of the courtyards to the immense round towers and shining muzzles of the brass cannons that kept watch over the countryside. Strength, beauty, piety--a miracle in itself, centuries old, the holiest place in Russia. Finally, a fitting home for the Tsarista and the Naryshkin household.

"If Sophia were to wage war now, she would be fighting against the Holy Father himself!"

"You are correct, Lady. I believe we made a wise decision regarding Troitsky."

"Wise?" The Tsarista grinned. "You are far too modest. It was brilliant, simply. Praise be, Boris! You have succeeded where I could not. How long has it been since I felt so hopeful?"

"You are far too kind, Tsarista." Boris bowed, looking pleased. "Providence was in our favor, certainly."

The Tsarista felt wonderful. Surrounded again in opulence, Natalya's mind seemed clearer, focused and ready to face the Patriarch. Natalya was convinced that when the time came to do her part, she would succeed.

She'd often dreamt of plodding tirelessly through drifts of snow, a swaddled baby clutched to her breast, fighting her way toward a destination she could neither see nor reach. Now, suddenly, the skies were clearing and the drifts around her were melting into puddles. Her destination lay just ahead, and the baby she once clutched in her arms had become a man, ready to challenge what she could not.

Soon, Peter will carry me.

"Joachim is a reasonable man," she announced confidently. "And we are of like mind on many issues. He favors me, I know, for my beliefs if nothing else. He will be receptive, without question. Would you agree?"

"Yes, Lady. Given the floods of Lutherans and Papal Latins coming into Moscow, we may not need his personal favor."

"Agreed."

"The Church has struggled too long with Sophia's progressive aims. Joachim would no doubt like to see her disgraced."

Natalya nodded, staring out at the courtyard but now seeing only the future unfolding before her. The long wait seemed finally to be at an end; the time had come to undo what Sophia had done. The conservatives would have their reign, led by the wisdom of the Naryshkin clan.

"Not only the Church," she offered, imagining the faces of Shein and the boyars. "The Duma will rejoice at the thought!"

"Yes..." Boris answered, his voice falling away. "And the Duma blames my cousin Vasily."

She paused, considering Boris' tone. Discretion was necessary here.

"With all due respect to your fine family, Boris, your cousin the Prince is far too progressive in his policy."

"We all admit to his mistakes, Tsarista," he replied, crossing his arms. "I would, however, like to mention--in our defense--that the Golitsyn family name graces every service roster at Preobrazhenskoe. Lady, we have decidedly thrown in our lot with the Naryshkins and our esteemed comrades in the Duma."

"You needn't defend yourself, Boris," she told him in a reassuring voice. "Your service is as good as gold and your loyalty unquestioned. I shouldn't blame you for wanting leniency for your cousin."

"With respect, Lady, I merely wish his many accomplishments during the Regency to be considered in any charges."

"They will, certainly. Best, however, to keep your family in good standing and let your cousin stand up for his own decisions. We will do what we must, Boris."

He lowered his eyes. "Yes, Tsarista."

"Take heart, friend. She has undoubtedly influenced him--preyed on his weakness to engender his support. Sophia is the one who wishes to parade herself as an autocrat before the embassies--and this 'Eternal Peace' with Poland was an act of arrogance! They may oppose him politically, but Vasily still has friends in the Duma. And Boris, you are right about the Pope's bloody Latins; they preach heresy in our streets. Joachim will remain with us in heart and mind whatever his opinion of Peter."

"Yes, Lady. I would strongly advise keeping to the issue of the Latins in your audience with the Patriarch."

Natalya paused for a moment, considering his words. "Do you think the Tsarevich such an unpalatable subject?"

"Certainly not, Tsarista--"

"I understand Peter's relationship with the Patriarch far better than you, Boris."

"Indeed."

"I am aware that Peter misses an occasional ceremony, and we've discussed many times his affinity for socializing with his foreign tutors. But his transgressions have hardly equaled an offense that could overcome a threat of this nature. Politics aside, how can the Patriarch not take pity on him?"

Golitsyn shrank a bit. "I apologize, Tsarista. I meant only to suggest that we…minimize the discussion of the night in question. I do not think it wise to arouse suspicion about the assassination plot."

"The punishment will go where the influence does not," the Tsarista responded, looking at him. "Shaklovity and Medvedev will be accused and Peter will be Tsar. The Patriarch will follow."

"If all goes well, yes," he replied.

"Good, then." She nodded to him, hoping to ease his worry. "We will concern ourselves first with the Patriarch. I agree with you--better to lead Joachim away from any thoughts of conspiracy. But Boris, do you not see? Think. Joachim is already ours."

"Of course, Lady." Golitsyn raised his hands in surrender. "I am, regrettably, an incurable pessimist."

"Yes, you are. Fear not, however. I will be the bridge between Peter's inconsistencies and Joachim's assent. Where is the Tsarevich?"

"With his wife, I believe."

"Is he dressed and ready?"

Golitsyn nodded. "Yes, Tsarista."

"Nothing too ostentatious, I hope. Peter must appear… pitiable."

"I have seen to it myself, Lady."

"Good, good. And his temperament?"

Golitsyn paused. “Much better, I think. The Tsarevich’s discussions with his Uncle Lev have been most beneficial…along with your presence, of course, Lady.”

“We mustn’t let him become too fearful, Boris. There are hills yet to climb.”

“Yes, Lady. Thankfully, the deceptions are at an end.”

“Very good. Have Peter sent to me. I must speak with him again before the Patriarch arrives.”

He bowed slightly. “I will fetch him myself, Lady.”

Natalya waited until the door was shut to turn back to the window, exhaling and reminding herself of all that was right in her world.

Peter will succeed with Joachim, she thought, imagining the two walking arm in arm. *He can rise to the moment when he chooses. Now, as ever, he listens to his mother.*

She’d spent over an hour with him speaking of his frantic ride to Troitsky, and though she’d seen trepidation in his eyes, Natalya’s instinct assured her that no irrevocable damage had been done to his spirit. Peter was all he had been before--smart and healthy--yet now very aware of his position, understanding his true relationship with the Regent.

Despite his fear and the fits of anger, Peter’s demeanor at Troitsky had greatly impressed Mother Natalya. The event had changed him, without question, his words and mannerisms taking on a decidedly mature air. He had been speaking of Ivan, thinking of ascension, dwelling on Sophia’s methods more than her motives.

The days of the ‘play’ army were over. This much seemed obvious now, even to Peter.

And so my child becomes a man.

When she allowed her mind to linger on the process, it seemed cruel to her--deceiving Peter so blatantly while knowing the fear he'd experienced. His suffering had been the worst part of the conspiracy, and Natalya had known from the beginning that it was her responsibility to restore him should he be emotionally damaged. For the moment, the repercussions seemed slight and the outcome acceptable, if not beneficial.

Her mind worked with impatience now, sorting out the details, preparing to face the Patriarch. She wondered what he had been told before leaving Moscow. News came that he had been sent by the Regent to resolve the 'misunderstanding', sent like a dog to do her dirty work and retrieve the Tsarevich. Sophia no doubt wished to align herself with the Patriarch now, or at the very least, to equal Natalya's standing in the eyes of the Church.

But Natalya knew better. The Holy Father was on their side, in both righteousness and favor. There could be no question.

There was still work to be done, certainly, but Lady Natalya had been alive long enough to recognize the blessings of Providence on her family.

We were right to act, she thought, her mind flashing to thoughts of Evdokia and the grandchild yet to be born. *Peter stands at his strongest point.*

Too anxious to sit, she stood silently at the window and waited, imagining what her conversation with the Patriarch would be.

In what seemed only a few moments, the door opened, again without a knock.

Peter looked at her and entered with a kind half-smile, ducking his head beneath the low entry. He looked wonderful in his 'respectful-but-sympathetic' clothes, the traditional white silk kaftan lending a divine air to his appearance.

"Mother…"

"With respect to your greencoats, Peter, you have always looked handsome in white."

He looked down at himself, shrugging. "Do I look acceptable? I would imagine that all the etiquette in Europe could not aid in telling what to wear for such a circumstance."

"You look just right, Peter. Raise your chin--you needn't be worried. Now, come give your mother a kiss…"

He grinned amiably and approached, kissing her cheeks respectfully before falling into her arms. She hugged him tightly, responding to what remained of the little boy inside the man, doing her best to convey a feeling of warmth and security.

"The Patriarch has never been fond of me, Mother."

"Perhaps," she said, standing him before her and looking into his wide eyes. "But this is a new road we travel, Peter. Sophia has entered into the domain of the Church. You will do well. Be honest with him and make no assumptions or accusations. A tsar must always remain above the rumors."

Peter hesitated, biting his lip. "I should refrain from mentioning Sophia, then? At all?"

"Yes," Natalya replied firmly, "unless Joachim mentions her first. Still, you mustn't make any accusations. If he asks your opinion, say only that you cannot understand why anyone would do such a thing. Keep Sophia's name out of the conversation. The Patriarch likes to feel as though he's making his own decisions."

"I will do my best, Mother. I admit, my anger for Sophia grows with each moment."

"You must hold back, Peter. With the Patriarch, you must play the part of the lamb for now. Given the past between the two of you, this is the wisest course. He cannot refuse you this way."

A knock on the door interrupted the Tsarista's response.

"Come."

Boris stepped back through the door, bowing upon entry. "Tsarista, Tsarevich. The Patriarch is near."

Natalya turned to receive him. "Join us for a moment, Boris. I am concerned with the Strel'tsy. I worry they will make another attempt on his life. What do you say?"

Golitsyn kept his serious demeanor, shaking his head slightly. "Certainly not. They would be fools to further incriminate themselves." He paused, raising a finger. "My opinion, of course. Yet I would put nothing past Sophia, particularly where Fedor Shaklovity is concerned. But if you are discussing the Strel'tsy, then I'm sure Peter has told you of his notions concerning their defeat."

She looked to Peter. "Notions? He has mentioned nothing in that regard."

"I think his idea is quite good. No, exceptional. Exceptional indeed! Tsarevich, have you thought any more on the subject of the Strel'tsy colonels?"

"I think of nothing else," Peter replied simply.

"If you will favor us, Tsarevich, I am certain your mother would like to hear."

"Well, the plan is not truly complete until I can see all the way to the end," Peter began, addressing his mother, "still, it is far better than any other solution I can find."

She tilted her head with interest, watching as the sorrowful look left Peter's face. It pleased her, knowing that such subjects intrigued him.

"The notion itself came from the depths of my worry and sorrow," he continued. "I was desolate, despairing over the bloody Strel'tsy and wondering if I'd ever be rid of them. For a moment, I imagined the tables turned and pictured myself as Sophia, controlling the Strel'tsy mob with my own hand. I thought of how it would be to command the ranks instead of fearing them. I pictured myself at their fore…and suddenly realized how simple the solution would be. Now, if only I could see the end!"

They waited as the Tsarevich paused, his eyes staring out the window, fixed in the distance.

"I realized, Mother, that I don't need to dream of commanding the Strel'tsy. I may not have their hearts, but by right, I am Tsarevich, and I do, ultimately, have their command. They were created by my father to protect the throne. If I am to be Tsar, then the Strel'tsy already belong to me!"

She grinned, her heart leaping at the sound of his passion and the strength of his speech. A glance at Boris revealed that he felt the same; the Counselor was practically beaming with pride.

"My notion is this…" Peter turned away from the window and spun back around to face them, his face alight with thought. "If I command the Strel'tsy, then I should rightly give them some orders. Don't you think? If I ordered a few regiments to accompany me here at Troitsky--as a security measure, of course--would they not be compelled to obey?"

From the corner of her eye, the Tsarista could see Golitsyn nodding. Inside, beneath her royal exterior, she giggled like a child at the sight of Peter.

"I would begin by summoning the best of their command--enough to send a message. Then another, and another--do you see?"

"You will steal Sophia's army from beneath her," Natalya burst forth, unable to contain her enthusiasm.

Peter shrugged, offering a determined grin. "At best, yes. Still, I told you I've been unable to predict the end. And if the Strel'tsy defy me, I may be left weaker than before."

"She will certainly command them to remain in Moscow," Golitsyn added.

"Yes. It will be your order against hers, Peter. A test of loyalty. She will claim that you intend to usurp Ivan's rightful place."

Peter nodded thoughtfully, running a hand through his unkempt locks. "I must show all of Moscow that I intend to do no such thing. We were made co-tsars and so we shall remain. Perhaps a letter, one delivered only to Ivan? I will convey the truth of our situation and ask him to join me in spirit."

Golitsyn beamed. "An excellent notion, Tsarevich."

"Truly?" Peter smiled. "I thought so myself!"

Her heart near bursting with pride, she placed a comforting hand on his shoulder. "You know, Peter, we love you and have the greatest faith in you. All of Russia waits. Keep your chin high, remember your greater purpose and allow the rest to come naturally. May the Holy Father bless your every step."

His eyes softened in her gaze. "You are my dearest thought, Mother. I promise not to disappoint."

"You will succeed," she answered, taking his hands. "Providence dictates it so. You are ready for Joachim, I think."

Peter grinned, his eyes bearing mischief this time. "I am glad you think so, Mother." He glanced toward the window. "Because the Patriarch's entourage has arrived."

"What?" She moved to the window, looking out toward the entrance path, her eyes immediately catching the brightly colored robes of the Moscow clergy. "Why didn't you say something?"

Peter shrugged and kissed her cheek. "I was in the middle of explaining and thought it best to finish. If we plan to invite Joachim to stay, who can tell how long it will be before we can speak plainly again."

Suddenly anxious, Natalya smoothed her dress and took a final glance at her reflection in the window.

Now is my turn, she thought, breathing deeply to fight the nervous feeling. *Joachim will stand by Peter's side. We will have them greet visitors together.*

"Let us go," she commanded with a wave of the hand. "We must be waiting for him."

"Wait!" Peter held up a hand, waving his finger. "Mother, we cannot possibly think of leaving until you've told me what you think of my idea!"

She paused, staring at him. "I think you are brilliant, my dear son, and your ideas equally so. If I'm not mistaken, Counselor Golitsyn agrees."

Boris nodded. "Indeed. We will discuss the finer points, of course."

Peter clapped his hands victoriously, nodding.

"Have you considered who you will recruit first?"

"I have." Peter smiled, clapping again as he moved toward the corridor. "A military man knows that an initial assault must be significant and overwhelming. If I wish to make an impression, I must act boldly. For this, there is only one choice--Sophia's best and most loyal. I will take her sharpest blade first." He posed, brandishing an imaginary sword. "Let her threaten me with no army!"

Outside Moscow, The Monastery of Troitskaya-Sergeeva

August 21, 1689

"I appreciate the indulgence of a private audience, Your Holiness."

Patriarch Joachim looked back at Tsarista Natalya, nodding slowly in acknowledgement. The lady bore her usual gracious countenance, but today seemed possessed with a hopeful spirit, her words and gestures bearing a sense of relief. Admittedly, the Patriarch shared her sentiment.

"Your clan has been through much," Joachim replied, his words calm and balanced. "I think it only fitting to hear your grievances. I do, however, intend to speak with the Tsarevich privately. Please,≈sit."

"Certainly, Your Holiness." The Tsarista bowed and took the chair opposite Joachim, her eyes quickly returning to meet his.

Natalya's look was captivating in its strength, her understated wardrobe having long ago surrendered to the stern visage which resided atop it. A wise face, commanding in both calm and anger. Even with the passage of years she had retained a semblance of her youthful beauty, her once striking look now tempered kindly by age and the bloody years of Kremlin politics. Natalya was still quite attractive in the eyes of the Patriarch, for her fortitude if for nothing else.

Strong, dutiful, quiet. In Joachim's eyes, the qualities of a fine Russian woman. For Natalya, two of three had somehow been enough.

"Peter was greatly disturbed by this act of treachery," she continued mournfully, her air of satisfaction suddenly absent. "His spirit, however, remains strong. To be truthful, Your Holiness, I fear taxing him further until he has a few days to recuperate."

I should have expected her to shield the boy, he told himself, wondering at the Tsarista's serene look. *Yet given Troitsky and my presence, should they not feel relieved?*

"His need for privacy is understood. I agree that certain issues may be too…difficult for the Tsarevich to contemplate in his current condition. I must nonetheless speak with him."

"Of course," she replied without hesitation, offering a kind glance. "We will comply with your request, Your Holiness."

Joachim had grown accustomed to acknowledging the powerful women in the Kremlin, and Natalya had grown through the years to be a truly valuable ally and supporter. She was a beacon of sorts, her figure the very image and inspiration of Naryshkin opposition, her status the solid ground upon which so many Duma members stood.

It was generally agreed, even by Joachim himself, that Peter would become a suitable Tsar. For now, however, it was the Tsarista who ruled the Naryshkin clan. If the Regent were forced out, it would be Natalya who claimed the reins.

"I will begin by offering my sympathies and my counsel in this time of trial," he told her. "I think it very wise that Peter chose Troitsky as his destination. I am curious. Had he planned to come here in the event of such trouble?"

The Tsarista paused, her face unchanging. "I certainly never discussed it with him, Your Holiness. I do, however, think that considering the history and reputation of Troitsky, it seems only fitting that a future Tsar should come here. Peter was always taught to hold this holy fortress in a place of reverence in his heart."

"Ah, yes."

Reverence? The Patriarch thought. *The boy has an abundance of everything else!*

"Peter was inconsolable," she continued, "and rightly believed that remaining at Preobrazhenskoe could cost him his life. It must have been the guiding hand of the Holy Father that brought him to this bastion of safety."

"I see. I trust the Abbot has kept you well."

"Everyone has been most generous," she replied kindly. "We seek only protection from those who seek to harm us. I thank the Holy Father and, of course, Your Holiness, for providing us this sanctuary. Who knows what might have happened."

"I am relieved that you and your family are safe, Tsarista, but I have come with the sole intent of offering counsel in this matter and nothing more. As you may know, the Regent requested my intervention in resolving what she considers a 'gross misunderstanding'. I informed her that I would offer no appeal on behalf of the Regency, nor would I act as liaison for her office. I act only on behalf of the Church."

Natalya frowned, her rounded face drooping. "In truth, Your Holiness, I knew that Sophia was desperate, but could never have guessed she would…"

"You think Sophia responsible, then?"

The Tsarista paused. "Forgive me, Father. I misspoke. We offer no accusations."

"I understand," he returned calmly. "But in truth, I would like to hear what you believe. No one knows Sophia as you do. In your pious heart, Lady Natalya, do you believe this treachery was ordered by the Regent?"

She paused, her brow knitting in thought. "Your Holiness, given my past with the Regent, I fear greatly that my answer will be taken as bitterness. As you well know, Sophia and I differ on almost every issue, from the colors of the Palace tapestry to the finer points of her policy. Should you ask, I am certain that the chambermaids would tell you horrid tales of our arguments in the Kremlin. Shouting matches, most. The topic of dispute, I suppose, would be whatever we fancied at the moment, changing with our moods. Your Holiness, I was wantonly cruel at times--may the Holy Father forgive my anger. My temper, I admit, gets the best of me, particularly when addressing Sophia's unnatural affinity for Latins! It is quite distressing being in her presence so continually, I assure you."

"I can imagine so."

She presses to win my support, he thought, his calm exterior unchanging. *I must allow her to believe that my loyalty is yet to be won. There may be even more ground to be gained.*

"I know, Your Holiness," the Tsarista paused, sighing. "I have failed to answer your question. I fear I cannot do so without seeming devious."

"No harm is taken from the past, Tsarista. You have a righteous spirit and you defend your beliefs."

"Yes, yes!" She offered a relieved smile. "You do know me well, Your Holiness. I am encouraged by your words."

"I ask only your opinion, Lady."

"I will not accuse the Regent," she said, her expression growing cold again. "Should this become necessary, it will be done in a proper way. I will say, however, that I know of no one else who would wish to harm Peter. The Strel'tsy have always been our tormentors, and Sophia the master of their leash. Truly, would it be sensible to accuse anyone else?"

"You are most persuasive, Tsarista."

"Your presence here nourishes my soul," Natalya continued, "though I fear that she will pursue us like a wolf after blood. And despite what you may have heard about Peter's army, his Preobrazhensky are little match for that mob of musketeers that serves the Regent. I can still remember the day you named Peter Tsar--do you remember, Your Holiness? Do you recall the bloodshed that followed?"

"Certainly," Joachim answered thinking back. The events of seven years earlier remained a bitter memory, scarcely forgotten. "We must hope that the hearts of the musketeers have changed in these seven summers. Moscow is not as it used to be, Lady. The topic of the Regent's competence has been well-discussed lately, even amongst her loyal mob."

"It is true; they blame Prince Golitsyn for the war."

"And Peter has shown well lately," he added, trying to be complimentary. "There is no question that he has become the favorite son. Even the most loyal Strel'tsy turns to applaud and praise him."

She nodded slightly, still looking troubled. "But the scoundrel that leads them? Surely, their minds remain clouded by the treachery of their Commander."

"Agreed," he answered firmly. "Fedor Shaklovity has been a persistent opponent."

"Your Holiness, I dare say that no figure casts a greater shadow over my family." Natalya's look grew dark, her eyes mournful and angry. "And though his dagger is yet to caress the skin of our throats, he has been wounding us for years with his words. Attacking my poor Peter from the time he was a child with his speeches and public accusations of heresy!"

The Tsarista was lost in her anger, but the Patriarch sat back and listened, knowing that her long complaints almost always led to a greater summation, and then a plan of action. Joachim was in the business of granting requests and had learned to be patient when listening. Natalya was still in want of something and was preparing him for her request.

"I certainly do not wish to insult you, Your Holiness, so I needn't remind you that the Commander's traitorous talk has been witnessed by many in Moscow, including, I expect, his own officers. And that monk, Medvedev? Well, I trust that you know he is worse…"

"I do," the Patriarch replied, bristling inside at the thought of Sylvester Medvedev. "In light of your honesty, Lady, I will admit that I have rarely had such dispute with one of my own calling."

"And certainly," she interjected promptly, "no one questions your leadership. It saddens me to know that a debauched monk like Medvedev is speaking against the Patriarch himself. I understand your distress, Your Holiness. These are burdens we must bear--like Shaklovity and the Strel'tsy, and even Prince V.V.! We are helpless against their presence as long as Sophia clutches her Regency."

He felt the sting of her comments, but did not blame the Tsarista. Medvedev's behavior had been a problem he had willingly overlooked, dust swept under the rug that he was now compelled to clean.

"Your Holiness, I have never been one for gossip or rumors," she pressed, her glare locked on him. "My family has suffered the treachery of such talk, and I have no desire to bear false witness. When the life of my child rests in the balance, however, I feel no shame in listening to everything I might. Considering this, Your Holiness, I think it my duty to tell you that Shaklovity and Medvedev are the names I hear in connection with this incident. Given the show of troops in Moscow on that night, I think it quite obvious that something was planned, rumor or not. No one but Shaklovity has the influence to summon such a force!"

Natalya was convincing, and despite what had seemed an honest response from Sophia, the circumstantial evidence was decidedly stacked against the Regency.

He allowed his mind to wander through the possibilities of what could be. The thought was wholly enticing--a Moscow without Sophia and the Miloslavskys, finally free of Vasily Golitsyn and the Regent's progressive policies. A regime led by the sensible morality of the Naryshkins.

A pious woman.

Natalya will allow me my right and no one despises foreigners more.

How much we could accomplish! But do we think ourselves past the Strel'tsy? I must remind her: the Kremlin is still delivered the traditional way...at the point of a sword.

Joachim quieted his rising anticipation and held to his duty, knowing there was more to say.

"The Regent claims that the armed Strel'tsy were meant as an escort," he told her. "Sophia was very firm on this point."

"I would not expect her to confess anything else," the Tsarista said, shaking her head sadly. "An escort for one of her pilgrimages? Sophia has responded the same in a letter to Peter; I am certain he would allow you to read it. But, Your Holiness, so many men for such an endeavor? Has she ever called so many men to service the Kremlin?"

The Patriarch shook his head definitively. "No. Not since the day of her ascension to the Regency. Even then, it could be said that the Strel'tsy called themselves."

"And Peter's chamberlain?" she asked, pressing. "Was he not beaten and interrogated? He was sent on a routine duty, a task of little consequence in Moscow. He was no threat, certainly. Where was the call for such action?"

Shaklovity, the Patriarch thought, his mind returning again to the image of the Strel'tsy Commander. *Was he preparing for battle or bracing in defense?*

"The Regent blames these difficulties on a letter that circulated through Moscow. It suggested that Peter was preparing to take the Kremlin."

Natalya frowned. "Yes, Your Holiness. I have been told many times of this letter, and I admit I have difficulty understanding how it mitigates our suffering. Surely, anyone who knows of the Preobrazhensky realizes that they are hardly a match for a single brigade, much less the whole of the Strel'tsy."

"Nonetheless," he countered, "the Regent claims that the Strel'tsy were agitated by the letter. Thank the Holy Father--the musketeers are hesitant to stand against Peter for fear of their mortal souls. The guards who arrested your chamberlain were acting on their own. This, it seems, is the position Sophia wishes to take."

"If the Strel'tsy hesitate, then Sophia must be truly desperate," Natalya stated, her tone sharp and bitter. "I cannot claim to know what happened in Moscow on that night, for I was not there. I do know, Your Holiness, that our Peter was pulled from his bed and forced to flee for his life! Let Sophia and her rats twist the truth and talk of anonymous letters while proclaiming their innocence…they cannot deny what has happened!"

Joachim leaned forward, adopting a reassuring look. "Please, Tsarista, calm yourself. I had no intention of disturbing you so."

"You have my apologies," she returned immediately, wiping away a tear. "You could never disturb us, Your Holiness, you are the light of hope in this horrid, dark time. I have waited anxiously for your arrival. I regret that now, when I finally have you here, my fear makes me melancholy and contentious."

He grinned like a father, nodding and staring into her eyes to comfort her. The Tsarista held his gaze like a statue, her eyes welling with tears.

"We are defenseless, Your Holiness," she continued, now bearing a supreme calm, her words measured and sad. "Only these mighty walls prevent us from becoming the victims of the Strel'tsy assassins. Now, just as Peter stands ready, we are forced to fear for our lives. You are our salvation, Your Holiness."

She stood from her seat and dropped to a knee before him, her eyes downcast. "We humbly ask your help in our plight. We ask that you remain here at Troitsky so that our Peter may outlive Sophia's designs."

"Please, Tsarista, rise. You are a pious woman; your gesture is greatly appreciated."

He watched as she rose and stood before him, her face now bearing a grateful look.

And so, the Church is left to cast its die...

Finally, Joachim stood at the long awaited crossroads. He had often ruminated on the end of the Regency and had long ago decided that the Church must be kept above the fray. It was at this moment, then, that the Patriarch thought not of Peter, Sophia, or the future of Russia, but searched instead for the answer that would provide him the smoothest path through the transition.

If I return to Moscow, they will expect me to come bearing a glorious resolution.

That, or I could be seen as an emissary of the Naryshkins.

This conflict is long from finished. Better not to infuriate the Strel'tsy. My presence at Troitsky will be represented only as devotion to the Church. Let Sophia untangle the rest!

"I will remain here," he announced, watching as the Tsarista's face brightened. "As a representative of the Church. I can only hope that my presence will aid in the security of you and your family, Lady Natalya. Divine right must not be challenged. I expect that these giant walls must have been constructed with such a task in mind."

"Oh, thank you, Your Holiness! You have our undying gratitude!"

The decision was not difficult.

He rose to stand with her, his thoughts churning. "I fear your elation may be premature, Lady. There is still much to consider."

She dipped her head respectfully. "My joy comes only from the thought of my Peter safe here at Troitsky. As for anything else that you may need, I am at your disposal, Your Holiness."

You must control your mischievous boy, he thought, wondering how Peter would react when removed from the shackles of the Regency. *He remains disinterested in the important things and is far too enamored with his foreign mentors.*

"I will speak frankly, Tsarista, for I feel the situation requires it. Please bear in mind that it is not my intent to insult you when I suggest that Peter's disposition still gives me pause."

"Oh?"

He could see the change in her face as he approached the subject, her eyes growing cold for a moment. Natalya was known for being fiercely protective of her son, even when facing the evidence of his shortcomings. Thankfully, she was also a reasonable woman and through her trials had grown to be a shrewd judge of situations.

Natalya could recognize the appropriate and thus proved to be a sensible negotiator.

A miracle, it seemed, for a woman to have learned so much about politics. Joachim would readily admit that Natalya's skills had matured, her aims executed in incredible fashion, orders delivered from seclusion. She could debate calmly on a myriad of issues. The subject of Russia's favorite son, however, was a subject best danced around.

"Your Holiness, if I may..." She spoke before he had the chance to qualify his statement, placing a hand on his arm. "I understand that in the past, Peter has fallen short of your high standards of devotion, particularly where it concerns his attendance."

"Lady, I--"

"We have spoken of this before, Your Holiness. I have always shared your concerns, though in truth I believed his high spirits to be a symptom of youth and his martial exploits understandable in light of the Regency. Today, however, is a new day. You yourself would admit that Peter's conduct this summer has been much improved."

Posturing for the throne, he thought. *Guided by Natalya.*

"I would agree."

"And though I hate to say so, I believe this frightful incident may have served a greater purpose. He has been affected, no question--yet he seems stronger somehow, more certain of his position."

"The Holy Father guides all," he answered, placing a hand over hers. "And if I may, Lady, I do not wish to be misunderstood. I meant only to suggest that Peter is still a bit naïve when it comes to the finer aspects of governing. To be more direct, I would feel greatly reassured if I knew that Russia would have the guiding hand of Tsarista Natalya to rely upon, to aid the young Tsars and guide the government through the more delicate matters."

The Tsarista looked up at him, her eyes still wet with tears, her face bearing a deeply serious, martyred look that proved her diplomatic skills were as sharp as ever.

"In the service of Russia, I am ever loyal. In the service of the Lord, I am ever devoted. And in the name of my son, my blood, I am ever committed, ever vigilant. I have no greater aspiration than to serve. Yes, Your Holiness. I will gladly play whatever role is required of me."

Joachim smiled down at the Tsarista, delivering his most benevolent look and nodding his understanding. Natalya was receptive, her eyes full of gratitude, her posture straightening in response. Little more needed to be said.

"Now I would very much like to speak with Tsarevich Peter."

"He awaits your counsel." Natalya nodded, offering her arm. "Allow me to lead you, Your Holiness."

Joachim took her arm and chatted politely as they walked, the conversation turning to the mundane subject of the warm summer weather. Inside, the Patriarch churned with troubles and worries, his thoughts returning again to the Strel'tsy.

And so the Naryshkins have an offence and the evidence to prove it…but who will contend with the mob?

Sophia will stand. If necessary, she will call her dogs. Surely, there is a plan. The Naryshkins cannot hope to defend themselves with accusations alone.

Moscow, The Great Sovereign's Palace of the Kremlin

August 23, 1689

"Tsykler?" Vasily almost choked on the words. "What?"

Sophia raised her palms. "Precisely my reaction! What can he mean?"

Vasily tossed the order back on the table, his eyes still wide in disbelief. "You know very well what he means to do! Is it not obvious?"

"He means to attack me with my own army? Is that it?"

She's lost her head, he thought. *Does she deceive herself?*

Prince V.V. Golitsyn exhaled, wishing he were somewhere else. The Naryshkins were running the game now, and whatever the events of the prior week, the rumors of treachery were suddenly etched as facts. There was still doubt in his mind concerning Sophia's participation--after all, Shaklovity had been begging for years to undertake something similar.

"He won't need to attack you, my dear. Do you think the rest of the Guard will be eager to face their brothers?"

"But Tsykler?" She fumed, her fists clenching in fury. "How brazen can he be to summon my greatest leader? My finest regiment, Vasily!"

"Your regiment?" Vasily stared at her, his tone souring. "The Strel'tsy serve the throne, Sophia. Tsykler's regiment belongs to Peter as much as it does to you. Perhaps even more so. After all, he is Tsar."

"Tsarevich." She scowled, brushing back her hair. "I am still Regent."

Vasily nodded sadly. "Yes…but not without an army."

"Tsykler's Regiment! The ones who lifted me to begin with! The same ones who gladly cut Peter's uncle to ribbons not seven years ago!"

"His choice of regiment is no mistake," he replied. "I see the Tsarista's hand in this."

"Without question," she agreed, pacing. "Naryshkin treachery. That wretch defies me at every turn. I have capitulated and provided for them--all of Russia knows I kept Natalya and her son alive! It was by my permission that they kept their heads all these years! Peter remains Tsarevich and their clan exists without persecution. What more can she want?"

"Back into the Kremlin, I suspect. You dwell in the past, Sophia, while the Tsarista looks to the future."

"I look to save the Regency from the treachery and ineptitude that surround me!" Sophia protested. "Deny it if you wish, Vasily, but there is a conspiracy afoot."

He frowned. "Deny it? Were there no conspiracy, I would not be standing here now!"

Sophia paused and turned suddenly, her face bearing a venomous stare that left no question where her anger would now be directed. "And your cousin?" she asked, baiting him. "What of long-suffering Boris?"

"What of him?" Vasily shrugged, knowing this was coming.

Sophia stepped closer, her breath tainted with wine. "He thrives on my disgrace! He stands by Natalya's side at this very moment, Vasily! I was kind enough to grant him promotions. You cannot deny that Boris gained far more than the other Naryshkin sympathizers. And after all this goodwill, he continues to advise the Naryshkins! I am told he was first to arrive at Troitsky to console the Tsarevich. No, Vasily, I cannot trust your cousin. For all we know, this plot may be of Boris' construct."

"Always on the attack," he replied sharply, glaring at her. "You are quick to snap at Boris, attacking when you should be thinking of defense."

"Defense?" Sophia returned his look, her face unyielding. "What do you know of it? It was your strategy of defense that led us into this difficulty."

"You see?" he returned, unafraid, having seen this face before. "You attack me now! You may insult my command abilities, but I will remind you that I have done nothing that would send Peter running to Troitsky."

"You advised me!" she snapped. "You told me to send the Patriarch."

"I agreed that you should request his assistance. Your standing with the Patriarch has been forged over the course of many years. Surely you don't mean to blame me for your poor reputation."

"I most certainly do! In this event, at the very least. And what of the rest? The boyars, the Strel'tsy colonels? Vasily, I have been carrying the burden of your generalship for the entire summer. You have turned the whole city of Moscow against me! Would I have been so quickly accused otherwise?"

"This," he said, extending a hand, "from the woman who shocked all of Russia with her performance at the Assumption

Cathedral! How could anyone forget the sight? Tell me, Sophia, which of the saints was it that you clutched to your bosom?"

"I won't be mocked, Vasily!"

"And wasn't it you who called for the victory parade?"

Her look hardened. "I did that on your behalf," she said. "To help restore your reputation."

He huffed in reply. "That spectacle was far more offensive than my failures in the south."

"Not in the eyes of the Strel'tsy…or the foreign officers."

She wishes to saddle me, he thought, his temper warming. *The more hysterical she becomes, the more guilt I will bear.*

He turned, calming his tone. "Since I see that you wish to speak the whole truth this evening, I will remind you that the Strel'tsy are still aching and sore from the execution of Hovanski. What has it been--just over a year since you executed him and put Shaklovity in his place?"

"You are cruel to bring Hovanski into this, Vasily. Have I not suffered enough at his hands? And you may remind yourself, my dear, I have made no decisions alone! You have been by my side from the beginning. You and your lovely little wife have benefitted enormously from our decisions!"

And now comes the jealousy, he thought, looking at her and relenting. Sophia's hair hung in strands, her face etched with anger and despair. Vasily relented, feeling a sudden rush of sympathy. She was troubled like never before, burdened with the grief of losing what she coveted most. Vasily knew well her reputation but had always thought her smile quite beautiful. Looking at her now, he wanted suddenly to bring it back, at least for a moment.

"I will proudly admit my part in the current administration," he began, softening his tone, "and can warmly profess my affection for you, my dear. My duty here has been a labor of love."

The words stopped Sophia before she could reply, her scowl melting quickly into a mournful look of gratitude.

"I am sincere, Sophia."

She stepped into his arms, embracing him with a grip that spoke of desperation, sobbing as she buried her face in his shoulder and held tightly. Despite her lust for the act itself, Sophia had never been one for long embraces, distributing her affections as she did her other emotions, in short effective bursts that left no question of her intent. On this occasion, however, Vasily felt something he'd never before experienced with Sophia--a fatherly connection, his tired arms holding a little girl as she cried. She held him for what seemed a long time, her hands clutching as though unwilling to let go. When she parted, she kissed him lightly, leaving his cheeks wet with her tears.

It was at once both a mournful and liberating rush that filled Vasily, his heart warming for what he thought might be the last time.

This journey is nearly finished. If not this, then something else. Peter will be Tsar before the year is out.

His days in the Duma taught him to always look ahead, to test the future with every thought and base his decisions on what would be, rather than what was. Given his success and personal wealth, Vasily considered himself quite capable of gauging the future and acting on his predictions. In their current situation, there seemed little to be gained other than, perhaps, a respite from the current trouble and, at best, a few more weeks of life for the Regency.

There was no question in his mind that she was fit to rule… and now, no denying that the brutal politics of Russia would force her out.

"We have accomplished much together," he told her, speaking proudly. "The embassies, the trade agreements, the Treaty of Eternal

Peace! Poland as a friend of Russia? This alone is much more than poor Tsar Alexis was able to achieve. This is to your credit, Sophia."

"How rarely we were appreciated."

"No matter. Such is the life of a progressive. Given time, we would have done much more. There is no question of that."

"Given time?" she asked, looking hurt. "You speak as though we are already undone! Is that truly what you believe?"

"Certainly not," he replied as though by instinct, his eyes immediately betraying his words.

As soon as it had arrived, her moment of sorrow was gone. Vasily could see the change in her face, the anger rising anew to take the stage.

"You lie to me," Sophia snapped, turning away. "What good are you if you lie? I can see what you're thinking, Vasily! I have known you too long for you to deceive me so!"

"I never claimed that we were undone," he replied in defense, tiring of her moods. "But if we cannot convince them of our innocence, then we must look to a rational compromise. I fear you may have to place blame on someone to satiate the hunger of curiosity… surrendering Fedor Shaklovity, for example."

She gave no response, offering only her back.

"Better to say that you had no knowledge of his plan and that Shaklovity acted on his own. This, at least in part, would exonerate you."

"But we would be admitting guilt, would we not?"

"Only in compromise," he added, hoping to persuade. "It is a difficult solution to bear. Yes, but one, I think, that removes you quite cleanly from blame. Would you be prepared to do this, Sophia?"

She turned back to him, her look bearing little expression. "I would not."

He delivered an extended sigh, nodding. "Very well. We will stick to our defense."

"Good."

"My advice, then, Lady, would be to comply with Peter's orders."

"And so I must simply send our best regiment to stand by his side?" She paced, huffing her frustration. "To defend him? Against what?"

"Against you," Vasily responded, his hope fading, his thoughts reaching beyond the concerns of the Regency. "Would you rather attack him? I think an assault on Troitsky would be quite memorable. That is, if you can get any of the Strel'tsy to actually engage."

"How can you be so light-hearted about our plight?"

"On the contrary," he told her, raising a finger, "I merely wish to impress upon you the truth of our trouble, the essence of our dilemma! Is that not my duty?"

"You don't have to take such pleasure in it."

"I take none, Sophia. Trust in this." He looked to the door, thinking of his wife and his journey home.

Better to be away from the Kremlin, he thought. *I will remain in Moscow only as long as it takes to decide this...*

"Fine, then. I will capitulate, again. I will send Colonel Tsykler to test the game of our Peter. Perhaps Prince Troekorov should go along with him to do what he can."

"Troekorov? Why?"

"His son is a member of Peter's 'play' army--some say a close friend of the Tsarevich. We have not yet tried to appeal to his sense of loyalty. Perhaps the elder can do us some good."

"Do as you wish," Vasily said, giving little merit to her notion. "But once he has Tsykler, I think it will take more than a friend of the family to pry him from Troitsky."

She shook her head, her eyes narrowing. "If you are correct, then we may hope for nothing more than clearing our names. Let Peter try to bewitch him; Tsykler will return to Moscow and the Strel'tsy will be stronger than ever."

"I pray you are correct, Sophia. The Regency may hang in the balance."

She scowled, shaking her head. "Without proof of my guilt, I refuse to compromise. If they wish to play games, then let us begin."

"Very well."

"I will see this resolved, Vasily. I will march myself to Troitsky if necessary! Do you understand? After all I have done for Russia, I refuse to be disgraced!"

"We will pray for success, my dear."

She will keep fighting and she will lose. Peter's ascendancy cannot be denied.

He listened for a while longer as Sophia vented her desperation, offering a reassuring comment where he could, trying his best not to counter her opinions or offer too much resistance. He nodded dutifully as she spoke, feigning continued interest while his thoughts wandered to more selfish worries.

Seven years later, and where am I now?

The face of the Regency. The best dressed, best accounted, best known man in all of Moscow. Prince Golitsyn's accolades numbered too many to count, his achievements notable even within such a prestigious family. He had earned his place and, with the exception of the Crimean campaigns, had succeeded at everything he'd tried. Even difficult Sophia seemed easily won and he'd willingly taken the opportunities she'd granted.

In his mind, they had been an exceptional pair, working in unison to turn the slow-moving gears of the Kremlin, pressing their ideas into movement and change, seeing the results of their actions etched into the history books. In their best years, there had been no greater joy for him than coming to the Kremlin and working with Sophia, forging policy and taking their breaks with wine and kisses. He respected no woman more.

But it all felt very different now, drifting in reckless pattern like snowflakes in the wind. There was little left to support them anymore, the boyars driven away by the abolition of the class system and the Church disillusioned with their openness to foreigners. Even the Strel'tsy were wavering now, driven by the failures against the Turks and the memory of past grievances. What began with Peter's exodus to Preobrazhenskoe seemed finally to be reaching its conclusion.

As for Sophia, she was moody and suspicious, her decisions more and more tainted by the opinions of other advisors. Increasingly, Vasily found himself feeling less like the face of the Regency and more like one of many masks that the Regent chose to wear.

I am used and played. All I have done, washed away in the wake of a single scandal. Did I not expect it to end?

Peter will call more regiments. He will drain her of support until she can no longer stand. There is no question that she will protest... but how long do I wish to be standing beside her? Would she give up Shaklovity before me?

Would they want Shaklovity over the face of the Regency--the man who bungled their precious campaign?

I will stay only as long as she needs me. They will execute anyone they suspect of conspiring.

He lingered for a while longer, sharing a cup of wine and talking, calming her with warmth and hopeful possibilities. Sophia was still so young--almost twenty years his junior--and it seemed to the Prince that hope was what she needed most. Using the talents he'd honed in the Duma, Vasily looked into her eyes as she talked, his thoughts far away, planning his exit from Moscow.

Outside Moscow, The Monastery of Troitskaya-Sergeeva

August 25, 1689

"Do we wait here, sir?"

Colonel Ivan Tsykler clenched his jaw, biting back a personal remark and staring up at the divine fortress that stood before them. Troitsky seemed bigger than he remembered, the regiment of Strel'tsy shrunken to mere insects at the sight of the massive white walls and cannon-filled towers. Like his men, the Colonel bore the weight of worry, the contemplative journey from Moscow followed by the intimidating sight of their pious destination.

The Holy Father could not hope to ignore such a place, he thought, shaking his head at the sight of it, silently acknowledging the wise strategy of the Naryshkins.

A man whose countenance matched his experience, Tsykler was accustomed to blood, driven by the call of duty and held fast to his profession by the security of rank. He was, above all else, a military man, capable of contending with any situation in the field. Had it been a battle he was expecting, the Colonel would have been ready, anxiously awaiting his chance. As it was, however, Ivan Tsykler found himself marching for a diplomatic cause, an effort for which he knew he was wholly unprepared.

Between the regiment and the Monastery, a small procession of greeting crept its way down the hill toward Tsykler, the group bearing the colors of the Preobrazhensky but moving without arms or escort. The party was led by an unrecognizable, diminutive figure clothed in civilian dress, his head topped with a large plumed hat.

Squinting in the morning sun, the Colonel dismounted, straightened his expression and turned to face the regiment.

"Ten of you will come with me," he ordered, pointing. "Kolov, Solubokov, Drenev…you four, you, you, and you, Nezhikov. The rest will wait here under command of Lieutenant Kolesnikov."

He motioned and Kolesnikov stepped forward, bearing the same confused look that graced the faces of the rest.

"Lieutenant."

"Sir?"

"You are to stand here in readiness," Tsykler told the young man, lowering his voice. "Be vigilant. Accept no commands but my own. Should I not return by sunset, you are to take the regiment back to Moscow and report to Commander Shaklovity."

Kolesnikov nodded his understanding. "Yes, sir."

"Keep a steady watch, Lieutenant. If you fail, you will answer to me."

"Yes, sir."

Tsykler turned back toward the Monastery, his heart pounding swiftly despite years of experience, his emotion equal parts anger and trepidation.

An insult or an honor? he wondered, staring at the small entourage. *Did I expect to be greeted by an army?*

He calmed his temper, remembering the importance of the moment. An imposition, perhaps, asking him to bear the burden of negotiation--but an honor, nonetheless, being called personally by the Tsarevich. Recognition, at the very least, that Ivan Tsykler's Stremyani was the finest regiment the Strel'tsy had to offer.

Called by the Tsarevich himself. Summoned to accompany and provide defense for the Naryshkins at Troitsky. A shrewd move, by any estimation. An order that Tsykler was compelled to follow.

And though in his heart he was reasonably sure of his safety, there lingered within the Colonel a pervasive suspicion, a fear that the atrocities of his past were coming home to roost.

The birth of the Regency was in his mind.

Tsykler had once reveled in the memories. His Stremyani had led the charge on behalf of Sophia--stirred the rebellion and stormed the Royal Palace on her command. It had been their demands that lifted Tsarevich Ivan to his rightful place and their blades that cut down any who opposed him. Tsykler could still remember the deaths of Matveev and the Naryshkins, his own blade having claimed its share of blood. Whatever his part, it was enough for the Colonel that all of Moscow realized who had been in command that day.

Ivan Tsykler, Strel'tsy leader, enemy of the Naryshkins. There was no question in Tsykler's mind that he had proven an intimidating figure for the Tsarevich in his youth, but how did the Colonel appear to the Tsarevich now that he was a young man, nearly ready to take his place? Would Peter seek revenge?

The Colonel had been well recompensed for his part in Sophia's ascension, and Tsykler had always proven a loyal supporter in both thought and action. In his heart, he was a Miloslavsky man and considered his service to be a crucial part of the Regency's success over the years. His contempt for the Naryshkins was real and his opposition heartfelt.

And yet, despite all his anger and fear, despite his inclinations and his history, the Colonel was wise enough to see that a new star was rising in Russia. Young Peter's strength was undeniable, his supporters growing to include everyone but the most fervent advocates of the Regency. Sophia's reign would soon be supplanted by Peter's, bringing a change that would see hundreds of promotions, every post emptied and refilled with a Naryshkin loyal. In such times, it seemed only rational to look toward the salvation of one's own career.

Some loyalties, Tsykler reasoned as the envoy bowed before him, *can be negotiated. Play the protector--not the aggressor. Better to position yourself well.*

"Colonel Tsykler, I greet you on behalf of Tsar Peter." The envoy smiled pleasantly. "I am to escort you inside. The Tsar awaits."

Already they call him Tsar.

Tsykler tipped his cap. "You have my thanks. If I may say so, you look familiar to me, son. May I ask your name?"

"Certainly. I am named Ivan Troekorov, Colonel."

"Ah, yes. The younger Troekorov, then."

"Yes, Colonel. The honor is mine."

As awkward as his stammering father.

Tsykler grinned a bit. "I have news that will interest you, son--should you not already know. Your father's procession rides behind us on the road. We outpaced them, certainly, but they will arrive soon enough."

"My father?"

"Yes. Prince Troekorov. He is your father, is he not?"

The young man nodded, his face weakening for a moment before resuming the diplomatic look. "The Tsar said not to keep you waiting. You are to be brought immediately to speak with him."

"Certainly," the Colonel answered sternly. "I will comply."

Troekorov turned and the Colonel followed, motioning for the selected musketeers to walk in his wake. They quietly fell in behind him, noticed but unacknowledged by the envoy.

It would be simply done and not unwarranted, he thought. *Once within those walls, they could cut my throat and say nothing more of it. All of Moscow would acknowledge my execution--and no one would question a thing!*

The polite walk to the gates seemed unbearably long, but once inside Tsykler was greeted immediately by the sight of the young Tsar and his entourage. The giant of a young man stood in his customary white shirt with knee-breeches and boots, his palms extended in greeting. As their eyes connected, Peter's round mustached face offered a smile that sang of victory.

Beside Peter, standing like a true compatriot, Patriarch Joachim offered a respectful look, his face bearing the importance of the moment. Yet, even with his headdress, the Patriarch seemed insignificant beside the Tsar, a mere ornament. Joachim offered no greeting as the Colonel removed his hat.

No words would be necessary. The Patriarch's presence at Peter's side was message enough for the Colonel.

He has played it well, the Colonel thought, masking his emotion. *God at his right hand and Tsykler at his left!*

The rest of the entourage proved a gallery of villains to the Colonel's eyes. Boris Golitsyn, Lev Naryshkin, Romodanovsky and others--all of them Naryshkin loyalists, many still bearing grudges from the past. More lurked in the wings, no doubt, ready to take their places in the new government.

Ambitious bastards. I've been the devil in their eyes. Do they come to see my end?

"Colonel? This way, sir."

Following Troekorov, he marched to greet the Tsar, his feet weighing more with each step. Peter's smile served to ease his fear, but the Colonel was now suddenly taken with the absurdity of the whole event and his own humiliating role.

"Thank you for your expediency, Colonel Tsykler." Peter's voice seemed to fill the courtyard, all others holding their tongues in expectant silence, their eyes fixed.

"My lord." Tsykler offered a respectful bow, lingering. "I come at your order."

Peter stepped forward, looking down at him. "As you can see, Colonel, your presence here is greatly appreciated. Rest assured that your regiment will be treated well by the Abbot."

"The balance remain outside, my lord," Tsykler answered honestly. "I did not seek to cause an incident. I brought only ten men with me…as a show of respect."

The ten men remained silent behind him, their eyes cast down, their muskets securely strapped to their backs. Tsykler now regretted bringing them, knowing it would have appeared more courageous to step inside the walls with no escort.

"Nezhikov," Peter said, scanning their number, "and Kolov? Is that correct?"

"Yes, my lord." Kolov answered.

"I do not recognize the rest," Peter said to Tsykler, placing a hand on his shoulder, "but it is good to know that we are not all strangers here."

The Tsar's hand remained on the Colonel's shoulder.

A trick of intimidation, a ploy used by Tsykler himself on occasion, now used with considerable ease by the young Tsar. Peter's grip was friendly but considerable, familiar enough to appear supportive when in truth it was an offence of rank, a too-familiar hand on the shoulder that left no question as to who was in command.

"As you can see, Colonel, I wish merely to speak with you." Peter spoke without restraint. "I have engaged no escort today and wish, as you do, that no incidents take place. And considering how many such incidents begin and end with muskets, I think we should leave them out altogether. Do you agree?"

"Indeed, my lord."

"In truth, I believe they are an offence to the sanctity of this place. You will understand if your men are disarmed. Mind you, I will personally see to your protection."

We do what we must, the Colonel thought, nodding his consent and motioning for his men to surrender their arms. Knowing that Peter's 'play' army was present at Troitsky, it seemed a small relief to see clergy members approaching to take the muskets.

Now, I am committed to negotiation, else I appear a coward!

"My wish is for you to feel as safe here as I do," Peter told him, his hand finally releasing its grip. "Your men will be fed and filled with wine for their trouble."

He looked to Boris. "As for the rest of you, you will have to wait to greet the Colonel personally. I wish to speak with him alone."

Despite the pained expression on the face of Golitsyn, Peter firmly and politely dismissed the rest of the entourage, including the Patriarch. They separated slowly from the Tsar as though reluctant to leave him, trickling back toward the Monastery and taking Tsykler's escort with them.

Soon, the two stood alone in the warmth of the daylight. In moments, the Colonel had gone from staring down a crowd to facing the young Tsar privately, without arms or escort, without even a roof over their heads. Alone in his rank, Tsykler felt both intimidated and intrigued. Peter smiled knowingly, as though ready to play out their conversation in a spot where the Holy Father could not miss it.

Would that I could manage, I could kill him right now! The Colonel nodded his appreciation. *Peter trusts that I won't attempt it...or perhaps he thinks he could take me.*

Either way, the move seemed one of courage and camaraderie to the Colonel, a display of confidence that made an immediate impression on the military man.

"I trust that you feel more comfortable without the nest of crows watching over us, Colonel."

"I admit, my lord, it is easier to breathe in their absence."

Peter nodded, chuckling. "Indeed. You have no idea what I go through, Colonel. You should come and dine with me sometime. I must persist while under the watchful eye of a roomful of them! Try swallowing your soup when you know you have an audience for every last slurp! Truly, I dine in private whenever possible."

Tsykler shifted awkwardly, not knowing how to respond.

"It is on this note that I will begin with an apology," Peter continued amiably, saving him the trouble. "I am certain that your journey was long and filled with consternation and I know that you likely seek nothing more at the moment than a meal and a cup of vodka, but I thought our business serious enough to warrant immediate discussion. Do you agree, Colonel?"

"Certainly, sire. I am not troubled a bit by my stomach."

"Excellent." Peter clapped his hands together. "Far better, I think, out here without the trappings and attendants--out in a place where we may clearly understand each other."

"I am no stranger to the field, my lord," Tsykler answered, "though I scarcely find myself in surroundings as pleasant as these. I am far more suited to the battlefield."

"You served under my father, did you not?"

Tsykler nodded. "I did, my lord. Proudly."

Peter stared into him, his eyes bearing weight. "This is a fine place for us to leave the rest behind and begin our serious discussion, Colonel. I will start by telling you that I have great and honest respect for men of your service. You have joined our brothers in campaigns as well as in the service of my family. You are an accomplished soldier and I would never think of dishonoring your record. I feel, however, that if anything is to be accomplished here, we must first speak of seven years ago."

Tsykler's heart went from a trot to a gallop in a moment's time, his resistance straining beneath the weight of the young man's stare.

"My lord?"

"We were both actors in the events of that year." Peter said, his tone deepening. "And we both know the role that the Stremyani Regiment played in the creation of the Regency."

"Yes, my lord."

"Despite the politeness of this discourse," the Tsar continued, "I refuse to act as though these things never happened. It was in part for this reason that I summoned you to Troitsky."

"I suspected as much, my lord."

"Well, I won't guess at your suspicions, but suffice it to say that you are quite safe here, Colonel. And I assure you, I did not call you here to answer for past transgressions. I wish merely to state the obvious. You and I have been positioned in opposing stances for too long. It does not have to be so. Your ranks were created by my father and have continued to serve the best interests of the Kremlin."

"The Strel'tsy serve the throne, my lord."

"Precisely. The Strel'tsy serve the throne--and so you have come. Trust that I know the importance of your presence, Colonel Tsykler. Graciously or otherwise, you stand here today because you are a man of duty and live to serve Mother Russia. Am I correct, Colonel?"

"Yes, my lord." Tsykler nodded back. "I am a patriot, if nothing else."

"For this, you have my respect," Peter said, the sun hiding behind his broad shoulders. "If you would, Colonel, I wish for you to forget for a moment all that has occurred between the

Naryshkins and Miloslavskys, all our allegiances and political stances. If you can, I would like you to forget all the trappings and see us now, in the moment that we currently enjoy, with the past far behind us and the future snapping at our toes. See us in this very moment, as a mere couple. Two men, two patriots who have in their hands the potential of an entire country. Consider me, Colonel, without my family. Do me the respect of considering my opinion as a solitary man. As Peter Alexeevich. This you can do for a fellow Russian."

Tsykler's paused, his response caught in his throat, his tongue made useless by the Tsar's frank address.

"My lord?"

"I was born into my position. A Naryshkin, left to bear the weight of all that had happened before. And whatever the trial, I have pressed to become something worthy of my position. I do not pretend to know what is said among your men about my worthiness or my fortitude, but I would assume that many feel me unready. I know there are those who would cast me as a shadow of my mother and my clan, as a child who has not been through enough. You think we are traveling from one regency to another, this time led by your opponents."

"My lord, I--"

"I am no longer a child, Colonel." Peter stopped, his stare deepening. "I am a man with my own opinions, a man who finds himself sitting astride an enormous dilemma. You are aware, I'm sure--just over a week ago, I was saved from an assassination attempt. There is belief, now, that the plot was conceived by Commander Shaklovity."

Tsykler held firm at the news, knowing that Peter was examining his expression for signs of guilt.

"I understand your loyalties to the Regent," Peter continued, his tone bearing authority, "but I will advise you now that the Regency nears its end. Given what has happened, I will no longer consent to be governed by Sophia."

Peter paused, allowing the words to linger in Tsykler's ears. The Colonel failed to hold his stony expression, his face betraying an inward buzz of anticipation.

Tsykler's initial fears had been soothed by the words of the Tsar; were he scheduled to be executed, the discussion would have been unnecessary. The Colonel was expecting a cold, public reception and had instead found himself warmly received, greeted immediately and granted privacy as a show of respect. Now Tsykler found himself warming, drawn by the demeanor of the Tsar and his own thoughts of the future.

Peter was persuasive, in presence alone, and imminently likeable. The Colonel had heard tales of the young Tsar's undeniable pull, but meeting the man, he now realized the truth of the rumor. The young man was driven by an energy all his own, a force which he was apparently quite comfortable extending. Here, now, in the presence of the crown, basking in the attention of Russia's favorite son, the Colonel's mind returned again and again to one dominating thought.

My promotion will be considerable. He needs me.

Like a falcon taking wing, Tsykler's thoughts were soaring high above the moment, his attention focused on the prosperity of the future.

What can Sophia possibly do for me now?

"Make no mistake, Colonel," Peter continued, raising his voice a bit, "This is no attempt to usurp power. I know this is of concern to you, but I cannot usurp what my brother and I already rightfully possess. This is truth. Ivan and I are both of age and have been performing our duties for years. I wish it to be clear to you and your men, Colonel Tsykler, that I have no intention of denying my brother his rightful place. Sophia will step down and we will continue to reign as co-tsars. Ivan, of course, will remain the senior. On this, I give you my word."

The boy will not be contained, Tsykler thought, his decision made. *He is more than ready.*

Tsykler bowed. "My lord, I am certain the Strel'tsy will be relieved to hear of your intentions."

"Our lives will soon change, Colonel. A change promised by the Holy Father and enacted by men like ourselves. This is my belief: As men, we act because God has placed us in the position to do so, a position that few others hold. Some men strive their entire lives to affect the world and others, men like ourselves, find themselves born in the enviable position to do so. As men, we act because we can. As patriots, we act because our country demands it. In your words, Colonel, the Strel'tsy serve the throne. I wish for this relationship to continue.

"I commanded you to come to Troitsky," Peter continued, "and you obeyed dutifully. Now I will beseech you as a man, not as a commander, and ask that you join in the defense of my brother and me. I ask that you continue to stand in defense of the throne, in the place where Russia needs you most. I wish for you to remain here at Troitsky until this situation is resolved. I assure you, Colonel, yours will not be the only regiment I call to my side. Being the most prominent and revered, you were, however, the obvious choice to be the first. "

Tsykler bowed again before the giant, his smile genuine. "I am honored by your flattery, my lord. The Stremyani strive to be the elite."

"Successfully," Peter added, nodding his approval. "And there is no question--there will be great need for capable souls in the new administration. We must move away from these family obligations and fill our ranks with those best suited to the post. In this, I must say that I concur with Prince Vasily and my half-sister Sophia. Do you agree, General?"

General? Tsykler mused, wondering at the Tsar's slip of the tongue.

"My lord, I would agree with your estimation and say that I, personally, am more than willing to do my part in the service of the Motherland. I am, however, yet a colonel."

"Colonel?"

"My lord, I believe you mistakenly called me 'General'."

"Did I?" Peter knit his brow, shrugging. "Well, considering that we were discussing promotions, I don't find it a bit odd. Soon enough, I expect. There is much to be resolved first. In all honesty, Colonel Tsykler, I wish this to be decided here and now--the better for both of us. You must tell me your evaluation of all I have said and give me your answer."

You play at war, and now at diplomacy, he thought, looking up at the Tsar. *Do you play at winning my loyalty as well?*

A new flower of suspicion bloomed within the Colonel, his baser instincts rising to warn of treachery. The Tsar was smarter than he'd expected--more forceful in his speech, brighter and more confident, ready by any estimation to take the throne.

The rumors spoke of a disobedient heir who, despite his capabilities, was impious and immature. Tsykler saw only a shrewd young man, unafraid and willing to play the game.

The boy could change his mind.

He could wait until he is rid of Sophia…or shovel me in with Shaklovity! How easy it would be to dismantle my regiment and put me up for trial!

The fear returned in that instant, rising to claim the thoughts of the Colonel and refocus him in the present.

I must secure my safety while I still can and I must get it in writing.

Standing like a child before the young man, his heart beating furiously, the military man composed his response.

"Tsar Peter, I will say that your speech is well-taken and I am truly grateful for the audience. If I may, I would also like to express my gratitude for the honorable manner in which my men and I have been received. I suspect that you have been in the company of enough old soldiers to know their peculiar ways."

Peter offered a grin and a nod but said nothing, waiting for the Colonel to continue.

"Regrettably, my lord, I must begin by stating my innocence in the matter of your delivery to Troitsky. I will swear by my life itself that I was occupied on that evening and that I know nothing of the traitorous plot."

"You are not a suspect," Peter returned. "Of this I have been assured. Please, continue."

"Thank the Holy Father. That news comes as a great relief, my lord." Tsykler hesitated, looking back at the Tsar. "Still…I know the power of rumors and false accusations. I worry that what is now my innocence can turn with a single lie and make me a guilty man. There would be others, as well--those who would seek to harm my regiment for our betrayal--members of the Miloslavsky clan who would surely spread a litany of lies should they be unable to cut our throats."

Peter remained silent, waiting for the rest.

"You have convinced me, my lord, that duty compels us to serve the throne, in the name of Tsars Ivan and Peter. I will remain here, in your service, my lord, but I would humbly ask a favor in return."

Peter's expression did not change. "You seek to insure your safety?" he asked.

The Colonel nodded. "I do, my lord."

"Then you need not worry," he replied immediately. "I will personally insure your safety, Colonel."

"I am grateful, sire, but if I may, I--"

"If it is treason that concerns you," Peter interjected, "you may rest assured that your name will not appear in connection with the attempt on my life. I do not suspect you, Colonel. You have my word."

Tsykler hesitated, leaving his worried frown in place. Eyes squinting as though he were in pain, the Colonel bowed slightly, showing his palms. "I am at your service, and the last thing I desire would be to offend you now by seeming ungrateful. I must, however, speak my mind, particularly in such an important moment."

"By all means, Colonel. Tell me your thoughts."

"I mean no insult when I say that with due respect to your word, my lord, there are still those who will disbelieve the tale of our reconciliation." Tsykler measured his words, treading carefully. "I would think that something more official, a written order, perhaps, would be far more convincing to those who might pursue me."

His words lingered in the air between them and for a moment he thought he'd stepped too far.

Do I ask too much? Stand behind your words, boy!

Peter's visage remained still for a moment before widening quickly into a broad grin. A smile followed, a hearty expression that seemed almost mocking in nature.

"You are wise to suggest it," Peter answered, his voice even and calm. "If you desire a written order to confirm my word, then you shall certainly have it. This is easily done, Colonel."

Tsykler relaxed, the knots inside him slowly loosening. "You have my gratitude, my lord."

"There is one last issue," Peter said. "We would ask of you, in the course of your duty, that you answer questions and divulge anything you might know regarding the conspirators. Are you amenable to this, Colonel?"

Tsykler thought again of Shaklovity, seeing the writing on the wall.

They will question and they will find enough in Fedor's past to incriminate him twice over. What damage can my contribution possibly do? They will execute Shaklovity. Fedor will die, with or without me.

With Peter's favor, I could take his place. Sixteen regiments at my beck and call. Strel'tsy Commander Tsykler.

"I will offer what I can, my lord," he answered. "Russia deserves nothing less."

Moscow, The Throne Room of the Faceted Palace in the Kremlin

August 26, 1689

The walls of the Palace echoed with the sound of twenty cautious feet--ten pairs, all of them clad in heavy leather boots, the clatter of their steps unopposed by the customary rumble of activity. The air carried a chill despite the season. The Palace lurked today, awaiting their arrival.

Fedor Shaklovity marched ahead of the reluctant group, his hand still clutching the order that summoned the remaining Russian colonels to the Regent's side.

More a request than a command, Sophia's call came in response to the dire news that Tsar Peter had written the colonels, ordering them to leave Moscow and attend him at Troitsky. Handwritten orders, the parchment bearing the signature of the Tsar.

Now Sophia called them to her side in the hope of countermanding Peter's order and securing their loyalty. Afraid of her temper, the colonels had been reluctant to comply, leaving no question in Fedor's mind that they were prepared to obey the Tsar and head out for Troitsky.

Shaklovity had convinced them to hear her words before leaving. The rest would be up to Sophia.

"Step quickly, gentlemen," he called back. "Dragging your feet will do you no good."

"Be assured, Commander," Colonel Kiprusov responded from behind, "we move as quickly as duty commands."

I have already lost their respect, he thought. *Without Tsykler to lead them, they become a rabble of boys!*

Sober and hungry, weary from thinking of the future, Fedor found himself in the worst mood possible. He screamed and raged within, restless, his emotions trapped hopelessly between anger and despair. There was no question now--his name, along with that of the monk Medvedev, was being circulated throughout the city, each word serving to reinforce the impression of guilt. Unable to defend themselves against a storm of rumors, he and the monk now stood as the prime suspects in the conspiracy to murder the Tsar.

And though Shaklovity felt no particular fondness for any of the Strel'tsy colonels, he understood the importance of this moment. Losing the colonels to Peter could prove a damning blow to the Regency--and a death sentence for anyone accused of plotting the crime.

Sophia will remain above suspicion. Would she sacrifice me to save the Regency? Need I ask?

His mind reeled, enrapt with what seemed the obvious outcome, chasing any possibility to avoid thoughts of a blade at his neck.

Medvedev spoke of leaving Moscow. Perhaps he will take the blame.

No--they will find him and bring him back.

I will be incriminated with or without him.

Damn Tsykler and that fool Joachim! They will lure the entire city to Peter's side!

Commander Shaklovity was a brutal and pragmatic soul and could easily figure the odds. With the Strel'tsy commanders at

Peter's side, there would be no need for the Tsarevich to return to his Fort at Preobrazhenskoe. From Troitsky, Peter would forgo the military and pursue his moral advantage, focusing on the alleged assassination attempt. Any and all investigations would begin with Peter's most vocal opponents, Shaklovity and Medvedev.

Still, there had been no official charges. Peter's game, apparently, was still concerned with the acquisition of the Strel'tsy command.

And so Fedor did his best to refocus on the task at hand, reminding himself that for the moment, the fate of the Regency was inseparable from his own.

Pausing at the massive golden doors of the Faceted Chamber, Fedor turned to address the group, maintaining an even stare.

"My comrades."

Better to disregard politeness, he thought, sensing hesitance in their stares.

"There will be far better moments to express my gratitude," he said, looking over the group, "so I will hold my accolades and simply say that in the coming days, we shall no doubt discover the true heart of the Strel'tsy!"

Dubious glances passed between the colonels. Kiprusov offered a venomous glare.

"I mean no insult, officers," Fedor continued, stiffening, "but be forewarned--the Regent still holds sway here in Moscow. She stands in the midst of a treacherous conspiracy, one from which we are obliged to defend her."

He thought of Tsykler, wondering if it would be wise to mention him.

"Make no mistake, colonels, this is a Naryshkin conspiracy, a plot to seize power and devalue our ranks! Despite the traitorous acts that have already occurred, our duty requires that we remain here in Moscow."

"Tsykler was not a traitor," Kiprusov answered, his face bearing defiance. "His orders came from the crown...sir. As do ours."

"I meant no offense to Colonel Tsykler," Shaklovity responded, scolding himself, "nor did I mention him. Colonel Tsykler has obviously been manipulated by circumstance and had no other wise course of action. There is no question that the Tsarevich keeps the Colonel against his will. Do you think Tsykler would abandon us? Would you follow him like dogs into captivity?"

Calm yourself, he thought, his temper slipping. *The bastards will defend Tsykler to the bitter end!*

"Gentlemen, the Regent is much maligned of late and remains innocent of the Naryshkins' wild allegations. Still, she is understandably...affected by this ordeal and will certainly be spitting fire. I pray you to indulge her and listen with your hearts open and your duty in mind."

"We arrived as ordered by the Regent," Kiprusov answered. "Is this not dutiful enough, sir?"

Shaklovity glared but did not snap back, knowing that a storm awaited.

"Certainly. For this, I am confident she will be grateful. As I said before, the Regent is your true benefactor. Do not forget who your enemies are, gentlemen."

Their allegiance hangs by a thread, he thought, reluctantly admitting the truth. *Sophia would be furious to know I'd angered them.*

"Let us proceed."

He motioned to the guard and the doors opened before them.

Can the Strel'tsy be so easily swayed? Sophia will straighten their collars!

His back to the wavering line of military men, Shaklovity stepped into the Chamber.

"You are welcome, Commander."

Sophia stood before the throne, dressed in a red silk letnik adorned with wide borders of embroidered satin, her hair pinned beneath a traditional headdress. Her rounded face depicted calm nobility, her chin lifted confidently as she watched the colonels form a line, saluting one by one as they met her stare. Sophia offered slight but significant nods and glances, remaining in stately character throughout.

The actor rises to meet the role, he thought, filling with pride. *Sophia has considered her approach...I should never have doubted her!*

"My lady," Shaklovity announced, bowing deeply. "The pride of your Strel'tsy command, reporting as ordered."

"We are pleased to see you, loyal comrades." Sophia's voice rang even and strong, her tone carrying authority. "Of all Moscow's treasures, you are the most honored and vital. Officers and native sons, you are the heart of the city and the strength of the Kremlin. We speak now on behalf of the throne and the Miloslavsky faithful, those who have so dearly counted on your support in years past.

"Our loyalty is hardest pressed in times of trouble," she continued without pause, as though working from memory. "Thus we thought it only fitting to call upon you to address this latest ploy on the part of our adversaries."

Fedor heard no sound from behind, wondering if the colonels were receptive. The Regent's face offered no indication of the success of her words.

She looked beautiful to him, standing tall like a pillar of grace, her look warm enough to seem fair and cold enough to provoke fear. At her best, Sophia was an incomparably hard woman.

They will respect her, he thought, his hopes lifting a bit.

"We will begin by stating simply that the Regency is innocent of these deceitful rumors, and we caution you, our strength, to recognize that no official charges have been levied. The Tsarevich himself acts on rumors, lies placed in his head by those who would see our beloved Ivan stripped of his right. These simple accusations have dark motives behind them, and we fear that the Patriarch himself has fallen victim to their persuasion. Now, as for Colonel Tsykler--"

"I have voiced our suspicions," Fedor blurted, interrupting her, "about Tsykler being held against his will, Regent."

She stared at him for a moment, her eyes quickly moving away to address the group.

"Commander Shaklovity believes that Colonel Tsykler is an unwilling guest of the Naryshkins," she said, her calm persisting. "Of this, we have no proof. I do think it likely, however, considering the Colonel's loyalty to our cause. We would be foolish to think that the Colonel would be easily broken. But officers, we must discuss the reason for your presence here today. I have been told of the letters you possess, the requests from Tsarevich Peter that you attend him at Troitsky."

Her words lingered in the echo of the high cross-vaulted ceiling, the colonels lined up before her like tin soldiers. Fedor closed his eyes for a moment, silently mouthing a prayer.

"We would remind you," she continued, stepping forward, "that your duty remains here, in Moscow. Here, with your people. The Naryshkins play at weakening us, but we refuse to allow it."

Now, as if on cue, Fedor could hear the shifting of feet and sighs coming from behind, the subtle sounds of discontent. Already, it seemed, the colonels were resisting, knowing where the Regent would ultimately arrive.

Sophia walked down the line, addressing the colonels individually as she spoke. "Comrades, these documents have no official authority. They could well be forgeries. Trust, however, that the Regency endures and that we will continue to perform our duties until the day that Russia requires us to step down. The throne will not respond to lies and treachery…and neither will the Strel'tsy."

Here it comes, he thought, asking the Holy Father for assistance. *Please let her prevail!*

"We will ask that you remain in Moscow," she stated broadly, pausing to insure that all were listening. "The throne requests the presence of the Strel'tsy. We ask you to disregard all other orders."

The colonels' respectful quiet was shattered all at once, as the military men began to voice their concern. The line behind Fedor buzzed with whispers and murmured comment. He turned to see the colonels bearing worried looks, appealing to each other for assistance. From their ranks, Colonel Kiprusov stepped forward.

"May I speak, my lady?"

Sophia turned to face Kiprusov, striding politely to his place. "Certainly, Colonel."

The Colonel produced one of the handwritten orders from his pocket, holding it out as though it were a saber. His wide, bearded face carried a mortally serious look.

"Our orders, Regent--they come from the Tsar himself. They bear his signature."

Fedor's soul sagged within him, the truth striking home.

He looked to Sophia, watching as the diplomatic calm faded from her expression, replaced by the bitter scowl he'd seen so many times before. The corners of her lips turned bitterly to mouth her furious response.

"Peter is still the Tsarevich," she answered sharply. "As I am still Regent."

"If you please, Regent," Kiprusov pressed, "Tsarevich Peter shares the throne with Tsarevich Ivan. And the Strel'tsy serve the throne. This is without question."

"And now, after all that has happened, you feel obliged to obey the orders of that boy?" Sophia pointed angrily. "You act on rumor and accusation, Colonel! You would march your troops willingly into captivity? Can you not see the truth of this?"

Kiprusov maintained, standing proudly. "We are all obliged, Lady. Compelled. None wish to ponder what it would mean to ignore the personal commands of the Tsarevich. Regent, I--"

"You defiant little man! How would you like to consider the repercussions of disobeying me?"

"My lady?"

"You will address me as Regent, Colonel! You will remember who has lifted all of you from the gutters where you lurked not ten years ago! Your orders, gentlemen, are unfounded and very likely forgeries. They will be disregarded. You will cancel all plans of departure and return to the Kremlin barracks--where you will remain!"

Sophia's face bore the full weight of her anger now, her hateful stare searching the eyes of her defiant command. Shaklovity stood frozen, unwilling to add to her tirade for fear of breaking its rhythm, the hole within him growing despite her vehement defense.

"But Regent, you mean to keep us in the Kremlin barracks?"

The colonels offered another murmured chorus of discontent, voicing their dissent. Only those under Sophia's direct scrutiny held their tongues.

She stepped back to stand before the double-seated throne, turning slowly to face the group. All eyes upon her, Sophia took a deep breath, never breaking her stare.

"None of you will leave Moscow," she told them, raising a hand to her throat. "Or I promise I will have your heads! The same goes for your men. Is this clear enough?"

Kiprusov's eyes narrowed, his stance never changing. "Yes, Regent. Quite clear."

"I warn you," she followed quickly, her voice like a sharpened blade. "Do not defy me. I will not hesitate to act. You are dismissed."

With a look, Shaklovity motioned for the colonels to exit, his own face reflecting none of the Regent's anger. They filed past him like beaten dogs, bitterly shocked and hanging their sorry heads, looking up at him as though he'd betrayed them. For the moment, at least, the situation had been remedied. The colonels would remain in Moscow.

It would have been foolish, however, to assume that Sophia's threats would carry no repercussions. These were, after all, local militia, soldiers who'd come from a far less civilized military background than their foreign counterparts. Their anger would remain and would eventually have to be answered.

"You will be compensated," Sophia announced as they exited, her appeal falling on wounded ears. "As always, your obedience will be well rewarded."

They made no more protest, but their footsteps told the story of their minds. The Strel'tsy would remain, but grudgingly.

She does what she must, Fedor thought watching as the colonels stomped away. He remained behind as the doors closed, waiting for his opportunity to speak with her alone.

Will she fight so hard for poor Shaklovity?

"I did not ask that you remain behind," she told him, her voice still carrying anger. "I have no desire to hear your complaint now."

"No complaint, Lady," he responded kindly, approaching her. "On the contrary, I want to commend you for your strength and resolve."

"I was a bear. Just as I'd feared I would be. But Fedor, how else was I to respond?"

"You have done just the right thing, Lady. They left you with no other option."

"The Regency will not stand for their exit," she stated, shaking her head. "I did not wish to threaten, but with their love of old Tsykler, how would we ever have convinced them? Tell me, Fedor, will they stay?"

She looked at him with sympathetic eyes, and he wanted to tell her she was right.

"For now, Lady," he replied, trying to sound confident. "We must pray that your words are enough to keep them in Moscow."

"Was I not kind enough?"

"You were as you should be," he replied. "How could you have responded otherwise--with so much at stake. I believe you have done the best in your power, Sophia."

She began to pace, enrapt in thought. "Would I have the Tsarevich take my entire army with a few handwritten letters? Does Natalya think me so timid?"

"They test you. They remain at Troitsky to further their conspiracy, Lady. With no officers, we are hardly capable of defending ourselves--against rumors as well as cannons! Had he won the army, Peter's next move would be to press the accusations."

She turned, glaring at him. "You think of yourself! Don't you, Fedor?"

"Would you expect otherwise?" he said, his own temper finally making an entrance. "The whole of Moscow thinks I'm sending assassins to kill Peter! Half of them think I was plotting to do it myself!"

"There have been no official charges from Troitsky."

Shaklovity chuckled with disgust. "Charges? Lady, the charges have all been made! A piece of parchment may make them official, but the villains in this charade have already been chosen."

"I have heard nothing of Father Medvedev…"

"Nor will you," he answered, frowning at the thought of his wayward accomplice. "He cowers in silence, waiting for the axe to fall. If I know Sylvester well enough, I would say that he plans to leave Moscow. I, unfortunately, have no such luxury."

Sophia's face dropped. "You wouldn't think of leaving me, would you, Fedor?"

Shaklovity sighed, looking into her eyes. "Never, Lady. You have my word that I will remain, though I do not expect the Tsarevich to seek my support. My summons will be of a different nature."

She needs me, he thought, watching her reaction closely. *I must make her fear her own demise.*

"Your summons will be ignored," she said, nodding as though she could make it true. "I will not let them take you, Fedor. Trust in this. It would only be an admission of guilt and we have done nothing but our duty."

"I am at your mercy, Sophia…" He moved closer, arms outstretched. Sophia stepped back, away from his embrace, the frown telling him it was not the right time.

And though the Regent's lips were speaking the words he wanted to hear, the practical soul within Shaklovity could not come to peace with her promises. Sophia was too much of an optimist, carrying belief that verged on denial when the situation became critical. She would respond as her temper demanded and fight like a lion to salvage her Regency.

But what of Shaklovity? How easily my death could become the solution to her problems…

Were he asked what she could have done differently, Fedor could not have given an answer. The standoff continued, and for better or worse, the colonels would now be confined to Moscow. With luck, Peter would abandon his charade and return to Preobrazhenskoe.

But beneath the thin layer of hope, in his cold and practical heart, Shaklovity's fear still loomed, dark and deadly, whispering to him that the ordeal would end only with the removal of his pitiful head.

Outside Moscow, The Monastery of Troitskaya-Sergeeva

August 27, 1689

"Everyone will address you as Tsar now. And you must demand it. Just as in the letters..."

Boris Golitsyn spoke to Peter but nodded to himself, his thoughts consumed by details.

Rarely had the young ruler sought his private counsel, but on this occasion Golitsyn had seen it coming. Peter was fearless and willing to take action, but only in the midst of crisis was the young Tsar realizing where the real family work was done. Overcome by the myriad of concerns, enduring the endless procession of supporters and well-wishers, Peter had come in polite fashion, seeking a private conversation. Boris had been flattered, but consented in a routine manner.

Now he stood alone with the Tsar, offering his opinions and gaining great satisfaction from the fact that Peter was listening. Gone was the petulant wit and defiant attitude, replaced in the young man by a simmering calm, a noble anger reminiscent of his father.

"Do you think she has seen them?" Peter asked, the talk of Sophia bringing a serious look to his face. "The orders summoning the colonels, I mean?"

"Certainly. Given the delay in their arrival, I would say that either the Regent or the Prince was directly involved."

"Do the colonels defy me, then?"

"A difficult question to answer, sire. Colonel Tsykler remarked that the delay was to be expected. I tend to disagree."

"Tell me."

Boris shrugged. "Well, sire, were we speaking of the foreign colonels, we might suppose that the Regent appealed to their mercenary instincts or simply paid them more to remain in Moscow. But your letters were sent to native sons; their hearts and reputations are deeply engaged in this matter. In truth, I expected them to follow Colonel Tsykler willingly. It appears now that we may have other conditions."

The lack of news from Moscow was disheartening. Despite the procession of nobles and well-wishers who flocked to the Monastery, Boris knew that their recent victories would mean nothing if the remainder of the Strel'tsy refused to comply with the young Tsar's orders. Peter's attempt to rally the entirety of the Strel'tsy command had been a bold move, seeming more shrewd than risky at the time. Now, Boris found himself wondering if the ploy had been wise.

"Sophia has made an appeal, then." Peter stood from his chair, brushing the hair from his eyes. "She played to their loyalties, no doubt. The colonels see the meaning in delivering me only ten men each. Had I sent for the entire regiment, it would surely have been considered a call to arms."

"Quite true, sire. I see no reason to question your method."

Peter cocked his head. "I questioned nothing, Counselor."

"Of course not, sire. I meant to say that the Strel'tsy are an unpredictable lot. Whatever the delay, I expect we will know soon."

The young Tsar nodded. "I sent Troekorov out to the gates to receive the couriers."

"Oh?"

"He was quite shaken by the appearance of his father, you know. Recovered now, of course, but I thought he might drop from lack of air when he first saw his papa stepping humbly across the threshold. I don't know whether Sophia is being clever or simply grasping for ideas. Did she truly think that sending Troekorov could affect my mood? She plays at madness…or at least smiles at it."

"The Regent has undoubtedly heard of the support for you pouring in from Moscow, sire. Troitsky has never seen so many visitors. With the Duma quieted, Sophia is surely noticing the difference. Everyone seeks your favor."

Peter grinned a bit. "Indeed. I'm grateful that Mother and Uncle Lev are willing to share the burden of the well-wishing. Most of them have their eyes fixed on the future."

"They have come, sire, and in that, there is little difference. They are cautious, perhaps, but not half-hearted. Trust that the Boyar Council sympathizes with your cause."

"Yes, yes--but we must know of the Strel'tsy. There lies our solution, eh?"

"We will know in time, sire," Boris responded, enjoying the Tsar's reaction. "Respectfully, there are other matters requiring your attention and--"

"Without question," Peter snapped, cutting him short. "I must finish my letter to Ivan."

"Certainly, sire, but I was thinking more of the writ of official charges."

Peter paused, exhaling. "In truth, I had hoped to win the Strel'tsy before accusing their Commander of treason. Do you think it wise to act now, Boris?"

Golitsyn tensed a bit, having expected no resistance.

The sooner he is charged, the sooner we part from the night in question. Better to act now, as though there were no question of Fedor's guilt.

"I think it very wise," Boris finally responded, nodding with a dramatic air. "I fear that Shaklovity is the snake that whispers in the ear of the Regent. Freeing Sophia from her advisors may be the best way to see her acting with reason. And certainly, Shaklovity's arrest could very well sway the remainder of the Strel'tsy."

"Or enrage them further," Peter added, quick to counter him.

"I think it unlikely, sire," Boris responded immediately, knowing how difficult the young Tsar was to convince. "The rank and file hold no undue affection for Commander Shaklovity. Like the rest of the city, they look to the future, sire. They seek to find a comfortable place within your reign."

"Our reign," he answered. "Ivan will be Tsar as well."

"Yes, of course, sire."

Peter looked at him, thinking it through. "But if the Strel'tsy are so eager to capitulate, then where are our colonels?"

A knock sounded on the chamber door.

"We may have our answer," Boris said, moving to open it.

Ivan Troekorov, the younger, stood on the opposite side of the door, his bright eyes traced with a look of concern. Golitsyn nodded to him and ushered him into the room, closing the door behind him. A bit out of breath, Troekorov fell to a knee before Peter.

"My lord, the courier has arrived."

"Quite good, Ivan." Peter moved to lift him by the arm. "Stand up, stand up--tell me what has happened. What did the courier report?"

"The Regent has confined the colonels to quarters, sire. She ordered the command to remain in Moscow and promised to behead all who disobey."

Peter's eyes narrowed. "And the colonels obeyed?"

Troekorov nodded meekly. "Yes, sire. They protested, but did as she ordered. Their men are deserting, sire. Fifteen lost during the night."

Deserters? Golitsyn's mood improved quite suddenly, his own elation equaled by the apparent distress of the Tsar.

"She counters my order?" Peter paced, his anger awakened. "Who does she think the Strel'tsy serve?"

Deserters mean support among the Strel'tsy. The charges against Shaklovity and Medvedev will hit them like cannon shot!

"She tests my will, Boris, not that of the Strel'tsy! How dare she leave this on the shoulders of the colonels!"

"It seems the Regent has drawn the battle lines herself, sire." Golitsyn offered a reassuring look. "We could not have asked for a better situation."

Peter's pacing stopped. "Your meaning?"

"Well, sire...put simply, the question is not whether the throne rules the Strel'tsy, but rather who rules the throne. We wish to leave no question that you have ascended to your rightful place and that your word comes before that of the Regent. We also seek to win the native Strel'tsy sons. Her ultimatum offers the opportunity for both. "

Peter's eyes widened suddenly, his face brightening. "Yes...yes! Of course, Boris! We will draft another round of orders for the colonels, but this time I will equal Sophia's punishment!"

"Yes, sire!"

"They will come immediately to Troitsky or be executed as traitors! Let her force their defiance now!"

Boris smiled confidently, nodding his reassurance. There was no question; the boy had always been sharp, but feeling the connection of thought, Golitsyn could not deny that Peter had a wonderfully politic mind. When focused, he was as shrewd a thinker as could be found in the Duma. Aside from his progressive inclinations, there was little to question.

I must commend him for his initiative.

"Given such an order, they will surely comply, sire. All of Moscow will know who commands the Strel'tsy."

"And if they refuse?"

Golitsyn waved away the question. "Unlikely, sire. You have the Patriarch, the Duma, and Mother Russia herself standing behind you. Who will they fear more? The answer is quite obvious. To put it plainly: your executioner's axe is bigger than hers, my lord."

Peter stared for a moment, then burst out laughing. "Quite good, Boris! We must wait for your wit, but when it finally arrives, it comes bearing a tremendous punch!"

"You flatter in excess, sire."

"Hah! You see? There is another!"

Troekorov was grinning now as well, waiting expectantly for an order from the Tsar. Peter walked over to pat him on the shoulder, looking down with affection.

"Good work, my friend. Wait outside, and I'll have a message shortly for you to send back with the courier."

"Yes, my lord." Troekorov bowed and turned for the door.

Peter's smile faded as he closed the door behind the young officer. "You will help me write the orders, Boris. I don't wish them to misread my poor handwriting."

"I am at your service, my lord."

"We shall also put ourselves to the task of my letter to Ivan." Peter hovered over the desk in the corner of the room, shuffling through the parchment. "I have much of it finished already, but you may offer your opinion."

As the Tsar searched for his letter, Boris watched, his mind clinging to more personal thoughts than Ivan's enlightenment. Still there remained the question of his cousin Vasily and what would ultimately become of Sophia's favorite.

Boris had always prided himself in his devotion to his family and was adamant about declaring all of his clan, with the exception of Prince Vasily, to be supporters of Natalya, Peter, and the Naryshkins. As of yet, the Prince remained free of any accusations in the matter. Given his proximity to the Regent, however, it seemed unlikely that he could remain so forever.

Golitsyn cleared his throat, reassuring himself. "Sire, if I may…"

"I know it's here somewhere," Peter replied without looking up, still enrapt in his search. "If you may what, Boris?"

"If I may re-direct our conversation, sire, to once again address the subject of the charges. Personally, I believe that Shaklovity and the monk pose the potential for further danger. They are not without their pockets of support, and I expect that the remaining Miloslavsky faithful will rally to their side. The more expeditiously they are charged and arrested, the sooner the Regent will feel pressured to step aside."

It felt a bit inappropriate, speaking in such blunt terms, but Peter seemed to appreciate his candor.

The Tsar looked up, the letter found and in hand. "Here it is! Somewhat unreadable, granted, but I'll sort out the ugly bits."

"Sire?"

"Yes, Boris?"

"The accused will be arrested and brought here…to Troitsky. If it is agreeable with you, of course, sire."

"Here?" Peter's lips turned to a grin. "Sophia's dog on a leash--that will certainly be a sight to see! But what of the other conspirators? What of the assassins themselves, and what shall I do with Sophia? Do we charge her?"

"This is left to your discretion, Tsar, but if I may suggest--"

"Of course, Boris. That's why I called you here."

"Charging the Regent with an attempt on your life would require a definitive outcome--either her trial and execution, or her absolution. Once charged, she would no doubt offer protest. And though it is apparent that Shaklovity is involved, we have nothing that would indicate that Sophia spurred him into action. In fact, it is widely believed that his prior transgressions were all committed on his own. Sophia would gain sympathy, and some would no doubt view your action as vindictive."

"I have no wish for her head," Peter said, hesitating.

"This is your decision to make, sire."

"And the assassins?"

Boris shifted. "Not yet found, sire. We are still trying to determine their identity. At the appropriate time, I assure you they will be charged as well."

Peter stared for a moment, his look taken by Golitsyn as suspicion. The boy seemed too thoughtful not to have ruminated on the assassination plot and too quick not to have guessed that something was afoot.

Has he guessed what has happened? Golitsyn wondered, his own look unchanging. *With such an enticing future, does he truly care how we arrived at this moment?*

Peter tilted his head. "You press the subject of the charges, Boris."

"Sire?"

"You push to have Shaklovity in irons," Peter said frankly, "and I know why."

Boris' throat tightened, his lips unready to respond.

"Sire? I press because I feel our cause in need."

"You press to protect your cousin Vasily," Peter countered quickly. "The mighty Prince V.V.! Am I not right?"

Golitsyn's stomach loosened its nervous clench, his bout of fear remedied as suddenly as it had afflicted him. Boris cleared his throat before resuming.

"Though the word 'protect' implies that I think him guilty, I assure you that I am of quite the opposite mind on the subject."

"Certainly, Boris."

"I do, however, know the power of rumor and accusation," Boris continued, his words finally flowing, "and with respect, sire, I fear that he may be wrongfully entrapped by lies and resentment. In turn, I must think of the rest of my clan and stand in their defense. I would remind you that Vasily is the only one of my family who supports, or has ever supported, the Miloslavskys."

"Yes, a common fact."

"In his own right, my cousin has persisted in a lifetime of service to the throne--and though many of us have often felt his loyalties to be misguided, we are still able to recognize his achievements. The return of Kiev is the first to come to mind, but as you well know, sire, there are many others."

"I would agree."

"Certainly his service in the Duma cannot be underestimated, and to my knowledge, he has never been one to disparage you personally--"

"Stop, Boris! Enough!" Peter held up his hands in surrender, exhaling with a groan. "You don't need to recount his personal history!

I'm fully aware of Prince V.V.'s role. Your cousin is well-acquainted with Patrick Gordon, you know."

"Yes, sire."

"Gordon respects the Prince as a man, but has little faith in his ability to command. And you have always been the one to tell me, Boris: the pikes of the Strel'tsy follow their greatest complaints. Prince Vasily's mismanagement of the Crimean Campaigns must be addressed if the Strel'tsy are to be ultimately won. The bitterness over the war is foremost in their minds."

Natalya pushes him, Boris thought, staring back at the Tsar.

"If he remains above the talk of treason, then surely his poor generalship can earn him only a small penalty."

Peter stood from his place, stepping closer, his size immediately threatening. "Understand me well, Boris! Prince V.V. has been standing beside my half-sister for the entirety of her Regency--lying in her bed despite his wife, claiming what he could in accolade, filling his substantial coffers and becoming the very face of the government. Neither he nor Sophia could have achieved such heights alone. So I do not begrudge him his place or his credit, Boris, but he was her bloody partner in this--in every step, including the murder of my family! The two will exit the Regency as they entered…together."

"Sire, if I--"

"And if Sophia is to remain in Moscow, then Vasily must leave it. I will hear nothing more."

"Yes, sire."

Boris stood quiet for a moment, trying to assimilate all that had just been said.

"Sire, are you saying that you have no plan to seek Sophia's head?"

Peter paused before speaking. "At the moment, I have no inclination to do so. Could I see the future, I might know what the end result will really be. I think it better to keep her in Moscow where I may keep watch over her. Mother has spoken of retiring her to the Novodevichi Convent and I think it fitting. After all, Sophia has donated enough to possess her own wing--let her rot there."

Golitsyn bowed, putting aside his worries and trying to regain his diplomatic feet. There was much to be happy about, including his impressions of the young Tsar's passion and initiative. In this, Boris knew his work had been done. Peter's mind was thinking ahead, already removed from the thoughts of assassination and looking to Sophia's destiny.

Merciful, Golitsyn thought, bowing again to show his understanding. *He will keep Sophia right beneath his nose. But what of Vasily?*

Peter walked to the carved wooden cabinet and opened the doors, producing a flagon of vodka and two silver cups. Walking back to the desk, he set down the cups and reached out with his long arm to pull a second chair alongside his own.

"Boris, sit," he offered, pointing to the chair. "We will have a drink and set to work. There is much to do, and I'm still in great need of your assistance."

Boris moved to the chair and sat obediently.

"First, to the task of writing the official charges against Shaklovity and Medvedev--that should make you happy!" Peter poured the drinks, offering one. "Here you go--bottoms up--that's right. How is your handwriting, Boris? Good, as I recall, yes? Good, then. Once the charges are finished, we'll set to writing those orders. Sophia will surely read them, so we must consider every word!"

Golitsyn held his tongue and listened as the Tsar spoke, soaking up the torrent of words and ideas that emerged from the energetic young mind. There was no question--Peter's time with the foreign tutors had cultivated his political ability, and his tongue could match his wit without fail. Natalya was loath to hear of her son's political leanings, but there was no doubt in Boris' mind that, given the chance, Peter could turn out to be more progressive than either Alexis or Sophia. The first years of his reign would have to be tightly managed.

Soon, they will bring the Strel'tsy Commander in chains, he thought, staring at the scrawl that Peter called handwriting.

When the Strel'tsy colonels arrive, we will have an undeniable advantage. If Sophia forces them to stay, she will have a riot on her hands.

The ball was rolling now, the distant future at their fingertips. After all the questions and doubts, the Regent's exit seemed inevitable. And despite Peter's shortcomings, there was no question in the Counselor's mind that their faith in him was well placed.

As for his own status, Boris considered himself to be well-positioned for the change, better, perhaps, than any of the other Naryshkin supporters. And though he realized that prominent posts in Russia were often the most precarious, it seemed far better to be in a position from which he could save himself should the conspiracy be revealed.

I must take the lead in Shaklovity's interrogation, he thought, his mind rushing back to thoughts of the conspiracy. *We must be done with him quickly!*

Moscow, The Great Sovereign's Palace of The Kremlin

September 6, 1689

"They are gone, Regent. Gone to Troitsky."

"How many?"

"Five or six colonels, including Kiprusov. Who knows how many men accompanying them--a rabble like that is hard to count. I would guess around a hundred men. We'd been losing men during the night, but this was like a damned parade of them, deserting all at once and knowing there was safety in it!"

"I should execute the rest for allowing them to leave!" Sophia snapped in reply, her head spinning with failure. Shaklovity looked like a beaten dog before her, his gaze weak with fatigue.

"The orders from the Tsar were quite strict and promised execution."

"And so they run off into the night! Apparently, death by my executioner is preferable to that of Peter's!"

"I hear that he summoned some of the Moscow nobles as well, though I don't expect that he threatened to take their heads."

She reached for the goblet of wine she'd left sitting earlier, drinking deeply in an attempt to ease her aching head. The waiting had proven the most difficult part of the ordeal; never before had she been so acutely aware of her restrictions. Considering the nature of the scandal, few were willing to provide her the information she so desperately needed. By the time Fedor arrived, Sophia was ranting and bitter, ready to fight.

Tonight his news came as no surprise.

"Peter sent notice to the Kremlin this time," she commented, holding up the letter. "Official notice to Tsarevich Ivan and to me that he has commanded the colonels. I sent Ivan's tutor, Bucharev, to explain that the soldiers were delayed and to beg for reconciliation."

"You send a tutor to beg for peace?" Shaklovity asked, absent his decorum. "After all the others were turned away."

"And who else could I send? You, Fedor?"

"It would make no difference. Not even the ghost of old Alexis himself could convince the boy. What was it that Peter told old Troekorov?"

"That he no longer consents to be governed by a woman," came a voice from the doorway.

Shaklovity turned to look. "Ah, yes. At long last, Prince Golitsyn makes his entrance!"

"Vasily!"

Vasily stepped into the room with a stern look, closing the door behind him. "You would be wise to keep the door shut," he said, wiping his forehead with a handkerchief. "I could hear you arguing all the way down the corridor."

"No matter now," Sophia commented, wanting him to hear the distress in her tone. "There is no one left to hear us."

"The tutor was sent back to Moscow," Vasily told her, speaking as though it were no surprise. "The Tsarevich refused to see him."

She turned away, holding back an urge to cry out in rage. With the departure of the Strel'tsy colonels, the truth was too obvious to deny. In a matter of mere weeks, she had been defamed--her strength made weakness, her position obsolete. Even those who hated Peter seemed compelled by the power of his name. Sophia wiped at her eyes, unwilling to show her fear.

She could remember standing in Red Square and looking up at the beautifully painted domes of Saint Basil's, feeling as though all of Moscow belonged to her, staring at the Kremlin and knowing that she, Sophia Miloslavsky, ruled within its mighty walls.

No longer did this familiarity rest within the heart of the Regent. The Kremlin had become suddenly unfriendly, of late seeming more a cage than a castle. What had once belonged to her now seemed little more than State property. Even her personal items seemed foreign and inappropriate, a condition of disenchantment that only increased in the long stretches of time spent alone in her chambers.

And now she stood with both of them, Shaklovity and Prince Vasily--the constructors of her success, the guardians of her strength, her lovers, now stripped of all their influence and bravery, left with only fearful doubt in the face of Peter's ambition.

"What of the foreign colonels?" she asked, straightening her posture and turning back to face them. "Do we still possess their service?"

"The Tsarevich has made no overtures to the foreign colonels," the Prince replied, hesitating. "As of yet…"

"You are still well-liked by the majority, Vasily, despite the trouble in the Crimea. Gordon and the others still have respect for you. I would think that you could do something to…secure their presence in Moscow."

Vasily frowned. "My orders are quickly overruled by those of the Tsarevich. Today's mass exodus is proof enough."

"The good Prince knows," Shaklovity huffed. "Peter will summon the foreign officers in time. Why should we not expect so?"

"He may not require them," Golitsyn replied, looking back to Sophia. "The departure of our colonels puts us in dire circumstance, Regent."

"He couldn't possibly be thinking of attacking Moscow. Does he plan to come marching through the gates with the Strel'tsy at his back? If so, then he wishes our heads!"

"He wishes to leave you with no support, my lady."

Fedor nodded again. "Yes. He wishes to leave you with no defense--no one to sound the alarm bell when he comes calling for your head!"

Sophia froze at the thought, despising him for bringing it up so crudely.

"This is lunacy," she said, rubbing her forehead to ease the throbbing. "He cannot rightfully pluck me from my place without some charge."

"You've heard his charge!" Shaklovity shouted at her. "He is of age and no longer consents to be governed by you, my lady! With the Patriarch and the Strel'tsy in his right and left pockets, he needs no other charge!"

Within, she struggled, unwilling to surrender hope. The Regency was still officially in place and Ivan's needs would never change, despite his age. And though it remained only a distant glimmer of light in what had become a long dark tunnel, Sophia nonetheless chose to cling to her faith and press for a solution.

"I am innocent," she told them, lowering her tone, "and cannot rightfully be removed by mere accusations. Peter rallies support without charging me and refuses to see my envoys."

Fedor sighed. "He will continue to do so--"

"Do not interrupt me, Commander." She glared without mercy.

Fedor stared back, his scowl fading slowly. "You have my apologies, Regent. You understand, I hope…the passions of an innocent man."

Vasily stared over at him. "Innocent?"

"Of this crime?" Shaklovity asked, bearing offence. "Of course I am. I planned no attempt on Peter's life."

"Yes, but you talked of it often."

"You press my patience," Fedor snapped back at him. "I stand falsely accused and no one in this Palace is in more danger than I."

"Quiet, Fedor!" she shouted back, her voice towering above all else. "I will not hear it! No charges have been made--there must certainly be a reason. Peter turns away my envoys but neither attacks nor makes charges. He is expecting something else…"

And then, in what seemed a rather obvious revelation, the idea sprang to mind.

"We will travel to Troitsky," she said, thinking aloud. "Peter seeks my personal attention. I always intimidated that boy--as a man he is no different to me. I will speak with him and all will be resolved."

Fedor sprang to life, twitching with anger. "Impossible! Regent, he will arrest us on the spot!"

"Ridiculous," she responded. "You forget, he is with the Patriarch."

"Precisely! My lady, the Patriarch is no friend. I will be arrested!"

She waved away his comment, her decision made. "Don't be foolish, Fedor. I wouldn't let them take you." She turned to the Prince. "Vasily, your thoughts?"

"I loathe the thought of it," he replied drolly, "but your idea is valid, Regent. Perhaps the Naryshkins are simply seeking a better position."

"Good, then," she said, feeling much better. "Fedor, I shall rely on you to make the arrangements for travel."

He shook his head. "Lady, we must at least take an escort. Considering their numbers and the Monastery itself, a regiment or more."

"One regiment," she relented, her mind already moving forward. "Unnecessary, but you have my permission. I suppose we must appear strong. Make the arrangements, Fedor, and be quick because you'll need your rest. When Peter and the Patriarch greet us, trust that you will be standing right beside me!"

Outside Moscow, The Village of Vozdvizhenskoe

September 10, 1689

Resting comfortably only eight miles away from the great Monastery of Troitskaya-Sergeeva, the small village of Vozdvizhenskoe sat along the road that led to the great landmark, proudly facilitating the comings and goings of the esteemed figures who passed through their humble midst. Somewhat larger than most, the small community was traditionally quiet and hard-working. Captain Ivan Buturlin had been told that Vozdvizhenskoe was a sleepy little village. As his small troop of musketeers approached on the cool September afternoon, however, the villagers appeared in numbers, wide awake and curious about the day's events.

"The whole lot of them," Buturlin mumbled to himself, staring at the lines of gossiping babushkas. The gathering of peasants stretched toward them, reaching out to encompass the soldiers, their questions and calls sounding from every dwelling in the village.

My actions will be noted, Ivan thought, looking down at the marks of rank on his green Preobrazhensky coat. *I cannot fail. Peter has put his trust in me.*

"Stay tight," he called back to the men, raising a pointed finger through the crowd to show them the direction. "And hold your tongues!"

The peasants shouted Peter's name in support, reaching out their hands to touch the soldiers and pat them on their unsteady backs. Tempered by trepidation, the men limited their responses to uneasy smiles and nods, happy to receive the support but still nearly petrified at the thought of what was to come. Like Buturlin, the men were stricken, their attention held captive by their task.

A simple request by words alone. Tsar Peter's commands were clear. The Regent and her party were to be denied access to the road to Troitsky. No one was to pass.

Their departure had been fervent and glorious, fists raised in loyalty and unstoppable desire, their company setting out to make history in the name of Tsar Peter. Buturlin had eagerly complied with the order, proud to be selected for such service. Similarly, his men were Preobrazhensky recruits, green and fearless by ignorance. With luck, their spirit would be enough to overcome the will of the Regent.

Buturlin remained unconvinced.

Peter thinks me capable, he mused, the accolades of the villagers having little effect. *I must show myself to be so.*

And where can Troekorov be? Does he expect me to call down Sophia myself?

The thought was troubling. Buturlin, of course, had never been in a position to exchange words with the Regent or Prince Golitsyn, and though his enthusiasm was great, he neared the moment of truth with his confidence fading…and without Troekorov.

"Bless you, Captain!"

"Bless you and Tsar Peter!"

"Good work, Captain! The Holy Father stands with you!"

Do they expect a battle? he wondered, nodding his acknowledgment as he pressed through the crowd. *Do we? If the village knew of our coming, what of the Regent?*

They moved in single file, breaking free from the group of well-wishers and heading for the opposite edge of the village. A few of the young men remained with them, falling in stride and proudly patting their chests.

They welcome the new Tsar! If only Peter were here to see it!

Will they be so supportive when the Regent arrives?

Ivan took a deep breath, struggling against the ache in his stomach, trying to look courageous. His friendship with Peter had always been his greatest treasure, his pride and prosperity, the future that awaited so many in his lowly position. He'd been granted rank and importance by the Tsar and now was his time to repay the debt.

I should speak to them, he thought, halting his pace and turning to face his men. *Peter would certainly do as much.*

A hunched babushka in a pale blue kerchief had been following at her own pace and now descended upon the Captain, taking his hand in her rigid grasp.

"Blessings upon you! Bless Tsar Peter!"

He looked down at her, forcing a grin.

The company was gathering around, watching as he addressed the old woman.

"You have our faith!" she told him, her voice a shrill drone of local dialect. "Should you die, we will bury you with respect. The Holy Father will know of your sacrifice."

"Spaciba, babushka." He nodded, prying her hand from his, placing a hand on her shoulder to lead her to the side. Gratefully, she complied, finding a place at the edge of the road.

"A new friend, Captain?" came the call from among the men, the comment promptly followed by a round of chuckles.

Buturlin glared at them, not caring who spoke the words.

"I am relieved to see you so confident, for it seems that an old woman has figured our chances better than we have. Straighten up, the lot of you!"

The company re-formed before him, their smiles fading quickly. Friends, most of them, some that he'd known since childhood, compatriots in the cause of Peter's ascension. Their green coats matched their experience; fresh and untested, handsome but lacking the seasoned look of veterans, each longing to make his mark in the field. A few were good shots and a few others capable in close quarters, but none stood ready for an armed encounter with a Strel'tsy battalion. They stared back at him with devoted, willing faces, looking to his lead.

He'd spoken at length with the Tsar before his departure, a conversation that left Ivan feeling as though he could conquer all of Europe, bursting with pride and certain that he would succeed. Peter delivered his orders with an infectious air of confidence, an affect that left the recipient feeling as though his task would be simple and easily performed. Ivan was empowered in his presence and now tried to summon inspiration with thoughts of Peter's forceful grin.

"Do not let the compliments fool you," he told them, raising his voice only enough for the company. "We have done nothing yet. Our task remains vital and we stand under the orders of the Tsar himself. Can you think of facing the Tsar in failure?"

His words had an immediate effect, the men's faces sobering, stern with determination.

"We must prevent the Regent's party from reaching Troitsky," he continued, pacing his words so that every one of them might hear, "but you are to do nothing without my lead. Am I understood? Keep your fingers off your triggers unless I give the command."

"But..."

"What is it, Yuri?"

The soldier's face paled. "Do you expect that...we'll really have to fight, sir?"

He wanted to snap back at the recruit, but held his temper.

"We cannot know," the Captain replied honestly, unable to form a more suitable response. "Had he expected trouble, I would think the Tsar would have sent more of us. Perhaps that is why he wanted us to stop her in the village instead of in the field. Still, we are equipped with muskets and tasked to use them should the situation call for it."

This is my burden. Knowing what order to give.

Where is Troekorov? How could he do this to me?

The sound of hoof beats reached their ears through the murmurs of the villagers, and Ivan looked up to see a peasant arriving on a work horse, his face flushed and desperate.

"Just up the road," the man shouted down from atop the mount, pointing furiously. "The Regent brings a regiment, and Commander Shaklovity to lead them! Prince Golitsyn walks at her side!"

A regiment? Two thousand at her back?

Holy Father, help us.

The eyes of the company looked to Captain Buturlin. He stiffened his posture and scanned the group, trying to look each one in the eye.

"We have our orders, comrades. Be not afraid at the sight of Sophia's might--our commands come from a higher authority. Muster your courage in the name of the Tsar. Think of what he would do in your place! We cannot fail."

Still dumb-struck by the thought of facing an entire regiment of Strel'tsy, the company responded little, producing only a few nods of awareness. Around them, the villagers renewed their banter, calling Peter's name and speaking prayers.

"Form a line across the road," the Captain ordered, pointing to the places where he wanted the men to stand. "Here, here, here… yes, you see. Arms' length…good. I want your muskets off your backs and in your hands."

The men took their places, nervously checking their muskets, forming a human wall across the narrow dirt road and blocking the Regent's only path through the village. Not enough men to hold back an army, surely, but Peter had spoken of the meaning of such action and seemed to believe that Sophia's offence at being confronted would be great enough to send her back to Moscow.

Would the Regent really call for blood before a hundred witnesses?

I must believe in the Tsar, he thought, steeling himself. *He said I would have more than enough men…*

Troekorov, there is still time!

The moments slowed to a crawl, a creeping procession of anxious thoughts that left the company silent and expectant, some whispering prayers and others lost in thought. All eyes remained fixed on the road ahead.

Ivan looked down at his gloved hands, knowing that he was trembling beneath the cover but glad that he didn't have a musket of his own. His polished sword remained sheathed.

Do I show my blade? Better to have an order to read. I should have thought to bring a blank piece of parchment! Without an official order, Commander Shaklovity will have our heads!

Troekorov leaves me alone!

Buturlin drew his sword, feeling better with it in hand.

Drifting in on the cool autumn wind, the sound of marching steps was the first indication of the Regent's arrival, a faint, rhythmic sound that quickly grew to reflect the size of the opposing force.

An entire regiment, he thought, *still loyal and eager to impress the Regent.*

"Hold until you hear my command!" he shouted down the line. "Do not raise your muskets!"

Ivan took a deep breath, saying a silent prayer. He focused on the road ahead, rehearsing his lines beneath his breath.

What do I have to fear? She's a woman--not a bear! My words carry the weight of the Tsar and the Patriarch.

The Regent's party crested the final hill, the footsteps finally given form.

Buturlin watched as they slowly filled the road before him, indistinct figures growing clearer with each approaching step.

Leading the procession, Regent Sophia Alexeevna walked proudly, chin up and bearing a look of serenity. She walked with reverence, appearing as though she were on a pilgrimage--her red shuba lined with fur, her hair suitably covered and topped with a headdress usually reserved for special ceremonies.

On her left, the recognizable figure of Fedor Shaklovity, his deep eyes passionless, his uniform betraying the bearded animal within.

On the right, Prince V.V. Golitsyn, typically dressed in his European style, wearing the wide-brimmed, plumed hat that had become his trademark. His face reflected none of the Regent's serenity, graced only by a squint-eyed scowl as he stared across at the company of Preobrazhensky blocking his path.

A regiment of Strel'tsy followed in the Regent's wake, loosely formed but looking deadly, armed with long axes and muskets of their own, many of them smiling as they saw the paltry size of their opposition.

Relieved not to see Tsykler standing in my place, he thought.

The village remained captivated. Held in their places by the Regent's sizeable escort, no peasants rushed to greet her. Their tongues, thankfully, were not as timid, as the hum of conversation continued. They rushed to find places along the side of the road, hoping for a better view of the fight.

Buturlin hesitated, wondering who would be first to speak, wondering if he were obliged to approach the party.

Walking to the center of the road, Captain Buturlin gripped his sword and waited.

They seemed desperately close before Commander Shaklovity finally raised a hand, calling the procession to a halt.

Within musket range, surely…

The Regent motioned to Golitsyn, her look unchanged. The Prince leaned in to receive her words before stepping forward.

"What is the meaning of this?" Golitsyn asked in a loud, authoritative tone, looking them over. "Who is in command here?"

"I am, sir" Ivan raised his voice, "Captain Buturlin of the Preobrazhensky Regiment."

Golitsyn's lip curled in disdain. "What is the meaning of this, Captain? As you can see, this is the party of the Regent and no one here answers to the authority of the Preobrazhensky."

"Our orders come from Tsar Peter," he replied, locking eyes with the politician. "We are dispatched with orders to tell the Regent that Tsar Peter refuses to see her."

Prince Golitsyn paused, offering a confused look before turning back to the Regent. Around them, the catcalls began from the windows and the street, sounds of laughter and cries blessing Peter's name.

Sophia's demeanor seemed shaken but still composed; she forced a smile and took a step forward, her eyes finding those of Buturlin.

An odd moment, staring into the eyes of the most infamous woman in Russia, a figure whom he'd only seen at a distance. Now she was here, the monster they all feared, her presence intimidating and her gaze bearing down directly on the Captain. In a single glance, he understood her influence.

The villagers quieted in anticipation of her response. The Regent paused, hesitating as though knowing that she was being watched. Raising a hand, she smiled once more.

"I shall certainly go to Troitsky. Captain, move your men out of my path."

Buturlin's chest tightened, his heart pumping furiously.

No other course, he thought, raising his sword.

The company responded appropriately, raising their rifles to ready position. With barrels pointed at her, the Regent's jaw dropped open in surprise.

"Don't be a fool!" Golitsyn shouted back at him. "We have a regiment at our backs. Surely you see what you face! You will all die. And I am quite certain that the Tsarevich did not intend for you to commit murder here today."

"By order of the Tsar," Buturlin shouted back, ignoring the Prince's words, "I command you to return to Moscow. You are forbidden from coming to Troitsky."

"I fear you will not live to regret this choice, Captain." The Prince shrugged and shook his head, motioning to Shaklovity.

"You have no authority," Sophia told him, her tone bearing insult. "Am I to take orders from a group of boys? Show me your orders, Captain, or step aside."

For Peter, then...we make our stand.

Ivan cleared his throat, his sword still held high. "I will not yield, Regent."

The village could bear no more. From the edge of the road, the babushkas began to shout, praising Peter and calling for Sophia to leave. Following suit, the rest of the village raised the level of their banter, the shouts and catcalls rising to a crescendo. They now shouted unafraid at the Regent, staring back as she turned to survey their ranks. Some held their hands to their chests, clutching imaginary icons and mocking her performance at the Cathedral. Others shouted support to Buturlin and his greencoats, the cries of Peter's name raining down on the Regent and her entourage.

Angrily, she turned and whispered to Commander Shaklovity. Golitsyn joined the conversation, nodding and pointing over at Buturlin.

We're done, Ivan thought, taking no solace from the chorus of support. *She's given the order.*

From behind him, the sound of hoof beats.

Spinning, Ivan turned to see Troekorov, mounted and galloping toward them, his look frantic. Buturlin could see the pale parchment of the order clutched in his hand.

Troekorov! Thank the Holy Father!

As the entire company watched, Troekorov leapt from the horse and ran to Ivan's side, placing a hand on his shoulder. Troekorov's eyes went wide at the sight of the raised muskets.

"Ivan--what has happened?"

"Prince Troekorov!"

"Tell them," Ivan whispered to him, pointing to the orders. "I am disbelieved."

"It is I, sir." Troekorov offered an awkward bow. "Regent, Prince Golitsyn, Commander Shaklovity. I bring an order from the Tsar, written only this afternoon. Regrettably, I must tell you that the Tsar will not see any of you. You are to return to Moscow."

He held up the parchment, the sight drawing a small cheer from the villagers.

Buturlin glanced down the line once again, his adamant stare warning the men to hold.

Sophia appeared stricken at the sight of the order. She glared back, her face flushed with embarrassment, her benevolent grin lost in the wake of her failure. Prince Golitsyn leaned in to speak to her, the chorus cackling with laughter as the Regent wagged a finger at him. Shaklovity stood nearby brooding, seeming quite disturbed by the calls of traitor assailing him. He stepped forward to join the conversation.

Her choice is simple now, Buturlin thought. *Still she struggles.*

Troekorov looked back at him. "I'm sorry, my friend. I rode as fast as I could."

"You were wise to seek the order," Buturlin answered quietly. "Tardy, but wise. If not for those scribbles, our lives would surely be forfeit."

And quite suddenly, it was over.

With no further regard for Buturlin, Troekorov or the musket barrels, the Regent and her procession turned their backs on the unreceptive audience and started back down the road to their waiting carriage to begin their trip back to Moscow.

Buturlin lowered his arm, motioning for the company to shoulder their weapons.

Beside him, Troekorov grinned widely, looking proud.

"Well…that was simple…"

"You owe me a drink," Buturlin told him, glaring. "Two or three, perhaps."

"We will drink with the Tsar--to our victory. Be assured of that, Ivan."

They waited patiently in the road, watching until the Regent and her troops were long out of sight before turning and heading back to Troitsky. The journey home would be a short one, their pace spurred by the thought of achievement and the sight of Peter's satisfaction.

Moscow, The Kremlin

The Early Hours of September 11, 1689

The carriage arrived in the dark, quiet hours of the early morning, rolling to a halt before the steps of the Terem Palace.

Vasily was the first to emerge, stumbling as he stepped into the courtyard, his legs so weary he wondered if they would hold him. Despite the late hour of the journey, he had slept little, kept awake by worry and the constant rattling of Sophia and Commander Shaklovity.

He turned immediately, reaching out to take Sophia's hand and help her down, fielding her wounded glance with the same even countenance he had shown throughout the trip. Given the circumstances, it seemed best to remain calm in her presence. In truth, the Prince was equally disturbed but could see that the Regent's emotions were dominating her now. Led by fear, her comments were taking an odd tone. In her current mood, she was capable of making damning mistakes.

"I should have known I would have no support," she said, looking up at the Red Staircase. "Not a soul to greet us."

"It is quite late," Golitsyn replied evenly. "And our arrival is unexpected. I, for one, am glad to arrive discreetly."

"Yes, I would think you would be," she snapped in reply, glaring. "You have a reputation to protect! Perhaps you are thinking of your future, Vasily? Unfortunate, your selfish interests will have to wait. You will accompany me. Both of you."

Shaklovity nodded his consent and the Prince did the same, unwilling to engage Sophia on meaningless subjects. They moved behind her, commanding their legs to work after the long ride, keeping pace with her hurried steps.

Vasily looked at her. *I have no reputation anymore. Her name has consumed me!*

The situation was unthinkable. Never would he have guessed that the Regency could crumble so fast. The false accusations had blossomed into a tangled choking vine, now mixed in a mass of weeds too formidable to simply hack away, a morass beyond his control. For days, Vasily had been denying his intuition, holding out hope that a suitable remedy could be found--something to pacify the Naryshkins into negotiation. Now, in the wake of their retreat from Troitsky, it seemed obvious that Sophia's time was at an end.

And with it, my entire career…

All my work, he thought, lamenting his fate as they passed over the threshold. *All my efforts, wiped clean in a month's time!*

"Vasily, you will call for my friends and supporters," Sophia shouted back at him, not slowing her pace. "I must speak with those who still have faith in me. Immediately! This cannot wait!"

"But Sophia, the hour is still early."

"Rouse them from sleep if you must!" she shouted, turning to face him. "No one else must be swayed. You know the Tsarista, Vasily. She is busily writing letters as we speak, calling for my dignity to be delivered to her in a basket! We cannot lose any more of our trusted to the Naryshkins."

"And Tsarevich Ivan? Must he attend as well?"

"No," she replied immediately. "Only my friends and supporters, those still loyal to the Miloslavsky name. The Tsarevich need not be bothered."

Vasily racked his mind to form a list, wondering who would stand for Sophia.

"I will do my best," the Prince answered, resigning himself to the task.

Vasily glanced at Shaklovity for support, receiving only a sour expression.

"Do you question me, Vasily?" Sophia's stare bore through him. "You were so quiet in the carriage! If you had something worthwhile to offer, surely you would have done so."

"There was certainly enough said in the carriage without my participation," he replied. "My concern, Lady, is for your welfare, both body and mind. I will certainly summon your supporters, but do you think it wise to see them without having rested? None of us has slept. I think it better to see your friends in a few hours' time, when you are at rested and at your best."

"Do not patronize me, Vasily. Do you think me a child?"

"Certainly not."

"Really, you sound like a nursemaid!"

"Your temper controls you, Sophia."

"Hah!" she huffed in response, looking a bit wounded. "After this betrayal, how can it not?"

"You are too weary--too angry to keep your wits about you. We must act reasonably if we wish to retain our--"

"Reason?" Sophia stepped into him, her breath warm in his face. "After all I have been through, you now wish me to be reasonable? You think me a hysterical woman, I suppose."

Vasily shook his head, trying to soften his look. “Perhaps just a few hours rest…you’ve been through so much in the last day.”

She stared at him, pausing. “I forgive your weakness, Vasily.”

“What?”

“And I know that you think you have my best interests in mind, but you are respectfully wrong. Your advice has kept us silent and that silence has damned us! I will see my supporters as soon as possible! You will see just how calm this hysterical woman can be!”

Shaklovity took a step forward. “Lady, I will summon the Strel’tsy colonels who remain. Shall I call the foreign officers as well?”

Sophia paused, thinking, as though she’d forgotten. “I suppose they are my strength now, yes?”

“They are mercenaries,” Golitsyn interjected. “Their loyalty has been purchased. Not a one has complained since this debacle began. Leave them in their houses at this early hour! Better not to anger them.”

She turned her head as though not listening to him. “Commander?”

Shaklovity nodded cautiously. “I would agree with Prince Golitsyn. The foreign colonels will remain in place as long as their contracts hold them. Better not to waste your heartfelt appeals.”

“Good, then,” she replied, turning back down the corridor without waiting. “The two of you have your duties. Bring everyone to the foot of the Red Staircase. No…perhaps the Faceted Chamber would be more fitting. Yes, the throne room at sunrise. I must prepare.”

The two of them stood watching as the Regent continued out of sight, her steps paced and confident. Exhaling, Vasily looked over at his counterpart, trying to sense Shaklovity’s opinion.

"The situation has grown too severe," he commented, "Even for Sophia. Do you think she adopts this lunacy by choice?"

Shaklovity frowned, shaking his head. "That woman is genuine. If she is mad, then she comes by it naturally. After how she's been treated…"

"She still has the strength of her family name; we mustn't let her lose that by scolding the few remaining faithful."

"Scolding?" Shaklovity waved away the comment. "Bah! You have it wrong! Perhaps you are the lunatic, Golitsyn. Sophia means to pull them to her breast and rock them to sleep with a lullaby!"

"Her flagging support will not suffice. Peter will have the throne. Do you mean to question her, or will you simply follow whatever order she gives?"

Visibly offended, Shaklovity stepped closer, leaning in, his tired eyes singing with rage.

"Medvedev has plans to leave Moscow--to run for his life! Smart bastard, he is. You see, Prince, I do not possess that luxury. I cannot run nor make an appeal. I think only of keeping my head attached to my shoulders…and cannot save myself! I have decided, sir, that the Regent is my only salvation. My head, so to speak, lies in her hands. If she bids me to pull the stars from the sky, then I must endeavor to do so."

Vasily backed away, turning his head from the Commander's sour breath.

Shaklovity is no fool, he thought. *Though flight may be his only hope.*

His will be the order that breaks the Regency.

Peter will call for his head, and Sophia will finally be made to comply, personally, with an order from the Tsar. This will be the end.

"I believe you are falsely accused," the Prince told him, lowering his voice, taking a more diplomatic approach. "I fear, however, that the facts of the crime become irrelevant in the face of Naryshkin will. We are both targets, Commander. And both dependent on Sophia's welfare."

Shaklovity nodded, calming. "Your point is taken, Prince."

"For my part, you may trust that I will offer nothing to incriminate you."

"Appreciated, sir."

"Still, we must protect her reputation, Fedor, even now."

"I would not think to do otherwise…"

"Good then," Vasily answered, feeling a bit better. Shaklovity was a brute, but shrewd enough to act responsibly.

"We have little time."

"Indeed. The throne room at sunrise, then,"

The two parted without regard and set out to accomplish their tasks. Vasily brushed the dirt from his stockings and straightened his wig before leaving for the houses of Sophia's remaining friends and political supporters, putting on his diplomatic face. He traveled without escort, thinking a more discreet approach to be the most effective.

Sophia's faithful were more amenable than expected. He was greeted with courteous smiles, and his humble request threw the households into a flurry of activity as they prepared for the unexpected audience. Vasily did his best to appeal to their sense of self-importance, speaking as though Sophia considered each a treasure and making it seem as if the Regent favored them above all others. Believing themselves special in the eyes of the Regent, most seemed honored by the request, apparently led by the belief that the crisis had finally come to a resolution. The Prince said little of the nature of the audience, stating only that the Regent was calling for her dearest and most trusted friends.

The news of Medvedev's impending flight from Moscow remained present in his mind, plaguing Vasily with predictions of the future, leaving him guessing at his own fate. There was no question: should Peter and the Naryshkins desire it, Shaklovity would be executed.

But how far is the young Tsar willing to go?

Prince Golitsyn smiled with his customary politic regard as he solicited the Miloslavsky faithful, his outward guise masking the tumult within, his heart pounding at the thought of what would come next. He performed his task well, and soon Sophia's dearest were arriving in carriages and on horseback, well-dressed and smiling, bearing only the slightest trepidation regarding the situation itself.

Shaklovity had been hard at work as well; the majority of the remaining Strel'tsy colonels were present and waiting in Cathedral Square, their horses breathing clouds of steam in the cold morning air. Their line seemed pitifully short but stood straight and tall, the beleaguered Guards taking refuge in the call to service. The Prince had heard rumblings that Shaklovity no longer had the confidence of the Strel'tsy dregs, but on this morning the Commander stood with his men, their faces showing few signs of distress.

The procession into the Palace was led by Golitsyn himself, a small parade of twenty or so Moscow notables, a showing he hoped would pacify the Regent. The first rays of glaring morning sun were upon them as they passed through the entrance and into the distinctive shadows of the Palace.

Sophia stood in full regal dress before the double throne, her face clean and smooth, bearing no angry flush or worried expression. She smiled in angelic fashion as the guests were led into the elaborate ceremonial Chamber, nodding her welcome to several of them. In her hands, a large golden crucifix, held to her chest in pious regard. She waited until everyone was in place before speaking.

"My friends, my beloved family, your presence here is a joy to me, even in these dark times. I take solace in the fact that some things here in Moscow are still as they should be.

"In light of Tsarevich Peter's unexplained retreat to Troitsky, I took it upon myself, as Regent and caretaker of our beloved country, to travel to the Monastery in an attempt to remedy the condition, whatever it might be. Despite the treacherous rumors and accusations, I chose to act as my position commands and offer my assistance. This is, after all, my duty as Regent."

Vasily stood quietly, watching Sophia as she surveyed the group, her eyes connecting with each in turn. With the exception of the recent incident at the Cathedral, Sophia had never lost face with her most trusted. Now, with the lot of them standing before her, she seemed renewed. For the first time in weeks she appeared to be comfortable, whole again.

"Our journey was an embarrassment and a failure," she continued loudly, her tone darkening, "our progress halted before we ever reached Troitsky. They almost shot at me at Vozdvizhenskoe. Many people rode out after me with muskets and bows…it was with difficulty that I got away and hastened to Moscow."

She paused for a moment, lifting her chin, taking in the audible gasp that filled the spacious Chamber.

"The Naryshkins and Lopukhins are making a plot to kill the Tsarevich Ivan Alexeevich," Sophia announced, "and are even aiming at my head."

Murmurs of protest rippled through the group. Sophia raised a hand in response, acknowledging their concern and shaking her head sadly.

She lies, Vasily thought, staring through an astonished pallor, glancing over at Shaklovity but seeing no reaction. *She plays the Naryshkins' game!*

"I will collect the regiments and talk to them myself," Sophia turned to the colonels, standing proudly in her moment of sympathy. "Obey us and do not go to Troitsky. I trust in you."

She stepped from her place, still clutching the cross. "Whom shall I trust rather than you, O faithful supporters? Will you also run away?"

She moved to the front of the group, holding out the crucifix before her.

"Kiss the cross first."

With a severe look, she motioned for them to approach.

One by one, the guests began to step forward, each in turn taking a knee and placing his lips on the cross. The process seemed unbearably long but Sophia waited to speak until all in the room had complied. For his part, Vasily obeyed, offering no odd glances or gestures that might have countered her aims.

When the last of them had kneeled before her, Sophia kissed the cross herself, offering a sad attempt at a gracious smile. He'd never seen her cry in public, but there were tears in her eyes now, trailing down her cheeks as she nodded her thanks.

"Now if you try to run away, the cross will not let you go. When letters come from Troitsky, do not read them. Bring them to the Palace."

The massive doors of the cavernous Chamber sprung open, the booming sound startling the lot and sending Shaklovity spinning on his heels.

The group turned to see a solitary figure dressed in Strel'tsy uniform, his hands bearing a folded piece of parchment.

Colonel Ivan Nechaev.

Vasily recognized the face immediately. Nechaev was a proud Strel'tsy leader, one of the summoned colonels, well known to the soldiers present in the throne room. Like most Strel'tsy officers,

Nechaev had been passed his rank by his father, a Moscow tradition that made the Strel'tsy command a matter of legacy and tradition. Nechaev had come from Troitsky, no doubt, sent by Tsar Peter in the wake of the latest Naryshkin victory.

Vasily glanced over to see the reaction of Shaklovity and his Strel'tsy, noting the sudden alarm on the faces of the colonels. Their eyes widened at the sight of their comrade.

The Regent placed the crucifix on the throne and turned to pounce on the Colonel, stomping down from her place to confront him.

"By what right do you interrupt us?"

"By order of Tsar Peter," Nechaev answered, stiff-jawed and firm. "I bring official letters from the Tsar, one to be delivered to you, Regent…and a second has been delivered to Tsar Ivan."

"What is this?" She closed in on the Colonel, appearing as though she meant to maul him. Vasily stepped from his place, moving to stand at her side.

The Colonel opened the parchment and began to read:

"Whereas the evidence of the night of August 17th has proven--"

"Stop!" Sophia reached out a hand, snatching the letter away from the Colonel, turning her back as she examined it. The Colonel stood stiffly and made no attempt to reclaim it.

Vasily peered over her shoulder, the Chamber held in silent shock as the two surveyed the letter together.

It was short and direct, the words announcing the existence of a plot against Peter and naming the leading conspirators. The letter called for the immediate arrest of Father Sylvester Medvedev and Commander Fedor Shaklovity.

The axe falls, Vasily thought, looking over at Sophia. Her eyes narrowed in anger as she forced the letter into his grasp.

"I cannot accept this!" she shouted, her countenance broken, the graceful calm replaced by the fire that raged within her. "I cannot know that this is authentic!"

The company stood in silent captivity, watching as the Regent exploded before them.

"We are betrayed at every turn--taunted by those who would have our head!"

As the Regent exhaled her fury, Vasily scanned the letter, searching again for any mention of his own name. Gratefully, he found nothing that seemed to implicate him.

Shaklovity moved from his place, too curious to remain standing at attention. Passing the Regent, he attempted to search the contents of the letter.

Vasily quickly folded the parchment, gripping it firmly lest it be snatched away. Stepping back, he looked up at Shaklovity.

"Prince Vasily, what does it say?" Commander Shaklovity growled the question, his tone bearing weight. "Tell me. I have the right."

Vasily stared back. "The letter is meant for the Regent, Commander."

Shaklovity sneered, turning to address Sophia.

"Regent, if I may..."

She looked past the Commander, her eyes connecting with Vasily. "Tell him, Vasily."

The Prince took a deep breath, holding out a palm to halt the Commander.

"It is an order for your arrest, Commander. Father Medvedev as well."

Shaklovity paled, his face draining of blood, his anger fading into a look of utter shock. Vasily watched as the realization crept over and through the Strel'tsy veteran. Slumping, the Commander turned to look at Nechaev.

"And Tsykler? He agrees with this?"

Colonel Nechaev said nothing, his eyes locked, avoiding the gaze of the Commander.

Sophia stepped forward in Fedor's place, towering over the Colonel. "How dare you take upon yourself such a duty?"

"I am here because I am ordered to be," Nechaev answered without hesitation. "I dare not disobey Tsar Peter."

Spoken quite plainly, the words were enough to separate Sophia from the last of her composure.

Dressed in her robes of state, her headdress slanted and unable to contain her hair, Sophia grabbed the Colonel by his collar and pulled him close, looking as though she hoped to devour him.

"You are a traitorous coward!" Sophia hissed, her eyes boring through him. "We shall see how obedient you are with your head removed!"

With a single push, the Colonel was on the floor, cowering before the Regent but offering no apology.

Raging, she turned to the stunned line of Strel'tsy colonels. "Take him away and cut off his head at the earliest convenience! We shall deliver it to Peter as a gift!"

The Strel'tsy colonels lifted Nechaev from his place and tied his hands securely, promising to deliver him to the executioner.

The Prince needed no more prodding. He stepped forward, waving Shaklovity over to Sophia's side and motioning for the rest of the guests to exit through the doors. Shocked beyond comment, the guests marched out of the Faceted Chamber without a word, their heads hanging in defeat, their tongues waiting patiently to tell others of what they had seen.

In moments, they were alone again, the three of them--clutching the letter and trying to assimilate the tragic events of the past day.

Moscow, Red Square

The Afternoon of September 11, 1689

Having been awakened yet again by the tumultuous events within the Kremlin, the crowded Square stirred with anger, the citizens of Moscow provoked one too many times by the pride of the Regent.

General Patrick Gordon stood in the shadows at the edge of the Square, his customary calm unnoticed by the gathering rabble of soldiers. He waited, listening and watching, his eyes searching their midst for a sign of leadership among the raised voices, his curiosity piqued as he wondered at the dynamics of the mob.

Quickly the ranks of local Strel'tsy filled Red Square before him, their figures lacking proper uniforms, their clenched fists bearing all manner of weapons. Drawn by news of Commander Shaklovity's guilt, the men gathered in anger and confusion, suddenly unsure of their position, lacking the familiar faces that had once guided their violent course.

"They circle like dogs. You would do well to stand away, Patrick, lest they think you ready to lead."

Diechmann's familiar voice came from behind, his accent unmistakable.

"I hold no fear," General Gordon replied, turning to offer his greetings. "The Strel'tsy would never call upon a foreigner to assist them with such important domestic matters."

"When I heard the rumors, my curiosity brought me here." The German offered his hand. "You seem unshaken by all this rebellion."

Gordon frowned a bit. "You have been here less than a year, Captain. This is your first serious turn with Moscow politics."

"So…the rumors are true? The Regent refuses to give up Shaklovity?"

Gordon nodded, his eyes still searching the scattered ranks. "And the Strel'tsy are apparently intent on delivering him to the Tsar."

"They cannot stand behind a traitor." Diechmann looked concerned. "They gather out of fear, then."

"With their own commander standing accused of treason, how else can they maintain any sense of legitimacy?"

The Square filled like a tide pool in a storm. They crept from their homes, joining the collective swirl of able bodies, gaining strength from the raised voices of their comrades. Gordon could see the men growing erect, building their courage with angry words, fingers pointed toward the Palace and calling for action. They found solace in the chaos of Red Square, fathers and sons gathering around the remaining native colonels.

For his part, Gordon remained aloof, unwilling to participate in the crude politics of the Moscow militia. And though his rank named him as a General of the Strel'tsy Guard, Gordon gladly leaned on his mercenary status, choosing not to participate in the growing furor. These were not the same soldiers he led into battle. This was the second face of the Strel'tsy, the same mob that had placed Sophia on the throne years before.

Today there was no question of their loyalty. The Strel'tsy stood against her, provoked by rumors that the Regent was refusing to turn over Shaklovity. The charges against him had been clearly defined and were delivered in the name of Tsar Peter.

"Sons of sons," Gordon commented, watching the gathering with ongoing interest. "These are men who have been passed the right by their fathers--by tradition itself. This is the peculiar difference between the Moscow Strel'tsy and the men who go by the same name elsewhere. This is their game, Otto--not ours."

The Captain nodded. "I see."

"Given what has happened, I would think it a relief."

"What? Sir?"

"They are angry and fearful, yes, but their spirit today comes from a sense of relief. Since the departure of Tsykler and the other Russian commanders, this group has been without direction, without orders--questioning their place. A bad place for a soldier to be. Now, finally, they have an order to follow."

"From Tsar Peter, no less!"

"Yes, finally a task to tell them that the Strel'tsy still matter. A clear order calling for the arrest of Shaklovity. With Tsykler resting his head at Troitsky and the Patriarch as well? No, there is no question now. Shaklovity must fall."

Diechmann shook his head a bit. "To think, all those days spent waiting and wondering if Peter's Preobrazhensky would attack Moscow. And now, without a single drop of blood, Peter eliminates Shaklovity and does it with the Moscow Strel'tsy!"

"A masterful bit of politics. Even the best would have to admit that the Naryshkin blade is as sharp as ever. Peter has performed a miraculous feat of daring."

"I would agree with you," Diechmann replied, hesitating, "though I find it curious that Shaklovity and the Regent would ever seek to murder Peter at all…and in such sloppy fashion!"

Gordon thought back to the beginning, the odd night when troops filled the streets and Peter was sent fleeing to Troitsky. "It does seem curious, but we cannot afford to confuse the truth with the facts, my friend. It matters not if an assassination attempt occurred--it matters only that the people are convinced."

"From the look of things, all of Moscow believes."

"Aye. We have only to deal with what is before us."

"You will advise me, then, General Gordon? I admit, I am unsure of my duties," Diechmann said, leaning in as though ashamed of his words. "Perhaps I should be envious of the Strel'tsy and their mission, for I admit I do not know my own."

"And what of the other colonels?" Gordon asked, realizing he had not spoken with them since the previous day.

"They talk of mercenary pride and tell me that we serve only the throne and that we have been issued no orders. They tell me to sit and have a drink of wine to calm my spirit."

"They are practiced--and right to do so," Gordon replied, nodding. "We have no part in these local matters. At the moment, our rank means little in Red Square. Be thankful and let the Russians do what they must."

"They also mention your name, General."

"Oh?"

"I was told that, if I am still feeling put off, I should speak with you."

"And so I may assume that you are..."

"Put off?" Diechmann shrugged. "Yes, still, a bit, General. They say you've been to speak with Tsar Peter."

"As I have," Gordon answered affirmatively. "Not to Troitsky, of course--our meeting was in Preobrazhenskoe. I met with Tsarevich Peter, but much has changed since that day."

Diechmann's eyes widened. "Not to assume, but do you have an inkling of the Tsar's intentions--his capability and his will?"

"Do you ask if he is prepared to rule, or whether he intends to take the throne?"

"Either," Diechmann replied. "Both."

"I cannot know his true intent, of course, but I would say that if you wish proof, you only need look at the scene before you. Listen to the cries of 'Tsar Peter' rising from their midst!"

His words brought their attention back to the Square, the smaller groups of armed Strel'tsy now coming together, gathering around the most senior members.

Fresh from his appearance at Sophia's latest appeal, the elder Troekorov stood like a statue on the Lobnoye Mesto, the Place of the Brow, elevating himself on the executioner's pedestal so as to be seen at the back of the crowd. He waited for the scattered pieces to come together before speaking. The Russian colonels did their part, gathering the stinking mass of angry men and then taking their places by Troekorov's side.

"You see?" Gordon huffed. "Order from chaos. They have done this before."

"So they mean to march on the Kremlin?"

"Aye, the most direct route to the Regent's ear. A hundred pikes can be most persuasive. You were not here to remember the events that placed Sophia on the throne, or the furor when Commander Hovanski was executed."

"And what if the Regent still refuses?"

"She will not refuse the mob," Gordon answered, watching. "Not if she wishes to remain in the Kremlin. Ivan is of age. He will not serve as her shield anymore."

Diechmann looked anxious, his temperament skewed by talk of the mob. "Your advice then? Shaklovity will fall, and then?"

Gordon thought of the odd string of events that brought the Naryshkin cause to this fateful moment. From Troitsky, Peter had summoned the Patriarch and then the Strel'tsy colonels, removing any foundation of support that the Regent might have. He'd rebuked her efforts at diplomacy, basking in the advantage given to him by the accusations. Shrewdly, Peter's decisions had kept Sophia in chains, unable to offer any defense without condemning herself.

"Given the progression of events, there is no question in my mind that Tsar Peter and the rest of the Naryshkins have yet to make their final advance. Without Shaklovity, without her Strel'tsy, there seems no hope for the Regency."

"I was told that Sophia has gone mad! She has arrested Nechaev and calls for his head. She calls it a plot to murder Ivan and refuses to leave the Kremlin."

"She certainly refuses to leave, though I doubt she has so suddenly gone mad. As for Nechaev, she should have known better. His arrest fuels this fire. Nechaev is one of their own. Our own."

"But what is our calling, General? How are we to present ourselves?"

"Be patient, friend. We are hired soldiers and little more. Our regiments will follow where ordered. Think of this as a game of chess--a game between Peter and the Regent. We are merely a piece that is yet to be moved. We wait to play our part."

Diechmann paused. "But who controls us?"

"Those who pay us. The throne, of course," Gordon answered. "In this instance, I suppose it could be either party. Still, Sophia's time to act has almost passed."

The Captain frowned, still unsatisfied.

"I see you remain troubled, so I will offer this," Gordon said, placing a hand on his shoulder. "In my time, I have never been so impressed with a young man. Peter has the broad spirit of a Russian and the clever mind of a European. I believe he will be fair with his brother Ivan and, given time, will be good for Russia."

"There is no question."

"All personal judgments aside," Gordon continued, "I was received well and was told by Tsarevich Peter that he would call for the foreign commanders when we were needed. Do you understand? We have orders, Captain, and they are to wait."

Diechmann grinned, looking a bit relieved. "And you feel the orders to be given in good faith?"

"I do."

"Excellent, then," he answered, exhaling. "I will gladly follow your lead, Patrick."

Gordon scratched at his chin, watching as Troekorov offered an impassioned speech to the gathered Strel'tsy. His crude stanzas met with roaring support, his furor growing with every word. The angst of the summer was bleeding out into the sweat and the cries of the plain-clothed soldiers, their pride growing as they stood shoulder to shoulder with their brothers and friends.

The sight was somehow comforting.

It seemed odd, to reach inside himself and find no trepidation or worry. In its place Patrick found reassurance, hope, and a bemused sense of justice. The mob had placed Sophia on the throne--now it would do its part in pulling her from it.

She was an extraordinary woman, without question. She had seemed a monster on her way to power but had proven an effective ruler. In another country, in a more sane circumstance, she might have been truly great; her longevity was an accomplishment in itself.

But this was Russia, and Sophia was a woman. She would no doubt respond to Shaklovity's charges, but her options were now reduced to pandering to the boyars or gambling with the loyalty of the Strel'tsy.

A month ago they were calling him Tsarevich. Now the men in the streets cried Tsar Peter's name, their fists raised in response to Troekorov's provocation.

"To be honest," Gordon continued, his eyes never leaving the mob, "I have very specific opinions regarding the beauty of Peter's trap. I have just recently come to understand the progression of events, and I believe our foreign-led regiments to be the final piece of Peter's puzzle. Beyond the issue of V.V. Golitsyn, who must certainly be charged, Peter has little left to accomplish. It is my opinion that he will call for us soon."

"It is a relief to hear it," the Captain replied. "I was right to seek you out."

"Patience is our aim now, Diechmann. Take a deep breath and enjoy the spectacle. Satiate your curiosity. Think of it as a lesson in Russian politics. After all, this day will be spoken of for years to come."

They watched as Troekorov hopped down from his place and pointed toward the Kremlin, spurring the mob into motion.

Moscow, The Great Sovereign's Palace of the Kremlin

Shortly Thereafter, September 11, 1689

"They mean to take the Commander away in chains, sire."

"How many are out there?"

"A few hundred, sire. Likely more."

Prince Vasily straightened his collar and rubbed at his aching temples, wishing he had more time. Sophia remained defiant, unwilling to listen to his counsel, her temperament flashing back and forth from furious to maudlin. She'd ranted and cried, trying desperately to find safety, searching for balance within the chaos surrounding her. Unwilling to surrender Shaklovity to the Strel'tsy, she now found herself at odds with the army she had once called her own.

No more hiding in the passageways. I must go back and tell her that we have no more time.

Vasily, as always, found himself placed precariously in the center of the controversy. He'd reasoned and pleaded with the Regent, one moment listing the facts like an advisor, the next pulling her weeping form from his breast, trying his best to console the woman within the ruler. The result was heart-rending and torturous, his rational mind knowing that her worst fears were indeed coming to light.

There must be a reckoning. We should be grateful that we have Shaklovity to give up. He is a dead man now--his death may save us both!

"And Medvedev?" he asked, clearing his throat. "What of the monk?"

"He cannot be found in the city, sire." The attendant lowered his eyes. "I was told that he left Moscow in the middle of the night, without accompaniment."

"The Strel'tsy will catch up with him soon. No doubt they will be searching. Tell me, Dmitri, and speak the truth. Did the Strel'tsy mention my name? Did you hear anything that might lead you to believe they want more than the Commander?"

The attendant paused. "No, sire, I heard nothing of your name. But they talk about sounding the alarm bell, sire."

Sounding the alarm bell…

The phrase itself was enough to make boyars shiver in their stockings, the traditional password for riot and murder, a call that would send the Strel'tsy into a sudden and destructive frenzy. Once delivered, no one would be safe from the chaos. The words were used as the ultimate threat by the crude militia and, though rarely put into action, were taken very seriously by all. It had been seven years since the last occurrence.

"We must be very cautious, Dmitri. We could easily be caught up in this--any of us."

"Yes, my lord."

"You must ready a carriage immediately--horses at the least--in the event that we need to escape the Kremlin. Discreetly, mind you. You may ride with me."

He will flee at the first sign of danger, he thought, looking into Dmitri's fearful eyes. *I must insure his loyalty.*

Lacking time to think of anything better, Vasily twisted off the ring on his right middle finger. Taking Dmitri's hand, he placed the ring firmly in the attendant's palm.

"You may use this to insure our success in escaping the city. You have my gratitude and my promise to fill your pockets when this is finished. Go now, Dmitri, secure our passage. Do not fail me. We leave Moscow tonight, regardless of the alarm bell!"

The attendant bowed before running back down the passageway, already clutching far more than his services were worth. He was loyal enough to consider trustworthy, but on this afternoon Vasily knew there would be no guarantees.

We will leave for Troitsky. I will make my appeal to Peter. I should have obeyed cousin Boris' counsel days ago.

He felt in his pocket for the letters, reassured at finding them.

Boris Golitsyn had written from Troitsky almost as soon as the trouble began, asking cousin Vasily to make a journey out to plead his case with the young Tsarevich. Boris had been kind to mention that no one suspected V.V. of the treachery, but added that an audience with Peter could help to ease any remaining suspicion as Peter was determined to take his place on the throne. This suggestion seemed ludicrous when first made, but Vasily had seen the circumstances line themselves up and was convinced that no more good could come from waiting at Sophia's side. As distasteful as it seemed, he would heed Boris' advice.

I will bow to Peter and apologize again for the damnable campaigns, but I'll never be able to apologize for my part in the slaughter of 1682. After what I've done to him I can only pray he will have enough mercy to set me free.

Frowning, he turned for the Regent's chambers, knowing his counsel was desperately needed, realizing that it would likely be the last of their official decisions, the pitiful yelp that would end their grand political history.

It will be a shame in the eyes of many, he told himself, thinking of the progress made. *The Turks aside, we exceeded every expectation; even Tsar Alexis would have been proud! The broad-minded girl held her ground against every opponent, and Prince Golitsyn was always there to finish the matter in decisive and stylish fashion.*

We are villains, now. Practically criminals, we are left to plead for our lives. Is Sophia prepared for this?

There were too many questions left unanswered. Despite Boris' reassurance, there were still the matters of Peter's temperament and the extent of Naryshkin will to destroy the Miloslavsky supporters. And now, the threat of the Strel'tsy, more deadly and immediate than any other.

He entered without knocking, finding the Regent and Commander Shaklovity locked in embrace. Fedor's head was at her breast, her hands stroking his hair as if he were a child. Sophia's eyes bore the tired, empty glare of mourning.

Seeing Vasily, Shaklovity lifted his head and stepped away from Sophia, raising a hand as though trying to relieve any offense. The Commander's stare was lifeless, his posture sagging and beaten, the arrogant lift of his chin hardly enough to shake his pitiful demeanor.

"Forgive me, Prince Golitsyn," Shaklovity offered. "I do not mean to stand in your place, sir. I never did, in fact…"

"The Strel'tsy are at the gates," Vasily announced regretfully.

"We know," Sophia answered. "They've been gathering in the Square all morning. Idiots chattering and frothing at the mouth, their imaginations spurred by rumors and treachery!"

"They will soon be inside, Sophia."

She crossed her arms, casting a wounded look. "I have weathered the demands of the Strel'tsy before--and prevailed! You know this."

"And you know the consequences of sounding the alarm bell."

Her eyes widened. "Will they?"

"Perhaps not," he replied. "But they have offered the threat, which is more than enough."

"They test me!" She scowled back at him. "They dare to test me when I provide them all that they have! After all the Commander's good service, they would have him in chains at the whim of the Naryshkins! I cannot capitulate."

Watched by Fedor's venomous glare, Vasily paced across to where Sophia stood, reaching out a hand to place on her shoulder.

"They are deadly serious, Sophia."

"You needn't tell me," she snapped, pulling away from his touch. "They would claim the liberty of their own most loyal soldier! Who has worked more diligently, with more persistence and loyalty than Fedor? None of those rats! I will order them to stand down."

"There is no more argument on this day," he pressed, wanting desperately to coerce her into reason. "There is no negotiation with the mob, Sophia. Either you surrender Commander Shaklovity or risk the lives of everyone in the Kremlin."

"No!" she screamed, her voice cracking into shreds, her temper radiating from her crimson face. "You fool! Do you know what it means if we surrender Fedor?"

"Of course."

"It means that we are complicit, connected to their imaginary assassins and this demonic plot to stain our reputations! If we agree, we are as much as guilty!"

Vasily turned to Shaklovity. "Apparently, the Regent is determined to die on your behalf."

Shaklovity straightened in his chair. "Do you accuse me, Golitsyn? In my last moments of freedom, you expect me to bear such insult! Is that what I am? A stinking coward? Do you think me so little that I would allow her to take the blow of the axe for me?"

Shaklovity's words cut through the chamber, silencing Sophia. She looked at him, her eyes melting into piteous regret.

"You will not have to, poor Fedor. I have promised to protect you."

"Sophia," the Prince pleaded, staring into the heat of her gaze, "you cannot hope to do so! Do you expect to stroll out there and command them from the top of the Staircase as you did years ago? The Miloslavskys will be the ones dropping this time, I assure you."

"I will not hear it, Vasily! The Strel'tsy are mine and they will obey."

"They serve the throne, Sophia, and are persuaded by an order from the boy they now call Tsar!"

"You wound me with your words!"

Vasily's heart sank, thin but pervasive threads of fear stringing through his temperament. The Regent seemed determined to hold out until the bitter end. With or without her consent, Shaklovity would have to be taken. If there were any hope for survival, it now lay in capitulation.

This, he reasoned, would be his final official act.

With luck, Fedor's guilty conscience will be enough to counter Sophia's foolishness.

He turned to the Commander. "You expect to surrender, then?"

"Of course," Shaklovity spat. "What kind of--"

"He does not! Will not!" Sophia interrupted, moving between them. "Did you come here to counsel or to torment me?"

"I came, Regent, to tell you how little time we have."

The sounds of raised voices could be heard from Cathedral Square. Hurried footsteps approached from the corridor, as though called by his warning.

A slight knock preceded the entry of two chambermaids, little more than young girls. Their faces were red and traced with tears. They fell to their knees at the sight of the Regent.

"My lady! Forgive us, but the musketeers are at the entrance! They shout for blood!"

"Off with you!" Sophia shouted back at them, scowling. "Back to work and bother me no more!"

The chambermaids subdued their tears long enough to flee, their footsteps sounding again as they ran back down the corridor.

Too much risk to bear. Does she not see it? Surely, this pious woman cannot fail to see the truth!

Prince Golitsyn stared down at the Commander, their eyes connecting in a momentary glimpse of understanding. Rising to his feet, Shaklovity nodded his acknowledgement.

Shaklovity will do it--for Sophia, perhaps.

"What are you doing?" She rushed to Fedor's side, grasping his sleeve. "I refuse to allow it, Fedor!"

Commander Shaklovity looked back at her, his weary eyes connecting. "Your blessed support is more than I deserve, Lady. As honored as I am by your defense of my righteous cause, I would be equally dishonored should I leave you to carry the burden."

"Your burden is mine, Fedor!"

"No, Lady. You must remain, and I must pay the bloody toll. The alarm bell must be answered. Thirty years have taught me as much. Lady, I have been called a wolf, a serpent, a rat…and these names may fit me and be justified. I could not, however, live with being named a coward. I am innocent, but I go in your name."

"Vasily!" she snapped, turning. "You would force him to go?"

Vasily shook his head calmly, knowing the Commander's mind was made. "No, Lady. I will escort him into custody."

"I will accompany you," she said, brushing back her hair and wiping at her eyes. "They will know my anger!"

"You will remain here," he told her, stiffening his tone, "where you will be safe. You will wait for my return."

"I will not."

He moved toward her, taking her hand. "Sophia, you must. If there is still a chance of saving the Regency, it may very well come through our civil treatment of these charges. With respect to the Commander, there is risk in involving you any further in this matter."

Shaklovity nodded his assent.

"You must now distance yourself from these charges," Vasily continued, his eyes pleading. "We cannot risk an incident that would serve to prove otherwise."

Moments later, the two were walking down the corridor toward the source of the clamor, free of Sophia and her tears, the Commander accepting his final free steps with the strength of a martyr.

"There is still your interrogation," the Prince said, wanting to offer some slight reassurance. "After all, there is nothing but rumor to convict you."

"Rumor is more than enough in this case," the Commander replied, his tone bearing resignation. "You know this, Prince Golitsyn."

Vasily sighed and nodded mournfully, wondering if he dare broach the topic further.

Will he turn me out? A few simple words from Shaklovity would have my head on a stake! Questioning his loyalty will only anger him.

"I wish to show you my respect for your conduct, Fedor. You have always been a credit to our cause. Strange, really, that it took until this moment for us to--"

"Speak no more," Shaklovity ordered, looking away. "This is not done for you."

"I certainly wa--"

"Move on."

As they descended to the lower floors, the clatter of rebellion grew louder and louder, the sound making it obvious that the Strel'tsy had gathered at the bottom of the Staircase. As they reached the final turn, the Commander stopped suddenly.

"Here, Vasily! Stop here."

Shaklovity tore a strip from his shirt-tail and handed it to Golitsyn before holding out his wrists.

"Here, bind my hands. If they see you leading me as a prisoner, your chances will improve."

"Are you certain?"

"Do it!" he barked in reply, spurring Vasily into movement. "Better you face the State than the mob!"

Golitsyn quickly bound his wrists with the cloth, obeying Shaklovity's direction to make it tight.

"What will you do?" the Commander asked, looking up at him. "When I am gone, what is your next move, Prince? Will you flee like Medvedev?"

"I will remain by the Regent's side," he replied nobly, "and endeavor to see her through this…transition."

"Oh?" Shaklovity looked at him as though he didn't believe. "Good, that. Nothing Sophia has done that you haven't, eh? Be careful you're not next."

"The Holy Father willing, I will not be."

They turned into the Holy Vestibule, the head of the Red Staircase awaiting them, the clamor of Strel'tsy anger ringing from every corner.

Shaklovity wiped his beard and held out his chin proudly. "Safe travels, Comrade Golitsyn."

"Safe travels to you, Commander."

Spotted immediately, the Strel'tsy musketeers ran to form a circle around the two, weapons drawn and ready. Their hungry looks made Vasily grateful for the torn strip of cloth.

Moscow, The Great Sovereign's Palace of the Kremlin

Moments Later, September 11, 1689

He found Sophia in her bedchamber, dressed and waiting, her face still carrying a flush but no longer bearing the tearful look. She stood immediately, rushing to greet him.

"Oh, Vasily!" She moved into his arms. "I knew you would return! Give me a kiss!"

He kissed her, allowing himself to succumb to her passion, feeling the fragility within her sturdy figure as she clung to him. Sophia's voice was calm, but her embrace spoke of desperation.

"They are gone, then? The trouble is finished?"

"The Strel'tsy have departed, yes. I cannot speak to the trouble."

"The two of us, together," she whispered, her lips on his neck. "You have always been the sun that breaks through the clouds. And now, when things are at their worst, you save me again."

She pulled away, smiling back at him.

"Sophia, I--"

"When the two of you left, my spirit went with you, Vasily. I was broken…standing here crying, praying, lamenting the loss of poor Fedor, imagining the horrors that await him, thinking of what the bloodthirsty Naryshkin interrogators would do, but even more than that, I was selfishly worrying about my own tragedy, allowing myself to dwell on the worst thoughts."

"Sophia--"

"But you must wait! Let me finish, my love!" She offered another kiss. "It was your words that changed me. I thought of your wise words, urging me to distance myself from the charges. You spoke of saving the Regency, did you not? I can see, Vasily! In the end, poor, brave Fedor will be the one to save us. His blood will wash away the suspicion and doubt. Our respectful presence will acknowledge his guilt and the matter will be finished.

"They have their perpetrator now," she continued before he could speak, "and though it tears at my heart to see Fedor carried into their hands, perhaps his sacrifice will rid them of their thirst. Surely, the Patriarch would be reluctant to support anything more."

"I would not be quick to guess at the intentions of the Patriarch."

"We were not named in the charges, Vasily! With Fedor in custody, there is little more of which we can be accused! With the matter finished, so is our trouble. The rest can be cured with politics. I was lost until I understood your meaning."

She is lost in denial, he thought, his conscience crying in regret but knowing that false optimism would serve her spirit better than despair.

I must allow her this moment of belief.

"I am happy to see your spirits up," he replied, his voice warm and strong. "We will certainly need to show Moscow this same bright face in the days to come. You are quite beautiful when you choose to smile."

"I am not." she replied, grinning with a blush. "Yet you have always been kind enough to say it."

"And I have always been sincere."

She smiled graciously. "I can recall Natalya once shouting at me that she wondered how a man like you could ever be so loyal to me. I remember being quite angry and shouting back that our loyalty was to each other--and to Russia. We have always been a pair, Vasily. This is the truth. I would proudly tell your wife the same."

Prince Vasily thought of his wife, waiting in the country, her simple life about to be changed forever. There was little question. Even if Peter were lenient, Prince Vasily and his household would be leaving Moscow for good. His wife and children would accept this fate along with him. Sophia would be left alone in Moscow, accompanied only by her dwindling list of family members.

"We must speak of the future, Sophia. We are still very much on the defensive--"

"I know, yes! I am not yet finished telling you." She stood before him, flushed with hope. "There is still much work to do--restoring our reputation, showing the people…showing the Strel'tsy that the Regency remains!

"I will deliver a heartfelt address," she continued, pressing to convince him. "A speech so pure and kind that they cannot help but sympathize. From the Red Staircase, I think, surrounded by the Strel'tsy and the most loyal members of the Duma. Surely, you can aid me in gathering the right people."

"The Strel'tsy and the Duma in the same audience?"

"Of course. You're right, of course." She paced now. "I shall have to give the speech in Red Square, and more than once! Two--no, three times--once to my supporters, once to the Strel'tsy, and finally to the people of Moscow. They shall see me and know I have survived the accusations. I am capable of this!"

He hesitated, not wanting to deflate her. "Do you think, perhaps, something more intimate might be more persuasive? You could, for example, summon the nobles for individual audiences and speak with them personally. One at a time, I think you might have great success. And with enough gifts, the loyalties of the Strel'tsy could likely be purchased. They are better swayed with coin than words."

"Oh, there will certainly be gifts," she replied immediately, her eyes bright. "Those who attend must be treated well. I will serve vodka, perhaps, and deliver my speech with Ivan at my side! And there will be more than just words, Vasily. The Strel'tsy will certainly see their compensation. Their gifts will be promised and delivered. I must prepare a list of those who are most deserving."

Prince Vasily forced a grin, knowing there was little for him to do now besides offering his support. He stared for a moment at the window, praying that his carriage would be ready and waiting. He quietly resolved to find a horse and proceed alone should it not arrive; one way or another, he would leave Moscow as soon as he left Sophia's side.

There was little time to waste. Shaklovity was on his way to Troitsky and would arrive sometime before morning. With luck, his interrogation would wait until the afternoon.

I must make it to Troitsky before Fedor has the opportunity to speak.

I must arrive and make my appeal in the morning. Peter will question the timing, but with Boris' good faith, he will at least hear my words. I should have gone sooner.

It now seemed obvious that he should have heeded his cousin's warnings when the letters were first delivered. Coming on the heels of Shaklovity's arrival, Vasily knew that his appearance at Troitsky would be seen as an act of desperation.

Still, despite the repercussions, Prince Vasily could not blame himself for staying. To this day--to this very moment--Sophia proved to be the most compelling figure in his life, a woman beyond compare. She was greater in his eyes than his own loving wife and had always been able to command his loyalty with little more than a glance. Their love had been more than simple convenience, and as he looked into her eyes, Vasily realized how dearly he would miss her.

"You must be sure to make the speech dignified," he told her, "and without any ill will or direct insult to the Tsarista or the Naryshkins."

"Without question." She frowned a bit. "Do you think me incapable of such tact? Surely you know I can hold my temper when I choose."

"I merely meant to suggest that there will be another time for avenging Fedor. Now, you must worry solely about your good name."

"My good name," she echoed, "and the security of the Regency."

He nodded reluctantly. "Yes, and that."

"Perhaps you should speak as well, Vasily! Yes! The members of the Duma would respect it."

"I will not," he answered abruptly, raising a palm. "This is your day, Sophia. And far too many Strel'tsy still loathe me for what happened on the campaign. My words could only detract from the potency of your sentiment."

She took his hand, raising it to her cheek. "Don't be silly, love, your words and my words are the same. You and I are one in the eyes of Moscow."

There was truth in what she said, the notion of it leaving him with an unsettling feeling, the better part of him knowing that his political career would end along with the Regency. Association and affiliation played a large part in the management of Russia; stepping across family lines to support Sophia's regime had been a decision full of risk and reward.

Vasily could see it all now. Peter would reign and Ivan would sit in his shadow as everyone expected. The Naryshkins would take Russia once and for all, claiming a rightful victory over the Miloslavskys. They had played a baiting game of chess, summoning the knights and pawns, winning the bishop and now claiming the queen in a brilliant endgame. Checkmate awaited them, only a few moves away.

He could wait no more. His defense of Sophia was bred from years of trust and complicity, his presence secured by genuine, heartfelt emotion. Had he loved her less, Vasily would have retired at the end of the campaign. Now, grudgingly, he would have to turn his back on Sophia and leave her to the Naryshkins.

"Vasily? What is that look?"

"Look?" he replied, waking from his thoughts. "I was thinking, my dear."

"Of what?"

"Of you," he replied, gazing into her eyes, sensing the fear beneath her happy exterior. "How many times did we stand in this very chamber, Sophia, planning the future, knowing that our simple discussions would bloom and grow into policy."

"And we shall do it again, my love. The two of us! Ivan is grown but still not a man. It is no secret that his condition cannot improve."

"Peter wants his throne, Sophia."

"But Russia needs us still, Vasily! You'll see. After my speech, we will return to our duties. Peter may not need us, but Ivan certainly does. This has been our duty. They have no more charges to raise against us!"

He moved to respond but held his tongue, fighting the instinct to contradict her. In her heart, Sophia surely knew the truth.

I must agree with her, he thought, nodding as though he understood. *She has been through too much to deny her this last bit of hope.*

"You will be wonderful. I know it."

"You will be proud, Vasily."

"With Peter at Troitsky, there is still much you can do to secure your support. You are still well-acquainted with the Novodevichi Convent, are you not?"

"Of course! I have given them more than anyone else--my donations are a mark of record! But why do you ask of the Convent?"

He cleared his throat. "I merely thought, in the absence of the Patriarch, it may benefit you to show the support of the Church. You may not be Joachim's favorite, but you are far more pious and devout than Peter. The sight of the Holy Father's favored would no doubt echo among the musketeers."

She paused, nodding. "A wise notion. I will send a letter requesting the presence of the Abbess. You see? Together we will survive this!"

Vasily thought again of his wife, missing her soft touch and understanding words, eager to be back at home and away from Moscow. Already the walls of the Kremlin grew cold and unfamiliar--the fortress that had once hosted his greatest achievements now transformed into a dungeon, a giant stone prison meant to hold him until his execution.

You must stop your bleeding heart, he told himself, welcoming her embrace. *If there is anyone capable of surviving this, it is Regent Sophia Alexeevna Miloslavsky. She is young enough to enjoy her life and wise enough to regain her place should the opportunity arise.*

Soon there will be heirs. The people will take comfort in the lineage. Peter will stand astride the country and Ivan will wither away into his illness. The Regency will be little more than a memory, a page in a history that we can no longer change.

We have only our lives. She will hate me at first, and in time, understand. Somehow, she will understand.

"You are a remarkable woman," he told her, offering a final kiss before pulling away. "I shall always carry you in my heart."

She slapped him on the shoulder. "Hush, before I have to pull you into bed! You speak as though you're going to be carried away by the Guard!"

"No," he returned, forcing a smile, "You have much to do. I will depart, but I plan to make every effort to avoid the Strel'tsy. At least for tonight."

"Be cautious, my love. Tomorrow is an important day."

"None more important," he replied. "As always, Regent, you have my devotion."

He bowed before exiting, closing the door behind him.

And just like that, it was finished.

It felt strange leaving the Kremlin, walking away from Sophia without feeling obligated to return, leaving her without offering some kind of final farewell. There was no question that he would think of her often, and he knew that in the days to come there would perhaps be regret when he considered how he exited her life. Yet, as he marched down the Red Staircase and out into the evening, Prince Vasily raised his chin to meet the cool wind, secure in the decision he had made.

In a matter of minutes Vasily was sitting in his carriage, headed out of Moscow toward Troitsky, his cousin's letters in hand. Finally, the end was upon them. And however grim the prospect, the thought of his impending audience with Peter came as something of a relief. After all the waiting and indecision, his appeal would be made and his fate decided.

Outside Moscow, The Monastery of Troitskaya-Sergeeva

The Early Morning of September 12, 1689

"Commander Shaklovity has arrived, sire. He comes bearing chains."

Boris made the announcement with pride, not bothering to hide his satisfaction. After all the time spent planning and worrying, it seemed a great cathartic relief to gloat and smile over their victory.

More than anyone here at Troitsky, Golitsyn knew that he was responsible.

"I believe Boris is attempting to be witty, sire." Lev Naryshkin chuckled beside him.

"A rare occurrence," Peter replied, rolling his eyes a bit. "And you are far too late with the news. I was awake to greet them and saw Shaklovity while you were still sleeping. I didn't speak to him, of course."

Predictably, the young Tsar was up early and eager to proceed with the day's events. Golitsyn had attempted to outlast Sophia's standoff but fell asleep in the early morning, just before Shaklovity was delivered.

"Then you heard of the events at the Kremlin…the difficulty in acquiring the Commander."

"Which difficulty?" Peter paused, staring. "That Sophia hesitated to give him away? That the Strel'tsy almost sounded the alarm bell?"

"Yes."

"As I heard," Naryshkin added, "they were well along the way to sacking the Kremlin!"

Peter nodded, shrugging. "Oh, I'm quite aware. They say she never appeared. She's seen what happens to those at the top of the Staircase. I was told that Sophia enlisted your poor cousin Vasily to march Shaklovity down to his captors. Can you imagine the sight? What a blow it must have been! If only we could have seen it ourselves! Eh, Boris? I suppose that few would expect Sophia to surrender him willingly, but it does seem a fortuitous surprise."

Peter's disdain for Vasily seemed obvious, still.

"The Strel'tsy line up behind you, Peter. There were many calling your name. Those who delivered the Commander have joined the ranks under Colonel Tsykler. The Strel'tsy in Moscow are calm again."

"Calm at present," Boris added, raising a finger. "Though I suspect the remaining few will be quite nervous to see General Gordon and the foreign officers depart. As for the event itself, I was told that Prince Golitsyn cooperated fully with the Strel'tsy musketeers."

"Oh?"

"He had little choice, it seems," Naryshkin interjected. "They were beckoning from the foot of the Red Staircase, and I expect Golitsyn was wondering if he would be carried off as well! It was, however, a gallant attempt at defending your cousin."

Offended, Boris glared back at Lev, desperately wanting to reach out and choke him.

The drunken fool! He disgraces me for sport--with my family name at stake!

"I was merely stating the truth," Boris answered quickly. "And I think it quite obvious that Prince Vasily was instrumental in bringing about the Regent's compliance. Tell me, who else would so sway her opinions?"

"Granted, he was likely responsible." Lev conceded, nodding. "Likely also, that he was sitting in her lap with his head resting on her bosom!"

The Counselor grimaced, his anger uncontainable for a moment.

"Lev! Must you?"

Boris could see Peter staring now. The Tsar was well aware of the friction between the two and disapproved completely. Both he and Naryshkin had received reprimands from the young ruler, though if asked, Boris would say that he had been treated far worse than his young counterpart. Lev was closer to Peter in age and shared the young Tsar's propensity for drink. And above all else, Lev was a Naryshkin.

"I refuse to hear your bickering today," the Tsar said, his glare moving from Lev to Boris and back again.

"My apologies, Peter." Naryshkin offered a slight, apologetic bow. "I merely mean to suggest that the Prince is at the command of the Regent, whatever the rest may claim. His support among the army has dwindled to nothing, and his respect in the Duma is naught but a ghost! Surely, Vasily would have thought his own neck at risk. It will be curious to hear what Shaklovity reveals."

"Vasily has not been charged," Boris countered, defending his cousin. "There has been no evidence against him!"

"Not yet," Lev teased, shrugging. "Old Shaklovity may decide that he needs company on the executioner's block."

"You are cruel to suggest so--"

"Hush!" Peter silenced both with a word, the boy scolding the men with a pointed finger. "The two of you are like cats--you prattle and wail without ever striking a blow. I want the interrogation to commence as soon as the prisoner is prepared. No rest for him. We must find the truth of this matter."

Shaklovity will not confess to what he did not do. The issue must be quickly buried and his head quickly removed.

Golitsyn took a breath, trying to exhale away his frustration, reminding himself that they were almost finished. All his efforts, guided by the favor of the Holy Father and the grace of good fortune, culminating in this interrogation. With Shaklovity's death, the conspiracy would become fact and Sophia's fate would be sealed. History would not remember, but the Tsarista would know that, without Boris Golitsyn, none of this would have been possible.

Recognition was unimportant at this moment. He would gain his reputation as he always had--through his work. With a Naryshkin government in Moscow, the benefits would be considerable, for Boris and his entire family. The worries and fears would soon be in his past, with nothing but prosperity in the future. All that remained was the issue of cousin Vasily.

"I would like to offer my services," Boris began politely, looking to Peter, "as chief interrogator."

He caught Naryshkin's look of approval, but remained focused on the Tsar. Peter was stoic and listening.

"My lord, I possess more information than anyone regarding this issue, and given that they may be inflammatory, the Commander's words must be kept close. I would gladly perform this task."

"Do so," Peter said with a gesture, nodding. "Begin today. And bring me the transcripts as soon as the interrogation ends. No doubt you will ask the right questions, Boris. I only hope you are strict enough to manage the torture."

Ah! The reasonable boy!

Boris relaxed a bit. "I am most capable, sire. We will get what we need."

He will give me a confession or die resisting.

"Good." Peter stared for a moment. "The task in good hands with you, Boris. I am certain Mother would agree."

"My thanks, sire."

"I am very eager to discover the truth," the young Tsar continued, "and we must consider any and all conspirators, not just Medvedev. Do what you must, but not at the risk of his life. The prisoner must survive the interrogation."

"Certainly," Boris answered with confidence, his spirits eased at the thought of the interrogation. "I will do my utmost to gain his confession."

"Indeed," Lev huffed, his tone thick with petulance. "And we should not be surprised when Prince Vasily remains unmentioned."

"No more." Peter glared now, quieting him. "On the matter of Vasily Golitsyn, my mind is already made."

Naryshkin bowed. "I will hold my comments for his trial."

Already made his mind?

Boris paled at the words. Peter's disdain for Golitsyn was no secret, but the boy seemed to possess a sense of justice and in his time at Troitsky had not seemed bent on bringing down Vasily. On the contrary, Peter seemed to understand Boris' awkward position and generally recognized the Golitsyn clan as Naryshkin supporters.

But Peter was not the type to reverse his decisions. With Vasily still in Moscow, there was no legitimate way of voicing opinion without seeming to pose as an advocate.

"Sire? Certainly it would be best to hold judgment until after the interrogation…"

"Your clan loyalty is no doubt commendable," Peter said to him, speaking quite directly, "but you fail to understand the breadth of his offence."

"Surely his service has earned him some consideration, sire."

"We have discussed this, Boris." Peter shook his head. "Prince Golitsyn has been standing beside Sophia from the very beginning, seconding every opinion, giving voice and force to every policy. That fattened mule has been staring down his nose and chastising our family for the whole of the Regency, posturing himself against our clan and passing veiled insults that he thought I couldn't understand. He has lost the faith of the Duma, the army, and has failed in his command on two consecutive campaigns."

Peter paused, stepping closer, his gaze serious. "But more than all this, Boris, your cousin was a participant on that bloody day, executing the orders of Sophia and her list, calling for the heads of Matveev and Uncle Ivan. Whatever I may see in my lifetime, Boris, I will never forget that day. Your cousin should be grateful--I will be far more merciful with his clan than he was with mine."

Golitsyn lowered his eyes. "Understood, sire--"

"Allow me to finish!"

Boris straightened respectfully, obeying.

"Unless Shaklovity incriminates him, I will not pursue your cousin for treason," Peter continued angrily. "In this, your family may feel secure. But neither will I bow to negotiate away his transgressions! Now, I told you I have no suspicions of treason. I've heard that Sophia was playing Shaklovity as well as your cousin, pitting them against each other. Given his failures, Vasily will certainly be seen as a desperate man, but I cannot envision his plotting with Shaklovity.

"Still, there remains the trouble of his presence. If Sophia is to remain in Moscow upon her retirement, then Prince Vasily must go.

This much is simple, Boris. Your cousin has played his part, received his accolade, and must now suffer through the results of his association with Sophia. I will bear nothing less."

He thought of his letters, disappointed that Vasily had neglected to take his advice and face Peter in person.

"I want you to know, Boris, that I understand your position and I respect your loyalty. Truly! The lot of us should be fortunate enough to have a clan member as diligent and loyal as you. I blame you for nothing and carry no ill will against your esteemed family for the actions of Prince Vasily."

Is all this conjecture for naught? Peter respects my family. Should I be distancing myself from Vasily instead of pleading his case?

Boris reminded himself that there were limits to such loyalties, even where family members were concerned. Vasily, despite his enormous success, had always been the black sheep, and Boris the respectable public servant. The remainder of the family was firmly aligned behind him now, and Natalya would secure their place in the new Naryshkin government.

Thank the Holy Father for Natalya! She will keep us above the scandal. I shall take my place and soon Vasily will be forgotten.

"Your mercy is appreciated, sire," he answered. "The Golitsyn clan remains devoted to your cause and that of the Naryshkins."

After all this time, after all I have done to create him, I must stand here crying my devotion like a concubine! Surely Lev is satisfied!

"Your devotion has never been in question," Peter said, his tone softening. "I've hurt your feelings, haven't I, Boris? Yes, I can see it in your face. Mother would slay me if she thought I afforded you anything but esteem for your service. Besides, this is a day for celebration--you said it yourself!"

Boris nodded, forcing a grin. "Indeed. We have struggled to arrive at this moment."

Peter nodded back, his face brightening. "Good, then. I wish for the two of you to embrace as brothers and for the three of us to drink to our good fortune!"

"Ah!" Naryshkin applauded. "Now that is an edict that I will certainly support…at least the part about drinking!"

The Tsar moved to the table, pouring three short cups of vodka. Before handing them away, he looked back to insure that the two would shake hands. Noting his interest, Boris grudgingly accepted. For the moment, at least, Lev's gaze bore no malice.

I should enjoy the victory, Boris told himself, accepting the cup and raising it to match Peter. *I deserve a moment of triumph.*

The Tsar paused in reflection before beginning.

"To the memory of all the poor souls lost in Sophia's wake…"

They drank, the fine vodka sending a warm rush through him.

Holding up a finger to prevent them from speaking, Peter quickly poured another round. The three raised the cups again.

"To my Mother, Natalya, the Naryshkins, and all who stand with us…"

"Here, here." Naryshkin grinned before gladly downing his second. "We will all be grateful to see that traitor's head in a basket!"

"What?" Peter raised a hand, looking to Lev. "You have me mistaken, Uncle Lev. I intend for Fedor Shaklovity's head to remain where it is."

The two hesitated, rendered collectively speechless by Peter's words.

What? Is he mad?

Boris' brow clenched in consternation. "Sire?"

"You heard me, Boris. I do not wish to be seen as the same bloody sort as Sophia. I do not wish Commander Shaklovity to be executed, confession or not."

Golitsyn's instincts spurred him. "But, sire, this is treason!"

"I am aware, Boris. We must be merciful, nonetheless."

"Mercy, perhaps for some of the conspirators. But for Shaklovity?"

"Think of it, Peter," Naryshkin stepped forward, equally concerned. "Even in exile, he would be an embarrassment...and a danger."

Peter crossed his arms. "I no longer fear the Strel'tsy. My mercy will only secure their loyalty."

"Hardly, sire!" Boris snapped, his emotion slipping. "The execution of traitors is a matter of law. How can you expect to gain respect if Shaklovity is allowed to live?"

"Have another cup, Boris, and I will explain."

Boris capitulated, wondering at the difficulties this happy day had produced.

We will tell the Tsarista. The boy's irrational thoughts will be quelled by his mother.

Gratefully, a knock on the massive double doors interrupted their third toast.

"Peter?"

Recognizing his mother's voice, the Tsar downed his cup and motioned for the other two to do the same. Boris set his cup on the table, eager to see the Tsarista.

Naryshkin put his cup down and rushed across to open the door. Dressed in her customary dark gown, Lady Natalya entered unattended. Her dark eyes warmed at the sight of Peter.

"My darling..."

He moved to embrace her. "Mother. Is something wrong?"

"No, nothing wrong," she answered. "But the Patriarch comes to speak with you. I would have accompanied him, but I thought it best to give you a moment's warning."

"Let him come," Peter told her. "I don't mind his endless questions. But for what purpose this time, Mother?"

Natalya nodded her greetings to Boris and Lev. "He comes to discuss the prisoner. He has specific wishes regarding the process. I believe he wishes the executions to take place here at Troitsky."

"An appropriate subject, Tsarista," Boris said, using the opportunity. "Peter was just telling us that he has no intention of executing the traitors."

"What?" Natalya frowned immediately. "What do you mean?"

"I refuse to leave a wake of blood like Sophia," Peter said, now speaking only to Natalya. "You remember that day better than any of us, Mother."

"I do, and this is much different." Natalya reached up to place a hand on his shoulder. Smiling, she tugged gently on his brown locks. "Your sentiment is well appreciated, but there is simply no other way. This is treason, Peter."

"Just as I was trying to relate, Tsarista."

Sounds from the corridor announced the imminent entrance of the Patriarch.

"The subject will wait," Natalya told them, allowing her glare to linger on Peter. Boris straightened and took a step backward.

The Patriarch entered in his richly embroidered velvet cope, flanked on either side by the highest ranking abbots. His tall miter sat like a tower atop his head, the Holy Father's way of insuring that no one would rise above him. Yet even when wearing it, Joachim could not surpass Peter in height.

"Tsar Peter."

"Your Holiness." Peter bowed slightly in respect, his gaze never leaving that of Joachim. "It appears that our time at Troitsky may soon come to an end."

"All in the hands of providence," Joachim replied, his words typically paced. "I am pleased to see the arrival of the prisoner and a resolution on the horizon."

"Your Holiness? Would you prefer that I clear the room?" Peter asked, gesturing toward Boris and Lev. "I can provide privacy, if you prefer."

"No," Joachim responded, looking at each of them. "I believe everyone here is in confidence. My issue bears import, but is not so indelicate that your mother may not listen."

He looked down at Natalya, smiling as a friend, his look returned in kind by the Tsarista. Peter seemed pleased and nodded his assent.

"Please, then, of what do you wish to speak?"

Knowing he commanded the attention of the room, the Patriarch paused deliberately and straightened the sleeves of his robe, taking his time just as he had done countless times before the congregation. Boris had to admit that Patriarch Joachim, though he was not known for his mind or his wit, had a sense of the dramatic about him, one which played well with the Muscovites. He seemed everything that he was and never compromised his appearance or his reputation.

"Executions," Joachim began, looking back at Peter. "A subject that is thankfully foreign to me. Though in light of the events of the past month--the treachery which befell you, your period of sanctuary and the eventual arrest--I feel that perhaps it would be best if the executions took place here at Troitsky. I would appreciate it, as a favor to the Church."

"Your generosity is appreciated, Your Holiness," Peter replied, "But I believe you may have misunderstood--"

"He means to say that the interrogation has not yet taken place," Boris blurted out in interruption, his cheeks flushing.

"With my apologies, I would add that the prisoner has not yet been convicted."

The Patriarch paused a moment, then offered a small shrug. "Well, all in time, yes? I see no reason why we shouldn't discuss the execution. The act itself would not take place within the Monastery walls, of course. I would like it to occur just outside, with the walls in the background. I think it would be a fitting place to mark this bit of history."

"Your Holiness," Peter began again, calling off Boris with a steely glance. "I do not wish to execute the conspirators. I would rather have them exiled. I will not have our ascension marked by a group execution."

Joachim's face reflected his surprise. "Tsar Peter, you cannot mean what you say."

"Only a moment ago did I hear of this," Natalya told Joachim, breaking her silence. "Peter was merely thinking aloud, wishing that he could save us the pain of eight years ago. I reminded him, Your Holiness, that these circumstances are different."

"They certainly are, Tsarista." Joachim looked to Peter. "I will readily commend you on your merciful notions, Peter. You would do well to carry such thoughtfulness with you on the throne. But the attempt on your life was not merely an attempt to murder Peter Alexeevich, it was an attempt to disrupt the rightful progression of rule, an affront to every Tsar who came before you and every one who will follow.

"But more than this," Joachim continued, his hands remaining still, "An attempt on the life of the Tsar is a challenge to the will of the Holy Father himself. You know this Peter. This is a law greater than that of Russia, one that cannot be surpassed by the word of any Tsar. Those who tried to kill you must be executed. There is no compromise. Do you understand?"

Peter scowled a bit, looking toward his mother. "I do, Your Holiness," he relented, managing his temper well. "Though I think it a bad omen to begin with such blood."

"Not at all," Joachim replied with confidence. "I expect there is little capable of staining your return to the throne. Many have been waiting to see you and your brother rule as you were meant to do. There is much work to be done; repairing the damage that the Regent inflicted will be a considerable task."

"Your support has been our strength, Your Holiness." Natalya kneeled to kiss his hand. "I know you will continue to provide counsel in the days to come."

"We are all driven by duty, Tsarista," Joachim told her. "Ah, yes, that reminds me--my abbots reported a visitor at the east gate, requesting an audience with Tsar Peter."

Peter looked up, still angry. "A visitor?"

"Prince Vasily," the Patriarch told him, speaking as though amused. "Traveling alone, asking kindly to see you, sire. In deference to you, I ordered him kept him outside the walls of the Monastery. You may call on him if and when you wish."

The news struck him well. Peter's face transformed into a grin, then again into a raucous laugh. "Yes! Now there is something to lift our spirits! Prince Vasily has come to make his appeal! This will save us the trouble of finding him. I will certainly call on him, but not just yet. Let us make him wait a bit!"

With the lightening of Peter's mood, the mood of the room lifted, and soon they were passing polite congratulations and talking of what Moscow would become.

Boris slipped away from the group, his mind on family matters, his worry re-doubling.

Now he arrives? What could he hope to gain by making his appeal at this late hour?

Sophia is finished, then--and Vasily along with her. His words must match those of the prisoner. Insulting! After all the work, our family name may rest on the words of that bastard Shaklovity!

I must be quick, he thought, his mind already enrapt in the interrogation. *I will leave no room for conjecture or argument. With the grace of the Patriarch, Shaklovity's head will soon be delivered!*

Outside Moscow, The Village of Vozdvizhenskoe

The Morning of September 12, 1689

"My lord? A cup of broth, perhaps?" the cobbler wrung his hands, unsure of how to please his unexpected guest. "I have little else here at the shop, I'm afraid."

"Nothing," Prince Vasily answered, wallowing in humiliation, hungry but unwilling to engage the commoner in conversation. The cobbler had been kind enough, but overly eager to interject himself, as though wishing to hear the tale of the great Vasily's treatment at the hands of the young Tsar.

They will know soon enough, he thought to himself. *They will all laugh at the story of how Tsar Peter made Prince Vasily wait for hours in a tradesman's shop!*

"Vodka," he said pointing. "Surely a man like you has some vodka."

"No, my lord."

"Are you certain?"

"Yes, my lord.

Hours? I'll be lucky if he doesn't leave me here overnight!

He sat on the hard wooden bench, staring down at his mud-streaked stockings, knowing how horrid he must look. His entire ensemble was coated in road dirt and spotted by rain, his white lace cravat stained and drooping, his once formidable wig flopping down into his eyes, ruined and ridiculous. The stylish European clothes had never been well received by the peasantry and were undoubtedly amusing in such soiled condition. Still, as much as he would have liked to blame his stylish dress for the disdain of the locals, Prince Vasily knew that it was his disgrace and not his appearance that so amused them on this day.

He could hear the villagers laughing as he rode back into Vozdvizhenskoe, a strange and forlorn figure creeping into their midst to wait after being turned away from Troitsky. Dressed in his light blue justaucorps and waistcoat, the Prince was an oddity, a wounded peacock stumbling into the pig pen. Embarrassed, he held his tongue and kept his head down, looking only for a place to wait for Tsarevich Peter's summons.

The indistinct cobbler's shop seemed discreet enough and a suitable place to hide from the curious eyes of the villagers. Once hidden, however, Vasily found himself miserable, wishing he'd chosen to endure the ridicule and find the tavern. Still cold with the chill of the rain, he removed his wig and shook away the droplets, trying to ignore the groans of hunger rising from his neglected belly.

Not even a crust--and he keeps the vodka from me! he thought, glaring at the man. *What a fool I was to think I would be allowed my dignity!*

The day, or rather the night, had begun quite differently.

He'd left Moscow in an optimistic mood, passing the gates without incident under the cover of darkness. Sophia lingered in his mind, but Vasily kept his course by reminding himself of his duty to his family and thinking of what might ultimately happen to him if he remained in the city.

His ride to Troitsky had been full of hope, driven by thoughts of negotiation, spurred by the prospect of restoring his reputation and somehow retaining his dignity. He'd practiced his words and responses, imagining what the audience might be like, carefully rehearsing his speech so as not to forget a single point. And whether it was his sanguine disposition or the open air of the road, Vasily's confidence grew as he neared the Monastery grounds.

In his greatcoat he bore the letters from his cousin Boris requesting his presence and a lengthy speech, written in his own hand. The defense was eloquent enough, he thought, reciting a long list of his service to Russia and a humble admission of his shortcomings in the recent campaigns. He'd done his best to list his many achievements while still remaining dutiful to the cause, just the words he thought Peter and the Naryshkins were eager to hear.

And, after all, there was cousin Boris.

Boris would be present, certainly, and would likely speak in his behalf--in light of recent events, there was no question that his words carried weight. Tsarista Natalya was a dour and disapproving woman, but Vasily knew that her ill will toward him was equaled by her fondness for Boris. The Tsarista would listen to Boris, and Peter, as always, would listen to his mother. There still seemed a definitive glimmer of hope, despite the Tsarevich's posturing.

He looked up to see that the cobbler had returned, rubbing his hands.

"Yes?" Vasily glared.

"I've sent the boy, my lord," he announced meekly. "Soon you will have vodka and some bread."

"You are most hospitable," the Prince replied curtly, "but I do not expect to be here long."

"My family will be happy to provide what you need, my lord."

"Yes, very well."

I should be more gracious. I need friends, of whatever sort. And my carriage back...

It seemed ridiculous now.

Brimming with confidence at the sight of the morning light, Vasily had ordered the carriage to halt at Vozdvizhenskoe, thinking it better to approach the Monastery alone so as to appear a more humble and pitiable figure. He took a single horse and commanded the carriage to return to Moscow, setting off for the Monastery with a buoyant spirit.

His ride was glorious at first, mounted astride the great animal, denying the weather and thinking only of his purpose. He enjoyed the feeling of independence, galloping down this well-traveled road without his entourage, both literally and politically alone, traveling without the escort Peter and the others would expect. He imagined his approach and thought of how the abbots and the Patriarch would speak of his humility and praise his change of heart. At worst, a pitiable entrance could only aid his cause.

It took longer than expected to arrive. The towering white walls of the Monastery were a welcome sight. Somewhere within waited Peter and the answers to the questions Vasily had been asking himself for days. How deeply was he implicated? What role was he given in this charade of accusations? And most important of all: what was his punishment to be? It felt both reassuring and frightening to know that the wait was over.

His arrival had been without fanfare--a lone rider approaching the shining fortress of God, riding with a humble bend in his posture and mournful regret etched on his face. He was greeted only by the sight of two guards, but kept his sympathetic look

He dismounted at the sight of the two Preobrazhensky sentries. They stared curiously at first, their faces changing to surprise when they finally recognized his face. As though acting on orders, the sentries instructed him to wait outside the gates.

I should have been admitted, he thought immediately, his eyes scanning the high walls and armed towers. *They knew enough to meet Sophia up the road. Certainly their spies knew of my arrival! Surely, they are waiting!*

It was nearly an hour before a green-coated soldier appeared with two abbots at his side. He recognized the soldier as the younger Troekorov.

"Prince Golitsyn." Troekorov's face bore no hospitable air. "Your arrival is unexpected."

"Good day to you, friend." Vasily offered a humble bow. "I arrive without escort and bear no ill will. You see I am alone."

"You deliver a message from the Regent?"

"No, no. I come alone and on my own behalf," he replied, hiding his angst. "A matter of importance--I seek an audience with Tsarevich Peter."

Troekorov paused, staring without expression. Vasily held his posture, unflinching, ignoring the first droplets of rain.

"I will deliver your request to the Tsar," Troekorov said finally. "You are to wait in Vozdvizhenskoe for a reply."

Vasily could remember his heart shrinking, his confidence ebbing away in a single moment.

"But it lies miles up the road!"

"Correct," Troekorov replied. "You are to wait there, Commander."

Vasily sighed, clasping his hands and forcing a grin. "If you please, sir, I bring no escort or entourage. Surely I am no threat to wait here quietly."

Troekorov shook his head, his expression unchanging. "Not possible, Commander. You are to wait in Vozdvizhenskoe. Your request will be delivered."

"Yes…but perhaps, if you would…" His desperation alive, Vasily reached into his pocket and produced the letters, holding them out for Troekorov to see. "I was invited here by my cousin Boris. He requested that I come to Troitsky."

Troekorov took the letters, perusing them before placing them in his own pocket. "These will be taken into consideration."

"If you would call upon my cousin, Counselor Boris Golitsyn," Vasily pressed, "I am certain he would allow me to stay in his care--until a time that my audience could be arranged, of course."

"I cannot make such decisions," Troekorov told him plainly, giving no ground. "My duty is to deliver orders from the Tsar. You are to wait in Vozdvizhenskoe until you are summoned, Commander."

"Outside the gates, then? I could wait here."

"In Vozdvizhenskoe, sir."

"Wait a moment, friend! Does my cousin know I have arrived? You know him, son. Tell him I am here. He will want to speak with me."

No reply. Ignoring his words, Troekorov turned and stepped back inside the gates, the abbots following closely behind. The sentries re-appeared, securing the iron latches before retaking their posts.

Troekorov was gone, and with him any possibility of protest. All that remained was the looming white walls and the road back to Vozdvizhenskoe.

He felt ridiculous. Prince V.V. Golitsyn, a man who only weeks before had been considered the most influential in all of Russia now begging like a peasant child outside the gates of the Monastery. Inside, the Naryshkins laughed along with the clergy, knowing that Prince Vasily had come to plead for his life. The thought was maddening, but there remained little else to do but return to the village and wait for Peter's call.

At least, he remembered thinking, *I will still have my audience.*

As the minutes in the cobbler's shop passed, it was this thought that kept him hopeful and focused.

This sort of game is routine for Peter, he reminded himself, trying to reconcile his current position with his chance for success. *He wishes to embarrass me--so be it. He will let me know who is Tsar and then allow me to resign gracefully. I desire only my wife and my property to exist. The Duma need never hear my name again.*

He thought of Sophia, wondering if she were yet aware of his absence. She would be enraged at his departure, but Sophia would live and would one day come to understand.

Yet, of all the questions surrounding his audience with Peter, there seemed one certainty: he had seen the Regent's face for the last time.

Sophia will survive. I must think of myself now, and my own family. If I can escape with my head and my gold, Boris can carry the name as far as he likes! My time in politics is at an end--Peter will see to that. But if I concede and offer my resignation from all posts? I will have to leave Moscow, surely...but to be completely rid of me? What more could Peter and the Tsarista want?

I look hideous, he thought, staring down at himself, *but my speech will be a work of beauty!*

Knowing his appearance could scarcely be recovered, Vasily produced his notes and began studying, working and re-working the lines of his appeal, murmuring under his breath as he practiced them in his head.

As promised, the cobbler produced some vodka and bread. Vasily gratefully indulged, and by the bottom of the second cup, he was shaking away the chill of the rain and feeling much better about his chances.

"I am a man of words, you see," he told the shopkeeper, holding out his cup to be filled. "I made my name through politics and the practice of coercion…in the name of our homeland, of course. All of Moscow knows this. They know me for this."

"Yes, my lord." The cobbler poured another cup, wisely holding his tongue.

"You see?" Vasily sipped at the third cup. "That's what I admire about men of your make, friend. You know when to shut up and let a man speak. I can speak, friend--and I will! This time, I refuse to be modest. Let all the Naryshkins cringe as they listen to my litany of service! By the time I am finished, none will be able to question me!"

Coerced by the drink, weariness crept in, leaving the Prince dozing on his bench, his back slumped against the wall. He drifted, his words fading as he mumbled the lines of his appeal.

"Sleep if you like," the cobbler told him. "I will wake you if someone comes."

"Not necessary," Vasily said, wiping his chin and attempting to sit up. "I was only resting for a moment, saving my strength for more important matters…"

And with that, he slept.

Moscow, Cathedral Square, The Red Staircase

The Late Afternoon of September 12, 1689

To Patrick Gordon, it seemed an appropriate place for the Regent to make her final appeal.

The Red Staircase had been the site of Sophia's initial, bloody victory, a perch from which she remained both woman and Regent. She had presented herself here dozens of times since that infamous day, using the traditional backdrop to her best advantage. Now, only seven years after her ascension, the opulent stage would be hosting her political demise.

"Quite the gathering, General."

"They are fearful, and rightly so," Gordon answered, surveying the scene. "This transition has been hard on the Russians. They like to know their place."

The large crowd gathered at the foot of the Red Staircase was common in nature, a cross section of the Moscow populace joined together as a public audience for Regent Sophia. Cautious and curious, the merchants, civil servants and clergy buzzed with anticipation, the third such group to visit the Kremlin on this day.

"She gave the speech to the Strel'tsy this morning," Diechmann commented, "and then repeated her exact words to the Duma earlier this afternoon. The servants say as much. Will we get the same address?"

"We may assume it will be the same," Gordon replied, "although I am more interested in why we were not invited to attend this morning with the rest of the Guard."

Gordon waited at the fringe of the crowd, the foreign mercenary officers present and standing nearby. They were unsettled and anxious after waiting nearly a month to be called into service, and in their presence, Patrick realized how much they needed his leadership.

For the local Strel'tsy, loyalty was a matter of emotion and pride. Their support for the throne was granted as a kind of gift, one which could be easily withdrawn. For the foreign mercenaries, loyalty was far less personal--a matter of money. Quite simply, they were contracted to serve the government.

A month ago this had meant serving the Regency. Now the colonels wondered at the identity of the legitimate government and looked to Gordon for leadership.

"They continue to arrive. This will be Sophia's biggest audience."

"I was told that she pardoned Nechaev."

"Aye, I heard the same. Good, at least, that she comes to her senses."

"She panders now," Diechmann replied, "and the Strel'tsy are through with her. Shaklovity is proof enough. If Peter came riding back with Tsykler and the Patriarch by his side, who would stop him? Would she truly call upon us?"

"No more worries about that," Gordon told him, raising a finger. "I will have you perform a duty for me, Diechmann--one which I think you will be quite glad to do."

He waved for the Captain to step closer, leaning in to speak in his ear.

"I have received an order from Tsarevich Peter," he continued, "delivered just as I arrived inside the gates. It is addressed to all foreign generals, colonels, and other officers in the service of the throne. It tells of the existence of a plot on the life of the Tsarevich and names Shaklovity and the monk Medvedev as conspirators. It also commands that we come to Troitsky, fully armed and on horseback."

"Hah! We--"

"Hear me out, Diechmann. We have been standing without orders for too long. My efforts to engage Prince Golitsyn have been fruitless and we continue to languish without orders from the Kremlin.

"My decision is made," Patrick told him, his tone bearing weight. "If the Keeper of the Great Seal cannot issue a command, then the regime is near collapse. Peter is our commander now, and it is unlikely there is anything Sophia could say this evening to change my mind. You and the other officers must make a choice you can live with, Diechmann, but I will tell you that I intend to leave for Troitsky tonight and arrive by morning."

"Excellent news!" Diechmann beamed. "I will certainly be alongside you!"

"Accompany me if you wish, and tell the rest the same. I will show them the order if they desire proof."

"I will, sir! The rest will come, I'm certain."

Inspired, Captain Diechmann turned to spread the word, Sophia's impending speech all but forgotten. He circulated through the foreign officers, grasping the arm of each before leaning in to speak.

Gordon took a deep breath and pulled his pipe from his pocket, watching their reactions. Judging by the response, he would have much company on his overnight journey to the Monastery. It seemed a great relief finally to have a mission, particularly one that required so little risk.

He nodded to himself, thinking of the outcome, knowing he had done everything according to his duty.

When the trouble first began, Gordon declared that without an order from the Tsars, none of his officers would act. And despite his growing respect for Tsarevich Peter, Gordon had remained true to his word, knowing his duty under contract, acting with the interests of his fellow mercenaries at heart. The Europeans followed his lead, remaining quiet in the Sloboda, more than willing to let him take the credit or the blame for their fate.

Unlike the boisterous Strel'tsy crowds he had witnessed in Red Square, the citizens gathered to see Sophia were cautiously quiet for their number, subdued by the prospect of what they were about to witness. They murmured their curiosity in small groups, the rumors about the Regent's first two audiences keeping everyone enrapt. He looked over their midst, noting the diversity of emotion--the Miloslavsky faithful bearing mournful stares as they wondered at their fate, the Naryshkin loyals smiling at the prospect of what was to come.

Peter's ascension would mean far more than a change of portraits and currency. With Sophia's departure, the Naryshkin clan would take its destined place, bringing a change to hundreds of posts and professions. Those who held high positions in the Regency would lose their influence, replaced by men who bore the family names appearing on Peter's Preobrazhensky and Semyonovsky rosters.

As he watched, Gordon thought of the flood of hopes and fears working in the hearts of the Muscovites. So much at stake for so many, all of them connected to the struggle, their Russian outlook making any change a difficult emotional process. By comparison, his own course seemed quite clear. Still holding his pipe, he crossed himself and quietly thanked God that he was born a Scotsman.

With no fanfare or introduction, the Regent and Tsarevich Ivan appeared at the top of the Staircase, flanked only by their attendants. Prince Golitsyn was nowhere to be seen.

The Regent was dressed in a white silk sarafan embroidered with gold and silver threads, an angelic contrast to her customary red. Her face was powdered, her hair pinned back and covered appropriately, a jewel-encrusted headdress resting atop her head. She bore a hopeful, friendly look, stepping forward with her arms spread like a Greek orator, her eyes slowly scanning the crowd below her.

Tsarevich Ivan was his usual docile self, his half-grown beard making the hunched young man look much older than his years. The two had once been inseparable in the eyes of Russia, but on this day they seemed mismatched and incongruous. The crowd quieted at the sight of them, only a few offering any kind of supportive applause.

Diechmann's efforts were paying off. From the crowd the foreign officers were emerging, one by one, to stand by Gordon, offering signals of assent. He puffed his pipe and nodded to each, feeling justified by their arrival. Gordon would have to include himself among those who looked forward to Peter's ascension; and though he would scarcely admit it, he was nonetheless eager to once again be in the company of the young Tsar.

"We stand with you, General Gordon."

"You have my gratitude. Now let us listen."

The Regent bowed slightly to Tsarevich Ivan before beginning, her familiar voice elevated so that all would hear.

"Evil-minded people…" she began, pausing in distress, speaking loudly but with passion, "have used all means to make me and the Tsar Ivan quarrel with my younger brother. They have sown discord, jealousy and trouble. They have hired people to talk of a plot against the life of the younger tsar and of other people.

"Out of jealousy of the great services of Fedor Shaklovity and of his constant care, day and night, for the safety and prosperity of the empire, they have given him out to be the chief of the conspiracy, if one existed."

The crowd murmured, but remained captive.

"To settle the matter and to find out the reason for this accusation, I went myself to Troitsky, but was kept back by the advice of the evil counselors whom my brother has had about him and was not allowed to go farther. After being insulted in this way, I was obliged to come home."

Diechmann tapped the shoulder of his coat, whispering. "General, all present have been notified. All those I spoke with have chosen to accompany you."

"Good man." Gordon nodded, his attention still fixed on Sophia. "Tell me, Diechmann, do my eyes deceive me or is that Tsarevich Ivan serving cups of vodka?"

Diechmann squinted, a grin creeping sadly across his face. "No question, sir. Would you look at that sight? You speak the truth, General."

The young Tsarevich had made his way down the red-carpeted Staircase and was carrying cups of vodka, handing them to the members of the crowd as Sophia spoke. He spilled a bit in his uneven gait, looking a pitiful sight.

"A horrible decision," he commented, shaking his head. "He is nearly blind. She demeans him. Cups of loyalty, he offers."

"Are we all to toast to the health of the Regency?"

From her place at the top of the Red Staircase, the Regent continued.

"You all well know how I have managed these seven years; how I took on myself the Regency in these most unquiet times; how I have concluded a famous and true peace with the Christian rulers, our neighbors, and how the enemies of the Christian religion have been brought by my arms into terror and confusion. For your services you have received great reward and I have always shown you my favor. I cannot believe that you will betray me and will believe the inventions of enemies of the general peace and prosperity. It is not the life of Fedor Shaklovity that they want, but my life, and that of my brother."

Her words rang out, offering little in immediate effect, leaving most without direction.

Applauded by a few, the Regent offered her thanks and called for Colonel Nechaev to be brought before the crowd.

His chains removed, the beleaguered Colonel was soon standing beside her at the top of the Staircase, holding a cup of vodka and receiving a very public pardon.

"Nechaev," Diechmann commented, pointing.

"Yes. In her rage, the Regent called for his head--and then gave it back to him."

"A most generous act, given the circumstances," Diechmann grinned.

"Certainly," Gordon nodded. "After all, she still has her immortal soul to consider…as do we all, I suppose."

"Aye, sir. And your reflections on the Regent's words? Did they change your opinion?"

"It was a long and fine speech," Gordon replied, "But I remain resolved."

He looked up to where Sophia stood, knowing it would likely be the last time. Scanning the attendants and supporters, he suspected that Prince Golitsyn had already fled to plead his innocence to the Naryshkins.

It would not be surprising, Patrick thought, watching as Sophia greeted the crowd and raised a cup. *Prince Vasily will certainly be charged. If not for treason then something else, something strong enough to chase him from Moscow forever. Better to appeal to Peter while Sophia still sits.*

Shaklovity travels as well. The Commander heads to his death, knowing he lives his last hours.

Three of us, he mused, *on our way to the Tsar's feet--one by choice, one by arrest, and one by command. All compelled, all at his ultimate mercy.*

Good, to be the mercenary and not the actor.

"The Regency is ineffective," Gordon said, speaking loudly enough to be heard by the other officers. "I will ignore any orders from the Kremlin and proceed to Troitsky on order of Tsar Peter. We will leave as soon as we are prepared, officers--at the gate of the Spasskia Tower. Do not delay."

Again, we make history. We must hope that Peter lives up to his reputation.

"Given what I have seen here today, our departure may be the decisive break." Gordon nodded, his military tone masking his satisfaction. "Either way, I am confident that we act in the interest of our agreement. You have my gratitude, gentlemen. Peter will certainly welcome us."

Outside Moscow, The Monastery of Troitskaya-Sergeeva

September 12, 1689

"Your accomplices are not hard to name," Boris said, looking down at his notes. "Finding them, however, proves far more difficult."

"You say 'accomplices'," Shaklovity breathed through the pain, forcing a chuckle. "You speak as though you hold my confession."

I do not need your full confession, Boris thought, staring back at the accused. *I need only a few guilty phrases…*

Before him, the former Commander of the Strel'tsy sat bound and bleeding, wearily shaking away the effects of the knout. Thus far, the interrogation had proven fruitless.

"Your accomplices exist regardless of your confession," Boris told him. "Their guilt is yours."

Shaklovity leaned forward as far as his straps would allow, pursing his parched lips to spit on the floor. "I will remind you, Counselor, that I deny any involvement in this conspiracy."

"Do you deny that Father Medvedev has fled Moscow?"

"His flight does not surprise me," Shaklovity replied, "but he runs because of your accusation."

"So you claim that Medvedev is innocent?"

"If accused of being my accomplice, then yes, he is innocent! He cannot be accomplice to a crime that did not occur. Would you beat me again to know? Perhaps you should question yourself, Counselor."

Boris held his tongue, knowing he should stay away from such discourse. In the corner of the room, the Tsar's scribe scratched away, writing down the minutes word for word--nothing would escape his dutiful ears. Later, Boris would present the results to Peter and gracefully field what was sure to be a long list of questions. Talk of conspiracy would only complicate and could be disastrous.

We are too close to see it fail now, he thought, reminding himself how difficult it would be for the Commander's ramblings to actually convince Peter. *Natalya will be present to see that Peter's thoughts are not allowed to roam too far...still, Peter is shrewd and will guess at the slightest implication!*

The Tsar must never know, Boris told himself, the thought alone strengthening his conviction to end Shaklovity's life. *We are still in fine position.*

It was hard for Boris to complain. He'd expected resistance from Shaklovity, but given the conspiracy, Golitsyn was still considering himself fortunate to find himself as interrogator, a position he'd lobbied for and been granted without question. The plan was almost complete, more perfect than he'd imagined. There seemed no better place from which to finish the necessary work and snip off what few loose ends remained.

As for the accused, Golitsyn had little sympathy. The man was a perpetual thorn in the side of the Naryshkin clan and knew how to use his Strel'tsy to intimidate on behalf of the Regent. More than this, Shaklovity was vocal and liked to criticize Peter and Natalya in public; there were few in Moscow who had not heard one of the Commander's impassioned speeches. Shaklovity may not have been guilty, but he was far from innocent. This had been considered from the beginning.

It seemed a bit odd now, seeing the plan come together and having to stand before Shaklovity as interrogator, the Commander's exoneration in the hands of the one man who would never absolve him.

Nothing has changed, Boris reminded himself, staring.

"Have I not been merciful?" he said, stepping closer. "It was hardly a beating in my eyes."

Shaklovity chuckled. "Why don't we trade places, and I'll ask you the same."

"I am too easy on you. I cannot decide if it is your rank, your name, or perhaps your history of service that provokes my sympathy, but whatever the cause, I have been far too lenient, Commander Shaklovity."

"You have been yourself," Shaklovity returned looking up at him. "A Naryshkin sheep to the very end. Cousin Boris, the finest they own."

"We will start simply," Boris began, ignoring the comment. "Do you at least admit to being acquainted with the monk Sylvester Medvedev?"

"Yes. Of course. I would be a fool to deny it."

"Good, then. In the course of this acquaintance, then, do you admit to having seen Father Medvedev speak or preach against the Tsar and his mother Lady Natalya?"

Shaklovity glared. "It is common knowledge that Medvedev was a loyal supporter of the Miloslavskys…much like your cousin."

"The monk was a supporter, no question. But he went much farther than mere support. As did you, Commander. Do you deny your own participation?"

"What?"

Boris paused. "Do you deny the fact that you, along with Father Medvedev, have spoken against the Tsar and the Tsarista on many occasions--speeches in which you called them heretics and traitors to their country."

"You would hang me on my past! You bait me with talk of denial when you wish to speak of guilt!"

"I wish only for you to admit what you know is true."

Shaklovity groaned. "Listen to this, then, Counselor: I admit to no part of this conspiracy! You have what you want, what the Naryshkins want--you have a crime, a criminal, and the Regent is disgraced! Your precious heretic Peter will soon take the throne and you may all step comfortably into your new promotions! As it is, I play your culprit. In the end, you will execute me because you must. What more, Counselor, could you possibly want?"

Golitsyn hesitated, staring down at the man, imagining how difficult it would be. Shaklovity was drawn and weary, a feeble shadow of the man he'd always seemed, stripped of all rank and authority, now possessing only the bitterness for which he'd always been known. Sophia had always kept her dogs close, with Shaklovity as the meanest of the pack. Now, to see him sitting here bereft of her influence, stripped of his fangs--this vicious man now seemed rather pitiful.

"I want only to secure your confession, Commander."

Raising his chin, Golitsyn motioned to the scribe. The man stood from his place, stirring around in a leather satchel to produce a handful of parchment pages and a quill. These were placed on the table beside Shaklovity, his hands still bound helplessly at his sides.

The prisoner began to laugh, quietly at first, then turning his head to show Golitsyn the light in his eyes.

"A written confession? I'm in no position to write…"

"That will be arranged," Boris answered, stepping closer. "Your statement must be on record. You will give your full confession and sign your name--"

"You may repeat yourself as many times as you like, Counselor. The answer will be the same! I cannot confess to what I did not do!"

"And your accomplices? They are innocent as well?"

"I do not speak for Medvedev, but he is incapable of such treachery. Make no mistake--he did call your precious Tsarevich a heretic, as did I! Words, however, are the beginning and end of it. We are innocent of this concocted crime."

"Need I produce the knout again, Commander? Can you not be reasonable?"

"You will beat me, then, to gain your truth…"

The smile had faded from Shaklovity's face and the mention of the knout brought fear into his eyes. The face that stared back at Boris was one of grim despair.

"As a final insult," he continued, spitting again, "you would have me sign away my dignity--"

"I do not wish to hear of your dignity," Boris snapped, hardening his tone. "You have wished Peter dead on many occasions. Why should he not wish the same for you?"

Dignity. The word reminded him of cousin Vasily and the family name. Regrettably, Vasily had chosen to remain too long in Moscow, ignoring Boris' advice, clinging to his ill-fated allegiance to the Regent.

"And what of Sophia?" he asked, watching closely. "What was her part in this matter?"

"There was no matter," Shaklovity returned, "and the Regent is innocent. You may entrap me with my past, but you have no cause to accuse her! Why would you ask such a thing? Do you truly believe that I would turn on her?"

"And Prince V.V.?"

Shaklovity hesitated, craning his neck to stare. "Wait…yes, of course! You seek to leave your dear cousin out of the matter, is that it?"

Boris tensed, his stomach clutching. His eyes leapt to the scribe, still inking every word.

The bastard could implicate Vasily with a single phrase! I've walked into a trap!

"Regardless of our relation," Boris answered, maintaining his tone, "I am tasked with the investigation of this crime."

"Murder charge or not, cousin or not…I would wager you have something planned for Prince Golitsyn. Something special. Eh?"

Boris narrowed his eyes. "Was he involved, or was he not?"

The Commander paused again, coughing. "Some water, perhaps?"

He stalls! Does the think to bury Vasily?

Rumors spoke of Shaklovity and the Prince competing for Sophia's affection. Despite their allegiance, the two had always been considered rivals. Suddenly it seemed obvious that a man without hope would turn on those around him. If implicated in the murder plot, Vasily would undoubtedly face the executioner, with or without Peter's promise.

"No water. Answer the question. Was Prince Golitsyn involved in the conspiracy to murder Tsar Peter?"

He tensed again, awaiting a reply. Shaklovity scratched his bearded chin on his shoulder and coughed before beginning:

"As much as I would enjoy disappointing you, Counselor," he began, "I will tell you that your cousin Vasily had, to my knowledge, no part in any conspiracy against Peter, Lady Natalya or anyone else including the Turks! He is as loyal and innocent as the man before you."

"Ah."

Relief washed over Boris. He looked to the side to insure that the scribe was taking down the testimony.

"I have no trouble delivering your good news if it means confounding the Naryshkins," Shaklovity continued bitterly. "Let them dwell on the fact that Prince Vasily is innocent. Trust this, Counselor--your family name survives today, but they will find a way to stain it!"

Vasily is exonerated, Boris thought, ignoring the curses. *There is hope for him yet! I must go to Peter and secure this... Vasily will have his audience.*

"I will serve the punishment for your treachery," the Commander ranted, now enrapt in anger. "Naryshkin treachery, surely, for you alone are not shrewd enough to bring about my demise! Shaklovity--an innocent man!"

"Innocent?" Boris quipped with confidence. "You are far from it, Commander. We have witnesses who have seen and heard you calling for the heads of Peter and the Tsarista. In more than one instance! Surely you know this..."

"You need no witnesses!" Shaklovity shouted back, his face flushed. "I do not deny it! I speak my mind and I have called your beloved Tsar and Tsarista every name you can think of! I have contrived accusations and spread rumors whenever I liked! And yes, you Naryshkin devil, I have even threatened their lives!"

Bucking against his straps, Shaklovity grew suddenly quiet. "But make no mistake, sir--given all this, given all my words and deeds, I am still innocent of these charges. In this regard, I confess to nothing."

The Commander fell back into his chair, his eyes straying to the corner of the room.

Boris stepped back, looking to the scribe.

"We will stop for now," he announced. "We will resume in a few hours...and we will begin by composing a confession..."

Shaklovity exhaled, shaking his head.

"Go on." Boris motioned for the others to leave, nodding his assent as the scribe and the guards exited. "I will follow directly--and find us some food."

Soon, only he and Shaklovity remained, feeling like two giant figures in the small religious chamber. Even now, the man seemed somehow dangerous.

"You wish to speak to me alone, Herr Golitsyn?"

Boris stepped to his side. "You would do well to cooperate, Commander."

"You shall have to concoct your own confession," he replied wearily, still defiant. "I have no temper for lies anymore..."

"You said yourself that the outcome is already decided. And, with respect, you are correct. You will be executed and this is as certain as the setting of the sun. What matter is a little confession? It changes nothing for you. Truly, Commander, how much pride can you pretend to have left?"

Shaklovity's eyes flared. "We both know who put me here! Are you blind? My life is forfeit at your command, you bloody prig aristocrat--so do not play at being civil with me! You have everything else you want, including the innocence of your beloved cousin!" He fell back into the chair. "I am finished, you devil. You will get no confession!"

Regrettable. We shall have to be persistent.

Boris looked to the stack of blank parchment and then back at the Commander, his face absent of any anger.

"Sleep," he offered, "for you will surely need it. We will begin again soon, with the knout. I expect fifteen lashes will loosen your tongue and get you writing."

Outside Moscow, The Village of Vozdvizhenskoe

Later that Evening, September 12, 1689

"Prince Golitsyn? My lord?"

He awoke in a rush of disorientation, looking around the darkened room before recalling where **he** was. The man who stood before him was not the cobbler.

"Prince Golitsyn, you are a difficult man to find."

The younger Troekorov stared down at him, his face now bearing a curious grin. Behind him stood two other greencoats.

"What?" Vasily Golitsyn squinted, looking up at him. "You could have asked any of these peasants!"

Troekorov bowed slightly. "It seems I owe you an apology, sir. I see that you were sleeping. I will give you a moment to awaken."

Vasily sat up slowly from the hard wooden bench, blinking and rubbing his forehead. The empty cup sat before him, a testament to his aching head.

No crime to fall asleep, he thought, taking a deep breath. *What do they expect of me, being told to wait interminably in this horrid condition?*

He glared, brushing away the assistance of the greencoats as he rose to his feet.

"I assure you I am ready now, my boy. I have been given far too long to collect myself. You brought a carriage for transport?"

"No, sir," Troekorov replied, his grin fading. "I was not instructed to carry you back, merely to deliver the order. Your presence is requested at the Monastery, Commander. We will accompany you on horseback."

No carriage? The amusement continues...

"Very well, I will ride."

Peter will see me, at least. Finally, we can be through with this foolishness!

And though he'd been anxiously awaiting the moment of his release from Vozdvizhenskoe, Vasily was unable to enjoy it, his mood spoiled by the lack of civility. He felt dirty, his fashionable outfit soiled to the point of ridicule, his wig wilted and weather-beaten, still wet to the touch as he placed it back atop his head.

Vasily could sense the cobbler's eyes upon him, but did not acknowledge the glance nor offer a farewell as he stepped outside into the evening air. His clammy skin was greeted immediately by a cool breeze; already he could feel the tiny but persistent drops of rain carried by the wind. At best, the ride would be uncomfortable

He would make me wait until the sun sets, he thought, following Troekorov to where the horses were tied. *Peter and the rest will be drunk from supper by the time I arrive!*

The shadows of the clouded night did not deter the villagers from attending Golitsyn's departure; stepping from their homes and shops, they lined the roadside to watch. The darkness was gratefully enough to limit the catcalls and laughter, but a few adventurous souls were still present to voice their opinions. This time, Vasily found the comments much easier to ignore.

He fell in behind Troekorov with the two escorts following at his back, riding swiftly along the well-kept road that led to the

Monastery. Soon the discomfort of Vozdvizhenskoe was behind them and again Vasily could focus on his task.

Once again, he practiced his speech beneath his breath, pleased with how much he could recite from memory. There would likely be just one opportunity to speak, and Vasily wished to be well armed in his own defense.

He will give me voice, he thought, imagining Peter holding court from the confines of the Monastery, wondering if the crisis had changed the boy.

Even at his age, Peter is no fool. Surely he can see the political advantage in it…my friends still lurk in the Duma. I may have opposed them politically, but I was not the one who routinely engaged in shouting matches with the Tsarista!

The issue was quite clear. Feelings aside, it was time to separate his cause from that of Sophia and hope that Peter was progressive enough to grant a pardon. Had it not been for his cousin, Vasily might have thought his cause lost. It was said, however, that even the iron will of the Tsarista could be manipulated by Boris Golitsyn.

Ahead of him, Troekorov rode tall in his smart green tunic, armed and proud as he answered the call of the new Tsar. He seemed a child to Vasily, but there was little question that Troekorov was one of many, representing a whole caste of bright-eyed young men poised to take positions in the new regime. They would serve with the passion of their youth and die for Peter if the cause commanded. This, Sophia could never equal.

At forty-six, Vasily knew that he seemed a relic to these stallions. They were too young to consider his experience and too old to grant him any respect. Soon, Moscow would be flooded with new blood, young men who were eager to enact policies of their own. Now, more than ever, it was clear to him: there remained only one political option.

I will retire gracefully to the country. We'll go to Livonia if they wish us out of Russia. Better to be away from Moscow than to contend with this new pack of wolves.

Sophia crept into his thoughts. It seemed like yesterday that they celebrated peace with the Polish, realizing all they could achieve together. The two accomplished much and envisioned even more, grand ideas that had suddenly fallen to ashes,

Sophia, could our time be finished so quickly?

There were other opponents of the Naryshkins, the Strel'tsy colonels most notably, who had begun this conflict in the Miloslavsky camp and now were considered Peter's assets. The Tsar had welcomed the loyalties of Tsykler and his compatriots because they served a purpose. Thus far, his methods seemed rational and free of vengeful motives.

If they can forgive Colonel Tsykler, surely they will see my worth! With Boris' help, this should not be too difficult.

Perhaps I will keep my dignity after all...

He thought back to his relationship with the Tsarevich, seeking reassurance in the past, noting that his few contentious encounters with Peter had been cordially settled. For most of Vasily's career, Peter had been a mere child--only in the last few years had he dealt with the Tsarevich officially. Given Sophia's influence, it was impossible to say that Peter liked him, but Golitsyn had always believed that the Tsarevich approved of his aims and methods. The boy was a progressive at heart; his love of the Sloboda was proof enough of that.

Good then, he thought, breathing deeply, filling himself with the cool night air, *I will leave Sophia behind and save my name.*

I am a politician, a speaker, a diplomat! This is my forte! Were I another man, I would be right to be worried--but I am not! I am Prince Vasily Vasilyevich Golitsyn!

He spurred his horse a bit, moving up alongside Troekorov, determined to be riding in the front when they arrived. The boy looked over at him but said nothing, quickening his pace. Vasily gladly kept up.

As they neared the Monastery, he began to think again of his appearance, wondering if there were anything he could do to make himself more presentable. Despite their conservative leanings, the Naryshkins were known for their European sense of fashion and Vasily had selected his ensemble with the aim of impressing. Now it seemed a ridiculous thought, his outfit soaked with rain and splattered with mud.

No worry, he told himself, determined to remove his wig. *My appearance shall make me all the more pitiable. Boris will leap to my defense!*

The Troitsky Monastery soon appeared like a snowy mountain out of the night, eternally impressive but much less imposing in the darkness than in the light of day. He felt a sense of calm as he stared up at the massive towers, knowing that soon enough he would rest in comfort.

This time, a greeting party awaited in the form of three additional figures.

Boris? No, he's not there! More stable boys?

They slowed to a stop and dismounted at the gates, greeted by three more of Peter's greencoats. Saluting to Troekorov, the greencoats led the horses away.

"I wish to speak with my cousin Boris," Vasily said, turning to Troekorov. "I had expected him to be here to greet me, so if I could have just a moment with him before I meet with the Tsar…"

"I was told nothing in regard to your cousin." Troekorov replied curtly. "Had he intended to greet you, I assume he would have. He is not here, however."

"Yes, obviously." Vasily sighed, pulling the lifeless wig from his head, shaking it free of rain before replacing it. "I ask only for your consideration."

The gates opened, revealing Troitsky's massive inner courtyard.

"This way."

Falling into step, Golitsyn walked beside Troekorov as they moved toward the central Monastery buildings, the Cathedral's domes looming high above. Despite the late hour, abbots and other clerical workers waited in groups at the edge of the courtyard, their attention focused solely on the small procession, lips murmuring as they finally laid eyes on the Prince.

Look! he thought, straightening his shoulders, keeping his gaze forward and his expression stone. *Look upon the most influential man in Russia! I deserve such regard, you judgmental little sheep!*

Better to watch. You will see how a man like me survives! Peter's games are finished, and now we can negotiate.

There seemed nothing suspicious to him; Peter was known to keep late hours. Troekorov was performing his task with an expression of near-boredom and was making no attempt at conversation.

Troekorov led him to a side door of the largest building, opening it before turning to speak.

"Not much farther," he said, allowing Vasily to enter first.

"Will I at least be allowed a moment of time to compose myself? It is most embarrassing appearing this way..."

Troekorov did not reply, walking him down the long corridor and leading him into a noisy anteroom.

Crowded?

The room was filled with unfamiliar faces, some sitting, some standing, all of them turning to lay eyes on Prince Golitsyn. Too many people, it seemed, for such a confined space, his presence creating a ripple of whispered comments and sideways glances.

What is this? Another of Peter's insults?

Ignoring his surprise, Troekorov led Vasily to a chair that sat empty and apart, as though reserved for him.

"You are to wait here," Troekorov said, pointing to the chair. "Someone will come to collect you shortly."

"But...are you certain?" Vasily asked, hesitating. "I am to meet with the Tsar!"

"I am quite certain," Troekorov replied coolly. "And I know only that you are to wait here to be collected. Sit, if you please."

With this, Troekorov turned and walked away, leaving Vasily with no option but to sit and wait in the crowded room. His ire provoked, Golitsyn had nothing but cold stares for those who dared look at him.

And where is Boris? he wondered, weary but refusing to rest comfortably in his seat. *Surely, he waits with Peter. Perhaps he will testify on my behalf.*

But no official greeting? No sign of the Patriarch nor any of the Naryshkin favorites? Is this mere insult or should I be fearful?

Does he wish to show me my place? One last effort to be certain that I am humbled?

His mind raced with questions and fears. Soaked through from his stockings to his wig, Vasily shivered with cold, too far from the corner hearth to gain any advantage from its warmth.

A pitiable figure, indeed. Sophia would be ashamed to see me sitting here--like a dog waiting for scraps!

Something is not right...

A figure appeared at the top of the small staircase that dominated one end of the room, his hands holding a piece of new parchment. Vasily didn't recognize him, but his green jacket marked him as one of Peter's entourage.

"Prince V.V. Golitsyn?" the man called out in broad voice, as though shouting orders in the field.

"I am here."

The room silenced, the man stared down through steely eyes, his gaze finding Vasily.

"Commander Golitsyn, stand to hear your charges."

Charges? Holy Father…

Trembling now on the inside, Vasily rose to his feet, standing before the eyes of the entire room. "I am on my feet, sir. I gratefully acknowledge your hospitality."

"Prince Vasily Vasilyevich Golitsyn, Commander of the Army, you have been charged with the following offences against the State: You are charged with reporting directly to the Regent and not personally to the Tsars. Secondly, you are charged with forging the Regent's name on official documents in equality with those of the Tsars--"

"May I not speak?"

"Finally," the man continued without acknowledging him, "You are charged with causing harm and burdens to the government and people of Russia with your bad generalship in the Crimean Campaigns."

Vasily shrunk in his place, the crowded room growing even tighter around him. Defeat reigned in his heart.

"Do you hear me, Prince Golitsyn?"

"Aye…"

"From this moment forth, you are hereby stripped of the rank of boyar and relieved of your position as Commander of the Army. Furthermore, you are to be stripped of all titles, property and wealth, and exiled with your family to Siberia, where you will live the rest of your days. The government will provide a stipend of three rubles a month to support your family. Attempting to leave the country or returning to Moscow will bring a penalty of death."

Guards appeared on either side of him, ready to provide escort. Lightly, they gripped the sleeves of his coat.

"But I was to be allowed to speak! I was granted no audience!"

A cruel twitter passed through the room, the polite stares now turned to looks of mocking amusement.

This whole charade? Contrived for my humiliation?

I should have left Moscow when I had the chance.

"Do you understand your sentence, Prince Golitsyn?"

Finished, he pulled the wilted wig from his head and tossed it to the floor, placing his wrists together so the guards could bind them.

There was no need to answer. Vasily understood all too well.

Outside Moscow, The Monastery of Troitskaya-Sergeeva

The Early Morning of September 13, 1689

"I believe we have what we need."

Boris Golitsyn stepped back, allowing himself a moment to reflect on the breadth and depth of his success. It was late, surely, well after midnight, but the result had been well worth the effort. In his hands he held a confession, nine pages in length, penned in the hand of the accused.

"After all this," Shaklovity growled angrily from his seat, "you mock me? Why don't you have them use the knout again? It would be more humane."

"You seem in high enough spirits to speak with such passion."

"I am well-finished," he replied, lowering his head. "Plague me no more."

"How many times have you been standing in my place, Commander? Dozens, perhaps?"

Shaklovity grunted, not bothering to look up.

Impossible, almost, to think that even the details had worked out so perfectly, the pieces coming together so smoothly that he could not honestly take credit. It had been little more than a notion in the beginning, the plot falling together almost by chance.

Yet here he stood, interrogator of the prime conspiracy scapegoat, insuring that the final touches of this masterpiece would be well placed. The Patriarch and the Strel'tsy had fallen into line without difficulty. Peter stood ready to return to Moscow and claim his throne. And with a few strokes, Shaklovity's words would be delivered to Peter and his body to the executioner's block.

The prisoner was stinking and dirty, hair hanging in ropes past his eyes, his beard matted with dried blood. He'd been a worthy opponent, denying his involvement to the very end, protesting any participation in the events of that July evening. Even after being beaten, Shaklovity refused to claim any part in the plot, his utterances more concerned with talk of Naryshkin treachery.

A perilous course, Boris realized. The minutes were being scrupulously recorded by the scribe in the corner of the room. By request of the Tsar, the record was to be delivered to Peter when the interrogation was concluded. Peter would read every word and was more than bright enough to question the course of events--too much talk of conspiracy would no doubt make him suspicious.

The prisoner seemed intent on sniping, using every opportunity to accuse Boris and the Naryshkins of conspiracy. The more Boris pressed, the sharper Shaklovity's tongue became, at one point accusing him directly of sending the Preobrazhenskoe 'assassins'.

Shaklovity's denials were adamant and Boris soon realized that the safer tack would be to pursue the Commander's past. Whatever his part in the July events, there was no question that Shaklovity had been a public opponent of the Naryshkins, on occasion going so far as calling for the heads of Peter and his mother. He claimed that the Naryshkins were heretics and concocted rumors that Natalya was plotting against the lives of Sophia and Tsarevich Ivan.

And, of course, the letters--the inspiration for Boris' part in Peter's ascension. Shaklovity was guilty of penning anonymous letters threatening the lives of Ivan and the Regent. These notes were designed to implicate the Naryshkins in a plot to seize the throne, but were acknowledged little and only served to identify Commander Shaklovity as their enemy. He'd spoken loudly and in public. There were hundreds who could testify to Shaklovity's hatred for Peter.

After fifteen lashes, he was broken and ready to speak.

Shaklovity admitted plotting against Peter and Natalya in the past and confessed to penning the suspicious letters. Focusing on the past, Boris questioned him thoroughly, walking carefully through each reported incident, including everything in the record.

Leaving nothing to chance, a quill and parchment were placed before Shaklovity so that he could write the confession in his own hand. Together, they stepped through his litany of dissent, carefully recording each offense. The process was laborious but gratifying, and when they finally finished after midnight, the nine page confession was nothing less than a masterpiece of guilt. If he would not confess to the present, Shaklovity would be executed for his past.

Golitsyn felt confident in this stack of parchment. The sheer volume of it would outweigh any suspicious comments, and Boris would report personally to the Tsar.

Peter's victory will carry us through, he thought, staring down at Shaklovity's scrawled signature. *The remaining loose ends will be hidden by his hatred for Sophia.*

Prince Vasily had been exonerated by Shaklovity's silence. Despite what had been considered by most to be a rivalry, the Commander offered no words that would incriminate his counterpart, going as far as to claim that Vasily knew nothing of any plot against the Naryshkin house.

A relief for Boris, despite his cousin's failed attempt to win his freedom. At the very least, the Golitsyn name would bear no stain.

Without Vasily's implication in the murder, however, proving the Regent guilty seemed an insurmountable task.

And though the knout served to loosen Shaklovity's tongue concerning his own offences, he proved defiantly unwilling to say anything that might incriminate Sophia. Showing a brand of loyalty that Boris could grudgingly respect, the prisoner suffered and yet remained unflaggingly true to his lover, denying that she ever knew of his traitorous acts. Whatever his motive, Shaklovity's testimony kept Sophia far above suspicion.

Pausing, Golitsyn perused the confession once again, wondering if there was anything he had forgotten. The scribe waited, staring from his place, his sunken face showing the weariness of the long day. Boris stared at the stack beside him containing the minutes, trying to remember just what had been said, questioning whether his responses to the prisoner's accusations had been appropriate.

Those splashes of ink could be our undoing, Boris thought, his confidence waning a bit. *Did I defend myself too vigorously?*

Peter's suspicions must be kept at bay. I cannot bear the thought of explaining it all!

The answer, though troublesome, seemed simple enough. He would take the minutes to Peter in person and make a point of addressing Shaklovity's accusations.

I will make light of it, he reasoned, trying to picture the Tsar's reaction. *I will laugh at the thought of conspiracy.*

"How soon," Shaklovity uttered from his place, interrupting Boris' thoughts. "My execution….how soon?"

Within the week, surely. We must not hesitate to finish this.

"I cannot say," he answered evenly, "though I expect your judgment will be complete before the Tsar returns to Moscow. He refuses to set foot in the Kremlin until Sophia is gone."

A weary chuckle emerged from the Commander's chest, the beaten man finally staring up at him.

"With that," Shaklovity said, "I wish you good fortune. Sophia will not depart so willingly and you have no cause to remove her."

"No one remains to claim her right, Commander. The time has come for Peter and Ivan to rule Russia--the people know this, from the serfs to the last bloody Strel'tsy. You are a fool to think that girl's defiance carries weight anymore."

Shaklovity huffed, nodding. "I am a fool, certainly…"

"If you think you are to become a martyr, Commander, you are mistaken." After hours of interrogation, Boris' anger was finally making an appearance, drawn forth by his doubts and fears. He felt suddenly angry, despising Fedor for his defiance. "You will be executed without fanfare. Your headstone, if there is one, will read 'Shaklovity the traitor'."

"You know the truth," Shaklovity spat in response, his body capable of one last furious outburst. "My blood is on your hands."

"Your accusations are laughable, Commander. Nonetheless, may the Holy Father have mercy on your soul. We are finished here."

In the corner, the scribe dipped his quill and scratched down the final words. Holding his tongue, Boris stepped away from the accused, moving to address the attendant.

"It is late and we are both weary. I will collect all the parchment and deliver it to the Tsar with my report."

The scribe hesitated, then nodded. "As you wish, my lord."

"Do not trust your noble lord," Shaklovity shouted from his place, addressing the scribe. "He means to alter the record to save his family name! He is unscrupulous, my friend, I warn you!"

To Boris' distress, the scribe's eyes widened a bit. He paused before looking back up at Golitsyn.

Still dangerous. Especially dangerous now that he faces execution.

"Perhaps I should have replaced the gag," Boris said to the scribe, grinning at his own humor. "He will accuse the Patriarch himself before he is finished!"

The scribe nodded uneasily, collecting the parchment and delivering the pile into Golitsyn's hands.

We will leave together, Boris thought, staring down at the man. *Better not to offer any parting words.*

And with a single glance back at the accused, Boris led the scribe out into the passageway, closing the door behind them. A wave of relief passed through him as soon as he crossed the threshold.

"You've done an excellent job," he said to the scribe, patting his shoulder amiably. "In the morning when I deliver the reports, the Tsar will surely hear of your good service."

The man's face changed a bit. "But, my lord, my orders were to deliver the minutes to the Tsar upon completion."

"Your sense of duty is commendable, my boy, but it is long after midnight now. I do not wish to wake the Tsar. The minutes, and the confession, will be more than secure in my hands."

The man hesitated. "Sire, I do not wish to be punished by the Tsar for disobedience--"

"You are speaking to Boris Golitsyn, son." He hardened his stare. "I am in charge of this interrogation, and I assure you that you will not be punished. Quite the opposite, in fact. Don't be daft, boy. Off to sleep with you! I will send for you in the morning."

"Yes, my lord," the scribe replied, bowing away. "My apologies, my lord."

The scribe scuttled off down the passageway and Boris was left alone, triumphant, his hands holding the words that spelled Shaklovity's end and the dawn of Peter's reign. The Naryshkins would finally have their day, recouping all that had been taken from them seven years ago. Whatever the circumstance, Boris vowed to remember the bloody fashion in which Sophia had taken her place.

The wretch will know that we brought her down! he mused, enjoying the thought of Sophia's final exit. *Damn her achievements--she has stolen years from us all.*

The conspirators would be executed as well, the few Strel'tsy officers who had been foolish enough to partake in Shaklovity's heretical rants. The monk Medvedev was yet to be apprehended, but his absence from Moscow only served to prove his guilt. If found, he would no doubt meet the same fate as the others.

Boris' footsteps sounded in solitary rhythm as he made his way to his bedchamber, quick in his pace despite the long day's work. Lifted by thoughts of success, he decided to stay up a bit and peruse the minutes of the interrogation.

It shouldn't take long to read them. I'll be waiting for Peter when he awakens. He will know soon enough.

An execution in a monastery, he thought, grinning at the prospect. *Imagine, the Patriarch calling for the death blow! It will be as though the Holy Father himself has proclaimed Shaklovity guilty!*

Peter's mind will be on the future. I must discuss the interrogation, then move directly to Sophia…

As he neared his chamber door, his footsteps were countered by a second pair, approaching rapidly.

"Boris!"

He turned to find a red-faced Lev Naryshkin, winded from running.

"Lev?"

"The interrogation--"

"Yes, it is finished." He held up the stack of parchment. "Including, I may proudly add, a lengthy confession written in the hand of the accused--"

"Boris, listen!" Lev stepped very close, lowering his voice to a whisper. "I met that scribe of yours, walking swiftly and looking like a frightened pup. I stopped him to discover the trouble and he told me that Boris Golitsyn had taken the minutes to his room instead of delivering them to Peter! Now, I don't know what you're up to, but I certainly know what it appears--and that scribe is on his way to wake the Tsar!"

"What?" Boris' stomach folded with anxiety, his knees faint and weak.

"Are you trying to get us exiled, Boris? Would you like the same fate that awaits your cousin? Would you ruin everything we've done saving your family name?"

"I have no intention--"

"Your intentions are unimportant," Lev told him, grasping him roughly behind the neck. "If Peter thinks us guilty, we are lost!"

"We must go to him," Boris replied, his feet moving before the words escaped his lips. "We must see Peter now! Hurry!"

And so he ran, the heels of his shoes sending cannon-shot echoes through the Monastery, relentless in their pace. Naryshkin followed in kind, one hand atop his wig as he trailed along, struggling to keep up.

Holy Father, how simple a mistake! he thought, clutching the parchment to his chest as he tried to keep his balance. *All the progress I've made with Peter, wiped away in a single incident!*

And with the conspiracy, his neck and the family reputation on the line, Boris Golitsyn moved faster than he'd ever moved before.

As they neared Peter's door, the two slowed to a stop, attempting to catch their breath.

"We didn't see the scribe," Lev said, hands on his knees, "he's already inside."

Boris straightened his posture, collecting himself. "It won't matter now," he replied breathlessly. "I am here."

"I will leave you to your business, then. It would be best if the scribe did not see me."

"Indeed."

"I advise you not to attempt any rescue of your cousin."

"Your aid is greatly appreciated, Lev. Now please go."

The scribe was exiting as Boris entered the room, the man's face falling pale at the sight of him. Aware of the Tsar's curious gaze, Boris acknowledged the scribe pleasantly and waited for him to leave. Peter stood fully dressed in the doorway, his curly hair springing out at odd angles, his mouth twitching into a curious grin.

"Is there something I should know, Boris?" Peter asked without offering a greeting. The words sent a chill through him.

"Sire?"

"Why would this man come and tell me that you've absconded with the minutes?" Peter stared into him, the playful tone lost in the depths of his gaze. "Explain."

Speak carefully, Boris reminded himself. *Relax...*

"Sire, Commander Shaklovity was most imaginative in his protest. He made accusations and claims of conspiracy throughout the process! As I am related to Vasily, admittedly most of the accusations were pointed at me. The scribe was apparently swayed by all the talk of treachery. If you don't mind my asking, what was his trouble?"

Peter's eyes narrowed. "You took the minutes to bed with you. He believes you were about to alter the testimony to suit your cause."

Boris delivered an offended look, holding up the stack of parchment. "As you can see, sire, the testimony is quite lengthy, especially if you include the nine-page confession. I suppose I thought it too large and too important to present at this late hour. Upon returning to my chamber, however, I found I could not contain my enthusiasm and decided to risk waking you to present the good news to you right away. As I suspected, you had not yet retired."

"Certainly not," Peter answered, pacing a bit. "And my orders were to bring the testimony to me as soon as you were finished."

"Yes, sire."

"That is the purpose of employing the scribe."

"Yes, sire. I have your testimony right here."

Peter hesitated, staring him up and down as though trying to gauge his honesty with a glance, pausing finally to shake his head and stare at the stack of parchment.

"Nine pages, you say?"

"Written in his own hand, my lord."

Peter's long-awaited smile finally showed itself. "Truly?"

"We have everything we need," Boris replied, returning the smile. "I walked him through the past, through each and every public speech and letter. After a few lashes with the knout, he was generally cooperative. The list of charges is impressive, if I may say so."

"And Sophia?"

He lowered his eyes. "Regrettably, the Commander refused to implicate Sophia. His loyalty to her runs quite deep, as you know."

"Did you press him, Boris?"

"I did, sire. Yet the harder I pressed, the farther he placed the Regent from his crimes. He refused to admit that Sophia even knew of his dissent. Perhaps he thinks himself a champion, but he is resolved to die with Sophia's gratitude."

"I should have known he would defend her."

Boris shrugged. "No matter. We need nothing more to finish Sophia, sire. With the conspirators executed and the Strel'tsy standing down, your letter to Ivan will be more than enough to unseat her. Sophia's complicity was merely a hopeful chance."

"Yes," Peter answered, looking down at the pile. "We could hardly ask for more. You've done well, Boris. Your family will be quite proud of you when they take their places in the new administration."

"You have my humble thanks."

Strange, after all the years of mentoring, to hear the boy speak to him as though he were a child. Peter was growing into his position, his words and commands reflecting his burgeoning authority.

He thought of Vasily, knowing better than to mention his cousin. Vasily would suffer the fate of his actions, and the family would continue to prosper in Moscow without him. Of all things, Boris knew Lady Natalya would see to that.

"I shall be happy to tell the Tsarista of our success. She will be pleased, I think."

"You will tell her with me, or not at all," Peter responded, his mood lightening. "I want to see the look on her face when--"

The Tsar was interrupted by a pounding knock on the door, far too indelicate for an abbot.

Peter shrugged, looking to the windows. "The sun will soon be up, and I'm still gathering visitors. Come."

The door opened and Lev Naryshkin entered with a bow, his coat and hair unkempt.

"Uncle Lev!" Peter waved him in. "Come hear the news!"

"Not before I deliver news of my own," he answered stepping into the room. "Something I think you'll be most happy to hear, sire. Patrick Gordon and the foreign colonels approach Troitsky--with their regiments in tow!"

"My good fortune!" Peter leapt forward, embracing Naryshkin and kissing his cheek. "First Shaklovity, and then the arrival of dear General Gordon. This, Boris, is what we need to unseat her! Where is my tunic?"

Golitsyn reached for the coat. "Here, sire. Do you not wish the full uniform?"

Peter shook his head. "No time for that, Boris, we must ride out to meet him! I'll wear my greencoat and leave it at that. Who is coming with me? Lev?"

"Gladly."

"And Boris?"

"I will stay behind and prepare the abbots for their arrival."

Peter nodded. "Very good, suit yourself. I shall return with an army at my back!"

"Another army. The barracks are growing full, sire."

The Tsar shrugged, urging Naryshkin toward the door. "No worries, Boris--soon we will all be back in Moscow!"

Outside Moscow, On the Road to the Monastery of Troitskaya-Sergeeva

September 13, 1689

It felt good to be out of the city, particularly on such auspicious business. The slow, steady rhythm of hoof beats was a welcome respite from the buzz of Moscow, and amidst the darkness of the early morning hours, General Gordon found time to collect his thoughts and prepare for the important moments to come.

In his lifetime, Patrick Gordon had witnessed more than his share of history, playing a part in battles and skirmishes, acting as the mercenary while larger figures directed his action. He'd seen kings and tsars making agreements and had taken the lives of common men in the interest of power. Looking back, he could realize that his life had been consumed by such historical pursuit. But never had he played a role such as this. Never had Gordon been able to say that he had truly played a pivotal role.

Until now.

Riding beside him, the figure of Franz Lefort seemed a bit out of place at the head of the Strel'tsy ranks, though his presence was nonetheless welcomed by the other foreign colonels. While not an official part of the Russian military, Lefort did play his part in times of strife, most notably riding with Tsar Alexis against the Turks. His face was flushed from the chill of the cool morning breeze, his pleasant expression evident as always.

"It will be my first time seeing Troitsky."

"And likely the first time a Catholic ever set foot inside," Lefort countered, grinning. "I should expect it will be your last trip to Troitsky as well."

"I am pleased that you chose to accompany us, Captain Lefort."

"An honor, to be certain," he answered, raising a hand to his wide-brimmed hat. "More so today than on any other--a landmark occasion, this. Think! How they will talk of you in the histories! I can hear them now…row upon row of loyal patriots escaping Moscow, faithfully guided by the foreign colonels and the noble figure of General Patrick Gordon."

"Your historian is surely an Englishman," he replied, smirking a bit, "for the Russians would be loath to give me such praise."

"Perhaps," Lefort offered, shrugging atop his mount. "But Peter will be praised for this bit of shrewdness…and you along with him. You mustn't underestimate your importance in this, General."

"Oh?"

"This, here--what we're doing, what we accomplish at this moment--this is the decisive break, my friend!" Lefort gestured toward the army at their backs. "This may as well be all of Moscow riding out to join Peter! And with you at the front? Well, you're a mercenary. You and the rest of the ruddy heretic colonels serve the throne by contract. Europeans, yes. Russian Orthodox, no. But where would they be without you in time of war? Lost, my friend, without question. If General Gordon and the foreign colonels support Peter at Troitsky, then the throne must certainly belong to him."

Gordon knew it to be true. For Sophia, losing the foreign commanders meant losing her legitimacy. The men were more than willing, provoked by the defections of the Strel'tsy colonels, suddenly afraid to be caught on Sophia's side of the fight. She now possessed too few musketeers to provide an adequate defense for Moscow.

"After what has occurred in the last month, there can be no question," he said, avoiding the topic of his own notoriety. "Peter said he would call on me and I knew little more than that. Admittedly, I was a bit confused as the events first began to unfold, but I soon grew to see the beauty of the plan. I know not how much of this plan belongs to Peter and how much to the Tsarista and her counsel, but I am nonetheless quite impressed. They have managed to wrest the throne from Sophia without spilling a drop of blood."

"Yes, yes," Lefort agreed, "Tsykler, the Patriarch, the charges--all executed in brilliant fashion. And while I wouldn't doubt that the Tsarista was the one to seek the support of the Patriarch…still, I see much of Peter's personality in this."

"Indeed…" Gordon paused, thinking of the strict doctrine of the conservatives. "A clever course of action. I am encouraged to see Peter using his wits to solve such a problem. Many in his position would not have acted so shrewdly."

"Well said!" Lefort chuckled.

"This is odd for me, you know. Difficult, for an old dog to feel such hope."

"Nonsense. Peter has that way with people. He draws emotion from them, both good and bad…and you're not such an old dog, General. I suspect you still have a few good battles left in you."

"Perhaps," he answered, grinning at himself. "In my thoughts, I am still young and capable."

"You are a lion, sir, and you are good for Peter. It benefits him to know a man like you, an accomplished man, a military man, a European. From you, he learns the brand of dignity that the Russians cannot teach. In truth, General, I rely on the fact that your contributions to his welfare counter my detractions. Or should I say distractions? Either, I suppose. At any rate, I am surely guilty of both."

"Do not fool yourself, Captain. Tsar Peter is very fond of you and takes much from your lead."

"Well, where drink is concerned, I have no question."

"In more than that," Gordon answered speaking frankly. "You discount your influence. I have seen it firsthand. Through you, Peter has developed a taste for life."

Lefort shrugged modestly. "Peter comes by it naturally, I assure you. The boy has a coarse side, much talked about. This is true. Yet I believe it is the Old Russian in him, the gifts of his ancestors."

"Perhaps," Gordon replied, "but where else but within the comfort of your company could he speak so freely? Where else could he find such willing conversation and someone so receptive to his wit? No, Captain Lefort, the boy within the man needs a comrade like you."

"You flatter me," Lefort said with sincerity. "And I must ask you, as I have before, to call me Franz. In time, your formality will make me quite uncomfortable."

"Very well then. I shall make every attempt to address you as Franz."

"Good! I am grateful, sir. And I wish to extend an invitation. You must attend one of my parties. I am quite proud of my hospitality. I promise by the time it ends, we will surely be comrades."

"I shall try not to disappoint you," Gordon answered, his words provoking another chuckle from Lefort.

They rode in silence for a while, enjoying the peace of the early morning, their thoughts accompanied by steady hoof beats and the churning footfalls of the men. The slight breeze was cool enough to keep the horses comfortable and the ranks awake, making it a pleasant, if slightly disorganized, march. Gordon didn't mind; there was little need for discipline today. There had been no battle, yet the men behind him reeked of triumph, certain they had made the correct decision.

They rode for a long while before Lefort turned to address him again.

"I wish you to know," Franz said, his tone uncharacteristically serious, "that my interest in the Tsar is strictly personal and that I never intended to benefit from my association with him. I need nothing from the Tsar but his friendship. My ambition is merely... curious, at best."

Gordon hesitated, thinking of the truth in the words.

He nodded. "Your mansion in the Sloboda is said to be the finest--"

"A gift!" Lefort protested, lowering his voice to a strained whisper. "Generously given! Am I to turn down Peter when he is so gracious?"

For the first time ever, he saw Lefort in a state of distress and was immediately regretful that he'd been the cause.

"Franz, allow me to finish." Gordon raised a hand. "I intended to say that I understand how such gifts could affect others' opinions. I experienced a similar feeling when I first arrived in Moscow. Granted my post by Tsar Alexis, I was confident that I had earned the right to lead. I learned, however, that a Scot with a few bars on his shoulders bears very little authority without practice. Not only were the men unwilling to recognize my authority--they were disdainful, mistrusting. Only through time and consistency could I rise above this suspicion. I assure you, Franz, I know how swiftly foreigners are judged."

Lefort grinned. "I see."

"And I believe you are sincere when you speak of your friendship with Peter," he continued, not wishing to offend. "It is good for him, no question. In his position, I am sure the Tsar encounters few people who bear no personal or political motive."

"The rest are in awe of his size or his sharp tongue."

"Indeed. His position alone is enough to befuddle most. But with you, he is allowed an escape from the pretense and posturing. He may speak, drink, curse or spit as he wishes, without any fear of repercussion."

Franz paused, tilting his head a bit as though taking in the comment. "I am pleased to hear that you hold such an opinion of me, General. In fairness, I cannot, however, take credit for your kind words. I am, at heart, a selfish man--and I spend what time I can with Peter because I enjoy his company. If he benefits in any way from a man like me, well…that may only be taken as a sign of his good fortune."

Gordon allowed himself a grin, knowing that Franz liked to see the effects of his words on people. More humble than he'd expected, Lefort's cavalier nature was easily palatable, carrying with it an amiable air that seemed to surround him. Self-deprecating to the end, Franz seemed to provide an excellent model for someone in Peter's position.

"I am glad that you joined us, Franz. The Tsar will be overjoyed to see you."

"It is my pleasure, General. I must thank you again for inviting me," Franz replied broadly, "And yes, I shall be happy to see him as well. Moscow simply isn't the same without Peter. The city seems lifeless without his presence, pale to gray when he is absent."

"I would agree."

"With Peter, however, one cannot be sure. As much as I would like to think that he will come and sit in Moscow, it seems hard to believe that the boy will stay in one place. In my mind, he is likely to return to Fort Presburg and skip Moscow entirely."

"He will return for the Duma meetings, I would assume. And we mustn't forget--he has a child on the way."

"True, true."

Moscow will consume more time than he wishes, Gordon thought, thinking of the rigid schedule that would soon be imposed upon the Tsar. *The Duma, the clan, the Church. If he runs from his duties, they will look to the Tsarista.*

"I expect he will soon be a regular sight within the Kremlin walls…"

"If they can manage to pry Sophia from her throne," Lefort added, finishing his thought. "You may have to go in and fetch her, General."

Patrick frowned at the thought. "I would certainly hope not. I admit she will be reluctant to leave her comfortable surroundings."

"They won't think to execute her, will they?"

"I do not expect so," Patrick replied. "From what I have been told, the Naryshkins have neither the evidence nor the necessity to seek her head. Retired, Sophia is as good as dead, anyway."

"I am reminded--something I have been curious to know, sir. Of all these distinguished military men, you could be considered the closest to the Regent and Prince Vasily. There is no argument that you were on good terms with the Regency--a friend of Vasily Golitsyn, if I may go that far."

"Certainly," Gordon responded without hesitation. "I served with Prince Golitsyn for years."

"My thoughts exactly," Lefort returned. "Given your feelings toward the Prince and your obvious affection for Peter, I am more than interested to know your feelings on the end of the Regency."

Gordon waited a moment before answering, drawing in the early morning air. "I suppose I would say that the situation is as it should be. Peter is of age and very capable. The Regent may have thought she could linger forever, but it seems the right time for her to step down, regardless of the charges."

"Ha! I ask for your feelings and you give me rationality! This alone gives insight into your character, General, but what I am truly seeking is to know your opinions, your mood, if you will."

Patrick smirked at his inadequacy. "Very well, then. I would have to say that I am pleased for Peter's sake. He deserves a chance and I would guess that he could be very good for Russia. He is much like his father, but stands in no shadow.

"As for the Regent and Prince Vasily," he continued, craning his neck to check on the ranks, "I was not unhappy with their brand of politics. They accomplished much in their short time. Peace with Poland? Who would have considered it possible? Not to mention the treaty with the Chinese. Personally, Vasily is charming and Sophia quite the opposite, no question. Still, I see success in their endeavors. Despite the leanings of his clan, we may hope that Peter is equally progressive."

Lefort nodded his agreement. "You are pleased, then, to see the Naryshkins have their day?"

He frets over the Tsarista. His worries are the same as mine.

"I am pleased to see Tsar Peter have his day," he answered, emphasizing the correction. "Where Lady Natalya and the Naryshkins are concerned, I am always admittedly wary. Does that answer your question?"

"I meant no offence, General," Lefort replied apologetically, "only to weigh your opinion. There has been plenty of talk in the Sloboda concerning the Church, and I thought, well, having heard that you'd been through worse in England…"

"It was likely much different than what you've heard. I shall relate the entire tale to you over a drink sometime, but suffice it to say that I share the concerns of the Sloboda, especially as I am a Catholic. I would very much like to discuss topics such as this with Peter, but I fear I must be careful, for I do not yet know how to speak openly with him. You, Herr Lefort, are well-versed in this subject."

Franz offered a mock frown. "General, I am beginning to worry that you didn't invite me for my companionship."

No better time to address the subject, he thought, already decided. There had been questions in his mind about how much he would say to Lefort.

"Your companionship is well appreciated, Franz, but I fear that we may be facing dark days in the Sloboda. The Naryshkins stand ready to enact their agenda, and the Patriarch regularly sips tea with the Tsarista. There is talk of disallowing any immigration and imposing restrictions on religious buildings in the Sloboda. It is quite a simple thing to drum up charges against anyone considered a heretic. This, in part, is why I invited you to accompany us."

"So I am correct," Franz answered quietly. "No matter, I bear no offence. I am grateful to see the Tsar and the inside of Troitskaya-Sergeeva--and for your company, of course. Happy enough to do my part, though I would expect Peter to do what is right."

"He is young and distracted," Gordon answered, thinking of Peter. "The Naryshkins will accomplish much without his direct consent; the Tsarista can insure this. As for Tsar Ivan, we may expect that he will do what he is told."

"You speak the truth, General. I cannot doubt you. We both know that Peter needs little coercion in any regard, but I can tell you I will do my part. If piety is to become a crime, I am certainly the most legitimate man in Moscow. As far as the Tsarista, we shall have to hope for the best."

"Indeed."

Hope for the best. The words echoed in Patrick's mind, a short phrase that purely and succinctly summed up their position. With Peter to ultimately rely on, this seemed a good prospect.

"General, I can see it."

Gordon looked up, squinting in the dim light.

In the distance, still a shadow against the blue fade of the morning sky, the Troitskaya-Sergeeva Monastery awaited. Massive and serene, the structure seemed appropriate as the center of the Russian Orthodox faith, distinctive onion top domes resting safely behind the forbidding white fortress walls.

"She's a beautiful stack of bricks, that one," Lefort breathed.

"Truly remarkable!"

A slight murmur of appreciation rippled back through the ranks as they set their weary eyes on their destination. They reveled for a moment in the sight of their Russian monument, the giant structure that housed hundreds of monks in the service of the Church. For men of their faith, Gordon recognized it as a kind of military pilgrimage, as though he were delivering Peter's army to receive a blessing.

"And here is our benefactor…"

Down the hill they could see a small line of horses, riding out at regal pace to greet them. At their head, the unmistakable figure of Peter, the tousled mop of black hair atop his uniformed figure. Today, he wore the green coat of the Preobrazhensky.

Peter sat astride his great mount, motioning to the others before spurring and charging ahead, far too eager to remain shackled to the greeting party. Raising an arm he waved to the regiments.

Gordon lifted his chin and suppressed the urge to smile, not wishing to offend the Tsar. The young ruler's enthusiasm was highly infectious, the mere sight of him seeming to lift the hearts of the men. Shouts of 'Tsar Peter' came from the ranks behind him and Patrick quickly lifted his hat to signal a response.

Let them criticize him when his back is turned...but Peter is difficult to oppose face to face.

While remaining a man of faith, Gordon could hardly be called superstitious or be swayed by the persuasions of mysticism. And given his age and experience, there was little that truly amused or provoked the General anymore, much less inspired him. Until recently, he considered inspiration to be something from his past, a sentiment reserved for the young and the creative. Yet there was no question in his mind--the young Tsar had moved him. Despite his stubborn spirit, Gordon could feel the lure of the young man's personality.

"Quite a likeable lad."

"I was just thinking the same."

"Impatient--just as I remember him. At least the exile hasn't affected his spirit!"

Touched by the sun, the horizon had bloomed into a rose-colored sunrise, the first bright rays casting shadows through the ranks. The rain clouds of the previous night were sent retreating into the west, chased away by the impending dawn and the presence of the young ruler.

Solitary now, Peter's shimmering golden bay raced to meet them, kicking up mud in its wake.

"I have enjoyed our conversation, Franz."

"As have I, General."

"Please, you may call me Patrick."

He could sense Lefort's smile. "I shall endeavor to do so," he replied pleasantly.

As Peter closed the final distance between them, Gordon gave the command to halt, ordering the ranks to stand at attention to receive the Tsar. All complied willingly. Gordon and Lefort dismounted, removing their hats.

"General! You have been busy recruiting!"

"Yes, Tsar Peter," he answered, bowing respectfully as the enormous Akhal-Teke came to a halt before them. "But only one man…"

Smiling brighter than the sunrise, Peter leapt down from his mount and offered a salute to the troops before embracing Lefort.

"Franz! I didn't think this day could be any better, but here you are!"

"It is my honor, Tsar Peter." Lefort's face reflected his gratitude. "General Gordon was gracious enough to entreat my participation and I eagerly complied."

Peter turned to stare at Gordon, his gaze growing serious. "General?"

Ah, a sense of decorum!

Gordon offered a stern salute. At his cue, the rest of the officers followed suit.

"With your permission, Tsar, I present the Sloboda colonels and their Moscow regiments, reporting as ordered, ready to stand in defense of the throne."

Peter stared proudly for a moment before returning the salute. "Well done, General. I knew I could rely on you. Your service to Russia is well appreciated."

"I am honored," he returned with civility, bowing. "I serve the Tsar."

Beaming with satisfaction, Peter turned to walk down the line of colonels, saluting and speaking a few words to each. He moved with careful pace, giving each of them their time before moving on. Looking over, Lefort nodded his approval.

He has an instinct for these things, Patrick thought, watching as the military stares turned to looks of gratitude in Peter's presence.

The weary soldiers remained rigid throughout, wanting the young Tsar to recognize their devotion.

"Back on your horses," Peter announced when he had finished with the colonels, turning back to leap astride his own. "We shall see if the abbots have any nourishment for these loyal men! Oh, and something to drink for Admiral Lefort!"

"You have my gratitude, Tsar."

"And you mine, Franz."

The two mounted and fell in beside Peter, the lines of men following faithfully at their backs. Riding at least a head taller than either Gordon or Lefort, the Tsar leaned down from atop his horse to speak with them.

"I am grateful that you included Franz," Peter said to him. "It has been too long since I've seen him."

"When else would I have a chance to see inside Troitsky?" Lefort offered happily.

"You shall certainly see it on this day. I would think you two the first of your kind. In light of the situation, the Patriarch will comply."

"Captain Lefort was quite eager to join us," Gordon offered. "And I could hardly deny him his place."

"Hardly, sir. Your humble general invited me, Peter, as a favor to you."

Peter nodded. "I thought as much. You have my gratitude, Patrick, in more than you know."

"I simply wished to reunite two old friends," he replied. "Had you not returned, Franz might have died for lack of excitement."

Peter laughed. "Excellent, General! Something I might have expected Franz to say himself."

"Indeed." Lefort bore a mournful look. "Regrettably, I fear my presence may be affecting your best general."

"It is good, then, that you are a man of such positive influence."

"Certainly."

"After all," Peter said, turning to look at him. "We can't let Franz take credit for having all the wit, can we?"

"I would agree, sire. Military wit is dry but potent."

"Dry but potent," Lefort echoed. "Yes, I have known many military men of this description."

"Well, you have arrived at the height of excitement. It has been a long night, truly."

Gordon's grin faded. "Commander Shaklovity?"

"Has confessed to his crimes," Peter answered thoughtfully. "Nine pages worth, in his own hand. You will no doubt be here to witness his execution."

"Here, Tsar? He is to be executed at Troitsky?"

"Outside the walls," Peter answered, nodding. "The Patriarch would not bear staining the holy ground with traitorous blood."

The Naryshkins have waited years, Gordon thought. *They will not hesitate now.*

"As for Sophia," Peter continued, "I shall seek your counsel on this matter--both of you. I have prepared a letter to Ivan declaring our intentions. I have paved the path, I think. Displacing that vindictive sow may be troublesome, still."

"I cannot say that my advice in this matter is worthy, but nonetheless I am at your disposal, sire."

"As am I," seconded Lefort. "Particularly if there is a bit of refreshment involved."

"Ha!" Peter smiled down at him. "You are in luck, Franz. You cannot hope to fathom the size of the abbots' wine reserves!"

"I knew it! It shall be a pleasure to drink some blessed libation."

"There is so much to tell, my friends--so much work ahead of us. I shall need you both in the days to come. I do hope you plan on remaining in Moscow."

"You are speaking to the General, no doubt," Franz commented, "for it would be impossible to pry me from my residence. I may never leave Moscow again! Sire, I can safely promise to be as unmovable as the Regent herself."

"Good." The Tsar replied. "I am the better for knowing it, Franz."

The perfect opportunity, Gordon thought, sensing his turn. *Do I speak of it now?*

No--better to wait until we are alone.

"I have no plan to leave," he offered. "I am more than satisfied to serve you, Tsar Peter."

"Excellent. Just what I was hoping to hear. I wish you both to have prominent posts in the new administration. You shall lead the armies of Russia, Patrick. Only with a man of your strength can we hope to succeed against the Turks. As for Franz, he shall be known as Admiral Lefort and will command our navy."

"Navy, sire?"

Peter laughed at himself. "Before you think me a lunatic, know that there is still much work to do and much to speak of! I must tell you about the ship, and Lake Pleschev, and Archangel! Too much to account for with Sophia still sitting in the way. Troitsky may be a miracle, but I tire of it."

Gordon followed in pace, riding stunned by the Tsar's promises, knowing that Peter would keep his word. Until now, Patrick had thought little of his own gain.

Once Tsar, he will do as he pleases. He will collect friends and enemies, both.

As the greeting party finally reached the company, Peter raised a hand to halt the soldiers, turning to address the group. Tall astride his mount, he looked over the ranks, offering a stern Russian stare.

"I commend you for a mission well accomplished. You are all patriots in the service of Mother Russia! Do not forget your promise to her, and I will not forget you! Awaiting you as reward, there will be food, vodka, and dry clothes for all! Follow my lead!"

Peter smiled down mischievously at Gordon and Lefort.

"The morning sun inspires me," he said to them. "Gentlemen, see if you can keep up!"

Without another glance Peter waved his arm in the air and spurred his horse intently, galloping away down the hill.

With a roar of approval, the ranks set in motion, running at his heels as they shouted in triumph. No longer weary, the lines flooded past Gordon and Lefort, headed down to the great white fortress.

"And so it begins…"

Gordon paused to look around him, this newfound inspiration unlike anything he'd witnessed before, knowing that much more history would be made before this young man was finished.

Offering a shrug and an amused grin, Lefort gripped his reins tightly, bracing himself for the ride.

"Shall we?"

Moscow, The Great Sovereign's Palace of the Kremlin

September 17, 1689

The long corridors of the Palace remained quiet today, left empty save for the wordless presence of the servants and guards. Outside, the Square echoed no sounds of carriages or conversation, the boyars and diplomats safely stowed away in the hope of a quick remedy to the trouble.

A plague had come to the Kremlin. All of Russia's business had been suspended, set to resume only when a cure was found.

And alone in her chambers, wrapped in isolation and defeat sat Sophia Alexeevna Miloslavsky, the daughter of Tsar Alexis Romanov and the acting Regent of Russia, now thirty-two years old and still unmarried, knowing that the best of her life was over.

She had lost much in the last month--her lovers, her friends and the reins of the country. Somehow, it had all slipped from her grasp, and in so short a time. All her supporters were absent, even the male members of her own family proving too timid to stand in public support. Only now was Sophia realizing that her mourning would someday fade, but the loneliness that ruled her would be endless and eternal. For though time would no doubt harden her emotions, she would never find the kind of excitement that the Regency provided.

I am the sickness that plagues this city. I am the reason they stay away.

I am alone, as they wish me to be. After all I have done, they wish for me to suffer in silence.

The quiet bothered her most.

Not the quiet itself--had she wanted to talk, there were still many servants who would stand and listen to her speak. She could also still find a friendly ear in the sisters of Novodevichi and was grateful for their presence in her time of need. Yet while pleasant and somewhat comforting, their company lacked spirit and their words lacked import. They knew nothing of politics or the world. Their opinions held no weight. Rather, what Sophia was lacking was depth of meaning.

She'd been too awkward to be considered graceful--too opinionated to be called pleasant. She was too loud to be docile and too plain to command with her beauty. Her strengths lay outside the tiny Russian mold of womanhood, resting in her politic mind and persistently sharp tongue. She was adept at manipulating a conversation and could see enough of the forest to make shrewd decisions. Since her youth, Sophia had been able to contend with any man. Suddenly and brutally, she was being stripped of ever having the opportunity again.

If there is any worth to me, it will now be wasted. I have no greater purpose than the Regency.

Alone, and with the exception of her sisters, friendless. Sophia had known the Regency would not last forever, but would never have pictured herself in such pitiful condition. Vasily was gone, exiled, and Fedor condemned; losing them both at once was almost more than she could tolerate. Now, her words leapt from her lips with nowhere to land, her thoughts and emotions vanishing into air as soon as she spoke them.

My body will live but my spirit will waste away, untended. I shall have to be content with simple thoughts.

A short knock returned her to the moment.

"Come."

Her chambermaid appeared at the door, bearing a worried look.

"My lady, I--"

"What is it?"

"My lady, there is a visitor…from Troitsky."

Her body tensed at the words, her sense of dread renewed.

They've come to call for me, she thought, unable to respond quickly. *Peter has already written to Ivan. This summons is for me.*

"How many men?" she asked.

"Just a single messenger, my lady. Prince Troekorov."

Sophia stood from her chair. "What is his request?"

"He seeks an audience with Tsar Ivan. He said no more."

Sophia walked to the dressing table, lifting the hand mirror to check her face. Gazing at herself, she saw fatigue and sadness, tired eyes and flaccid features, the evidence of seven difficult and glorious years. She did not, however, see anything that resembled fear.

"Tell him that he must wait," she ordered. "Tsar Ivan will see him very shortly. Go, now. We will see him in the Faceted Chamber when the Tsar is ready."

"Yes, my lady."

The chambermaid disappeared back down the corridor, leaving Sophia alone. She dressed quickly in silence, calming her thoughts and thinking only of what she would say to her brother.

Ivan must be prepared.

She found him alone, standing and staring out the window, his posture marked by a permanent slouch in his shoulders. Ivan was not a small man, though he always seemed so; even when dressed in his finest robes, his downcast eyes and slumped stature belied his position. Never in the least had he seemed a fitting monarch.

"Ivan…"

He turned, his lips curling. "Sister. I was hoping to see you."

"Well, I am here, finally." She approached, reaching out a hand to touch his thickly bearded cheek, patting him like a puppy. "You look tired, Brother. Have you been spending late nights in the company of your wife?"

"No," Ivan shook his head. "I haven't seen her lately…especially at night."

"You are her husband, Ivan, and the Tsarevich. If she is not present then you must call for her. Do you understand?"

Ivan nodded, looking as though he'd done something wrong.

"You must persevere, Brother. Peter is soon to have a child, and you must have one, too. Russia depends upon you to provide a healthy son."

"Yes, Sister."

And if Mother had been able to do the same? she thought, looking at him. *None of this would have been possible.*

His disability had been her opportunity, his infirmity her foundation. She had certainly never rejoiced in the fact that her brother was half-witted, but there was no question that his condition had provided her a path to greatness. Through Ivan's inability, her own peculiarities had become necessary and valuable traits. Through Ivan, she had become notable and worthy, escaping the insignificance of the cloistered life. Their lots had been cast together, and like flowers in the steppes, one had withered so that the other could thrive.

All pride aside, Sophia had always known how much they had in common. She and Ivan were both disappointments, oddities in their royal family--Sophia, so unlike her beautiful and obedient mother, and Ivan, cursed from being even half the man that his father was. Neither had been what their family had expected or hoped for, yet together they had risen to significance. Proud of her achievements, Sophia would have gladly compared them with those of any tsar, knowing in her heart that Ivan was the catalyst for her reign.

He will live on, much as he did before. He has a wife now and, with God's blessing, a son. Peter will use him like a shield and Ivan will capitulate. He will sit and stare and become little more than a stick of furniture... but he will live.

"We must speak, Vanya."

"Oh?"

"A messenger awaits from Troitsky," she began, holding his glance, "The Naryshkins will call for me to step down as Regent. I have no Strel'tsy left to defend us, and we have no support in the Duma. Peter wishes to return to Moscow and he wishes for me to leave. Do you understand this, Ivan?"

His face changed a bit, losing a shade of brightness, his features falling. "You're leaving? Today?"

"Not today," she answered calmly, "but soon."

"This is about the letter, isn't it?" His features wavered, on the brink of tears.

"In part, yes, but you mustn't worry, Vanya. We will both be fine. The letter--may I read it again?"

"But why must you leave?" he asked, his usual lethargy shattered in the wake of her words. "I know Peter wants the Regency to end, but he can't just send you off into the snow like he did Vasily!"

"I will not be exiled," she said firmly, reaching out to pull him close. "Do not worry, little bear. I will ask your step-brother to allow me to retire. I have earned that much respect. I will be close, likely at the Novodevichi Convent."

"Are you certain?"

"Very," she replied, hugging him. "They would never send me to the same place as Vasily."

Teary-eyed, he gripped her, returning her embrace with a tight squeeze.

Poor Ivan will have no champion now, she thought, wondering how long his spirit would last. *His wife must treat him well or answer to me.*

Ivan will remain safe. At least, Peter will see to this.

Peter's affection for his step-brother was genuine; this she could not deny. She had seen them together enough times to know that Peter held the same tenderness for Ivan as she did, and whatever her complaint with the Tsarevich, she had never squabbled over his treatment of Ivan.

Some relief, then, knowing that Ivan would be taken care of. When the sickness finally claimed him, Ivan would die as Tsar, and the family name would become part of history. Even in death, it seemed, she would owe Ivan a debt, for as he would be remembered, so would the Regency.

"The letter, Ivan. The letter from Peter. Do you have it?"

He nodded, producing the parchment from his robe. "I carry it with me."

She took the fateful note and rested her eyes upon it for what seemed the hundredth time:

> '...And now, brother sovereign, the time has come for us to rule the realm entrusted to us by God since we are of age and we must not allow that third shameful personage our sister the Tsarevna Sophia Alexeevna to share the titles and government with us two male persons...'

The letter concluded that Ivan would remain the senior Tsar, as he had during the Regency. More important, Peter had included a shrewd request asking for permission to appoint new officials without Ivan's consent. It seemed a simple concession, but given the vast number of positions in the Kremlin, would mean the end of Miloslavsky support in every fashion. Peter would have the authority to promote his supporters to any and all posts, from Moscow to the Kazan. If he and his mother wished to erase the Regency's success, they would certainly have the means to do so.

The Naryshkins were bidding to control Russia, cutting every line of support for the Miloslavsky clan. Given his disability, Ivan would be unable to counter them politically. Still, there remained the hope for an heir.

I am finished, but Ivan may not be...

For a moment she looked to the future, finding solace in her visions.

Much can happen in time. If Peter's wife were to bear a girl or lose her child at birth, Ivan could still be the first to father an heir!

His children--or grandchildren perhaps--could still rise to rule someday. Much can happen! The Miloslavsky line needs only a seed of hope.

Though his wife claimed that he could perform his duties as a husband, there was still question as to whether Ivan was capable of fathering a healthy heir. Sophia's efforts to seek an outside contributor had been forgotten in the midst of scandal, and with Shaklovity and Golitsyn absent, there was no one she could possibly trust with such a delicate mission. Like the rest of her existence here, Ivan's fatherhood would have to be left in the hands of God. Her own influence would be limited to hope and prayer.

Now, even in the face of her own political extinction, Sophia could feel proud. She had done her part for the family, struggling every step of the way against custom and tradition.

They may call me a murderer, but Ivan sits on the throne because of me! Even when I depart, he will remain in the bed I've made for him.

"Will I be allowed to visit you?" Ivan asked, pulling her from her thoughts.

"Perhaps," she responded, seeing no sense in adding to his worry, "but not for a long while. You must learn to manage without me, Ivan. Praskovia will help you. You must look to your future as Tsar and to making yourself a father. This is my wish for you. Will you be a good brother and satisfy me?"

"Yes, Sister." He looked down, defeated. "But I want you to stay."

She pulled him to her chest once again, kissing him on the forehead. "I, too, wish to stay, little bear. Some things, however, cannot be. You know Peter's wishes. If I remain here, they will be angry and will seek to send me into exile. You don't want this for me, do you?"

"No, Sister. I just want it to be as before."

"You will be fine, Ivan. A fine, proud Tsar. Remember to keep your head up, eyes forward. You'll make me proud by giving me a beautiful new nephew."

"Yes, Sophia."

"Now come, Brother. You must receive this messenger from Troitsky. Today, I shall stand beside you instead of hiding behind the throne."

Sophia took his hand and they walked in silence to the Palace of Facets, the sound of their footsteps echoing throughout the empty Palace. He gripped her fingers tightly, pausing once to look at her and proclaim again that he did not want her to leave. Sophia kissed his cheek and placed her arm around him, explaining that her departure was God's will.

Half of her believed it. She'd always said that it would take the Holy Father himself to separate her from the Regency. On the day the Patriarch departed for Troitsky her prophetic words seemed laughably true. Of late, however, her opinion had changed. Now, it seemed impossible that this treachery had been destined by God. Surely, it was mere chance that brought her to the top of the mountain and back--the Holy Father could never be so cruel.

With Ivan finally settled in the throne, Sophia took her place beside him and called for the visitor.

Prince Troekorov entered without pretense, his familiar face bearing no ill will, but nonetheless renewing Sophia's ire.

Little bastard. Peter chooses him to remind me!

Troekorov seemed a harbinger of her downfall. He had been a courier during their failed negotiations and in command of the embarrassment at Vozdvizhenskoe. Now he stood before her again, empty-handed and without escort, his mere presence a declaration that the young Tsar had nothing to fear any more. Peter was a soldier now, and Troekorov his standard.

"I bring a message for Tsar Ivan from his brother Tsar Peter." Troekorov glanced at Ivan for a moment before refocusing his stare on Sophia.

She returned the glare in kind. "As Tsar Ivan has no other counsel, I will remain. As Regent, I think it my right."

Troekorov nodded his agreement. "You have no dispute from me, Lady Sophia."

"You will address me as Regent," she snapped in reply, her voice filling the vast Chamber. "For the present, at least."

"My apologies, Regent," he replied, his expression remaining flat. "If I may?"

"You may."

Troekorov turned his attention back to Ivan. "Tsar Ivan, your brother sends his warm regards and wishes to tell you that it is time for him to return to Moscow so that he may stand by your side as co-tsar. He will not return, however, while the Regent remains."

Ivan looked to Sophia, his visage mournful. She nodded her understanding and tilted her head to direct his attention back to the visitor.

"To enable his return," Troekorov continued, "Peter asks, Tsar Ivan, that you request Regent Sophia to leave the Kremlin for the Novodevichi Convent, where she will be safe and well-kept. Once this has been accomplished, Tsar Peter will return to Moscow."

She'd known it was coming, but the words were painful to hear. Novodevichi had been her charity and she its biggest benefactor, having donated large sums and commissioning several of its buildings. In this, Peter was being kind. Sophia would not be required to take the veil but would spend the rest of her life in comfort, well-kept, indeed, but unable to leave. She would remain in Moscow, right under Peter's nose, invisible and without voice.

Not knowing how to answer, Ivan looked to her again.

I shall accept my fate, she thought. *But I shall do it the way I have done everything else in this Regency--in my own time, at my own command. Let Peter wait a week or so.*

"I cannot possibly leave the Kremlin," she said, staring down Troekorov. "If I am to retire, I must have time to prepare. I am, after all, an important woman..."

Outside Moscow, The Monastery of Troitskaya-Sergeeva

September 18, 1689

The scaffold had been constructed in short time, rudimentary in its structure but more than adequate for the purpose. Set just outside the walls of the Troitsky Monastery, the executioner's block awaited its moment.

The crowd gathered for the morning's austere event was comprised of more clergy than was the custom, the abbots and monks joined by many curious peasants. Also well represented were the Moscow Strel'tsy, a majority of their rank and file still held by duty to their task at Troitsky. Finally, the nobility, present in small pockets gathered along the fringe, represented today by surprisingly few of the Naryshkin inner circle.

Knowing he would be one of the prominent family members present, Lev Naryshkin dressed appropriately, clothed in a green velvet justaucorps and waistcoat with white silk stockings, the ensemble topped with his finest wig and copiously plumed hat.

He didn't mind the attention. Lev enjoyed his notoriety, though his choice of European dress was made through preference and not originally intended as self-promotion. Still, it was true that his fashionable appearance made him more memorable and thus more notable--in a family like the Naryshkins, one had to strive to stand apart. Through looks, personality and style, Lev had always managed to do so. Now, with Peter's ascension, he knew he would be required to do much more than look good.

"So you are already promoted, so to speak."

Lev Naryshkin nodded. "Well, yes, the Tsar has promised me as much and the Tsarista is in accord."

"Ah, excellent."

"This was all agreed long ago, of course. If we are fortunate, we may all be comfortably installed in Moscow within the week."

"Truly?"

"Oh, yes. I shall soon begin preparations for the return. What a celebration it will be!"

"There are many who will benefit from your promotion, Lev. With you as Director of Foreign Affairs, the Duma will once again have an ally in the Palace."

Beside him, the bearded figure of Emilian Ukraintsev seemed content with the prospect of becoming personally involved with the new administration. One of Russia's few professional diplomats, Emilian was savvy where negotiation was concerned and his acumen had proven effective in avoiding international incidents. With the weight of Russia's foreign policy staring him in the face, Lev considered himself fortunate to have such friends.

For though Lev was a popular, stylish, and well-received gentleman, he was aware that his actual administrative skills were, as of yet, still untested. Not that he lacked confidence; with the influence of the Naryshkins and the affections of Tsar Peter in his favor, there seemed little that could initially derail his success. Still, Lev, more than anyone, was aware that the perception of his abilities was greatly exaggerated.

"I will be happy to have you in trust, Emilian. We will no doubt face our share of challenges."

Ukraintsev produced his tobacco pouch and began to stuff his pipe. "You know, my friend, I was not opposed to the efforts of the Regency."

"Nor should you have been."

"Though perhaps too far reaching, the Regent was wise to increase the number of embassies."

Lev nodded. "Certainly."

"And though I had my differences," Emilian proclaimed with an air of pride, "I cannot be made to cast away the progress that we made together. Our trade now stretches as far as China, and our embassies travel across the continent--and I have yet to mention Poland. I welcome you with open arms, Director, but I refuse to discount my prior achievements. Our efforts in Europe must continue. We cannot rest on the victory of the Eternal Peace."

Must he press so tirelessly? Lev groaned inwardly. *There will be plenty of time to worry ourselves with policy.*

"You are most correct," he said to the diplomat, nodding with a serious look. "And I would have you know that I am in agreement and that I trust in your opinion. In this instance, a man of your experience certainly knows best."

"Your words are a relief, sir."

"Nonsense! I shall cause no trouble." Lev patted his shoulder, wishing to be done with the discourse. "You needn't worry about my stepping in and changing things, Emilian. I want only to continue in the same successful manner that you just described--due, in no small part, to you, of course. Your counsel is well taken, I assure you. I shall continue to listen."

"Your confidence is appreciated," the diplomat replied graciously, his expression still lacking comfort. "I should ask your forgiveness; my approach lacks my usual finesse. Admittedly, I am anxious to know my place among the members of the new administration and eager to set to task."

All of them, Lev thought, grinning back amiably, *all of them hoping to win a new fortune. Let them dwell on the mundane if they wish. I have celebrations to plan!*

With the majority of his usual entourage remaining in Moscow, the time at Troitsky had seemed a lonely stretch, a necessary but unpleasant task that was soon to be finished. Kept away from the pleasures of the city, Lev had spent most of his time conversing with Peter's favorites and ordering specialties from the cooks. Weeks later, he now felt a bit thicker and far less interesting--it was time to return to Moscow.

"I shall be happy to be finished with this business," he declared, staring over at the still empty scaffold. "Personally, I believe the execution would have been far better received in Red Square…but I suppose there is something to be said for expediency."

Ukraintsev nodded. "I was told that the Patriarch insisted."

"Yes," Lev replied, full of responses but choosing to hold his tongue. "I was told the same."

No need to disparage the old bird, he thought, looking out over the abbots and monks. *If Joachim is shrewd enough to feather his own bed, why call him out?*

A voice from behind drew his attention.

"Now here's a true gentleman…perhaps we should address him as Director!"

He turned to see the unlikely pair of Tikhon Streshnev and Prince Fedor Romodanovsky, the former dressed impeccably in a traditional kaftan and bearing a pleasant smile, the latter clothed in a soiled Preobrazhensky uniform, displaying his characteristic scowl.

Despite the obvious differences, the two had much in common. Unflaggingly loyal, both counted themselves among Peter's inner circle, members of the Jolly Company, personal friends of the new

Tsar. As a result, both were prominently placed for advancement and were sure to receive key positions in the Naryshkin government.

"My friends!" he said, offering a greeting to both. "What a pleasure it is to have company in this circumstance."

"I wouldn't have missed it," Romodanovsky growled in his usual fashion. "I'll enjoy every bit."

"A happy occasion for all Russians," Streshnev added, bowing.

A boyar, Tikhon was an old friend of Tsar Alexis and served as one of Peter's guardians. His counsel was even and rational, his connections in the Kremlin considerable. Far less abrasive than the gruff Prince Romodanovsky, Tikhon was far more interesting in conversation and possessed a fatherly air that made his every word seem profound. He looked uncomfortable standing beside his hot-tempered companion.

"Two others, I hear, are to be executed along with the Commander. Co-conspirators."

"Good riddance to the traitors," Romodanovsky said, spitting on the ground. "They caught three Strel'tsy, as well. All three--knouted and had their tongues torn out. By now, they're halfway to Siberia."

Naryshkin winced, thinking of Boris and the conspiracy. The truth was buried now, never to emerge, all of it nestled comfortably beneath the holy robes of Patriarch Joachim. In Lev's mind, the plan had been a tremendous success. Shaklovity's death would be the proof.

A shame--not to be able to take credit for such a thing! At least Boris cannot deny me this bit of accolade...and the Tsarista.

"Your venom for the Strel'tsy persists?" Lev questioned, grinning. "It seems a bit odd. Do they not serve the Tsar now?"

Romodanovsky huffed, glaring back at him. "Do not mock me, friend. The blood of my father is as fresh in my memory as it was seven years ago. You wrong me to speak light of this."

"You have my apology," Lev said immediately, bowing, irritated with Fedor's persistent rancor but hardly inspired to engage. "I am too light-hearted, Prince. Your father's memory is revered in the halls of the Kremlin, Fedor. I would never seek to disgrace those honorable souls who perished in Sophia's bloody wake. You must forgive me."

He nodded a bit, scowling as he gazed at the ranks. "You, I can easily forgive, Lev. The Strel'tsy I cannot--will never trust!"

"You are a fair man, Fedor."

"Not likely," he responded, distracted, his attention still fixed on the Strel'tsy musketeers. "Only three in this conspiracy? Ridiculous! They should be killing the lot of them along with Shaklovity!"

"Your point is well taken," Lev offered, placing a hand on Romodanovsky's shoulder. "and I know many who, quite rightly, share your opinion. But with respect to your father, our own dear Ivan Naryshkin, Matveev and all the rest--we are embarking on a new regime, a new day. What will the Strel'tsy be without their Sophia?"

"A dim lot of bastards."

"They will be in service to the throne," he continued without stopping. "They are sworn to defend both Peter and Ivan. The war between the clans is finished and we are the victors. In time, surely all this venom will have worked its course. The Regency, now so fresh in our minds, will soon be naught but a mournful memory, a lesson learned where treachery is concerned. Do you not agree, Herr Streshnev?"

Streshnev paused a moment, holding the attention of the group. "You have given me much to agree with, so I will simply state what I am thinking."

"Please do."

He scratched at his beard. "The end of the Regency must be recognized," he began, "and then put away. Today's adversaries often become tomorrow's allies, and one must strive to adapt with grace. Sophia's old supporters are already fleeing the fire. Given that I see no Miloslavsky heirs or family members willing to stand against the Church, I would agree that the 'war', as you put it, is finished. But the Strel'tsy? Here I must side with Romodanovsky. Their traditions...their fraternity runs deeper than their loyalty to the Regent. To be truthful, I find it difficult to believe that they will ever truly see themselves aligned with the Tsar."

Romodanovsky huffed again. "You see?"

"Spoken like the learned counselor that he is," Lev interjected. "Cautious, not too confident--just the kind of advice Russia would want for the Tsar. Yes, caution is the correct path, but I would wager these same devils will be shouting Peter's name a year from now."

"You give them too much credit," Romodanovsky said, his anger still evident. "Wolves never lose the taste for blood."

"Perhaps," Lev countered, "but these Strel'tsy locals are more dog than wolf. They can be domesticated, made to obey a new master."

"Foolish. We should disband the whole lot," Romodanovsky pressed, still visibly angry. "The Preobrazhensky Guard is strong enough to protect the Tsar. That, or execute all the colonels and start from scratch!"

Typical, Lev thought, staring at the bullish Prince. *He heard nothing I said. How does Peter tolerate him?*

Tiring of conjecture, Lev was ready for the execution to commence.

"Fedor, my friend, I must apologize again, for I fear I have angered you and stirred your passions."

"Nothing I cannot do myself."

"Yes, perhaps, but on this occasion I am guilty and quite regretful. This is a time for celebration, and I should not be denying you the satisfaction you came here to find."

Romodanovsky nodded, cooling. "You're a right man, Lev--one of the Tsar's beloved family. I won't begrudge you an apology."

"Think of it, my friend," Lev clenched his fist, curling his lips. "Think! Shaklovity's head on the ground!"

"Yes…"

"This, the dog who dared call our pious Tsarista a heretic and the Tsar a devil--and called for their heads in the very same breath! I thank the Holy Father that Shaklovity was too great a coward to see his plans through. The Holy Father watches over us."

"Would that we could see Sophia's head rolling as well." Romodanovsky spit again. "We know she deserves it."

Ukraintsev flashed an offended look but said nothing, apparently unwilling to engage Romodanovsky. Streshnev said nothing, pretending to be interested in the activity around the scaffold.

Lev shook his head. "Your passions are well noted, but Sophia will not be executed. Certainly not. Even if the charges could be mustered, she would only become a martyr. There is Ivan to think of, of course--and what a terrible way to begin this glorious regime!"

"Here, here," Streshnev added. "As it was, Peter was most reluctant to execute the Commander."

"True," Romodanovsky finally relented, shrugging. "Pity, that. What for Sophia, then? Shall it be Siberia?"

Lev shrugged, unwilling to tell. "That decision belongs to the Tsar, and perhaps the Patriarch. All I know is that she will live."

"The crowd continues to gather," Ukraintsev commented to the rest, changing the subject. "Who knew there were so many villagers in Vozdvizhenskoe?"

"Not just Vozdvizhenskoe," Streshnev countered. "They come from farther, I expect."

"Quite a crowd for a beheading."

"The execution is not the attraction," the boyar continued proudly. "They wait for Shaklovity, but they have come to see the new Tsar. They are here for Peter."

"Of course."

"Astounding, I agree," Lev said to him, pointing. "Look at them all! This is terribly amusing! Tell me, Tikhon, did Peter's father ever garner such a crowd for a mere glimpse of him?"

Streshnev soured. "Tsar Alexis was quite popular in his time, may God rest his soul."

"Yes, certainly."

"Finally, the Patriarch makes his appearance!" Romodanovsky rolled his eyes, pointing.

Heads turned to watch the opening in the Troitsky gates, the entrance guarded by a split complement of former adversaries, red-coated Strel'tsy and green-coated Preobrazhensky standing together at attention. The murmuring crowd hushed to a dim buzz, villagers pointing and whispering.

From the light behind the tall green gates emerged two figures, side by side, their shapes unmistakable even in shadow. The silhouettes of the Patriarch and Tsarista Natalya moved slowly from the darkness of the gate and into the light of day. An odd, reverent moment of silent indecision was followed by cheers and applause as the crowd broke into an enthusiastic but respectful round of appreciation.

Clad in an exquisitely jeweled cope of gleaming golden damask, the Patriarch stood tall beside the plainly dressed Tsarista, her Polish clothes making her look a bit like a foreigner. The group behind them held no other notable family members but the Tsarista's statement was made with her presence alone, the stern, devout look on her face telling the crowd all they needed to know. As the supportive calls died down, the two found their seats beneath a canopy at the back of the setting.

Natalya is a gem, Lev thought, suddenly aware of the crowd's curios stares. *She wins them without a word…without a look!*

"The crowd is still buzzing," Streshnev commented. "Do you think they still await the Tsar?"

"Some do, though I expect the brighter among them have already figured that there is not an empty chair beside the Patriarch."

"Ah, yes…"

The crowd looks to Natalya, Lev thought, suddenly wanting to be the subject of attention. *I should make my own appearance.*

"Well?" he asked the others, straightening his sleeve. "Shall we greet the Tsarista?"

Naryshkin stepped first, moving toward where Natalya sat, knowing that the eyes of the crowd were on him. The group followed in tow, chins up and proud.

As he approached her, Lev maintained his serious look, removing his plumed hat and offering his best flourished bow. She offered a thankful nod, her expression hard but gracious, flawless in its subtlety.

Perfection! I could not have directed her better myself. He stepped back, his eyes reflecting family pride. *I could learn much from Natalya.*

Following his lead, the rest of the group bowed and nodded silently, paying their respects first to the Tsarista, then asking and receiving the blessing of the Patriarch. The entire process was completed quickly.

With a nod from the Patriarch, the gates opened again, this time revealing the shrunken form of the accused.

Led by a complement of Preobrazhensky and a few Troitsky abbots, Commander Fedor Shaklovity's head remained lowered, his dirty tangled locks hanging to hide his face. Hands tied and feet shackled, the prisoner offered no reaction to the crowd, not even a glance to satiate their curiosity.

Shaklovity's reception was notably quiet, the group offering only a few blunt jeers and murmuring at the sight of him. Many of the villagers had never seen him before, and the Strel'tsy present were unwilling to offer any response, eyes held forward in military stare.

A month ago they were taking orders from him, Lev mused, marveling at the speed at which Shaklovity had fallen. He thought of Boris and the interrogation, wondering what had gone through the mind of the Commander as he penned his lengthy confession.

All finished now. All for the best.

"Look at him," Lev said to the others, lowering his voice. "His hair looks simply hideous. If I were to go to my maker, I would at least have the sense to be properly groomed."

"He's groomed," Romodanovsky returned. "His shirt and trousers are clean, at least."

Lev waved away the comment. "Those were given to him. Hanging his hair in his eyes was by choice."

Romodanovsky chuckled. "You'd go to the block with your wig on! Eh, Naryshkin?"

He grinned at the thought. "Yes, if possible, I think I would. Although in my case, it would certainly be a waste of a very expensive wig."

The black-hooded figure of the executioner climbed the small set of steps and took his spot on the scaffold, waiting beside the chopping block. In his hand he held an axe that seemed small for its purpose.

"Large man, this one. Do we know him?"

Ukraintsev shook his head. "No. The man who used to perform the duty is too weak now, and they still haven't found a replacement. This young man is from a nearby village. Big enough, I would agree."

"A good executioner must be difficult to acquire. We must hope the Tsar has little use for their services. That, or consider hanging them."

"Hanging wouldn't do," Romodanovsky growled, now enrapt with the sight of Shaklovity. "Now be quiet at let me watch this man die."

Lev grinned, glancing over at the Tsarista before turning his attention back to the drama.

Led by a greencoat on either arm, the prisoner made his way up the creaking wood of the scaffold, the shackles allowing him only one step at a time. Once atop the platform, he received a final blessing from the abbots, nodding his head obediently as they spoke.

Lev could see the Commander's face between the dark strands of hair, the formerly intense visage now carrying only a calm expression.

Finally looking up, Shaklovity delivered a single, prolonged stare in the direction of the Strel'tsy colonels before lowering his head again and stepping to his place. The executioner's hand on his shoulder, the former Commander fell to his knees and rested his neck on the blood-stained wood of the block. A basket awaited his head.

The murmurs of the crowd fell to silence.

"Will there be no final words?" Emilian whispered to him.

"Not today," Lev returned in kind. "All has been said."

The hooded figure took his place beside the block, planting his feet firmly and readying his grip on the axe.

A sense of drama, this one, Lev thought.

As though burdened by the weight of the hushed audience's attention, the executioner took another moment to ready himself. Shaklovity remained still, his tangled hair the only thing visible to the crowd.

"I hope this man is good," Lev whispered, unable to contain his comment. "Removing a head is more difficult t--"

A hissing 'shhh' from Romodanovsky cut him off mid-sentence.

"My apologies."

Slowly, the executioner raised his weapon, taking careful aim.

The first blow was incomplete.

The crowd winced collectively, recoiling at the sight. From the rear, the villagers offered an amused cheer. Lev smiled at the sight; somehow, he had known it would be messy.

Blood flooded down onto the scaffold, staining the pale wood.

The executioner frantically wrenched his axe free from the flesh and raised it for a second blow.

Again, the result was less than desirable.

Lev shook his head, groaning. Beside him, Romodanovsky muttered the word 'beautiful' and slapped him on the back.

Five strikes later the goal was reached. Chopped free, Shaklovity's bloodied head finally made its long-awaited journey into the basket below. Appreciative of the effort, the crowd rewarded the despondent executioner with a polite round of applause.

"One down and two to go," Lev commented, unable to contain a grin. "He will get better with practice, surely."

Moscow, The Great Sovereign's Palace of the Kremlin

September 23, 1689

Regent Sophia stood alone.

The warmth of summer was all but gone now, the cold nights having returned as a prelude to the expected chill of fall. The Palace windows open wide, Regent Sophia waited in the cool breeze, staring out at the buildings of the Kremlin and surveying her domain for the final time.

Her hair lay about her shoulders, combed but unrestrained, the final touch of preparation remaining before her journey. She'd left it down all week, knowing that the rules at Novodevichi would never permit such leniency, even for an important resident like herself. For despite her Regency and all its glory, Sophia remained a woman and would have to abide by the restrictions placed upon her.

In her life, there had been countless difficulties to overcome, many of them conquered by sheer, willful indifference. In her mind, a monarch of any significance knew that action bests reaction and that, to lead, one must often put on blinders and press on despite all opposition. She had easily ignored the doubts of her competency in the early months of her reign and pushed forward despite

Naryshkin opposition. Yet, in the final throw, she had been unable to escape the inevitable.

It had been a week since Tsar Peter had sent for her removal, yet after hearing that he refused to set foot in Moscow while she remained in the Kremlin, it seemed an easy decision to stall her efforts and remain in place for an additional seven days. She remembered laughing at the thought of the Naryshkins waiting for her departure, yet in these final moments in the Palace she found herself mourning her loss more acutely than ever, the ghosts of the past still lurking.

Her laugh was hollow now, her kind look only a mask meant to hide her bitterness. Every hopeful thought seemed a ruse of self-deception, yet they arrived--the joyful memories and pleasant reminiscences, accompanied always by a thread of torturous hope, the distant notion that somehow, someway, she could regain what was lost.

She missed Vasily terribly. Sophia had been unable to sleep, finding herself pacing the floors in the early morning hours, her emotions moving from despair to anger and back again until fatigue finally claimed her. The sisters of Novodevichi had assured her that she would find peace and rest within the walls of the Convent. In truth, she doubted that she would ever truly rest again.

This morning she paced the floors a final time, her mind still spinning from the events of the summer. In three months' time, her security had been stripped and her Regency stolen, a mere matter of politics for the Tsarista and her followers. A simple accusation, a culpable perpetrator, and a willing jury. The process had been so well-executed that she could not help but wonder at the depth of the conspiracy. How long had the Naryshkins been plotting?

So quickly taken, she thought. *Could it be taken back with the same haste?*

Even now, there was still a part of her that clung to the notion of staying put in the Kremlin. And though she knew better, there still lurked deep down inside her a small part of her spirit that was in acute denial of the truth, still refusing to believe that the rest of her days would be spent chained to the Novodevichi Convent.

The child is not yet born. Recurrent thoughts kept her mind resting in fertile ground. *Were it to die…or be born a girl…*

Ivan remains. In Peter's absence, he would again need my aid.

Sickness, accidents, poisoning--the possibilities flooded into her mind in reassuring waves, hopeful thoughts of Peter's demise and the collapse of the Naryshkins.

The notion is not so odd, she told herself, clinging to possibilities. *I could rightly be brought back--more reason to keep my head.*

People die. Even heroes like Peter. I shall have to treasure this thought in the long, quiet hours.

The better part of her recognized her immediate defeat. Natalya and her progeny would win the throne for now and the Naryshkin loyal would take their coveted positions in the Kremlin.

Vasily had once told her that the Regency worked on borrowed time, and despite her denial, she had always replied that she understood. It was true. Peter's ascension had been a foregone conclusion. The boys were set in their lots, bound from infants to grow into their adult places. Even as children, one could see that Peter would grow into a healthy young Tsar and Ivan into a worthless invalid.

Looking back, it seemed ludicrous to think that the Regency would have lasted forever, and now in her vengeful state of mind, she found herself wondering whether she had actually believed it.

Was I so foolish to think it might last?

Was I a fool not to have murdered Peter when I had the chance?

I cannot be blamed for denying my fate.

Left with only bitter thoughts and unfulfilled goals, she did her best to keep from shouting as she directed the displacement of her remaining personal items. The Kremlin had retained only a bit of its former charm as the influx of new servants prepared the Palace for the arrival of the Tsar. The disconcerting quiet of the past month would now have been welcome.

Looking up, Sophia saw her chambermaid Inna standing before her, waiting patiently for her attention.

Have I been talking to myself?

"How long have you been standing there?" she asked, glaring.

"Only a moment, Lady."

"What is it?"

The chambermaid bowed without expression. "The escort awaits, at your convenience, Lady. And you have a visitor."

"Ah, Maria! Finally!"

"Yes, Lady."

The Regent had planned well for her younger sister's arrival. With or without the Regency, she was still the head of her beleaguered clan.

"What? Why didn't you simply allow her in?"

"I did not know if you wished to be bothered, Lady."

"Assist with my headdress," Sophia replied with a wave, fighting against her anger. "Then send in Maria, and inform the Abbess that I will only be another few moments."

"Yes, Lady," Inna replied immediately, moving to secure the headdress before curtseying and turning for the door.

Sophia watched the chambermaid escape the room, thinking ahead to the accommodations awaiting her at Novodevichi.

I will not be able to order around the sisters like this. I must learn to wear my pious face all day and night.

As the chief contributor to the Novodevichi coffers, Sophia would be provided a suite of well-appointed rooms, many decorated with items she had donated. And though her life would be Spartan and uneventful, Sophia would not be required to follow the strict doctrine of the Convent as the sisters did. A captive guest, she would remain in an appropriate place of honor.

Her time at the Convent would be restrictive, to say the least. Under the commands of Peter's order, Sophia would never be allowed to leave the Convent grounds, and the only visitors allowed her would be her female family members. Maria, her favorite and the closest of her sisters, would no doubt provide a vital link to the world outside the Convent.

"Sister, come kiss me!" She opened her arms at the sight of Maria, the smile returning to her face.

"Poor Sophia!" her sister fell into her arms, kissing her cheeks. "We have missed you so!"

"Well, you shall see much more of me in days to come. It is good to have you back in my arms, Maria. Here, let me look at you. By the flush of your cheeks, I can see you're in good health."

"And you, Sister," Maria replied, her face etched with concern. "You have endured so much."

Sophia lifted her chin. "I am steadied by prayer," she replied with a brave face. "Your presence is a great comfort, Maria. How are Ekaterina and the others?"

"Clamoring to see you," she replied. "Particularly Feodosia. She has gifts for you and wanted me to bring them today. I said it would be better when we visit the Convent."

"I will be happy to see her," Sophia told her, "...to see you all. I am quite distressed that I shall not be living with the family."

"As are we. But you are not forgotten, Sophia. There has been much talk of your suffering. You are always in our prayers."

The second youngest of Sophia's five surviving sisters, Maria was only three years her junior and had shared in her life as much as anyone in the family. Docile yet opinionated, Maria was much like her mother in both look and temperament. Years before, when Sophia had been called by the clan to champion Ivan, Maria had been her greatest support.

Now Maria stood with her hands folded, her eyes lowered, bearing no curiosity for the opulent decor of the Palace. Rather, she focused on Sophia, ignoring the finery that surrounded her as though the Palace itself had betrayed her.

Granted, it was an odd feeling being here, knowing that in mere hours the Naryshkins would be walking the same floors, celebrating their victory and changing things to suit their tastes. Sophia could picture Natalya's chin lifted in arrogant pride as she re-entered the Kremlin. The Tsarista, more than any of the rest, would revel in her defeat.

"Ekaterina has been quite worried," Maria said, her eyes averted as though she were embarrassed. "She believes we are forgotten, lost--that we shall surely lose our home. Could it be true?"

"I am hopeful the family will be allowed remain in Moscow," Sophia replied, her tone cooling. "Considering the black hearts of the Naryshkins, I suppose we should consider this merciful."

"But, Ivan--"

"Ivan's influence will not hold against the Tsarista and Peter."

Maria nodded, pulling a handkerchief from her sleeve and dabbing at her tears.

"You must tell Ekaterina to visit me as soon as possible," Sophia continued angrily. "There will be much I need her to do. If my sisters are to be cast out, then I will strive to allow you a bit of dignity. Better to leave of your own accord than to be escorted away by musketeers. If anything, I know this. For now, Maria, be grateful to the Holy Father that you still breathe!"

A small explosion, a bit of residual gunpowder within Sophia that found its way to the end of the barrel.

Maria recoiled, looking a bit intimidated. "I will tell Ekaterina, Sister. We will abide by your wishes."

Sophia paused, regretting her outburst, realizing that her sisters had rarely seen her at her worst. Turning away, she took a deep breath.

I am foolish to treat her so! Maria must be coddled, not whipped.

I will soon be at the mercy of their charity. My dear sisters will be my only link to the world.

Putting on a mournful face, Sophia turned back to Maria, taking her sister's cold, small hands into her own.

"Dear Sister, you must forgive me for my anger. I have been ill with worry--here, alone, praying--striving only to defend our name against those who would defile it. Please, Maria, understand that I am not myself, driven to this by the treachery of Peter and the Naryshkins."

"Sophia, you needn't--"

"Nonsense," Sophia continued. "I have shamed myself with my rudeness. They have stolen the Patriarch and the Regency from me, and now the Naryshkins have lowered me to hurting those I love. You must accept my apology."

"Of course, Sister," Maria replied immediately, softening as expected. "Poor Sophia, there is no reason to apologize. I am here to aid you, dear Sister. I was selfish to mention our condition."

"Not at all," she told her. "The concerns of our family are my life-blood and you are all in my prayers every day. You are a miracle to me, Maria…to our whole family! You have always been the kindest and most temperate of us, and it wounds me to think that Natalya Naryshkin could drive me to deepen your despair. After all, my sisters are my heart!"

Maria smiled modestly, reaching out to embrace her. Sophia reciprocated, squeezing her tightly.

"Don't worry, dear Sophia. Natalya Naryshkin could never stand between us!"

"Ah, my little Maria! I have sorely missed you!"

"I will visit you every day, Sister."

Sophia paused, ending the happy moment with a suddenly mournful look. She brought a hand to her lips as though she were about to cry.

"Sophia, what is it?"

"Oh, Sister, it is hard to explain. I am just grateful for all that God has given me."

"Good Sophia, even when you've been treated so horribly, you still prove an inspiration."

"With all I have lost," she answered, staring away as though delivering a soliloquy, "with all that has been taken from me, it would be a great comfort to think that I was still important to our family...to my sisters."

"And you are, Sophia! Of course you are! You remain our guiding light!"

Sophia closely watched her sister's response, paying more attention to her look than to her words, knowing that one could read every emotion in Maria's simple gaze. In her eyes, Sophia saw nothing to trouble her. The loyalty of her sisters was unquestioned, something she could rely on.

She will be of great use to me, Sophia thought, smiling humbly. *I must keep her comfortably in the palm of my hand.*

Guiding light. Ekaterina, Feodosia, Yevdokia, and Marfa will follow because they're obliged, but Maria will be my eyes and ears.

"I am prideful to worry of such things."

"Nonsense!" Maria objected, her look sincere. "I meant it when I said I would visit you."

"And I will be grateful." Sophia answered calmly, again changing her look to one of worry. "I will strive to do my best by all of you. Admittedly, I do have fears. The current plight of our family may require you to do more than simply visit, Sister."

"What?" Maria's face paled. "Of what do you speak?"

"Once the Naryshkins have settled…" She allowed her voice to trail off, as though lost in worry.

"Sophia? Please tell me--I promise I won't weep."

"Weep if you will." Sophia extended her chin proudly. "The Tsar fears and hates me--this is a fact. And worse, there is the Tsarista. She has carried her grudge for years and spent many seasons plotting my downfall. Now that she has succeeded, I fear that the Naryshkin lust for blood will not be satiated. This much is true: they will seek to discredit and bankrupt those who were closest to me. And this includes our family."

Her sister held captive by the words, Sophia continued.

"I was thinking that…" she hesitated dramatically. "No, it is too much. I cannot ask you to--"

"No, Sophia, please! I wish to help!" Maria came to life, her eyes wide. "You have done so much for all of us. It would make me proud to think I could help you!"

"I will be helpless at the Convent and must know what is happening in Moscow. I will certainly ask you to help me, to aid our cause…perhaps by delivering correspondence to those who might help us or carrying messages from others who might need my help. Were the situation not so desperate, I would certainly try to keep you away from such business."

"I will do whatever you ask, Sister," Maria re-stated, her face now bearing a serious stare. "My feelings for Lady Natalya and her son are no different than yours. I tire of being so helpless. Please, dear Sophia, do not deny me this chance to help!"

Sophia looked back at her, nodding in approval. "Very well, my dear. You make me very proud."

"Oh, thank you, Sophia! I will show you I am worthy of your trust."

"You have nothing to prove to me, dear girl."

Sophia embraced her sister again, feeling a bit more at ease. With Maria's confidence secure, her inspiration was taking root, finding fertile ground in her vengeful heart. With a few words, the impending isolation seemed much less restrictive.

I will find ways to communicate, she thought, the reassuring possibilities again claiming her thoughts. *Peter will never know! I will provide a willing ear for all those who oppose him.*

Thoughts of defeat must be put away. I am not finished.

Sophia exhaled, nodding. "It is time for my grand exit, I expect..."

"Grand is correct," Maria replied. "Wait until you see the numbers, Sister! Armed Strel'tsy in full dress line Cathedral Square and the nobles watch from the bottom of the Red Staircase--all in preparation for your departure. You deserve such respect."

"It is easy for them to offer it now."

My final public appearance, she thought, wondering how the historians would portray it. *My final trip down the Red Staircase.*

I will linger at the top before I take a step--in case they've forgotten how I arrived here! Let them remember and fear me!

Sophia looked down at herself, knowing she'd done her best to look the part; her plain black robe and simple headdress were pitiable yet regal, perfect for the occasion, bearing no visible pretense. She'd imagined her exit hundreds of times in the past week and believed it important to appear humble and graceful in these final moments.

"They will miss you when you are gone," Maria said, shaking her head.

"If only it were true," Sophia replied, her melancholy smile now quite sincere. "Will you escort me, Sister?"

Maria nodded. "I would be honored, Regent."

They walked out the doorway arm in arm, and Sophia was in the corridor before realizing that she'd forgotten to take a final look at her chambers.

As they reached the top of the Red Staircase, Sophia kept her promise and stopped, looking out over the crowd below.

Her audience remained strangely silent, offering neither applause nor dissent, their numbers frozen in blank expression as her gaze passed over them.

And what did I expect? she asked herself, lifting her chin. *Applause? A parade?*

My supporters are quieted by fear.

The Abbess stood in the arcade at the foot of the Staircase but made no effort to approach, wise enough to allow Sophia her final moment. Leaving Maria a step behind, Sophia walked to the edge, all her notions of parting speeches and profound exit lines lost in the silence of the crowd.

I demand their attention, but not their voice. So be it.

Holy Father, give me strength.

Let them see me, God, one final time! Let all of Moscow see the grace and calm with which Regent Sophia takes her punishment! Let the Abbess and the Convent revel in my piety! And should Peter slip…

Let the Naryshkins remember and be fearful.

Peter will regret not executing me.

Lifting her chin, the former Regent suppressed a scowl, maintaining her martyr's calm as she struck her final pose.

See your fallen Regent--proud and without shame!

Enjoy the moment, you traitorous lot. Sophia Miloslavsky is not yet finished.

Moscow, Franz Lefort's Mansion in the Sloboda

December 1689

"My heart is wholly in Moscow," Lefort said to him, speaking with pride, raising his tankard as though toasting his own words. "I think I shall never live in Europe again."

"And Moscow is equally fond of you, Franz." Van Keller grinned back at him.

There was little reason for complaint. The mansion buzzed around him, just as he liked. The guests laughed in luxury as they drank his ale and smoked tobacco from long pipes. A single violin played happy folk dances, coloring the smoky air with familiar melodies. Food was plentiful and the room was filled, as always, with men like Keller, the wealthiest and most influential Europeans in Moscow.

But most important, the room was populated with women--beautiful young Europeans from the foreign quarter who, unlike their invisible Russian counterparts, were friendly and willing to trade favors for favors.

In Lefort's mansion, there were two types of parties.

The first was a respectable type of gathering, filled with soldiers and merchants, respectable foreigners and their equally respectable wives and daughters. Western gowns were the style, polite conversation the main activity, and the levels of inebriation were kept to a tolerable minimum. In these instances, Lefort's mansion served as a private refuge for the foreign elite of the Sloboda, a luxurious taste of home that was otherwise unobtainable within Russia.

The second type of gathering was much less respectable and yet more frequently held, lavish parties filled with many of the same notable men but absent their honorable wives. On these occasions the mansion would be well-stocked with unflappable wenches, comely, sturdy women who did not take offense at crass language or the admiring touch of experienced hands. Their duty was to see that no man was unhappy and their efforts were always well-compensated with gifts or coin.

His parties and banquets were the stuff of legend. This, Lefort knew, was one of his strengths, an activity he engaged in gladly. He spared no expense and made it a point to share his good fortune with those around him. In his generosity, Franz Lefort was equaled only by Tsar Peter.

"Your mansion is exquisite, Franz." Van Keller nodded his approval as he looked around the room. One of the most respected of the Sloboda's citizens, the Dutchman Van Keller was fond of commenting on Lefort's good fortune.

"Coming from you, sir, that is truly a compliment," Franz returned amiably.

Van Keller looked around, nodding his approval. "You are a fortunate man, indeed."

"That I am, sir," Franz replied, nodding, "But not nearly as respected as a man like you."

"Well, I…"

"I was told that you were receiving news from The Hague--every week."

Van Keller attempted a modest shrug. "Well, yes. Every eight days, to be correct. I send many letters as well."

"Sending and receiving then, every eight days! No doubt maintaining your business dealings and, of course, keeping in contact with the news of the continent. You are a worldly man, certainly. I envy you there, friend!"

"Your generosity extends beyond the ale, Herr Lefort."

Van Keller paused, his attention drawn by the approach of a flaxen-haired beauty.

Anna Mons. Slender, soft-featured, the daughter of a Westphalian wine merchant, she was as sharp-minded as she was pretty and held her chin high despite a blemished reputation. She was a frequent guest at Lefort's more raucous gatherings and had even shared his bed on several occasions. Needless to say, he liked her immensely.

"Anna, my dear."

"Franz, my darling," she responded in kind, flashing a wide smile and taking his arm.

"You are enjoying yourself, I trust."

Anna offered a single nod. "As ever. Who could fail to enjoy themselves in this heaven on earth?"

"You are kind, my dear."

She kissed his cheek. "Franz, you must tell me--I was told that Tsar Peter is coming tonight. Is it true?"

Franz wrinkled his brow. "Hmm…I seem to be having some trouble with my memory. Kiss me again and we'll see if it returns…"

She kissed him, this time twice on the lips. "There, that should do it."

"Hmm." He shook his head a bit.

"Franz!" she smiled rapping him on his wide chest. "Tell me, please…"

He chuckled, pressing her warmth against him. "Yes, my dear, he shall be here. But don't ask me when, for the Tsar comes and goes as he likes."

"I expect he does," she replied, her mind working behind her pretty blue eyes. "Is it true that he stays up all night?"

"I suppose," he answered, "when the occasion calls for it."

"He is quite handsome now."

As the German girl daydreamed, Franz could see her thoughts as though they were written in the air.

She's quick and crass, he thought, examining her. *She can drink and talk--and make a man feel more like himself. Perhaps it's not such a bad idea…*

"I shall introduce you when he arrives," he told her, watching as her face brightened. "I think he would like you."

Anna hugged and kissed him again, thanking him before gliding back into the midst of the party, her slender curves drawing the attention of the room.

"You've had her, then?"

"What?"

Van Keller pointed to Anna's swaying backside. "You've had her?"

Franz raised an eyebrow. "Well, I'm certain I would remember, but not certain I would tell. Unlike the great Agamemnon, I refuse to walk on the curtains. It was curtains, wasn't it?"

Van Keller snorted. "You are wiser than you look, Lefort."

"And hungrier as well," he replied, patting Van Keller on the shoulder. "I know the cooks have been working hard. Shall we see if we can find something to eat?"

Not wanting to miss the Tsar's arrival, Van Keller was about to agree when Andrew Vinius appeared through the crowd. The

Dutch merchant was a good friend, a man who, like Lefort, had been in Russia for many years. He reached out to take Franz' hand.

"Well met, my friend."

Franz embraced him. "I looked for you, but didn't find you."

"I've just arrived, as has General Gordon."

"Gordon?"

He nodded. "We came in together, and he's still standing down there waiting for you. I think he was a bit put off by the naked ass that greeted us."

Franz laughed out loud, unable to contain himself. "I shouldn't be surprised. General Gordon has only attended my official functions. He's probably as red as a beet! Stranded in the battlefield! If you will excuse me, gentlemen, I must rescue him immediately."

He set off for the entry, leaving Vinius and Van Keller behind and realizing very quickly that others were walking in the same direction, a mass exodus of guests headed for the front doors. Had he not seen it before, Franz would have been surprised. As it was, he knew very well what was occurring.

"The Tsar has arrived," he said keeping his pace, excusing himself as he moved past the guests.

Lefort saw Patrick Gordon as soon as he reached the entry. As of yet, the Tsar was nowhere to be found.

The General was still wearing his greatcoat and looking a bit perturbed amongst the rush of activity. Around him, Franz' guests continued to socialize as they filled the grand entry and positioned themselves for the Tsar's arrival.

"Greetings, Captain Lefort."

Lefort stepped forward to grasp his hand. "General Gordon!"

"The Tsar's carriage has arrived," Gordon commented dryly. "If you could not otherwise tell."

"I am greatly pleased to see you, General. Please forgive the lack of…formality." He looked around him. "I assure you, my home is not always in such a chaotic state. When the Tsar visits, he usually arrives unannounced, without difficulty. Tonight, the entire Sloboda seemed to know of his intent."

Gordon nodded as though receiving vital information, his eyes kept politely away from the sights around him. The General was not known to be a prudish man, but his age and temperament were enough to keep him on the respectable invitation list and out of the special gatherings.

"I, too, heard about the Tsar's attendance tonight, and I recalled your once telling me I had an open invitation."

"So I did, General, and you are most welcome here. I regret not being present to greet you."

"Not to offend," Gordon said, leaning closer to be heard, "but Peter is quite difficult to find of late. Admittedly, I came tonight because I wished to see him."

"And so you shall," Franz replied, nodding toward the door. "And I'm not offended in the least, General. I am pleased enough that you are here. In fact, there is something I wish to discuss with you."

"Certainly," the General replied. "But it will have to wait. He has arrived."

With all eyes lingering on the entry, the buzz of the party rose to a curious crescendo before suddenly falling to a whisper at the sight of the Tsar. A few guests fell to one knee and were quickly waved back to their feet.

Peter stepped through the entry with a serious expression, scanning the silent room. He wore a blue knee-length justaucorps, his hair hanging in curls past his ears, his face shaven save for a still unimpressive moustache that rode upon his lip. With his eyes narrowed to angry slits, Peter strode aggressively toward Lefort.

Franz waited, the room cowering in doubt around him. Peter's glare quickly moved to meet his, the depths of his eyes bearing venom.

"I am mystified and confused!" Peter shouted, holding out his arms, turning to stare at the guests before returning his attention to Lefort.

"I am mystified," he repeated, bellowing. "You invite me to your home, Herr Lefort, and I arrive only to be mystified and confused! This I cannot bear. So I will ask a question, Herr Lefort. If you value your neck, you will hope that I like the answer!"

Lefort nodded his understanding, avoiding Peter's penetrating stare.

Moving with a sense of drama, Peter paused, looking first to one side of the room and then to the other, raising a hand to cup his ear as though waiting for one of them to speak. Now wrapped in utter silence, the guests offered nothing but shocked stares.

Peter stepped forward. "Tell me, Herr Lefort...you invited me to a party. Why are your guests so quiet?"

Lefort grinned, looking up to see a smile spreading across the Tsar's face.

Peter laughed, the room exploding around him in a relieved expression of joy, cheering as he took a short bow.

Lefort fell to a pleading knee. "They are not drunk enough, sire! In this duty, I have failed you!"

The Tsar's face grew serious again. Peter reached out his hand and placed it on Franz' head, pulling away the wig and setting it atop his own brown curls.

"You heard the words of your generous host," Peter announced to the room, raising a hand. "If you wish Herr Lefort to keep his head, you will begin enjoying yourselves immediately!"

The room exploded again, this time with a cheer and a collective toast for the Tsar. Franz was happy to see his servants on point, ready to hand Peter his first tankard. When the toast was finished, Lefort commanded the guests to return to their merriment, dispersing the group save for a few curious stragglers unable to separate themselves from the sight of Peter.

To this, he was well accustomed. In their time together, Franz had noticed the Tsar's captivating effect on people; in public there were always a few who would follow the Tsar simply to stare at him. If someone had charged them, they would gladly have paid for the opportunity.

"My friend!"

"You had them frightened for a moment, Tsar."

Peter embraced him, squeezing like a brother. "I couldn't help myself. They were all so quiet. I felt as though I were entering a cathedral."

"Word spread of your arrival," Franz replied. "I don't quite know how they all found out you would be present. I detest turning friends away at the door."

"No matter." Peter shrugged, looking around. "You know I don't mind a crowd--especially one as beautiful as this. Patrick?"

Finally spotting the General, Peter moved to greet him.

"I didn't see you standing there! Franz, why didn't you tell me he was here?"

Franz shrugged. "I suppose I thought the General would be self-evident."

"Admittedly, I have difficulty standing out in a crowd of this nature," Gordon answered. "If I fade into the walls, I suppose it is my own fault."

"Nonsense! You stand out in any crowd, General. I was simply not prepared to find you here."

"You are kind, sire."

"A wonderful surprise, truly."

"You have been difficult to find in Moscow," Gordon told him. "I am glad to find you here."

"As am I." Peter nodded. "There is much to tell, General. I've been busy, day and night. Have you heard of Lake Pleschev?"

"Yes. Not far away."

The ship, again, Franz thought. *He's become preoccupied with that relic*.

"Well, we are going to sail on it," Peter announced, crossing his arms. "I've already been there several times. I think it a perfect place to start--once we get a ship in the water."

"And the shipbuilding efforts, sire?"

The Tsar glowed with pride. "Progressing. A struggle, no doubt, but we're making progress. Even better, I'm thinking of purchasing a ship, a real and true warship from the Netherlands. The flag ship of our new navy. Am I right, Admiral?"

Lefort straightened, saluting. "Certainly, sire."

"This reminds me, I'm determined to learn the Dutch language and would speak with a merchant named Andrew Vinius," the Tsar said, looking about. "Is he present tonight?"

Lefort nodded. "He is, sire. I saw him only a moment ago, before you stopped the world by entering the room."

Peter grinned. "On this occasion, I only stopped the room, Franz. I suppose I must work my way up if I wish to stop the world."

Peter turned to General Gordon, smiling beneath his curls. "Patrick, I see too little of you."

"Tsar Peter, it is always good to see you, whatever the circumstance."

"You must tell me what you think of Franz's little parties."

He paused. "I have not been here long enough, but my first impression tells me that Captain Lefort is an unparalleled host. The accommodations are extraordinary. Were I a younger man, I might find more to enjoy."

Lefort smirked back at him. "Come now, General, there are many in our midst who are older than you. And you cannot possibly convince me that you have lost your taste for ale!"

"On that count, you are correct."

"Patrick is a happily married man," Peter added, "and sees to his wedding vows more diligently than other husbands."

"Aye, sire. The General is married to a Russian woman. She is far more loyal and dutiful than a Western wife. But I am crude to speak of her without asking. General Gordon, how is your fair wife?"

"She is well, thank you," Gordon replied, not showing offence. "I shall tell her that you asked after her. But I would expect that she exhibits my European manners as much as I drink her Russian vodka."

"Very good," Franz replied. "Let me see what I can do on that count."

Don't offend the General, Franz reminded himself, *especially not today.*

Inspired, Lefort turned and found a serving girl among the ranks of moving flesh and called for a round of drinks and pipes.

Soon, the Tsar was comfortably fitted with a second tankard of ale and a bowl full of tobacco. Peter had acquired a taste for smoking at Lefort's mansion and now puffed away contentedly, still intrigued with the novelty. Gordon's presence seemed to elevate the young ruler's spirits, and the three found much to talk about as they surveyed the scene.

"I am at home here," Peter told them, wiping the foam from his lips. "I am grateful for the retreat."

"The doors are always open, you know," Lefort replied. "My parties gain immeasurably in stature from your presence. You see how they all stare at you? Trust me--all of the Sloboda wants to be here tonight."

Peter's eyes lingered on the local girls. "I think your guest list appears perfect. So Franz, I can only assume that you've invited the General here to make an appeal."

Now he's done it. Lefort shrank a bit, somehow knowing that the Tsar would be the one to begin.

"Franz?" Gordon turned to face him.

"Well, yes, General, I--"

"Call me Patrick, please. We discussed this."

"Yes, Patrick. Thank you. Yes, well, I do have…something."

"I've never seen you speechless, Franz."

He grinned, realizing that he was blushing. "No, I suppose not. The more serious the topic, the more tongue-tied I am."

"Franz is in the amorous spirit," Peter said finally, speaking for him. "And his desires involve you, General. Well, your cousin, more specifically."

"My cousin?" Gordon's face changed a bit. "And Captain Lefort?"

"Franz…"

"My cousin and Franz?"

"It may be inappropriate given the circumstances, General, and you see that your cousin was certainly not invited to this particular gathering, but the two of us have made acquaintance and I believe she finds my company pleasurable."

The General paused. "Pleasurable?"

"In no crude or untoward way, I assure you," Franz appealed, trying to read Gordon's unchanging expression. "Our encounters have been formal, and quite by chance. I have the utmost respect for her, General--the very reason I wished to speak with you."

"Franz wishes to marry your young cousin," Peter blurted, bearing a wide smile. "There, Franz, I have spared you the agony."

Lefort looked back to the General, still not knowing what to expect. Gordon's stare lingered on him for a moment as though attempting to survey his character in one look, his expression still bearing no indication of his thoughts.

"How mighty you must be in the field, General! The opposition has no way of knowing your mind."

"I am not opposed," the General said finally, "given that she is not included in your baser pursuits."

"Oh, no!" Franz straightened honorably. "Certainly not! This is simply the case of a lonely man who wishes some company."

The General nodded. "She has her own mind, particularly here in Moscow. As her cousin, I cannot, of course, give her away, but your consideration is appreciated, Franz."

"It is settled, then," Peter exclaimed happily. "I shall pay for the wedding myself. The two of you will soon be related! Let us drink to it!"

"Here, here!"

As the tankards clashed, Lefort caught the General's gaze, lingering for a moment and seeing no resentment behind his smile.

My luck that Peter was here, Franz thought, drinking deeply.

"I must warn you, Franz," Gordon began, his look growing serious again, "you marry into a family of Catholics. The mood of the city turns against us. Had Charles of England not been beheaded, Tsar Alexis would not have allowed us at all."

The words caught Peter's attention, his expression falling cold. "You will remain, Patrick--as will all the Latins."

"Your words are appreciated, sire. I am not, however, reassured that the Patriarch will not act. I have heard rumor that Joachim seeks to expel all Jesuits."

Ah, so we come to the point, Franz thought. *The General's motive for attending. Gordon cannot help but talk politics.*

"Impossible." Peter waved off the comment. "You are in service to the State. Russia and the Tsar need you. I will not allow it. I will speak with my mother tomorrow."

"With all due respect, sire, I think your mother is aligned with the Patriarch on this issue."

"I am well aware of my mother's leanings, and there is no doubt she is unduly influenced by Joachim and his rigid views. Still, I cannot rightly see her overturning my father's commands."

"If the anger were limited to your mother and the Patriarch, we would have little problem. The disdain, however, seems to infect all of Moscow as well."

Peter reached out to place a hand on the General's shoulder. "We will speak, Patrick. Somewhere with less distraction."

"Yes, sire," Gordon offered a satisfied nod. "This is not the place for such topics. I shall bother you no more on this evening."

"I rely on your counsel, Patrick. There is a new stallion in the stables I wish to try. Perhaps we should ride in the morning."

"I would enjoy that, sire."

"Good, then! It is settled. Franz?"

"I will let the two of you ride without me," he told them, knowing his place. "I will be much better off in the restful throes of slumber."

"With the quality of this ale, I should think you'll be sleeping all day."

Franz took a drink. "Yes, it is good, isn't it?"

Peter struck a match and re-lit his long clay pipe, sending clouds of bittersweet smoke into the air. Raising a finger, he commanded their attention before blowing several perfect smoke rings sailing toward the ceiling.

The room was still rather full around them, the curiosity surrounding Peter's presence only mildly diminished with time. Happy to be in the presence of the Tsar, the merchants and soldiers remained in close proximity while attempting to mind their own business. The local girls were far less discreet, staring from the corners of the room and bravely passing flirtatious looks at the Tsar as they passed him. The Tsar surveyed their ranks with capricious interest, unable to focus on one before being distracted by another.

That is, until Anna Mons entered the room.

Franz knew it the moment he saw her.

She was exquisite and rough, stepping forward with confidence and shameless pride, fully dressed and still more beautiful than the others. He was stirred by the sight of her, his baser instincts crying out.

Her light eyes looked first to him, smiling, then focused on the Tsar. Approached by one of the Scots, she paused to talk.

"That one," Peter said, nudging him in his ribs. "Who is she?"

The boy has good taste for courtesans.

"That, my friend, is an exceptional girl. Her name is Anna Mons."

"Dutch?"

"German, sire, though she speaks Russian well. Her father is a wine merchant of moderate success. A fair man, I think. Of late, she has been a frequent guest."

Peter looked to him. "You've...been with her?"

"Well, sire, I hesitate to--"

"You have!" Peter chuckled.

"Not recently, sire. I find her quick-witted and fond of drink. This is more than enough to enjoy her company."

Peter shrugged. "I should like to meet her."

Franz grinned in return. "I thought you might."

He avoided the General's gaze as he captured Anna's, raising a hand to wave her over. With a knowing smile, she nodded her assent, moving to greet him.

"Beautiful, eh?"

"You have excellent taste, Franz."

As she approached, Anna lowered her eyes but did not fall to a knee, instead offering the back of her hand as a princess would. Peter set down his ale and leapt forward to kiss it, smiling down at her.

"Anna, is it?"

"Yes," she said, her eyes afire. "The Tsar, is it?"

"At present, yes," he answered, laughing. "I suppose it was my height that gave me away."

Franz chuckled. "Anna, may I present the Tsar of Russia."

She stared up, her glance never wavering. "I am honored."

"In this instance, I am certain the honor is mine," Peter replied, reaching down to her hand. "You are truly a delight to look upon."

"And you are as kind as they say…and as tall."

Peter laughed again. "I am, rather. Tall, I mean. It aids me greatly when trying to out-drink my comrades."

"Oh?" she reached out a finger to touch his chest. "I should like to see that."

"Gladly," he answered, "but I fear we shall have to find other willing participants. General Gordon does not engage in such base activity, and Franz is capable of putting any of us under the table. Never a fair fight."

Franz proudly puffed his chest. "We must all strive to be our best…"

Anna giggled, shaking her head. "No, no. I wish to participate, not to watch! I meant that I should like to challenge you myself."

And with that, the Tsar was captured. Peter laughed again, his face flashing with a look of wonder, his eyes devouring the willing beauty. She smiled back with potent effect.

He will enjoy her, Franz thought, watching the two. *She will challenge him much more than his pitiful Russian bride.*

Peter stepped forward, nodding before claiming a flagon of vodka and two silver cups from one of the tables. With a playful grin, he held them up for Anna to see. She nodded, balling up her fists as though challenging him.

Offering only a smile to his comrades, followed by the curious stares of the entire party, Peter took Anna by the hand and disappeared up the stairs.

"I admit, the girl can drink…"

"Among other things," the General commented, his tone souring.

"Do you disapprove of my companionship, General?"

Gordon shook his head a bit. "No, sir, though I often wonder at your methods."

"Methods? I have none, sir."

"Peter loves you above all others--this, in itself, is a great responsibility. I may question the value of all this, but I will readily admit that this company is pleasing to him, and that through you, Franz, Peter comes to love Europe. I am also told that only you can calm him down when he is angry, and that you plan your festivities so as not to interfere with his official schedule. You must be wary, however, of the individuals who surround him in the Kremlin. They frown on your friendship and think you a corruptor."

"This is nothing new."

"Perhaps," Gordon continued, "but this is a new regime. Tsarista Natalya is a presence now. Her words carry weight. You must be certain not to go too far, Franz. They will accuse you of much worse than you've done."

"Your concern is greatly appreciated, Patrick. But do you think a single German consort a step too far?"

"She offers him little of value."

"Oh?" Franz queried. "I would say the opposite. She's sharp enough to contend with him, and he could always use the calming effect of a woman's touch. She is little more than a game, a novelty. Besides, a consort could never hope to find herself in the Palace. She is sharp, but a common girl after all. If the Tsar is content, then so am I, Patrick."

"I understand, my friend. Just remember--they will look for reasons to tear you down. You must walk the line between pleasing Peter and ruining your name."

Franz laughed. "You must trust me more, Patrick, particularly if we are to be cousins! Here, let us share a loaf. I will get cups, Patrick, and we will drink and eat and talk. And worry not. Anna will treat him well. Trust that Peter is in very good hands."

"That," Patrick replied, "is precisely my worry. Let us have that drink."

Moscow, The Palace of Tsarista Natalya in the Kremlin

December 1689

Tsarista Natalya Naryshkin straightened her shoulders and looked down at herself, frowning at the sight of her new gown. It was of the latest style, having just arrived from the West; in this, it was more than adequate for her tastes. The neckline, however, was disagreeable, but keeping with fashion dictated tolerating the new trends. There were, however, so few women in Russia who knew of Western costume, it seemed no crime to have the dresses altered to suit her taste.

Far removed from the elegant gowns of the Paris courtesans, the Tsarista's brand of Western style was conservative and befitting her position, respectable black with long skirts and no bustle. And though in form her garb was not unlike many of the other aristocratic women, Natalya's wardrobe was, nonetheless, notably European and much remarked upon in private circles. She had always taken pride in this reputation, and on her return to Moscow, one of her first tasks was to send away for the latest designs.

Natalya's taste for Europe, however, ended with style.

Now settled back into the Kremlin, the Tsarista was a healthy woman of forty years--pious, strong-minded and unrelenting, well-aware of the fact that her son was not yet ready to take the reins by himself. With Peter carousing in the Sloboda and his child on the way, there was no question in her mind that both the Tsar and the Church still needed her influence. Europe, regrettably, brought more to Russia than fashion and art. After years of waiting, Natalya was eager to set to more important tasks--such as ridding Mother Russia of heretics.

"You needn't worry, Mother. You look beautiful."

"I'm not worried, dear," she told her daughter, smoothing the gown with her hands. "But the Patriarch must be given consideration, and this gown is too extravagant."

"I think it beautiful," Princess Natalya replied, reaching out to feel the fabric. "Mother, I want a dress like the girls in the Sloboda wear...brightly colored."

"And your bosom pressed to the heavens," she replied, frowning. "You do very well with what you have."

"Yes, but they are so pretty, Mother. All of the young girls in Europe wear them! Truly, I feel like an old woman in these sad gowns!"

Natalya looked at her, pausing as she examined her daughter. Not yet a woman but no longer a girl, little Natalya was competent and bright, well-received despite the fact that she possessed her brother's quick tongue.

"We shall see..." the Tsarista said finally, opening her arms to capture her daughter's embrace.

"Oh, thank you, Mother! Thank you! I shall begin choosing fabrics."

"You may, but I will be present when we speak to the seamstress. I won't have you looking like a courtesan. In the Cathedral, you will continue to wear what I choose."

"Of course, Mother." she hugged her again, pressing tightly. "I won't embarrass you, I promise."

Natalya smiled, kissing her. “No, I suppose not. Smooth your hair, dear. Compose yourself and let us go. We are expected.”

“Will I go with you to see the Patriarch?”

“No, child. But Tikhon Streshnev will accompany me, and he wishes to see you.”

With her ladies in tow, the Tsarista and her daughter set a slow, dignified pace as they moved through Cathedral Square. Natalya was now allowed the greatest respect and always moved with poise and calm.

Removed from her chambers, the Tsarista’s thoughts began to drift from the mundane to the serious, wondering about the real reason for Streshnev’s presence. A boyar and the new head of Home Affairs, Streshnev was an old friend of Tsar Alexis. A Naryshkin supporter, his appearance usually preceded a complaint.

He has come to talk of Peter’s disobedience, she thought, preparing herself to respond.

Tikhon Streshnev waited for her arrival, dressed respectably in his long fur-lined robe, bearing a well-intended look of admiration.

“Tikhon.”

“My lady, may I say you look radiant!” he bowed deeply, kissing her hand. “Both of you! ‘Tis like standing near the sun!”

“You are kind beyond your means, Tikhon. From an old friend, I can accept such flattery. Prince Cherkasky…”

Beside Streshnev, stoic and austere, stood Prince Mikhail Cherkasky. A true aristocrat, Cherkasky was known as a member of the Graybeards, a group of nobles who loyally followed Peter. Devoted to the ‘old ways’, they served the Tsar out of a sense of patriotism, often quite vocally. Not to be forgotten, the old guard continued to talk, and it was well known that the Graybeards disapproved of Peter’s recent activities.

Cherkasky kissed her hand. "Tsarista, it is a pleasure. You look in good health."

"Ah, finally an honest man. Have you chosen to accompany us, Prince?"

"Yes, if I may."

"Certainly. You are welcome."

Streshnev took little Natalya's hands, spreading them apart to look at her. "Princess Natalya? It is hard to believe! Fair of face, like your mother. You seem to grow each time I see you. Will you be as tall as your brother?"

"No, sir," she replied, shaking her head a bit. "At least I hope not. If I do, you may cut off my legs."

"Natalya!"

"Still our little Natalya. That will never change. I was present at the celebration of your birth, child. I remember when you were not much bigger than my hand!"

"Tikhon and your father were friends for many years," the Tsarista intervened, placing a hand on Natalya's shoulder. "Tikhon, we don't see as much of you as we would like."

He nodded mournfully. "I'm afraid my new duties offer me far less time for socializing. Regrettably I cannot say the same for others...."

The Tsarista soured, looking to her daughter. "Natalya, say your goodbyes and return to your duties. Take everyone with you. The gentlemen and I must not be late."

"Yes, Mother." Little Natalya offered a short curtsey and left with the attendants behind her. The Tsarista waited before resuming her stare.

"She hears enough about her brother," she commented, turning. "I should not have to worry about her collecting opinions from family friends."

Streshnev recoiled a bit, bowing. "My apologies for being so direct, my lady. We are perhaps too passionate about the subject."

"You've come to speak of Tsar Peter, then?" She tilted her head. "You as well, Prince Cherkasky?"

Cherkasky nodded timidly. "We simply sought an opportunity to voice our concerns, Lady Natalya. The topic, I think you'll find, is well related to your meeting with the Patriarch."

"Oh?" she feigned ignorance, turning to depart. "Well, you shall have to assail me as we walk for I cannot keep the Patriarch waiting."

"Of course, Tsarista."

The two positioned themselves on either side of her, each taking an arm. Together they moved toward the meeting, Natalya's strength emanating from the touch of her hand. She remained cold in expression, knowing what was coming.

"If I may begin, my lady, I must say that there are many who have great faith in the Tsar, and that his support is widespread, especially in light of the blessed event awaiting us. May I inquire as to the welfare of the Tsar's young wife?"

"Tsarina Evdokia is quite well, thank you," she answered, "and with the grace of the Holy Father, is looking forward to the day she becomes a mother."

"Soon, yes? I do hope I shall be invited to the celebration."

"You will, Tikhon, certainly. Knowing Peter, all of Moscow will be invited."

"There is no question--the Tsar loves all of Moscow."

Cherkasky huffed, drawing the Tsarista's glare.

"Prince?"

"Forgive me, Tsarista, but your words led my thoughts to the reason for our presence here today."

"Oh? Please tell."

"Well, my lady, it is not his love of Moscow, but his love of the foreign quarter that draws our concern. Of the two, I think it obvious which he prefers."

"You assume far too much," Natalya responded, disliking Cherkasky's tone. "His tutors all reside in the Sloboda and many are trusted friends of the crown. Mind you, I am not particularly pleased to hear that Peter chooses to linger there, but I am told that it is only on occasion."

"More than occasionally, Tsarista. Regrettably. He dines there two or three times a week and returns staggering drunk."

The news was a bit shocking, but she held her posture.

"And when were you last accused of being drunk, sir?" she asked, her words cutting sharply. "Last evening? This morning, perhaps?"

"If I may," Tikhon interceded respectfully, "It is, I believe, a matter of great delicacy, Tsarista. I would not speak unless certain, and I can say with the greatest reliability, Lady, that Tsar Peter has been seen walking arm in arm with girls from the Sloboda. Germans. To be truthful, Tsarista, they are girls who are well known to be courtesans."

"He is a young man," she told him, her temper hidden, "and he spends time in the company of young women. This is not unusual."

"No, Lady, but--"

"And surely he would not be the first Tsar to mingle with courtesans, would he?"

"Most definitely not, Tsarista."

Natalya made a point to stare at both of them, Cherkasky first. "Then with all due respect for your concerns, gentlemen, I would suggest that you concentrate on more pressing matters than the nature of the Tsar's relationships. Frankly, I find it inappropriate that you come to me with such talk."

"We meant no offence, Lady." Cherkasky tucked his chin, looking a bit offended himself.

Streshnev cringed. "'Tis not the nature of his activity that we are concerned with, my lady," he paused, pursing his lips, "rather, the company he keeps. To be specific, a close familiarity with those who practice heretical beliefs--Lutherans, Protestants, Latins. I know you are sympathetic to the cause. Were it another day, Lady, this brand of rumor might not be notable. Given the events of the past week, however, I think it only wise to consider the Tsar's reputation in Moscow."

He may be correct, she thought, her mind already partially occupied with the recent turmoil. *And to think--I was pleased to hear the news.*

Only days earlier, the city had been captivated by the death of a Protestant mystic, beaten and burned to death in Red Square along with his writings. Driven by anti-foreign sentiment and anger over the construction of new Lutheran temples, a mob of Russians went looking for a scapegoat in the Sloboda and found prophet Quirinus Kuhlman. Dragged back into Moscow half-naked and clutching the parchment that contained his life's work, Kuhlman was beaten and paraded around Red Square before being set afire.

At the time, the Tsarista could remember shrugging her shoulders and thinking that the people of Moscow were acting in accordance with their beliefs; the mystic's death was an unpleasant, unfortunate, but altogether understandable occurrence. Patriarch Joachim had been warning of the dangers of foreign influence, and given the goals of the Church and the new Naryshkin government, the incident seemed almost fortuitous.

Now, Streshnev's words put the event's meaning into question in her mind. It suddenly seemed obvious that those who frowned on foreigners might also oppose Peter.

It is far too early for Peter to develop such a reputation, she thought, looking back at them. *News travels fast from Moscow. Peter must be seen to be strong, unmovable!*

"Moscow is rife with bitterness, Tsarista."

"The subject rests on the lips of every citizen, and there is talk of burning down churches in the Sloboda. Many of the diplomats are returning home."

Natalya raised her chin. "And we may hope that they stay there," she commented, thinking ahead to her meeting with the Patriarch. "No, Tikhon, the passions of the people have not gone unnoticed. They call for us to act, and I think a response from the Kremlin would be the perfect remedy for the city's ill temper. It will, no doubt, be a difficult task to reverse the damage done by the Regent, but the Patriarch is determined to succeed. As ever, the Church has our full support."

Streshnev opened his mouth to speak but was silenced by the Tsarista's raised finger.

"I do not, however, wish you to spread such loose talk about the Tsar. Do not be selfish in your concern. If you wish to reprimand him, then do so to his face. Peter is a pious and devout soul and, despite his youthful tendencies, has proven diligent in his responsibilities. Tell me, Tikhon, has the Tsar failed to appear at the meetings of the Duma?"

"Not a single one, my lady."

"Good, then. I will tell you again, gentlemen, that your concern is appreciated, but you will leave the matters of my family to me and to no one else."

Tikhon bowed in deference. "I would think of nothing else, my lady. The welfare of Tsar Peter has been my calling since the day of his birth."

Do not scold them too much. We will surely need their loyalty.

She stared at him, offering an approving nod. "You are a good man, Tikhon. And the Tsar has always liked you; I think he would be receptive to your counsel."

"You flatter me, my lady."

As they neared the Palace of the Patriarch, the conversation turned to less important subjects like the weather, the two old dogs returning to their tricks of flattery and wit, happy to be seen escorting the Tsarista. She liked Streshnev despite his tightly-wound persona; he had been a capable mentor to Peter in his youth and was now respected enough in the Duma to carry considerable political weight. Cherkasky, though less influential individually, was nonetheless a well-respected veteran and, as a Graybeard, represented many others of his kind.

And so, as she walked between the two conversing, Natalya made certain to complement their expertise and laugh at their attempts at humor. She caressed their hands with her fingertips and smiled back when they offered hopeful grins and compliments. At times like this, Natalya often wondered just who was trying harder to impress.

For though she may have been the most influential and well-known woman in all of Russia, Natalya Naryshkin was still a woman. Her words now carried meaning, but to have any consequence, her commands would have to be carried out by men--men who wished to agree with what they were doing.

So many ideas and intentions--so many obstacles. The Tsarista was beginning to understand what Sophia had endured to achieve her political ends in the males-only world. Oddly, and quite without her intention, a new respect for the Regent was blooming within her.

The Patriarch stood waiting in his courtyard to greet them, along with a small group of priests. Dressed in a burgundy velvet fur-lined cope, he nodded respectfully as he locked eyes with the Tsarista, his black beard now showing streaks of gray, his gaze showing the signs of poor health.

Politely, Streshnev and Cherkasky said their goodbyes, kneeling to kiss the Patriarch's hand before shuffling away into the Square. The Tsarista bowed before him, receiving his blessing and waiting for him to speak.

"We are honored by your presence, Tsarista." Joachim spoke with his public voice, as though trying to call the four winds. "I hope we find you in good health."

He looks horrid. Wasting away beneath that robe.

"The honor is mine," she replied, "and yes, I am well, thank you, Your Holiness."

He motioned to the priests and they dispersed. "It may not be good for me, but I do appreciate breathing the open air. May we walk a bit?"

"Certainly, Your Holiness."

"It is not too cold, then?"

"I am quite comfortable. Living in Moscow, one becomes quite impervious to such things."

Joachim paused, then grinned. "Ah! Most amusing, yes."

They walked slowly through the courtyard, the Patriarch's hands clasped behind him, the Tsarista moving patiently beside him, slowing to match his creeping pace. She longed for a warm fire but wanted Joachim to be comfortable and speak freely. Rarely were their conversations held in such private circumstances, and she could only assume that there was something important to be said.

"Your Holiness, I would inquire into your health. If I may say so, you do not look well."

He looked down at her, his thin lips forming a half-grin. "Yes, my lady. Either you are good at spotting such things or I look much worse than I believe I do. It will pass, surely. In this I have faith. My body grows weak but my spirit remains strong, Tsarista."

"You shall be in my prayers, night and day."

"You have my gratitude, my lady. This has come and gone before. It will pass. Before we catch a chill, however, we should talk of why I called for you."

"I am always at your service, Your Holiness."

"I have called upon you, Lady, because you have always been a devout supporter. The Holy Father has blessed you with an understanding of our troubles and has given you the strength to carry the banner. You have heard of the burning in Red Square, have you not?"

"I have, Your Holiness."

"Then you have surely seen the flash of light, the same glimmer of opportunity that I have. The issue has come out into the open and is pleading to be addressed. This could very well be a crucial moment in our history, Tsarista. For we may try to tell the people what is right. We may try to force them, coerce them or bribe them to do what we wish, but when they come to the right by their own means, by their own thoughts and hearts, well…this is the work of the Holy Father! This is surely a sign, Tsarista."

Never had she seen the Patriarch so animated and intent, his gaze focused and certain. Enjoying the sight, she simply nodded and allowed him to finish.

"Our cause, our mission has come to a crossing in the road," he continued, speaking thoughtfully. "We may remain upon the same, conciliatory path or we may choose to seize our opportunity and take a new path, acting on the will of the people! There are so many ideas we have already discussed--mere notions that may now become policy. Do you see what I am saying, Tsarista?"

Still holding her devout gaze, Natalya nodded sternly. Joachim's claiming the mandate of the Russian people seemed a bit ridiculous to her, but there was no denying that the incident in Red Square provided opportunity. The people of Moscow, at least, were passionate about the foreign dilemma.

Perhaps it will be enough, she thought.

"I ask you, my lady, to consider the possibilities. Long have we sought a moratorium on the building of new Protestant churches, and the issue of our borders remains in the forefront of my mind. How many are we to allow in? How long will it be before the Protestants outnumber the Orthodox in Moscow? Not long, if one chooses to look around."

She couldn't help but agree. Her husband had been wise to import foreign generals to teach his armies and merchants to build Russia's trade. He had been clever enough to create the Sloboda to segregate these foreigners and tolerant enough to allow their churches and temples within its walls. Yet despite the fact that Alexis would likely have disagreed with her, the Patriarch's words made sense to Natalya. The urgency was real.

"You are wise, Your Holiness, and your words are well taken," she said finally, looking up at him. "The troubles of Russia belong to the Church as well. I wish to offer my assistance in any way I can."

"Good, then. Very good. You are a pious woman, Natalya. The Holy Father will repay your devotion. There are others we will need, of course."

"The Duma is in line," she answered plainly, thinking of Streshnev. "Their passions have been similarly stirred. I'm quite confident they will be receptive to policy changes concerning the foreign influence. I will, however, begin speaking with those closest to me to assure our success."

"And the Tsar?" he asked.

Natalya paused, tilting her head. "Your Holiness?"

"I do not wish to anger you, Tsarista, but there is much discussion over the extended time he spends in the Sloboda. When he misses ceremonies, I put it out of my mind, happy to have Tsar Ivan in his place. And as for Peter's drinking and women…well, these are things I would expect from a boy. The Church has always looked the other way on such matters. Perhaps he will grow out of these habits. I cannot say. I cannot predict the future of our Russia, so I must speak of what I know today.

"The Tsar has developed a great admiration for the West," he continued, "and as distasteful as it may be to me, I cannot change that fact. This is no reflection on you, Lady. Peter is strong-willed, and by most accounts, I would think his future bright. But given his friendships, his tastes--how will he react to our aims? It is not far-fetched to think he will oppose them; therefore, without intending any insult, Tsarista, I wish to know if you think Peter will stand against us."

Arriving for the first time, the thought struck her oddly. In all of her ruminations on Peter and the issue of heretics, never had she considered him their champion. Listening to the Patriarch speak, it seemed almost obvious that Peter would move to protect his friends. Yet even now, faced with the real possibility, the notion still seemed impossible. To others it may have appeared as if Peter defied everyone and everything, but Natalya knew that he was yet to cross his mother.

"Peter is enrapt in this new devotion to shipbuilding. When not obligated in Moscow, he's been spending most of his time at Lake Pleschev. He shows less interest than I would like, perhaps, in the matters of court, but he is young and still drawn by his passions. As for his friends, they are the elite of the group--generals, diplomats. They will remain in Moscow regardless of policy."

"The Tsar is young, yes. And full of fire. Standing against his clan, his own mother--this kind of passion could prove troublesome."

She looked at the Patriarch, her anger seeping out. "You asked me, Your Holiness, if I believed that Peter would stand against us. Let me say now that I will not allow him to do so. Some things a mother knows. I suppose you must simply trust that I speak in good faith."

Her words lingered in the air for a few moments, daring a response. As though unwilling to challenge her further, the Patriarch stared out to the horizon for a moment before offering a definitive nod.

Looking down at her, his eyes softened. "A bit cold, are you?"

"Yes," she answered, securing her hands back within her muff. "A bit, Your Holiness."

"Yes, so am I. Let us find some warmth, and we may speak of the details."

The Tsarista nodded in reply, falling in step beside him. The Patriarch's words were hopeful and his ideas promising, and with her in place as the field marshal of the Naryshkin government, there seemed little to oppose them. Yet as she walked back into the warmth and security of his Palace, Natalya found herself ill-tempered and angry, thinking only of what had been said about Peter.

Moscow, Red Square

February 23, 1690

The quiet shower of snowflakes floated soft and formless without any wind to alter its path, falling steadily to complement Moscow's customary white winter cloak. The weather was cold but calm, hardly enough to sour the spirits of the people lining the streets on this joyous day.

They cheered the birth of an heir--a boy, Alexi Petrovich Romanov, his name ringing throughout the crowd. The christening finished, the city stood ready to rejoice.

The celebration was the biggest Moscow had seen in years, an event so joyous as to dwarf the festivities that followed Tsar Peter's wedding ceremony only a year before. All of Moscow had come to celebrate, their presence beckoned by the church bells that sounded from every Cathedral in Moscow. In addition to the customary rituals, Peter had put his own twist on the events, calling for the city itself to join the festivities.

The streets of Moscow stood lined with banners bearing the newly re-designed Romanov Family Standard, a double-headed eagle holding a scepter and an orb, each of its two golden heads bearing a crown. Atop, a third crown with a ribbon tying both together, a sign to all that Peter and Ivan were unified in their rule.

Following the resplendent Patriarch and church officials of every station, the procession between the flags was led by two regiments of foreign-led Strel'tsy marching in formation, their rhythmic steps accompanied by the beat of an impressive corps of drummers. Behind followed a regiment of Peter's Preobrazhensky greencoats led by Colonels Buturlin and Bruce, their poorly timed march step countered by the proud expressions that graced their chilled faces.

In the wake of the musketeers followed a grand procession of decorated sleighs that carried nobles, family friends and members of the Boyar Council. Other notable Muscovites, most of them merchants and diplomats, trailed behind on foot, dressed in their finest fur-lined robes and headdresses, their commonly austere faces transformed today into bearded smiles and merriment.

Not to be forgotten, the people joined the Tsar to celebrate in the Square, entertained during the parade with dancing and the promise of free vodka. The parade was lengthy and well-received by the Muscovites, the day's events accompanied by the constant crackle of fireworks, a new passion of the Tsar.

A podium had been erected in Red Square, a platform from which noble speakers stepped forth to congratulate the Tsar on the birth of his son. The speeches varied in length and potency, but all received enthusiastic applause as they faithfully echoed the joyful tone of the event. Peter stood surveying the scene, receiving the kind words and embracing each of the speakers as they finished. He seemed settled and full of joy today, patient even when the speeches ran too long.

The Tsar looked handsome in his military tunic, his mane of hair neatly combed away from his face. He stared out at the crowd, his face bearing a look of calm appreciation, his manner reserved and appropriate. On this day, at least, Peter seemed free of his restless spirit.

From her place, Anna Mons could see the entire scene. And though she was quite fond of parties and celebrations, on this day there was little that amused her. She found herself growing irritable, her gaze still fixed on Peter's beautiful hair.

Anna looked extraordinary, as ever, her features alone enough to elevate the appearance of any ensemble, her angled, painted eyes captivating beneath the white fur of her hood. The matching white velvet cape lined with sable and generously trimmed with ermine helped her stand out even among her betters, the ensemble chosen specifically in the hope of catching Peter's eye.

The prospect was unlikely. Her position in the crowd was hardly one of prominence. With all the nobles and aspiring government officials present, she was forced to stand at a distance from the proceedings; being a resident of the Sloboda, even Lefort's escort was not enough to gain her a good view. Franz's invitation, however, was gladly received. Lefort's standing exceeded her own and being accompanied by one of Peter's favorites would keep her name on the lips of the city's inhabitants.

Anna was not averse to this kind of attention. On the contrary, she enjoyed receiving the sideways glances from the proper ladies, often attempting to catch their eyes in an attempt to embarrass. And though they stood strong in their moral posture, Anna could see the primal, female jealousy in the stares of the noble women, pure vitriol as they stared at her unparalleled beauty. To her, it seemed their past had been wasted, spent covered in burdensome Russian gowns and scarves.

By comparison, Anna was everything they were not. She was painted and combed, powdered and corseted, the personification of femininity, created as much for the pleasure of men as Russian women were for duty. It seemed almost unfair. Orthodox girls were pitifully plain by comparison and could never hope to rival her skills where lustful Russian men were concerned. A few moments in their midst and there was no question in Anna's mind--blemished or not, she was someone to be seen and envied.

She had taken care to appear beautiful today, knowing that she represented the Tsar. The boyars and nobles may have offered only nervous glances on important days such as this, but when arm in arm with the Tsar, they treated Anna as though she were a lady of importance.

He may still see me, she thought, her gaze never leaving the Tsar. *If not Peter, then all these other fools. Let them know that the Tsar's mistress is well cared for!*

"Enjoying the celebration, my dear?"

She turned to see Franz Lefort, a rosy-faced bear in his fur coat and hat, his large hands holding out two cups brimming with vodka.

"Should I be?" she answered, taking one of the cups with a nod.

"Certainly," he responded, sipping before taking a drink. "Very exciting, this. Russians are generally so sour--to see them rejoicing is most welcome, especially on a day as important as this."

"You left me standing here for far too long, Franz."

"People everywhere! A boyar was struck by a stray firework--I heard one of the rockets failed and came straight back at him!"

"Was he killed?"

"Hard to say," he replied, shrugging. "Though I doubt he will be attending the banquet. At any rate, the lines were troublesome and long. It isn't every day that the Kremlin serves vodka to the peasants."

"True."

Lefort raised a finger. "And, if you'll notice, I was careful on my return and managed not to waste a single drop! This alone is a remarkable accomplishment. Perhaps instead of lamenting, you should praise my skill."

"Where drink is concerned, I never doubt you, Franz."

"Good. To the health of the new Tsarevich, then." He raised his cup.

She countered weakly, touching her cup to his before putting it to her lips. The vodka was ice cold and pure, warming her body as it trailed down inside her. She drank deeply, finishing half the cup in one attempt, Peter's face creeping into her mind as soon as she closed her eyes.

I think of him whenever I taste vodka. Horses, snow, rubles…everything reminds me of Peter.

"Ah, you see that?" Franz held up his cup, turning it upside down. "Mine is already empty! A pity. Quite good, though, I admit. I hear the nobles received wine, but I'm much happier with the vodka."

"I suppose you shall be wanting me to share."

Lefort frowned immediately. "Oh, no, Lady Anna! I would never ask you to do such a thing. We shall not want for enjoyment; I am the type of man who plans ahead. Did you know they will soon be calling me Admiral?"

"Oh?" she grinned despite her mood.

"Indeed. Commander of the Navy. Nice, eh? Not that I'm overly fond of titles, but still, it does have a ring to it. Today, I shall command our libation."

Reaching inside the folds of his fur coat, Franz produced a silver-gilt flask filled with vodka. He showed it to her proudly.

"We should be discreet," he continued, quickly pulling the stopper. "I don't want to be mobbed by thirsty friends."

She frowned, slapping his shoulder. "Franz! You've been holding that treasure? Why did you waste all that time standing in line for two meager cups?"

He rolled his eyes. "Isn't it obvious? We honor the child, the parents, Russia herself! We drink to join in the celebration, of course. We owe it to Peter to have at least one cup with the rest of Moscow."

"I see."

"And now, we owe it to Peter to drink to his health...and to that of his wife and child."

"Good, then," she said, touching cups rudely with Franz. "I shall gladly drink to Peter, and no one else."

She took a gulp from the second cup, feeling warmth from the drink but little from her escort; Franz seemed contradictory today, displeased with her words. And witty or not, his hesitation was obvious.

He worries I will become an embarrassment. He feels responsible and doesn't want me to anger Peter.

He knows nothing of Peter's feelings for me. If he knew, there would be no worry.

Franz grimaced, shaking his head as he stomached the vodka. "So tell me, Anna, would you deny this newborn your good wishes?"

"Not the baby," she recanted, raising her cup half-heartedly, "but I would certainly exclude his mother."

He sighed. "I must say that I am surprised. You are far too cross, my dear. A bit mean-spirited. You generally provide such splendid company, but I must say that today you are proving to be quite tedious. Are you truly so jealous of the Tsarina?"

The question hit her oddly.

"Me?" she asked, a smile creeping across her lips. "Jealous of a little sullen cow like Evdokia? Really, Franz. Dowdy, needy, ugly--there is no comparison. Why, she barely speaks!"

Even as the words escaped her lips, Anna realized how hollow they sounded.

I am jealous then, she thought.

And what if I am? Do I not have the right?

"There is much more to envy than beauty," Lefort offered, his tone still friendly. "After all, Evdokia is Tsarina and the mother of Peter's child. The good wife of the beloved Tsar. The most notable or--if you consider Natalya--the second most notable woman in all of Russia. With respect to the fine trinkets Peter has given you, Anna, the Tsarina is the one who truly wears the gold."

"For now," she replied smartly.

He shook his fur-capped head, laughing out loud. "Oh, my! Anna, please don't tell me that you see yourself as Tsarina!"

She straightened. "And why not?"

"Let me see…you are German, Lutheran, the daughter of a merchant, and a courtesan. An exceptional companion, granted, but a courtesan, nonetheless. Lowly or not, you're a smart one--smart enough to know it cannot be."

"Peter is Tsar," she responded curtly. "He could make it so. He can do whatever he wishes."

"Oh?"

"If you can be an Admiral, Franz, then why should I not be Tsarina?"

He balked, hesitating. "Clever girl…"

"I think you press me to be contrary," she said, shaking a finger at him. "And not for my benefit."

"Untrue, my dear. I assure you, I detest seeing you in this humor."

Anna looked away. "The Tsarina may wear whatever ancient bit of cloth she pleases. She may cover it in gold and still not match my most frivolous gown. Peter gives me gifts as well--many of them. And he does it out of love, not because he is obliged to do so."

"I see."

"Little Dunka does not worry me," she continued, shaking her head. "I will, however, admit that I am distressed to see Peter having to march through ceremonies with his dull little provincial wife at his side. I don't know how he bears it! You know as well as I do, Franz, he is terribly bored with her. Peter deserves much better..."

"Peter deserves better?" Franz raised an eyebrow. "Or you, Tsarina Anna?"

She scowled purposefully at him, her angry look incapable of altering his amused grin.

"You should be more sympathetic," she said, playing hurt. "You are the one who introduced me to him. You, of all people, know how wonderful he is, how he affects people. I am not the first to fall in love."

"Certainly not," he answered plainly.

"So why, Franz, would you deny me a moment of weakness?"

"Because you're spoiling the day, my love. I told you--you're too cross. Try to enjoy the day! An impressive turnout, to be certain. It seems your love for Peter is infectious."

"The Strel'tsy in the parade are foreign-led," he said proudly. "An honor from the Tsar." He pointed. "There--do you see General Gordon? Stunning figure, indeed. Impressive, even at a distance. I shall have to tell him."

Anna finished her cup, looking up at him, the warm vodka now stirring her emotions.

"He prefers me, you know..."

Lefort nodded. "I am certain he does."

"The Tsarina writes him little love notes. No, not love notes--pity notes! Tragic little things, actually, in which she pleads for his company and scolds him for neglecting her. The letters only push him further away."

"Royal matches are rarely perfect," Franz replied. "And Evdokia was not chosen for her allure. As we are here celebrating the birth of a male heir to the throne, it would seem that Lady Natalya was quite correct in her choice. With respect to your personal dilemma, my dear, you must not forget how important this birth is to Russia. So, while there is no doubt that Peter is hardly thrilled with her company, it seems Evdokia is thus far a great success as Tsarina."

Her gaze clinging to Peter's image in the distance, she held back her anger, knowing that once offended, Lefort's feelings would be difficult to repair.

I wouldn't want to be removed from his guest list.

"How can you defend her?" she asked, finding his gaze. "You know that Evdokia disapproves of you!"

"She is not alone," he answered. "But yes, I am aware of the Tsarina's feelings. I would suggest that she simply doesn't know me well enough."

"Rubbish," Anna answered, shaking her head. "You know, Franz…your wit is considerable, but you cannot deny the truth. Little Lady Orthodoxy hates anyone who isn't like her. Do you enjoy the thought of her poisoning Peter against you?"

"Bah!" he waved the comment away. "Surely you don't believe that! Peter cannot be poisoned in that way. You are a treasure, even when you don't wish to be." He chuckled at her, amused at her tirade. The sight only provoked her anger.

"You are horrible, Franz! Now you laugh at me!"

"Calm down, child. Come give me a kiss on the cheek and I will refill your cup."

She nodded, offering him an apologetic smile before kissing him.

"I am not without feeling," Lefort explained, taking her cup and pouring another round. "You will sip this one…"

Anna smiled. "Yes, father."

"You know I approve of your relationship with the Tsar. You are good for him in your own way and there is no question that your life has benefitted from his favor."

She tried to speak, silenced by a raised finger.

"I believe we have much in common, you and I. Much. Think, dear--we are both guests in this country, both Western heretics, both terribly stylish and witty…and both of us love Peter, are loved by Peter, and in turn, are envied by the Tsarina and the rest of Russia."

She nodded, saying nothing.

"The difference between us? I have learned to cope with and appreciate his manner and his ways. He is generous beyond measure--to both of us. I am grateful and altogether unworthy. I expect nothing and am content, satisfied. Peter sees this, and it makes us closer. You may discount my words if you wish, but I will tell you plainly that if you seek to keep him, you must be content as well."

She looked down, feeling a bit ashamed. "I have tried--honestly, I have. The moments I spend with him are so glorious, so magical. It makes me miss him even more when he's gone. I have no way of knowing when he'll return, or if he'll want to see me when he does."

"I know how odd it feels," he said, his tone more sympathetic, "to think that you are so very important to him one moment then to find in the next that Peter has turned his attention away, ignoring you for something else. This is his way. He has more plans than time to pursue them and far too much to accomplish to worry himself with regret--not to mention the routine demands of the State. With Peter, we must take the time we are offered and ask nothing more. It would be unfair to him. Remember, my dear--within the walls of my house, you and I are nothing short of royalty. But in the face of all this?" He asked gesturing toward the crowd. "Here, Anna, we are little more than foreign friends.

"I realize that Peter makes you feel as though you are the only important thing in his world, but you must remember that no one can claim more than a part of him--and for this, we are fortunate. I have no better advice than this. Free yourself from these troubling thoughts and remember whose company you are in. I refuse to believe that the vodka has failed to do its job. Give in, my dear, and let us play!"

Better not to argue anymore. He is trying so hard.

"Your charm exceeds your taste in women, Franz. A lucky thing for me, perhaps, for you brought me to Peter's side. I owe you my kindness, at the least. And I am not drunk, if that is what you were thinking. Not nearly."

He beamed with satisfaction. "I am glad to hear it, Lady, for though the celebration is most official this afternoon, the party at my mansion this evening will be quite off the record!"

"Do you mean?"

Franz smirked and shrugged coyly. "We can never be certain, but if he has seen you in that ermine, I would expect a visit from Peter when the fireworks have all been burned."

Her spirit leapt. "Oh, Franz! Always the good host!"

She dropped the cup and wrapped her arms around him, standing on her toes to kiss him several times on the cheek.

"I shall need time to prepare, and we must do something special for him when he arrives!"

"Calm down, child--I am pledged to be married! You wouldn't want to ruin my reputation."

Anna laughed out loud, filling the cold air with the boisterous cackle for which she was known. "If you want a good reputation, then perhaps you shouldn't be seen with a German Lutheran merchant's daughter…oh, and a courtesan!"

"The best in all of Russia," he replied, grinning. "If you need proof, then ask the Tsar himself!"

Moscow, The Palace of Tsarista Natalya of the Kremlin

March 22, 1690

She could hear the sound of his boots long before he entered the room, Peter's extended stride unmistakable, the weight of his steps indicating a sour mood. Dressed in mourning out of respect for the former Patriarch, the Tsarista took a deep breath and braced for her son's arrival.

You are still his mother, she reminded herself, coughing into the small handkerchief she held. *He will bark and snap, but in the end he will do as his mother wishes.*

He entered alone as was his custom and, after delivering a short bow, turned to close the door. As he turned back, she could see the agitation in Peter's eyes.

"I assume you've summoned me to speak about the Patriarch," he said immediately, his posture demanding.

She lifted her chin "Among other things, yes."

"I knew it," he said, snapping his fingers. "I suspected you would call me for an appropriate scolding. I should have it and be done, then. It is such a long ride back to Lake Pleschev. I would like to be on my way."

"Do you wish to offend me?" she asked sharply. "You arrive without a proper greeting or offering your mother a kiss; then you assail me with rudeness and command me as though I were one of your little soldiers!"

Peter's eyes went immediately to the ground. "I apologize, Mother."

"You should know that I act only for your benefit. Trust in this, Peter, I cannot promise that the sun will rise tomorrow, but I do know that there are two things in your life that will always be. You will always be Tsar, and I will always be your mother."

"Forgive me, please." Peter stepped forward, offering an apologetic smile, moving to embrace her and kiss her cheek. "I expected you to be angry."

"Not angry," she said coolly, receiving his kiss, "but given the events of the last week, I would think that you would act with a bit more decorum. Especially considering your failure to attend the Patriarch's funeral service--may his soul rest in peace."

"I never attend funerals," he said, still unwilling to match her gaze. "You know this."

"You should have made an exception, Peter. Your absence at the funeral only served to renew conversation regarding your dinner with General Gordon."

Peter threw up his hands. "Again? Must I continue to be told of this? Had Joachim passed a month later instead of a week, my scandalous dinner would have been long forgotten."

"That's not true, Peter. In the days before his death, His Holiness was quite concerned."

He looked down at her, his obedient expression fading. "Surely, Mother, you don't mean to suggest that I caused poor Joachim's death…"

"Certainly not," she replied tersely, not holding his gaze, "And I do not wish to play games this morning. You know my meaning, Peter. After openly defying his wishes, not a week before his passing, you should have been there."

"I defied nothing!" he protested, shaking his head. "In fact, I followed the Patriarch's wishes exactly. He was opposed to a heretic's dining in the Palace and I promise, not a single grape crossed heretic lips! His wish was granted. Russia was saved. And with all respect to His Holiness' eternal soul, His Holiness should have been satisfied."

She had hoped that the unpleasantness would be forgotten, but Joachim's death brought the issue back to life.

Only a week before, Peter had invited Patrick Gordon to attend a dinner at Court, one of the many celebrations that followed in the wake of the birth of Alexis. The General had accepted the invitation, but upon hearing that a foreigner was invited to sit at the Tsar's table, Patriarch Joachim protested his inclusion.

Peter was furious but reluctantly withdrew his offer to the General, replacing it with an invitation to a private dinner at Peter's country home near Preobrazhenskoe. The Tsar skipped the Court event to dine with the General, and afterwards they rode side by side all the way back to Moscow.

A week later, the Patriarch was dead, a long illness finally claiming him. Left behind, a lengthy testament written in His Holiness' last days, urging the Tsar to end his contact with the heretical foreigners. Out of respect for the Patriarch, Natalya thought it her duty to address it.

"You embarrassed His Holiness," she said. "Purposely. He tried very hard to understand you and ultimately felt as though he'd failed."

"It was a ridiculous issue," he told her, calming. "A point of control. Just like his color-matching and the hundred other irrelevant rules he put in place. The next Patriarch must be more of a thinking man."

First things first, she thought.

"I assume you have read the testament left by His Holiness."

"I have," he replied, "And though his advice is no doubt well intended, I found little that I have not heard already."

"Peter…"

"No, truly, his sentiment is appreciated. But you know as well as I, Mother, that Joachim may have claimed to be saving me from the evils of the West, yet short of the ex-Strel'tsy Commander, there has been no one to draw more attention to my supposed shortcomings. Who was more critical of me? Name one, Mother."

She balked, not wanting to enter a verbal exchange. "I believe Tikhon Streshnev has expressed his concern as well."

Peter smiled. "Yes, I respect old Tikhon. When he's not drunk, he's a good Graybeard, but Russia would never prosper at the whims of old men. Patrick Gordon is to be High Commander of our armies! Yes, yes--he is good enough to win glory for Russia, yet unworthy of the Palace's borsht! Is this what I am to understand?"

"The issue is hardly so simple, Peter. You know this."

"I do," he responded. "And I capitulated. General Gordon was directly uninvited."

"And then re-invited to Preobrazhenskoe," she added, "on the same evening."

"Mother, I fear that you see this as an act of selfish disrespect, when I believe it to be quite the opposite. Joachim forced me to make a choice between disrespecting either the Church or General Gordon. Don't you see? If I dined in the country, I would be offending the Patriarch. If I dined in the Palace, I would be offending a friend and the Commander of our armies. Considering it was Joachim who forced this decision, the choice was simple."

"Are you so worried about the General's opinion?"

"Europeans are different, Mother."

"You have very high regard for General Gordon."

"I do," he replied simply. "As did my father. I am not the first to recognize Patrick's worth."

"You are correct," Natalya conceded. "Tsar Alexis--may God rest his soul--was quite fond of all his foreign imports. Gordon, in particular. It neither surprises nor disturbs me that you have come to rely on him as well."

"The General was the innocent in this tedious protest," Peter replied, cooling, "and I know he despises the thought of becoming a pawn. So scold me if you wish. Thanks to my dinner in the country, I gladly carry the blame while Gordon escapes any undeserved attention."

The General is a worthy mentor, but Peter must learn not to dote on his friends. They will consume all his time.

"You are a kind soul," she told him, "but as Tsar, your decisions must not only benefit your circle, they must serve your office and Russia."

"Your capacity for advice is unlimited, Mother, but you are wrong to think me so selfish."

He tires of my counsel.

"I never said th--"

"You should know that I did consider my office," he interrupted, now pacing. "I thought it a perfect opportunity to set a precedent. With one simple action, a mere dinner party, I showed the Patriarch that the Tsar takes advice from the Church, not orders."

Could he possibly have considered all this? Is he already so shrewd?

"In my mind," he continued without waiting for her response, "I believed that countering His Holiness could only strengthen my posture as Tsar. I am better prepared for the day when I receive a truly unreasonable suggestion. I should think you would be proud of me."

With this, Peter offered a wide, apologetic grin, the little boy still shining through the man. Natalya sighed, her resolve bending at the sight of his smile. His charisma was undeniable, particularly for his most loyal supporter.

"I have always been proud," she said, softening. "And you have always known how to achieve your goals despite the obstacles. Do you remember? When you were six and we forbade you from daggers, you complied and immediately began using mason's tools to battle your imaginary foes."

"Of course I remember," he answered. "I've thought of bringing back that spade a time or two; it was an excellent weapon when killing invisible Strel'tsy."

"You are like your father," she told him. "Both of you witty, both restless. Both, perhaps, a bit too progressive…"

She uttered the word, hoping Peter would understand her meaning. Her true dilemma was yet to be addressed, and the next subject was sure to touch a nerve in the fiery young Tsar. She knew her son well enough to worry.

He cleared his throat, straightening. "I am proud to hear you say it, Mother, but I have the distinct feeling that the serious part of our visit is not yet complete. You mean to lecture me about my support of Metropolitan Marcellus."

"I have been told that you have been…active."

"I have," he said simply.

"Such public division does not benefit the clan."

He shrugged a bit. "My opinion is shared by many in the clergy, Mother. The better-educated among them are all in favor of Marcellus."

"The younger clergy members."

"I was impressed," he continued, "and so it seemed quite natural. A sharp man, so unlike Joachim! The two are equal in terms of piety, certainly--so why not choose the man who better knows the world?"

"I am well aware of Metropolitan Marcellus' worldly nature," she replied, feeling defensive. "His travels abroad, and such."

"A scholar," Peter added with emphasis. "An educated man. Marcellus speaks several languages, you know."

"A notable quality," Natalya replied, unimpressed. "For a diplomat, perhaps, or even for a Tsar. But to lead the Church? To represent the very foundation of Russia's strength? For this, I believe we need a man of wisdom, not a scholar. Metropolitan Adrian is the correct choice, Peter--for Russia and for the Naryshkins. Metropolitan Adrian will see things through and fall in line with the wishes of his predecessors. After enduring the events of the last year, the people tire of complication. You provide them more than enough excitement, Peter. The Church must provide stability, constancy. Adrian will achieve this. Besides, Metropolitan Adrian is not so…"

"So what, Mother?" he asked aggressively. "So progressive? Is that what you mean to say?"

"As Patriarch, Adrian will be much like his predecessor. The transition will be smooth and the policies similar. The people take comfort in this--thus they support Adrian. And, of course, we may rely on the fact that Metropolitan Adrian will continue the good work that Joachim began."

"Which good work, Mother?" Peter bristled, scowling. "Are you speaking of color-coordinating the abbots? Or perhaps you're referring to burning priests in Red Square?"

"You would defend heretics, now?"

"I see no Latin churches in our midst, and none of our sturdy Russian brothers and sisters seems interested in converting. They are harmless, Mother."

"In their current numbers, perhaps," she commented, trying not to show her anger. "But if we continue to allow them to pour across our borders. How long before we become lost ourselves?"

"Ridiculous!" he burst out, rolling his eyes angrily. "The Church is in no danger of becoming lost--even the Tsar gets scolded for questioning its authority! Besides, these heretic foreigners are much needed in Russia! Without them, who would train our armies? Who would forge our treaties and keep our trade flowing? Who would bring you those Polish dresses you wear and the marble Uncle Lev uses to commission his new monastery? Who tutored your son, Mother? Heretics, perhaps, but these men own the shoulders on which we place the future of Russia! Father understood this--why don't you? Without the West, Mother, we are dead in the water--a ship without a sail!"

"You're shouting again," the Tsarista said in measured tone, her calm never breaking. "I will not be screamed at nor told what I do and do not understand."

Again, the Tsar quieted, his anger still present.

"Contrary to your beliefs," she continued, "I am not blind to the worth of our mercenary aid. You are quick to remind me that I chose foreign tutors for you, and despite your obstinacy, I do not regret my decision."

Natalya sighed, wishing she could make him understand.

"I was not always the buttoned-down conservative you imagine me to be," she told him. "You wouldn't remember, but I was a young Tsarina when your father brought the theatre company to Russia. I caused a scandal by requiring the noble ladies to attend the performance."

"I've heard that story."

"Well, I wasn't going to be alone," she said, thinking back to the proud look on Alexis' face. "So you may question my Polish gowns or my admiration for foreign tutors, but the Church is another matter. It is the foundation of Russia, the very authority that legitimizes your divine mandate, Peter. Respectfully, I have no intention of handing the Church over to a progressive. The Patriarch must represent the interests of Russia, not those of Europe."

"You speak as though he were a pagan! Marcellus is a well-respected man!"

"Perhaps," she replied, remaining firm, "but he is not the best choice for Patriarch."

"And this is your decision?"

I must be adamant. I must leave no room for argument.

"This is our decision, Peter. A clan decision."

"Just like that?" he asked, looking incredulous. "You would discount my wishes so quickly?"

"Your wishes have been well-considered," she replied in motherly tone. "I would see you safe and prosperous. My wish is for you to cease all exertion on Marcellus' behalf."

"This is hard to believe…"

Her own temper rising, Natalya allowed herself a moment of anger.

"I spend my days defending your honor," she began sharply, "and my nights consoling your neglected wife. I comment very little on your absences and your friendships with Westerners, even when you lavish them with land and estates. I am your greatest advocate and your most loyal subject. So if not for your clan or for the good of Russia, you will do this for me."

The silence following her words told of his acceptance. Peter would be angry but would soon be on to his next crusade, the bitterness forgotten in pursuit of another goal.

Peter looked at her without speaking, then looked away, clenching his jaw in frustration.

He is unaccustomed to being directed, she thought. *When I am gone, there will be no one capable of restraining him.*

"This is not your dinner with the General, Peter. At the risk of sounding distrustful, I must tell you that I will bear none of your clever disobedience. We must be finished today with the issue."

She waited calmly as he resumed his pacing, shaking his tousled head in disbelief as though he'd just been beaten in a fencing match.

He will never admit he was wrong. He needs only to agree.

Peter stopped, turning to face her. "I will not oppose Adrian's election but only out of my devotion for you, Mother. As for your part, you will smile and wish me safe travels when I go to Archangel. I know you've been against my taking this journey, but I think it only fair that you allow it…because I'm your son."

Ah! The next crusade, she thought, her spirits lifting.

"A bargain, then?" she asked.

"Of a kind," he replied, tilting his head. "I would prefer to consider it a mutual display of kindness and trust. Mother, I can't hope to learn anything of sailing when I'm sitting on a lake!"

"You enjoy this ship-building too much, I think."

"Untrue, Mother! Russia will need the seas for trade--a navy if we wish to--"

"A navy? Peter, we have no real port!"

He grinned back at her, his eyes alight. "Another difficulty I shall have to remedy. A real port? Perhaps I will take one from the Turks. Or Sweden! I must first get a ship afloat, of course. Did I tell you? I'm working with two shipwrights from the Netherlands--Timmerman and Houtman. You remember, surely. They are both quite capable."

The Tsarista grinned, thanking the Holy Father for her good fortune.

"We are agreed, then," she told him, grateful for his ambition. "You may travel to Archangel, but I refuse to hear of your going out on any poorly made ship, particularly one you've built yourself."

"Good." Peter nodded. "I promise you will hear nothing of it, Mother."

"You will promise to be careful," she added. "And you will promise not to stay away long. The Tsar is needed in the Kremlin."

"You're here, Mother--and the Kremlin has Ivan," Peter said. "I am quite grateful for him. And I'm certain his presence will be enough to make things official."

"He is not enough," Natalya responded. "You need to be in the Kremlin, Peter, for your office, if not for your reputation. There is greatness in you and I wish everyone to see it."

Peter raised a hand. "I sense another lecture coming, Mother, one which I have heard so many times, I think I could recite it myself."

"Very well," she said, waving him off. "I shall cease my tireless counsel. I suppose I cannot help myself."

He smiled, bowing a bit. "And you have my eternal gratitude."

Better to quit with one victory. Knowing Peter, I cannot hope to win more in a single day.

Taking her seat, the Tsarista exhaled, the restless feeling eased by the outcome of the conversation. Metropolitan Adrian would be elected and would serve God, Russia...and the Naryshkin clan.

As they talked of lesser subjects, the Tsarista found herself staring at Peter's charismatic visage, admiring his beauty and his shrewd mind, knowing she had done everything she could to prepare him for the future. He was clever and strong-minded, capable of contending politically. Even Peter's progressive leanings seemed to take on a charming and compassionate quality in her conservative eyes.

My son...my life...everything I could have hoped for. Better than Russia deserves--a gift to the country.

We have survived, and we prosper.

Not just the Tsar. Not just my son. The boy is capable of great things.

She daydreamed as Peter spoke of sails and oceans, thinking back to the celebration of his birth, remembering the accolades and prophesies, secure in the belief that she'd done her part.

Moscow, Franz Lefort's Estate in the Sloboda

May 1690

"Two, three, four--ah Alexashka!"

Alexander Danilovich Menshikov resisted the urge to gag and forced down the contents of the goblet, allowing the ice cold spirits to slide down his throat and into his body. The prickly sting of the vodka was followed by a consuming rush of warmth and an uninvited urge to cough.

"Alexashka? Are you all right?"

Oh, Holy Father, he prayed, enduring the burn. *In your mercy, I beg you to keep me from vomiting! Lord, I ask no more than this!*

"Certainly, sir." He straightened, clearing his throat and shaking off the twinge. "Never better!"

"Good, then!"

Tsar Peter stood smiling before him, clutching a large pitcher, ready to pour another. Surrounding them, a cast of masquerade masks and laughing faces, the room roaring in a cacophony of joy.

They watch to see my worth! Oh, please, Lord, make me strong enough!

A good Russian, Menshikov was a man who loved drink. Vodka was an old friend, and as did everyone from the Patriarch to the lowest serf, he drank the dark Russian beer known as kvass like water. Menshikov had been weaned on the taste and knew how important the ritual of drink was to his homeland. But never had he known the intense, devotional brand of drinking practiced by the Tsar and his Jolly Company.

This is only the initiation, he reminded himself, his head already swimming. *Someday I will stand and laugh at other poor initiates...*

The room was filled with faces, some of them familiar, some known only to him as foreign officers; through his service under Franz Lefort, Menshikov had come to know many of the Sloboda's favorite sons. This gathering, however, was a mix of foreign and Russian, old and young, the distinguished and the unimportant irrevocably bonded in the fraternity of drink and revelry, led by the giant figure of the Tsar. From the fringes they shouted to him.

"He is good to have another!"

"Hasn't proven anything yet!"

"Let us see how he shoots when he's drunk."

Peter reached out to refill his goblet, offering a reassuring wink. The Tsar was unmasked, but instead wore one of Lefort's loftiest wigs atop his curly brown locks, his face powdered to resemble a Western aristocrat. Raising a hand, he quieted the zoo in an instant.

"My friends, dear Alexashka is a loyal member of the Preobrazhensky ranks!" Peter addressed the group, allowing Menshikov a moment to recover. "A bombardier in the battles against the Polish King!"

The lot began to shout again, cheering their victories.

"Yes, yes! Where is the Polish King?" Peter turned, scanning the room. "Show yourself!"

The crowd parted to reveal the figure of Ivan Buturlin, the greencoat officer who bravely led the enemy armies in Peter's play battles. He stepped forward, smiling and raising his tankard of kvass to a chorus of boos.

"Now, now--leave him in peace," the Tsar scolded playfully. "Let the King drink and save his strength. He will need it when we face him this spring. Your Majesty..."

Buturlin looked on gravely as Peter knelt before him. Scarcely clinging to his head, the wig fell to the floor and was quickly snatched back by the Tsar. He fluffed it with his hand before putting it back atop his head.

"Now then. With deference to the King, I shall continue. Our Alexashka, Alexander Danilovich to most of you, attempts today to win the favor of Bacchus and enter the Drunken Synod. I assure you, friends, if he does well, our newly ordained Prince-Pope will appear in blessed form to complete the ceremony. Alexashka?"

"Yes, sir?" Menshikov answered, sober enough to remember not to use the word 'sire' in a meeting of the Jolly Company. Peter held no rank within this world and forgetting so would be an offense.

"Show us how versed you are and recite the first commandment of the Drunken Synod."

He is merciful, Menshikov thought, fighting the effects of the vodka. *He allows me a breath. I must not fail now!*

"The first commandment," Menshikov answered, raising his voice, "is that Bacchus be worshipped with strong and honorable drinking and receive his just dues."

Peter grinned, clapping. "Correct! All goblets are to be emptied promptly and all members are to get drunk every day."

"None are to go to bed sober!" Franz Lefort added from behind his mask, a wide smile creeping out beneath.

"Not without insulting the lot of us!" Peter quieted them again. "Bacchus is watching you, my friends, vigilant in his duty, testing your devotion! He requires no prayers or sacrifices--only your dedication to revelry and drink! Centuries ago our predecessor the Grand Prince Vladimir of Kiev declared it the Joy of the Russes. Now, Alexashka, show that you belong by proving him right!"

Peter reached down with the pitcher of vodka, pouring the goblet half full before pausing to look around the room.

"Fill it all the way!" Lefort shouted into the silence, his words followed by a collective cheer.

Shrugging, Peter filled the goblet to the top.

Now imbibed with the confidence of the first, Menshikov reached out and took the goblet, raising it to the group. After a wordless toast, he brought the goblet to his lips.

"One…two…three…four…"

The vodka was cold to the taste but burned as it flowed down into him.

"five…six…seven…"

He struggled against the urge to gag and resist, stomaching the spirits with a soldier's resolve.

"Eight…ni--"

With the last drop gone, Menshikov flipped the goblet and slammed it down.

The room burst out in joy again, this time for him. The Tsar grabbed a tankard of kvass and raised it to toast the room.

"To you, Alexashka! Service to Bacchus is, of course, a lifetime pursuit. Can you stand?"

Nodding, Menshikov placed his shaking legs beneath him and stood, managing even to take a slight bow as the group cheered.

"There! You see? Alexashka Danilovich is a born member!" Peter reached out to place a hand on his shoulder. "Fear not, my friend, the next course of the banquet will begin shortly. But before we may eat, we have some vital business awaiting us--another important event."

With the room in joyous flux around him, Menshikov found a chair along the wall and gratefully sat down. Beside him, a greencoat snoozed contentedly, his long pipe still resting in his mouth. Other greencoats patted Menshikov's shoulders and thrust a brimming tankard into his hands.

Peter paced for a moment, waiting for the room to quiet before resuming.

"Welcome, members of the Jolly Company--our All-Joking, All-Drunken Synod of Fools and Jesters! There is much to celebrate this day, and much call for reverence. We join here today for services to celebrate the election of our new Patriarch. Someone call for Patriarch Bacchus! As his first official act as Patriarch, today our Prince-Pope will crown a new Caesar!"

The cheers were deafening.

Even through the drunkenness, Menshikov could see the Tsar's game. Peter's support for the candidate Marcellus was not enough. The conservative Adrian, favorite of the Tsarista and an opponent of foreign intrusion, had been elected Patriarch and used his first speaking opportunity to condemn the plague of heretic foreigners. In response, Peter had elected his own patriarch, a Prince-Pope, a foolish mockery draped in thinly veiled Roman liturgy.

And though he had once believed that he could hold no higher respect for Peter, Menshikov was finding new admiration in each moment of each day.

Masked, the host of the event walked to the center of the circle, calling for a round of toasts. The group clapped and whistled at Lefort's generosity, knowing that the gatherings were planned and funded by none other than the Tsar. Peter, however, was never fond of receiving such accolade and offered the first toast to Lefort.

Menshikov raised his tankard along with the others but took only small drinks, knowing he would need to keep his feet. The elaborate day-long banquets were served in several courses, with breaks between for smoking, drinking and activities like ninepins or archery. Music and dancing filled the halls of Lefort's mansion, the men faithfully accompanied by women from the foreign quarter. He had been told that the meetings of the Jolly Company would often continue into a second or third day with the party-goers falling asleep in their places and continuing when they awakened.

Saving his strength, Menshikov thought, staring at the man in the chair beside him. *I should stand or I'll meet a similar fate.*

Shakily, Menshikov stood to his feet, managing while still holding his tankard.

The toasts continued for many rounds, as the members of the party rose to salute everyone from Bacchus to Peter's favorite jester, Turgenev. Menshikov persevered, maintaining his smile throughout. Finally, Peter commanded their attention again.

"Take your places, friends. The service is about to begin!"

The Tsar's words caused a flurry of activity as the members of the party scrambled to find their places, the hopelessly drunk left sitting bewildered in their seats. Peter's motley crew numbered in the dozens, and their usual banquet room was growing too small to comfortably accommodate them all. Given their current drunken state, however, the crowded hall was more than large enough. Arm in arm, piled one atop another with their pipes and tankards, the remainder of the company happily filled the empty corners.

The Tsar bowed deeply then stood with a grin, dragging his finger across his neck, commanding relative silence.

"The time has come to pay our respects to our great and holy leader, our kniaz-papa, our Prince-Pope, the Patriarch of all Iauza and Kukui, the exalted Patriarch Bacchus."

Behind him, Lefort and several others began singing a poorly coordinated imitation of a monk's prayer, their faces solemn and reverent.

The doors opened and the Prince-Pope, Patriarch Bacchus, entered along with a small entourage of cardinals and priests. Dressed in austere white robes, the Prince-Pope surveyed the group before moving slowly though them, his parchment hat flopping with each step. After only a few moments, Menshikov recognized the Pope as Nikita Zotov, one of the company's oldest members and a former tutor of the Tsar.

For his part, Zotov played the role perfectly. A long wooden pipe in each hand, he nodded serenely to all, passing out signs of blessing as he shuffled to his place. The Jolly Company reacted in kind, keeping their silence as though standing in a Cathedral.

Taking his place at the head of the group, the Prince-Pope extended his arms, crossing the two long pipes and blessing the congregation. An extended prayer to Bacchus followed, after which everyone was commanded to finish their tankards.

Still standing, Menshikov kept his eyes open as he tipped the tankard, worried that closing them might send him to the floor. Surviving the draught, he wiped his mouth with his sleeve and smiled along with the rest.

Peter moved to stand beside him, wrapping a giant arm around his shoulder. Menshikov straightened, trying not to appear drunk.

"Alexashka," he whispered, leaning down. "What do you think of my Drunken Synod?"

"I feel at home," he replied, knowing the words were slurred.

"Excellent!" Peter patted his back, gripping him behind the neck. "We will share many a good time here, Alexashka. And this is just the beginning! I have many plans for our little Company--not to mention the mock battles this spring! You shall see!"

With a wink, Peter leapt away again, back up to his place, nodding devoutly when summoned by the Prince-Pope.

"Be it known that all authority lies in the Prince-Pope," Peter began, growing very serious. "He is our light and our example, and only through his divine guidance may we ever hope to find our way. Today, by the grace of our beloved kniaz-papa, you will bear witness to the crowning of a new kniaz-kezar, our Prince-Caesar!"

The group responded with a shout, the room quaking under the sound. Inspired, Menshikov added his voice to the mix.

"Watch," the Tsar shouted above them, "as the miracle of ascension occurs before your eyes. By the divine grace of His holy light, our Caesar gains his right to rule. I present to you a monarch, a warrior and a prodigious eater--your beloved leader, the King of Presburg!"

The crowd parted again, this time to reveal the sour-faced, slouched figure of Prince Fedor Romodanovsky. One of the Tsar's most trusted, Fedor was the leader of the Russian side in Peter's mock battles, commanding his troops from small Fort Presburg on the grounds of Preobrazhenskoe.

Ever crusty, Romodanovsky was dressed oddly, his jacket turned inside-out, playing cards resting atop his shoulders like epaulets. Squirrels' tails dangled from his belted waist and his tri-cornered hat was turned comically backward. With a regal air, he looked over his subjects and offered a sneering smile.

"Your Majesty…" The Tsar fell to a knee, rising only when Romodanovsky acknowledged him.

Romodanovsky lifted his chin, strolling with a king's pace, his eyes never meeting those of the congregation. Attended by a full entourage of greencoats, he moved to take his place beside the Prince-Pope.

The group quieted again and the ceremony began. Led by Patriarch Bacchus, Romodanovsky was blessed, prayed for and toasted, receiving the accolades of the house, maintaining his austere look throughout. The Tsar had carefully planned each step of the ceremony, and his players never wavered in their parts, performing the scene just as Peter had written. Captivated, the audience members waited for every line, eager to play their part when called upon to pray or drink.

At the height of the ceremony, Romodanovsky kneeled before the Patriarch and a crown of fir branches was placed atop his head. The Prince-Pope stood before him, offering blessings and again making the sign of the cross with the two long pipes.

Now fully ascended, Romodanovsky was handed a tankard. He belched and held it to the sky, proposing the first of many toasts as Prince-Caesar.

"My first official order is for more ale!" he shouted, the ale splashing down into his hair. "To my favorite subject, Peter, and the Jolly Company! Pay your dues or I'll have your heads!"

With this, the King of Presburg received the greatest cheer of the evening, an ovation that continued for several minutes.

Menshikov swayed in place, his strength waning, the dizziness growing too severe to resist. The wondrous scene before him was growing indistinct beneath the effects of the vodka, the events blurring together in succession, his thoughts pleasantly muddled. Not alone, he took comfort in the fact that others were in worse condition, some already comfortably asleep on the floor or held up on the shoulders of their comrades.

I must last as long as I can, he repeated to himself, now concerned with more rational goals. *Whether I drop, or not--I must keep the vodka inside me!*

Satisfied with his reception, Romodanovsky called for the next course of the banquet to begin, his words stifled as Peter leapt up to stand beside him. The Tsar leaned close, whispering something in his ear before stepping away.

"We have changed our mind--as kings are wont to do! We have been told that a special display of fireworks has been prepared in our honor. We would see it now."

The words began a mass exodus from the great hall, the members of the Jolly Company rushing out to the courtyard, pushing to get the best place.

Hoping for a bit of food, Menshikov's spirits fell.

I can barely walk. How am I to manage?

As the room cleared, the Tsar returned again to his side, this time bearing a childlike grin.

"Fireworks, Alexashka! Better than any of us have seen before. Come, I know you'll be impressed!"

Menshikov stumbled, dizziness claiming him.

"Hah!" Peter wrapped an arm around his shoulder, steadying him. "You're well drunk, Alexashka! I would have it no other way."

"I am ready for the fireworks, sir."

Peter laughed, leading him to a chair. "Next time, Alexashka. Sleep now, and I'll wake you before the next course. Remember, I wish to beat you at ninepins--you had better save your strength for later!"

"I'm better than you think, sir."

"Yes, Alexashka," Peter replied, patting his spinning head. "I'm certain you are."

Now granted a pardon from the Tsar himself, Menshikov's last bit of resistance faded and he gratefully slumped into the chair to sleep.

Outside Moscow, Fort Presburg at Preobrazhenskoe

April 1691

The green-coated Preobrazhensky sentries stood at attention and saluted proudly as General Gordon entered the Fort, their presence here still considerable despite the Tsar's official residency at the Terem Palace in Moscow. Now the Tsar's personal guard, the majority were spending their time in the city providing escort for Peter.

These boys are devoutly loyal to Peter, he thought, riding through the gates and returning their salute. *Once trained properly, they will be fearsome in a campaign.*

So many issues--so many questions about the young Tsar's intentions. With all that had occurred in Moscow of late, it seemed a pleasant dream to think of focusing solely on war. The politics, however, persisted. Patrick was certain that there would be more rhetoric before he could again take the field.

One issue before the next, he reminded himself. *The Tsar still thinks me an unwilling captive.*

"General Gordon, to see the Tsar." He cleared his throat. "I am expected."

The dentchik bowed slightly. "Of course, General. Please enter."

As he crossed the threshold, the General could hear the distinct sound of Peter's raised voice, the shouts confined by the small rooms and low ceilings of the Fort. From the volume and intensity of the tirade, he could only assume that the Tsar was feeling better.

It was his first opportunity to see Peter since the Tsar's illness, a dangerous bout with fever that prevented contact with him for weeks and set most of the loyal Naryshkin supporters to packing. Peter had been so ill that the Naryshkins were contacting relatives in the country and readying for an exodus in case he should die. In a matter of days, the security of the Naryshkin government had been thrown into question.

Word of Peter's recovery sent waves of relief spreading throughout the city, all talk of Sophia's return quieted, at least until the next crisis. To Gordon, it seemed a great risk to keep the former Regent so close in Moscow. The Naryshkins had even gone so far as to remove Sophia's name from all public record, yet despite a lack of active family members, the Miloslavsky name still resonated in the corridors of the Kremlin Palaces.

From behind the dentchik, Fedor Golovin approached, his arms extended in greeting, his face bearing a look of discomfort.

"Ah, General Gordon!"

"Herr Golovin, I did not expect to see you."

A pleasant surprise. A boyar and an experienced diplomat, Golovin was one of Gordon's closest Russian friends and an advisor to the Tsar. A rational fellow, Golovin proved worthy company.

"Your arrival is quite timely, General. I am certain the Tsar's temper will be eased by your presence."

"Oh? And what is the trouble?" Gordon asked, removing his hat and smoothing his long hair. Knowing Peter, he had wisely left his wig behind for the trip to Fort Presburg.

"The Tsar found a cockroach crawling beneath his bed."

"Ah…"

Golovin shrugged. "Admittedly, I was not aware of the Tsar's…. position on cockroaches."

"He is strictly opposed, I take it."

"Indeed." Golovin waited patiently while the attendants took the General's tricorn and overcoat. "The Fort is not as well staffed as it might have been a year or so ago. It can become quite a scramble to accommodate one of the Tsar's unannounced trips. In any event, I am quite pleased to have you here. I think you may have arrived just in time to save an orderly."

"It can't be that bad, can it?"

"If you will follow me, sir."

They found the aforementioned dentchik standing with his eyes fixed on the ground, his posture bearing a shameful slump. Before him, the young Tsar of Russia towered in aggressive stance, his eyes bearing fire.

"Soon you will have them crawling in my food! They will be traversing the sheets and making camp in my boots!"

Looking up, Peter's face changed at the sight of Gordon, the look of rage fading.

"Patrick…General Gordon, it is a relief to see you. I am in need of command in my current efforts against cockroaches. My staff is apparently incapable of killing them!"

"I am happy to be here, Tsar," Gordon replied, "though I fear I will be of little use to you. The roaches are smarter than most Swedes, tougher than most Frenchmen and quicker than a starving Pole--difficult to hit with a musket."

"Despicable things," the Tsar replied, shaking his head, the anger still visible in his eyes. "Were it a bee, or even a spider, I could tolerate it more; those creatures have purpose. After all, the bee makes honey and the spider polices the other bugs. Some have even greater purpose--a silkworm, for example, or the worms that consume us and send us back to the soil. But cockroaches? They feed and multiply and do little else. They scuttle about without purpose…like nobles."

Peter raised a finger and nodded, looking to his dentchik. "You have a friend today in the General. He is a well-respected man and takes mercy on you. But I will not bear another incident. If I see another cockroach in this Fort, I will personally see you consume it! Am I understood?"

"Yes, sire," the man answered meekly, his posture quivering.

"Good, then. You are dismissed."

Without a single glance, the dentchik turned and made a restrained but hasty exit, his face bearing the astonished look of a man who'd just escaped the gallows. Peter seemed satisfied enough, exhaling the remainder of his frustration. As Gordon watched the dentchik slump away, he caught sight of a figure he had not yet noticed.

The vertical silhouette of Alexander Menshikov stood in the corner, tall and severe, bearing only a mild grin to indicate his amusement. Low-born and ambitious, Menshikov seemed more and more present in the Tsar's life, a willing drinking partner and friendly soundboard for Peter's passion. Menshikov was said to be illiterate but shrewd, willing to take orders and to perform the unpleasant tasks Peter would never ask of a foreigner. When Gordon first met Menshikov, he gave him no more consideration than any of Peter's other young dentchiks. Time, however, was proving the young peasant's loyalty to the Tsar, and the General was not surprised to find Menshikov in Peter's presence at any given time.

"Patrick, you remember Alexander Danilovich…"

"An honor to see you again, General." Menshikov approached, looking unsure whether to bow or salute.

"Herr Menshikov."

"I am truly blessed to be in such fine company, General," he said. "I promise you, sir, I do not deserve such good fortune as to be standing with the Tsar and the Commander of Russia's armies!"

"You are kind, sir. You served under Franz Lefort, am I correct?"

Menshikov nodded, shrugging. "Half-correct, sir. I didn't serve in a martial capacity--"

"He likely served more vodka than anything else," Peter interjected, smiling. "But I promise you, General, you wouldn't want to challenge him to a fistfight. Alexander is strong, and tougher than the soles of my boots!"

Menshikov grinned at the flattery, bowing his head in thanks.

"A captain in the Preobrazhensky Regiment, I will add."

"I should think him just the kind of man we need, then." The General nodded, eager to get to business. He could understand and tolerate Peter's young exploits, but to a man of Gordon's age and experience, the Tsar's rabble of loyal young wolves proved merely tedious.

Peter looked vibrant despite his recent illness, his face flushed and rosy, his eyes clear and sharp. Given the dire nature of the reports, it was quite a relief to see living proof of his recovery.

"Tsar?" he asked. "I trust you are feeling well again."

Peter nodded happily. "Much improved. Thank you, General. The physicians credit my resilience, but I tell you it was the private stock that pulled me through…that, and my anger for Sophia."

"Moscow takes solace in your recovery, Tsar."

"Half of Moscow," Peter replied quickly. "The other half was looking to bury me."

Menshikov scoffed. "You are better loved than that, sire."

"Perhaps," he responded, "but even through my sickness, I could hear Sophia's rats creeping around my feet. How happy she must have been to hear of my plight! I could picture her, waiting patiently in her Convent, praying for my last breath while her bloody comrades stood ready to cut down any who remained behind. Mother, Evdokia…my son!"

"All the more blessed that you are well again, sire. Admittedly, I briefly considered my own exodus."

"I cannot blame you, General." Peter stared, his gaze lost in thought. "It makes one realize how fragile the throne is."

"When the Tsar is ill, Russia is ill. Everyone must consider his place, I suppose."

"Well, the fear has passed. I am standing again, and all the stronger for it." The Tsar paced, stomping with his heels. "My opponents must think themselves unlucky, for they will not have another such opportunity to displace me. They tell me that too much air weighs on my health, but I feel much improved when I'm out here. Even better when I'm at the lake. We have much to discuss, General."

"Yes, sire."

The Tsar turned to Menshikov. "Alexander, I should think we are in the need of drink. Surely the General is thirsty after a long ride. Fetch us some vodka and cups."

With a dutiful nod, Menshikov turned and exited, his swift pace mirroring his devotion.

"Fedor, come closer." Peter motioned to Golovin, waving him over. "Given your diplomatic expertise, the General must hear what you think of my notion. Patrick, I know more important matters await us, but you simply must hear my thoughts. I would be much wiser for knowing your opinion."

"As ever, sire, I am at your disposal, though I fear my diplomatic skills are lacking."

"Nonsense, General! You are a statesman in every respect. From England to Poland, you are far better traveled than any man here."

"Perhaps," Gordon replied, "though I cannot say what I have gained from it."

"The General is a true warrior," Golovin added. "No boyar would ever be so humble."

"Were the vodka here, we would drink before business. Given its absence, I will tell you my notion and hope you won't think me still feverish."

Gordon offered a curious look, now wholly intrigued.

"As you may know," the Tsar began, "my illness was preceded by my journey to Archangel, a humbling experience, indeed. The beauty of the water cannot be described, nor the feeling of setting your feet on the deck of a real ship! To be away from Moscow, away from all this--farther than the Fort or Troitsky--I am better for having made the journey, my spirit renewed and my head filled with ideas. This, for a rocky trek across Russia! I realized much on this journey and found myself clinging to an idea."

Gordon held his tongue, knowing the Tsar was not finished. Golovin beamed up at Peter in admiration, his expression genuine. Whatever the notion, the boyar was apparently in favor.

"I propose a trip to Europe," Peter stated firmly, his eyes bright, "an embassy of grand size, with the purpose of collecting knowledge and developing the skills necessary to keep and hold Russia in this warring world. I speak of shipbuilding and artillery, carpentry and masonry, truly, all that we lack remains well within our grasp! I will bring fifty--no, a hundred young nobles--men whose minds have not yet hardened, boys willing to return and teach their comrades all they've learned."

"And you will lead this embassy?"

"Certainly not," Peter replied. "I will appoint someone worthy to lead the endeavor, though I will indeed be included in the traveling party. I will have the opportunity to attend to a few official matters along the way, of course. I imagine King Frederick would be quite stunned to see me sitting on his doorstep!"

"All of Europe will be quite stunned to see you," Golovin echoed. "A tsar has never traveled outside the borders."

Patrick hesitated, trying to assimilate it all. "Sire? You're not just thinking of ordering this embassy--you propose to accompany it? Through Europe?"

"Of course. I could hardly call for the embassy and then not go along!"

Gordon hesitated, unsure of how to respond. "Certainly this is unusual practice for the Tsar of Russia."

Peter grinned. "Yes! Think of it, Patrick--to see the docks in Amsterdam, the walls of Riga, perhaps even the bloody Tower of London! There are things in the West I could never hope to experience here. I will find craftsmen to hire as well, individuals willing to return to Russia to teach their craft. You would hardly believe how much I have benefitted from Timmerman and Houtman; Russia can benefit in the same fashion."

"Indeed." Gordon felt tongue-tied, his mind flooded with questions, his conscience not wanting to douse the Tsar's enthusiasm with skeptical thoughts.

To transport the Tsar and a hundred nobles through Europe? A trip of such enormity was hard to comprehend.

Sensing his hesitation, Peter frowned a bit, tilting his head as if trying to read the General's thoughts from the look on his face. As their eyes connected, the expression on the Tsar's face changed.

"Everyone out," Peter announced suddenly, pointing to the door. "Fedor, I must have some time with the General. Perhaps we will meet later for a drink."

"As you wish, sire." Fedor bowed respectfully, backing away. "General Gordon, I would hope to see you there."

"Perhaps another time, Herr Golovin," he replied. "I shall be back to Moscow as soon as the Tsar releases me. Your hospitality is appreciated, however. Please give my regards to your good wife."

Golovin bowed before taking his leave, the dentchiks exiting behind him. As the last of them vanished through the door, Menshikov reappeared in the entrance, holding a flagon of vodka and four pewter cups.

"Ah, Alexander! Always such impeccable timing."

"Sire?"

Peter shook his head. "Never mind. Come, bring the vodka. I suppose we can all have a taste before we speak."

They waited as Menshikov poured three cups and carefully passed them around.

"To new comrades," Peter said, touching his cup to theirs, "and to the sudden demise of any remaining cockroaches."

Menshikov quickly downed his cup and stood waiting to pour another, his face bearing a proud look.

"No time for another, my friend," Peter announced, patting his shoulder. "I have a task for you. I cannot bear to sleep here tonight knowing there are still cockroaches crawling about, and I cannot trust the competence of the staff. So you will supervise the dentchiks to insure their success."

Menshikov's proud look faded instantly, drooping into a dutiful scowl. "Yes, sire."

"What's that look, Alexander? You know how particular I am about things like this. I know I can trust you to come through."

"Yes, sire." Looking a bit offended, Menshikov bowed.

"Alexander?"

"Yes, sire?"

"Leave the vodka."

"Of course, sire."

Defeated, Menshikov set down the flagon and stomped toward the door, closing it sharply behind him. The Tsar waited quietly for his exit before turning back to Gordon.

"Alone, finally. This is much better, Patrick. I wish you to speak your mind, particularly where my great embassy is concerned. I could see the troubled look in your face. Fedor was quite supportive, but I am, of course, curious to hear your opinion."

Gordon hesitated, considering his reply. "Your aims are admirable, and I can understand your desire to travel--"

"There is a 'but' coming," Peter interrupted. "I hear it in your tone."

"I merely think there are concerns of…security if you wish to undertake such an expedition. There is a reason for a monarch to remain in state."

"Security?"

"Regrettably so." Gordon could see the disappointment in Peter's face.

"But Ivan is here to do his part, not to mention my mother--and the Naryshkins! As it is, I spend weeks away at Lake Pleschev without a single difficulty! Truly, Patrick, do you think we will be invaded in my absence?"

"With deference to the Turks," the General replied, "I was thinking more of your opponents at home."

"Yes, of course."

"Sire, your illness was a shock to the city, a warning to shake the overconfident from their comfortable beds. It was a stern reminder of how deeply they rely on your strength. When you are feverish, they prepare to flee the city out of fear. Respectfully, Tsar, I would worry about leaving Russia for fear of losing it."

Peter's enthusiasm waned, the acknowledgement of his understanding written on his face. His words had been blunt, and Gordon immediately regretted not thinking before speaking.

"I understand," Peter said, his gaze dropping. "You must think me a bit of a fool."

"Certainly not, sire."

"I may pretend that I am finished with Sophia, but I am not. I can remove her name from record, yet her presence still plagues me. You know, I despise her much more now than I did when she was lurking behind the throne. Before, she was only a bear, brooding and plodding around in her cave. Now she is worse, Patrick, a ghost that lurks over my shoulder, forever present, watching and waiting for my every misstep! Sophia sits, waiting, cursing my name--accomplishing much more from her little room at the Convent than we could ever think possible. She remains. Of this, I do not need to be reminded!"

Peter paced now, his worries awakened, his lingering suspicion still manufacturing angst.

Now I've angered him, Gordon thought, regretting raising the spectre of Sophia. *I should be more careful where I direct the conversation.*

"Please allow me to apologize, Tsar, for my ill manners. I lack diplomatic skills and I'm afraid my poorly worded thoughts are--"

"Do not apologize," Peter interrupted. "No call for an apology. And with all respect to your sense of decorum, you are, of course, a man of the highest regard and I mean this sincerely. I would hope, Patrick, that we could leave the Tsar out in the corridor when you and I speak alone. We both know well the restrictions of decorum, and I certainly wouldn't want you to bear the embarrassment of shouting my first name across the throne room. Still, in our private dealings--and in your heart--I would prefer that you call me Peter. We both know all too well that I am Tsar."

"You have my humble thanks," the General replied. "I know we have had this conversation before and regrettably, old habits are hard to break, particularly for an old soldier. I am honored, Peter, and shall endeavor to be more familiar."

"This pleases me, Patrick." Peter lifted the bottle, indicating that he would pour again. "The last thing I would want is to embarrass you. Here, let us have some more."

Oddly, the General felt for a moment as though he were a child and Peter his father, a willing subservience that rested in his trust of the character within the Tsar. Even at eighteen, Peter was capable of extending his personal authority, emanating an air of maturity and control that made people want to serve him. The young man was a natural artist when inspiring loyalty and carried the mantle of power quite naturally, as though it were fitted to him.

For the General, Peter's abundance of ability was no mystery. The Russians' prophecies may have been fulfilled, but the boy's shrewd, assertive nature seemed more attributable to the Tsarista than to God. Moreover, Peter had been carrying the burden of opposition from the time he was ten, living in constant fear, never truly knowing if he would survive to reign. As a result, the Tsar took nothing for granted and, despite his flip exterior, was quite serious at his core.

In Peter's presence, there was no question. His aggressive charms were too great for most to resist, his perseverance too solid to oppose. For those who remained outside his spell, there waited his fearsome temper.

This, surely, was part of what the world admired about young Peter--the spirit, the drive, the boyish verve that provoked him to create the Preobrazhensky and the Jolly Company. The Russians seemed to want a strong leader. Peter was applauded for his capable air and praised for his potential. In the shadow of such success, bitter opposition was certain to develop.

The boy is well-liked...and well-hated.

The two were tied in marriage, the anger as inescapable as the adoration. For beneath Peter's vivid personality churned an assertive drive, an ever-turning wheel that rolled on in great fury with little regard for what lay in its path. Not a bad trait for a monarch, perhaps, and certainly not for someone as innately compassionate as the Tsar. His leniency seemed to balance his stubbornness.

Yet General Gordon had been in Russia for many years and believed he knew the hearts of the Russians as well as any native-born citizen. He'd learned from his Russian wife the love of tradition and constancy, the longer view of life that all Easterners possessed. In his mind, there seemed no way that the sour, rooted Russians could remain in love with Peter's ambition.

His intentions are endless, his dreams spectacular. He is a vivid streak of color in a land of muddy brown.

"I do not mean to sour your ambition," Gordon told him as they finished the cups. "Truly, sire…er, Peter. You may think me a rather immovable old stick, but I see great value in your trip to Archangel and even more in this endeavor into Europe. I marvel at the thought, in fact. The more I think of it, the more astounding it becomes."

"Exactly!" Peter burst out, nodding.

"My intention, then, is not to drown your spirit. In my eyes, Russia has the world to gain from you. As you seek my counsel, however, I must remind you, with all respect, that you are training a bear."

Peter hesitated a moment before breaking out into a peal of laughter that filled the room to the ceiling.

"You have described my task perfectly!" the Tsar replied, his eyes beaming. "A wolf training a bear! You are the wisest man I know, Patrick."

"That, I am not," Gordon responded with a slight grin. "Though I would think you a lion, sire."

Peter hesitated, frowning. "Your meaning is appreciated, but I have been told that lions spend their days lying in the shade. I would much rather be a wolf. Then again, perhaps I am simply just a bear, and don't want to admit it."

The boy understands his place. I should do the same.

"In any case, I should limit my counsel to military matters," he told Peter, straightening a bit. "I have every belief that you will do what you feel is best for Russia."

"I have no other purpose," Peter replied, his tone bearing weight. "And to this cause, we must speak of your position, my friend. I was told that during my sickness you planned a return to your homeland…for both you and your family."

Gordon nodded honestly. "There was so little information available about your condition, sire--like many others, I was preparing for the worst. In truth, speaking frankly, I would have no reason to remain in Russia without Peter Alexeevich on the throne."

Peter paused, offering a grateful look. "And I can think of no one better to place in command of Russia's armies. But I am healthy now, and the throne is mine. Your contract is complete, and still I worry about the presence of my finest General--"

"Sire," he interrupted, "Peter, if I may--"

"You must allow me to finish, Patrick. Your service to Russia has been too noteworthy to ignore, and yet the conditions of your employment have been grossly unfair. I won't hear another word until I am finished."

Finally, the long-awaited topic arrived, the true reason for his presence in Preobrazhenskoe on this day. Having long ago considered his response, the General held his tongue, wishing to hear Peter speak.

"You were, of course, originally contracted by my father," the Tsar continued, "and were kept in service by Tsar Fedor when father passed. This was when the first offence occurred. It was Fedor's duty to release you, Patrick. Instead, he re-interpreted the term of your contract and kept you here. Given your talents, this was an understandable, yet dubious action. I am grateful for your presence, but you should have been allowed your leave."

Peter shook his head. "Again, when Sophia took power you made an appeal, requesting that you be released from your obligation and allowed to return to England. Despite what I assume was an amiable relationship with Prince Vasily and Sophia, you were again denied. This was the second offence, and for this I know you were quite distressed."

"Admittedly, yes," Patrick conceded. "I was not yet acquainted with you, sire."

"The response of a diplomat! And you say you lack the talent..."

"I feel I have done my best to accept my life here," he continued seriously, "if nothing else, my dear wife is proof of that."

"But you have longings for your home. I understand."

"Moscow is home, as well."

The General had arrived that morning knowing his course of action. Even after the scare surrounding Peter's illness, Gordon had made his decision to remain in Russia with Peter and, having seen the crisis through, was prepared to state his intentions.

As Commander, Gordon would have influence and responsibility greater than any he'd enjoyed before. His family would prosper and, barring the sudden death of the Tsar, would find a permanent home. There were battles to come, and Russia remained unprepared to defend herself. Here, in this odd, barbaric, orthodox empire a thousand miles away from home, Gordon had found a place where his talents were not only appreciated but were also sorely needed.

But it had not been promotion or prosperity that turned Patrick's opinion regarding his freedom. Even in the cool depths of his soldier heart, there was no denying: he had grown to believe in the young Tsar, to understand in some small way the complexity of Peter's character, to see beneath the extraordinary exterior and glimpse the soul of a true leader.

A friend and compatriot, a comrade of the most unlikely sort, this eighteen-year-old Russian monarch had grown familiar to Gordon in a matter of months. For the first time, after a life of being a mercenary, the General could honestly say that he had a cause to believe in, a purpose beyond mere duty. For this, Patrick could be loyal in both heart and mind. For Peter, if not for Russia.

And yet, as he reached the moment of his declaration, he was nonetheless curious to hear the Tsar's decision. If he desired, Peter could invoke the right of contract used by Fedor and Sophia to keep Gordon in Moscow. Later, Peter could apologize and claim that it was all for the sake of Russia and Gordon would have to understand.

In the old soldier's mind, however, the more likely scenario involved a different speech from Peter, one Gordon half-expected but could only hope to hear. As Peter lifted the flagon of vodka, the General felt confident in his choice, believing the Tsar was about to act with true nobility.

"We shall agree to be comrades," Peter said to him, raising the cup, "and to remain brothers in the eyes of the Holy Father, whatever his discretion may be. I shall treasure the memories of your role at Troitsky and our time together, but I refuse to keep you captive here."

The General sighed inwardly, his hopes affirmed.

How much better--to stay because I choose to!

"I know the perils to come," Peter continued, his tone warm with sincerity, "and trust when I say there is no man in this world I would rather have commanding our regiments. You are a good man, a worthy man, Patrick, and I do not need my father's recommendation to know it. But I will not have you against your will. Consider yourself no longer obliged to Russia. You are free to return home or go where you will."

The General held out his cup, pinching his fingers to indicate a small amount. Grinning back at him with a quizzical look, Peter poured accordingly.

"Before we met," Patrick began, pointing to indicate that Peter should pour one for himself, "I was told that if the Tsar offered me a drink, I should accept it."

"Who said that?" Peter asked. "Franz?"

"Indeed."

"Hah!" Peter chuckled again. "He is right."

"When I first heard these words," Gordon resumed, holding his cup without drinking, "I thought it some kind of warning, a caution on his behalf, to inform me that Tsarevich Peter despised those who refused to drink with him, or that his temper would show itself should I not be able to keep up. I know now that my assumptions were wrong and that I was looking at the situation with the eyes of a Western man. Lefort was not warning me; he was telling me to recognize an invitation when I saw it. I have learned from you, Peter, that to a Russian a toast is a kindness shared and that there are few higher honors for a man than to be invited to share the vodka of the Tsar."

Peter said nothing, grinning and nodding, holding up his cup and waiting for Gordon to finish.

"In light of this grand tradition, sire, I would tell you that I have decided to remain in Moscow and that I would be greatly honored to accept whatever post you see fit, provided I may serve you. I pledge my loyalty to Tsar Peter and to Russia. May all our enemies fall in despair."

"I am grateful, Commander."

Gordon lifted his cup, emotion taking him. "Show me then, my lord Peter! Honor me by sharing a toast and sealing our accord!"

Peter nodded and touched cups with the General. "To Mother Russia and her new Commander! To comrade Patrick Gordon!"

The vodka was cold and smooth, the taste of it something he would remember fondly for the rest of his days.

But the thing that would remain most prominent in his mind was the sight of Peter leaping into action as soon as the drinks were finished, moving with restless energy to grab his maps and begin conquering the next dilemma.

Tireless resolve, endless ingenuity--Peter was the proverbial unstoppable force. Whether Russia could bear him, only time could tell.

"There is so much to speak of," the Tsar commented, scrutinizing the maps.

"You refer to the Turks, I assume…"

"Or the Swedes," Peter replied without hesitation, his tone bearing no wit.

Images of the powerful Swedish navy came immediately to mind, their cannons capable of decimating entire cities from the water.

"Sire? The Swedes?"

"Well, not alone, certainly," Peter said, "but we cannot hope to prosper without trade, without being able to defend ourselves. This means having a port capable of trade. Russia must have a year-round port…and a navy."

"You look to the Black Sea, then? To Azov?"

"I would much rather have Riga and the Baltic Sea, but I suppose I must slay one dragon at a time."

Gordon relaxed a bit. "Agreed, sire. I would consider the threat from the Turks the most immediate, particularly considering the outcome of our last campaign."

"We will concern ourselves with the Turks, then," Peter said, sounding resigned. "But you, Patrick, must promise to make the journey out to Lake Pleschev to see our efforts. You may think it merely an amusement, but if you could see, you would be amazed at what has been accomplished."

"I know that your amusements have a way of becoming reality, Peter. I would never doubt the possibility. And you are wise to view the Swedes with a critical eye. They will not remain passive forever."

"They are spread too thin," Peter returned, newly inspired. "To invade them in Stockholm? One would have to be a fool to attempt such a thing. But to steal Riga, or even better, some little guarded territory that borders the sea? Well, suddenly the task seems less imposing, a mission within the realm of possibility."

As much as Gordon hated the thought of facing the Swedes, there was truth in the Tsar's estimation. If Russia were ever to match the greatness of even the meekest of European nations, she would require a port on the Baltic.

And so I begin a new journey...clinging on for dear life as this powerful horse carries me to God knows where.

Peter nodded to him, focused. "There is no question, Commander, I am far more attracted to the Swedish land. Have you heard anything of Charles the Twelfth?"

"The boy monarch?" Gordon shrugged slightly. "I hear that he is sharp and capable."

"Indeed," Peter countered, rolling his eyes. "I hear the same... and I think I might not like him."

And what if the rumors are true? he thought, considering Peter's reaction. *Is it possible? A Swedish monarch, a boy as bright and as assertive as Peter, soon to be in command of the world's largest army and deadliest navy, a military and social juggernaut at his back.*

"As young as you both are, there seems no doubt that you two will cross paths."

"I suspect so," the Tsar answered, his eyes distant. "He will learn much from me. The Swedes are far wealthier and better armed, but no Norseman can outlast the will of a Muscovite! What is your counsel, Commander?"

He would conquer every issue at once. He thinks not of tomorrow, but of the day beyond.

Gordon cleared his throat. "I am told that will is the measure of a man. In this, the Russians are blessed, indeed. Where the Swedes are concerned, however, I would advise restraint--or at the very least a collection of powerful allies. In terms of our immediate troubles, I would advise a well-considered campaign. I will not forget our disgrace in the steppes under Commander Golitsyn. Here, too, we must be careful and plan for success. Neither your father nor Sophia was able to claim victory at Azov."

"You will command this time," Peter replied with confidence, "and I will be by your side. Together, I am certain we can manage this. I already have notions on how to prevent the Turks from reinforcing from the sea. Sit, and we shall plan our victory."

The General sat, grateful to be off of his feet, intrigued with the Tsar's approach, wondering at the spirit with which Peter attacked his dreams.

They think him frivolous, that he fires cannons and plays with ships all day. Do they know he has already plotted the Turks' demise? The boy is ready to rule.

"Before we begin, sire, I do recall one other tidbit I heard about young King Charles."

"Oh?" Peter looked up curiously. "What is that?"

"I heard that young Charles is being compared to you, sire. Not physically, of course, but they say he is much like the young Russian Tsar."

"I am decided then," Peter said, looking back to the maps.

"Sire?"

"I am certain that I hate him."

Outside Moscow, Peter's Cabin at Preobrazhenskoe

February 1694

Peter stood, his thoughts disrupted by the sound of the wind against the windows, the rattling of the frames further cluttering his already troubled mind. The quill remained dry in his hand, the parchment on the desk before him empty save for the words 'My dear Fedor,'.

He blinked, wiping the tears from his weary eyes and trying to compose his thoughts. After retreating to Preobrazhenskoe in the hope of clearing his mind, the long stretch of solitude was only proving to muddle his grief and deepen his despair. Only General Gordon had been admitted to express his condolences and Peter had turned him away after only a few minutes.

Now, a long three days after the funeral, the Tsar found himself tiring of solitude, anxious and irritated, eager to satiate his rage.

Morning comes again, he thought. *Soon enough. Perhaps today I will return. I must attend to my sister…*

He looked out the window into the darkness, wondering at the hour. Sleepless and drunk, he'd been drifting between despair and anger for nearly a week, his vigil broken only the day before by an unaccompanied journey to visit his mother's tomb.

Even now, the memories filled him with despair.

Peter had been at a banquet in Moscow when he received the message that his mother's health was failing.

It seemed a blur now, though he remembered racing to her bedchamber, grieved to find her pale and full of whispered prayers. The physicians confirmed the worst. After only a two-day illness, Tsarista Natalya was dying.

His knees fell weak at the sight of her. Lady Natalya seemed smaller than ever before, a fragile white angel in the throes of her misery, lucid enough to kiss him and give him her final blessing. He nodded with tears in his eyes and held his face to her warm cheeks, lingering in her embrace long enough to whisper his unending love.

The memory of their last moments alone would be replayed in his mind for the rest of his life--forever interrupted by the infuriating memory of Patriarch Adrian's bold entrance. For as Peter lifted his head from his mother's breast, his eyes met those of His Holiness.

Adrian was neither young nor old, unremarkable in looks, lacking the cleverness to mask his emotions and absent the wizened appearance which might have given his words credibility. The sight of him sent Peter to his feet, the tears still welling in his eyes.

He stood over his mother, demanding to know why he'd been interrupted. The Patriarch advanced on him, cheeks red with bluster, scolding that the Tsar's Western clothes were inappropriate.

Peter could remember the holy man's lips curling in disgust as he stood in the presence of the failing Tsarista and spoke of clothing.

The comment had thrown him into a rage, a consuming rush of anger that had wiped away his final moments with his mother. He remembered wanting to strike the Patriarch, looking over at the icons on the wall and wondering which would best bludgeon His Holiness. In the end, Peter had stared down at the Patriarch with every bit of venom he possessed, expressing with his gaze that which he could not with his fists.

"I would think that His Holiness would have more important matters to deal with than tailoring!"

And with that, Peter's angry feet carried him out of the chamber and out of the Kremlin, not stopping until he reached the frozen sanctity of Preobrazhenskoe and his cabin at Fort Presburg.

Only hours later, a messenger arrived with news that Tsarista Natalya Kyrilovna Naryshkin had passed in her sleep.

The tears had come immediately, like a torrent. There had been very little he had ever regretted in his young life, but as Peter realized the error of his anger, he found himself penitent and ashamed, wishing he'd cast out Adrian as soon as he'd seen him, knowing he had robbed himself of precious time with his mother.

Overcome with grief, Peter remained at Preobrazhenskoe, alone, denying admittance to even the closest of friends. The tears continued without end, the shock of her sudden passing borne only with vodka and solitude. He drank and prayed, and when the day of the Tsarista's funeral arrived, Peter remained in his cabin, refusing to attend.

Now he sat alone amidst his memories, attempting to put his scattered and sorrowful thoughts into words.

The letter was intended for Fedor Apraksin, a trustworthy friend and sympathetic ear. As Tsar, it was difficult for Peter to express his sadness publicly, and Apraksin was a genuine and pious man whom he could trust with his feelings. Once determined to express himself, however, Peter found that he was at a loss for words, unable to translate his melancholy into prose.

He could still see her clearly in his mind, standing straight in her black gown, her porcelain white face bearing even expression, her lips standing ready to smile or scowl at her command.

Natalya's embrace had been unique, her hugs consuming and strong, expressing the deep emotion that her countenance and position could not.

The finest of the court, Peter thought, tossing down the quill and wiping his weary eyes. *Father knew it. The marriage was not arranged. He chose her personally because she was beautiful and remarkable.*

A pious woman, certainly, but possessing more depth than most Russian brides. Natalya's tastes had been Westernized by her youthful days in Matveev's household--her Polish gowns and love for baroque architecture was proof of that. Yet despite her Western leanings, within the heart of the progressive Tsarista was a devout love for Orthodox tradition and the ceremony of the Kremlin. Her strict adherence to the Church had glorified their family and safely guided the Naryshkin clan and her children through the pitfalls of the Court.

Mother reaps her reward, surely. She's done the Holy Father enough service to earn her own suite in heaven.

A wonder, compared to me. A pillar of temperance and patience.

Peter had visited her that morning, the day after the official services, traveling alone in search of some peace. He stood before the tomb but felt nothing of his mother in the air surrounding it, the sight of her name only serving to deepen his feeling of loss. He'd cried and said a few prayers before turning back toward Preobrazhenskoe.

Now he paced, restless and still alone, caught in the rare position of being helpless to act against that which tested him. He had persevered through the last few days, managing his grief as every man did, measuring the time in alternating bouts of anger and sadness. Still, there seemed little he could do besides outlasting the sadness, experiencing what he must. Gratefully, Peter knew enough to know that time would heal what crying did not.

His tears came not from regret--he'd done what he could to be an obedient and loving son and was satisfied in this respect. He was alone now, however. Despite the presence of a wife, a child, and many living family members, Peter had never felt so isolated. He cried because it had always been Natalya and Peter, the immovable mother and her unstoppable son.

Now there was only Peter, and the better part of him realized that there would never be a substitute for his mother's love.

For the present, his tears were as real as the stone upon which Natalya's name was carved, his grief tangible and permanent. And yet, in the quiet moments when he sat alone in the relative darkness of the cabin, the Tsar would experience another emotion, not contrary to his grief but separate from it, a small but potent feeling of relief and liberation.

A sense of freedom. Personal and political.

It came to him guiltily, distinct and different from his sorrow, the realization that he would no longer be guided or curtailed. Without Natalya, his course would be his own, his decisions questioned only by his own judgment.

There would be other freedoms, as well. The demands on his time, the long Church services and Kremlin ceremonies, all appearances would be optional now, leaving him time to attend to more important matters. Without his mother, there would be no shame in refusing.

It existed despite his guilt, yet as the days passed, Peter found himself more and more focused on the idea. The Tsarista had often claimed that he was a natural monarch, instructing that, whenever in doubt, Peter should rely on his instincts. Now that she was gone, there seemed nothing more natural than acting as he saw fit, disregarding the tedium of the Church in favor of court affairs.

The knock on the door came as Peter began his second attempt at the letter. A timid rap, belonging to a dentchik.

"What?" he shouted at the closed door.

"Sire? I apologize for disturbing you." The muffled voice drifted in. "Herr Golitsyn waits in the hope of speaking with you."

Peter stood from the desk without having written a word, tossing down the quill and wiping at his eyes. He'd given orders not to be disturbed, but the dentchiks recognized Boris' relationship with the Tsarista. Apparently, they felt the Counselor important enough to admit.

At this hour?

He suffers, like me.

Golitsyn is consistent, even if tedious. He mourns her with the same familiarity. Who better knew her mind? Perhaps I owe him a word...

"Sire?" the voice repeated from behind the door.

"Yes, send him in," Peter ordered, buttoning his shirt and taking a deep breath, trying to put the grief out of his mind.

Boris has seen me cry too many times. I may express my grief, but I must not weep, ever again. Now is the time for strength. This is the first day of many.

The door opened and the Counselor entered bearing a solemn look, his eyes sunken and weary. Boris stepped carefully, his movement paced and cautious as though entering the cave of a bear.

They fear my bitterness, Peter thought, staring at him. *They tiptoe around me because they fear I will explode.*

"Boris, please enter."

Boris bowed respectfully. "I apologize for the intrusion, Tsar. I realize the impudence in arriving at such an hour and expecting an audience. I was pacing the floors of my bedchamber and found myself wanting to be out of the city, outside in the night air. I'd been told you were here and thought you might still be awake…I thought, perhaps--"

"You are welcome," Peter told him, interrupting. "And to be honest, I was half-expecting you."

Boris bowed his head, kneeling. "Sire, you have my deepest and most heartfelt condolences. May God rest her soul, your mother was a paragon, a living miracle."

Peter nodded his thanks, dry-eyed. "Your kind words are appreciated, Boris. Mother was very fond of you. She considered you the closest of family friends."

"I am truly saddened by her passing. It has been my honor to serve your family, sire."

A respectful man, Peter thought. *Better to commend him.*

"There is no question," he began, "you have been loyal from the start--from the bloody beginning. No one could replace Papa Matveev in her eyes, of course, but Mother always took comfort in your counsel. In those first, bloody years of the Regency, I know you helped insure that I survived my childhood. For this, I am grateful."

Boris hesitated, seeming a bit stunned at the compliment. "Sire, your kind regard is appreciated. I consider my efforts doubly rewarded, both in service to the Naryshkins and Mother Russia."

"Good man." Peter nodded again in support. "Your shoes have always been on the right feet, Boris. A practical man is hard to find in Moscow. Mother knew this."

"We were all fortunate to survive Sophia's purge" Golitsyn returned, lost in memory, "and though I often feared for my life, sire, I--we--always had a cause, a purpose, a reason for pressing forth. There was a meaning to our actions that was greater than any one of us, including your mother. In a greater sense, one might say that this cause was the greatness of our homeland. But as individuals, moment to moment, in our hearts this cause was you, sire--your survival and ultimate ascension. In this, we succeeded. I know your mother was quite proud to see you take your place."

"You've been with us since I was a child."

"You were a joy to your mother, Peter. I can still remember you running through the corridors of the Terem brandishing a grub hoe! You'd hide from us, and we'd find you hours later in the kitchen cellars, chopping away at a hanging goose or a smoked boar!"

Peter grinned at the memory, his amusement fading quickly. "Much has changed," he replied. "I am no longer the little boy."

Golitsyn's wistful look evaporated. "No, Tsar. Certainly not. I meant no offense."

"Tell me of the funeral. What was it like?"

"Respectable, pious--if such a tragic and mournful event may be called beautiful, I would call it this. In any estimation, I believe the Tsarista would have approved."

"Approved of her own funeral?" Peter asked, growing suddenly irritable. "Not Mother. What was it like?"

Boris cleared his throat. "Her coffin was draped in black velvet, placed on a sledge for the journey from the Palace to the Convent chapel. His Holiness walked beside the coffin and behind him Tsar Ivan, preceded by a number of boyars and courtiers. All the while, the funeral knell tolled in the bell tower of St. John with the muffled peal, in the ancient manner. All in all, most reverent and fitting, I think."

"I am glad Ivan was present," Peter commented. "Did he walk the entire way?"

"He did," Boris answered, nodding, "Though his pace was admittedly slower than that of the coffin."

He grinned honestly for the first time in a week, thinking of Tsar Ivan in a race with the sledge. "Even the departed must wait for poor Ivan."

"Apparently, yes."

"Mother would not mind too much," he returned. "She was indulgent of Ivan and had great respect for the Kremlin ceremonies. I am pleased to know the service was worthy."

"Indeed. The only thing missing was you, Peter."

Peter scowled back at him. "You know I never attend funerals, Boris. Especially not Mother's!"

Boris nodded dutifully. "I understand, sire. I'm not suggesting that you should have processed beside the coffin…but a brief appearance at the funeral would certainly have been well received by the Boyar Council and the Patriarch."

Peter stared back, his temper swiftly and surely gaining control.

Within a week of her death, he comes to scold me, the Tsar thought, his fingers balling into fists. *My actions don't suit him, and he's come to re-direct!*

Before, he always answered to Mother. Who pulls Boris' strings now? The boyars? Or does he direct me out of habit?

And now, quite unexpectedly, a landmark moment seemed to have dropped on Peter's doorstep. He'd been talking of a new day, but it was suddenly obvious that to move forward, new boundaries would have to be established.

"Mind you, I certainly don't mean to suggest that you offended the memory of the Tsarista in any way," Boris continued, unaware of the impending explosion. "But I do think it good to remember how important these official appearances can be. Now that you are Tsar--"

"Now that I am Tsar," Peter shouted, silencing him, "I will receive your opinions only when I ask for them! Odd, in the eyes of the Holy Father, I have been Tsar from the time I was ten. In Sophia's eyes, I became Tsar when the Regency ended. But in the eyes of those closest and dearest to my cause, I am still a child! You speak as though I became Tsar just a week ago, when my mother closed her eyes for the final time! Is this what you believe, Boris?"

"No, sire! Tsar, you have my--"

"Your apology?" Peter raged back at him. "I do not seek your apology, Counselor. It serves me no purpose. What Russia requires is your obedience. What I require--what I will have, Counselor, is your deference!"

Boris averted his eyes shamefully. "Yes, Tsar. I humbly--"

"Do not offer your apologies now," Peter continued, aware that he was venting his grief, allowing his temper to claim what it could. "In your heart, Boris, you may always see me as a little boy who needs direction. And though I may never truly win your respect, I will, at the very least, command your tongue!"

Golitsyn recoiled, remaining silent for fear of being interrupted again. His downcast eyes reflected regret, but Peter knew the mind of the man.

It will take time for him to recognize me as I am now. Boris still sees through Mother's eyes.

"I will warn you once, Boris, and I won't be countered. If you know your place, you will keep it, but I won't be subjected to your daily critique of my habits and endeavors! As far as my appearances are concerned, the Kremlin ceremonies are off my list for good. I only attended them to please Mother. I will appear when and where I choose, and you will say nothing of it. Is this understood?"

"Yes, sire."

"And as for Adrian and the Church, I am certain His Holiness will manage with Tsar Ivan. Adrian should be grateful that the Holy Father provided an additional Tsar willing to endure long services! Blessed, indeed, I think."

And though there was a part of him that recognized he was pressing too hard, Peter continued, riding the rush of release and giving in to his temper, unlocking the emotional fetters and allowing the rant to continue. Personally, Boris seemed undeserving of such an attack. He was loyal until the bitter end and humble for a man of his station. In addition, his offence was defensible, as he had so often played the role of mentor.

But the Tsar could not let the moment pass. As true and good as he was, Boris was in need of direction, likely the first of many. Whatever his opinion, the Counselor would leave the room knowing, irrevocably and without question, who held the reins of Russia.

"You may tell the Duma that, as always, they can count on my regular attendance. This, I will continue regardless of my other habits in the Kremlin."

"The Boyar Council will be pleased, sire."

"They are never truly pleased to see me," Peter replied without humor. "A topic for another time, perhaps. For now, my friend, know that you are a trusted and respected member of our family."

He allowed the words to rest before resuming. "Know also that I will bear no more mothering from you, Boris. I will act as I please--as is my right. To be honest, I expect I will often be asking your opinion and seeking counsel. After all, this is your duty. But I warn you again--if you press me without solicitation, you will face my rage. Am I understood?"

Golitsyn bowed slightly, his eyes still averted. "Quite clearly, sire."

"Good, then." Peter hesitated, looking back to the table and the empty parchment. "Your kind words are appreciated. You have my thanks, now go away."

"May the Holy Father bless you, Tsar."

Peter softened, waving him away. "Go, Boris. We will speak tomorrow."

The Counselor bowed and moved to the door, offering a final nod of appreciation before exiting. As the door closed behind him, the Tsar's grief came rushing back to claim the void left by his anger.

Exhausted, Peter shuffled to the table, staring down at the page and wondering what he could say.

Fedor is but one of many. All of them former friends of the Tsarevich...now friends and subjects of the Tsar.

Peter had scolded Boris for speaking as though his reign were just beginning, but in reflection he could see that there was a measure of truth in the thought. The title had seemingly always belonged to him--the robes and palaces, ceremonies and banquets had always been a part of his life.

Yet Peter had realized it only as he stood looking at his mother's tomb. Until that moment, the moment of Natalya's passing, Peter had never truly been Tsar.

There were so many others like Apraksin, friends who had known the boy, comrades who had served him faithfully but would soon be asked to do much more.

More than mere parties and war-games. I will be asking them to serve, to work, to die, perhaps. They must know me as Peter, and as Tsar.

He thought of his friends and mentors, family members and political opponents, the countless list of seconds and supporters, boyars and graybeards, diplomats, merchants, priests and courtiers. From the squires to the Patriarch, from the chamberlains to the Cossacks of the Ukraine, all of Russia would soon know whom they served and precisely what was expected of them.

Too many, he thought. *Too many opinions. Impossible to please them all.*

I cannot contend with all of Russia.

I am the caretaker. I am the Tsar. This is my purpose.

Let Russia contend with me.

He paced now, his mind working, already set to thinking of the future. A Russia of Peter's choosing, without the Naryshkins or the Patriarch to curtail him.

His thoughts leapt from topic to topic, addressing his dreams and dilemmas with equal vigor, the possibilities flooding in endless stream.

First and foremost, there was the defense of Russia--a proper army with proper weapons, trained by the best Europe could offer. The Turks would not linger forever, and Vasily Golitsyn's failed campaigns would have to be avenged. This, Peter knew, would be his task.

Russia's enemies were few, but formidable. Like a storm on the horizon, the Swedes waited, their massive navy mocking the rest of the Baltic, their presence too close for Russia to ignore.

How long before they find us too tempting, and attack?

We must have a navy, he thought, more certain than ever. *Ultimately, a true port. We will import specialists and learn the craft.*

So much, it seemed, for Russia to learn.

And while the Tsar could be said to have loved his country more than he loved himself, he was nonetheless able to look upon it as a mother or father would a child, to take pride and applaud its glory while still expecting more. Russia still possessed no proper courts, and education was left in the hands of the clergy. Culturally, the capital city of Moscow was bereft of theaters and the icons that graced the walls were still painted in medieval style. The nobility shuffled around in long beards and ancient garb while the rest of Europe experienced an explosion of art and style.

All this, Peter knew. Western influence was more than wigs and buckled shoes, more than minuets and decorum. Western influence meant progress, new ideas in science and medicine, new tools and techniques in every field from carpentry to sailing. The world was changing and the dominance of the Western powers left no question as to the key.

Progress demands knowledge...and we are sorely lacking. What my father began, I shall finish. Once Russia gains her feet, we will show our ass to the West!

Russians are slow to change, he thought, repeating the phrase he'd been told a hundred times before. *I can lead, but they must learn to follow...or be left in the past. The danger lies not in accepting the ways of the west, but rather in denying their importance.*

He grinned to himself, thinking of General Gordon's well-intentioned warnings about the Russian temperament.

Patrick knows my mind. He knows I cannot bear to sit and watch while the country falls further behind.

The image of the General was an inspiration, and Peter found himself thinking of the Russia that might be, wondering how many of his notions were realistic.

So much I could change. So many ways to act. Russia must learn to live with a conscientious father. I will be demanding and the nation will rise to meet my expectations.

In her final moments, Lady Natalya had whispered that he should live a life without regret. As Peter recalled her words, it seemed suddenly obvious that the time for mourning was finished.

Lady Natalya would expect more of the Tsar.

Resolved, Peter knelt beside the table, allowing the grief to claim him one final time as he bowed his head to pray.

Holy Father, bless and keep her soul. Grant her the glory she deserves.

Heal our wounded spirits as we mourn her passing and suffer our loss.

Bless the Church and our Mother Russia, our backward little corner of the world. We are humble and hard-working, strong but ignorant. I pray, Holy Father, give our people the strength to overcome their fears and the faith to persevere in the face of change.

For this humble servant, I ask only for the strength to rise another day. May my temper be mild and my mercy great. I will not waste the gift of your benevolence. In your name, Holy Father, you have my faith and my vow.

Standing, the Tsar took a deep breath, feeling better as he exhaled.

Outside, the sky was beginning to lighten, the approach of a new day waking his weary spirit. Peter marched to the window and pushed it open, feeling the gust of cool air on his face. Still a dim shadow in the early morning light, the golden onion domes of Moscow waited in the distance.

As though delivered by the wind, the words of his letter came to him. Peter returned to the table, uncorking the inkwell and dabbing the quill before setting to work:

> 'It is hard for me to tell you how bereft and sad I feel; my hand is incapable of describing it fully or my heart of expressing it. So, like Noah, a little rested from my misfortune and leaving behind what cannot be restored, I write of what is alive.'

Suggested Reading

Listed below are writings and publications which I have used as the historical grounding of this fictional story of Peter the Great. Insofar as possible, I have attempted to provide a true picture of Tsar Peter, depending largely on the various historical and biographical works and their factual, usually similar, but sometimes differing, presentations of events and their characterizations of Peter and the many people surrounding him. I am very grateful to have had these magnificent sources from which to draw my story of Peter. I highly recommend these works to any reader who may wish to know more about Peter and late 17th and early 18th century Russia.

Anderson, M.S. *Peter the Great.* London and New York: Longman Group Limited, Second Edition, 1995.

Bushkovitch, Paul. *Peter the Great.* New York: Rowman and Littlefield Publishers, Inc., 2001.

———. *Peter the Great: The Struggle for Power, 1671-1725.* Cambridge: Cambridge University Press, 2001.

Cracraft, James. *The Revolution of Peter the Great.* Cambridge, Massachusetts and London: Harvard University Press, 2003.

DeJonge, Alex. *Fire and Water: A Life of Peter the Great.* New York: Coward, McCann and Geoghegan, 1979.

Duffy, James P. and Vincent L. Ricci. *Czars: Russia's Rulers for Over One Thousand Years.* New York: Barnes and Noble, 1995.

Durant, Will and Ariel. *The Story of Civilization: Part VII, The Age of Louis XIV.* New York: Simon and Schuster, 1963.

In the Russian Style. Edited by Jacqueline Onassis with the cooperation of the Metropolitan Museum of Art. New York: Viking Penguin, 1976.

Hughes, Lindsey. *Russia in the Age of Peter the Great.* New Haven and London: Yale University Press, 1998.

———. *Peter the Great.* New Haven and London: Yale University Press, 2002.

Klyuchevsky, Vasili. *Peter the Great.* Translated by Liliana Archibald. Boston: Beacon Press, 1958.

Kolchin, Peter. *Unfree Labor, American Slavery and Russian Serfdom.* Cambridge, Massachusetts and London: The Belknap Press of Harvard University Press, 1987.

Massie, Robert K. *Peter the Great, His Life and World.* New York: Random House Trade Paperbacks, 2011.

Montefiore, Simon Sebag. *The Romanovs 1613-1918.* New York: Alfred A. Knopf, 2016.

Pososhkov, Ivan. *The Book of Poverty and Wealth.* Edited and Translated by A.P. Vlasto and L.R. Letwitter. London: The Athlone Press, 1987.

Rodimzeva, Irina, Nikolai Rachmanov, and Alfons Raimann. *The Kremlin and Its Treasures.* New York: Rizzoli International Publications, Inc., 1987.

Tolstoy, Alexei. *Peter the Great Volume I.* Translated by Alex Miller. Moscow: Raduga Publishers. 1985.

Voyce, Arthur. *The Moscow Kremlin, Its History, Architecture and Art Treasures.* Berkley and Los Angeles: University of California Press, 1954.

Voltaire. *History of Charles XII, King of Sweden.* Translated by Winifred Todhunter, Edited by Ernest Rhys, London: J. M. Dent & Sons, Ltd. New York: E.P. Dutton & Co., 1978.

———. *The History of Peter the Great, Emperor of Russia.* ISBN-13-978-1533122186, 2016.

Warnes, David. *Chronicle of the Russian Tsars.* London: Thames and Hudson, 1999.

Yefimova, Luisa V., and Tatyana Aleshina. *Russian Elegance, Country and City Fashion from the 15th to the early 20th Century.* Moscow: Art-Rodnik Publishing House, 2011. Cambridge, UK: Vivays Publishing Ltd., 2011.

Summer Palaces of the Romanovs, Treasures from Tsarskoye Selo, The. Edited by Emmanuel Ducamp, Photographs by Marc Walter. London and New York: Thames and Hudson, 2012.

Kirk Anthony Vollack lives in Colorado where he teaches music and writes.

Made in the USA
San Bernardino, CA
27 December 2017